I0825161

AGNES SHARP *and the* WEDDING *to* DIE FOR

Books by the author

THE SHEEP DETECTIVE STORIES

Three Bags Full

Big Bad Wool

MISS SHARP INVESTIGATES

The Sunset Years of Agnes Sharp

Agnes Sharp and the Trip of a Lifetime

Agnes Sharp and the Wedding to Die For

AGNES SHARP *and the* WEDDING *to* DIE FOR

Leonie Swann

Translated from the German by Amy Bojang

First English translation published in 2026 by
Soho Press
227 W 17th Street
New York, NY 10011
www.sohopress.com

First published in German under the title *Tod in Mistletoe Manor*.

Names: Swann, Leonie, author | Bojang, Amy, translator
Title: Agnes Sharp and the wedding to die for / Leonie Swann ;
translated from the German by Amy Bojang.
Other titles: Tod in Mistletoe Manor. English
Description: New York, NY : Soho Crime, 2026. | Series: Miss Sharp investigates ; 3
Identifiers: LCCN 2025040867

ISBN 978-1-64129-711-0
eISBN 978-1-64129-712-7

Subjects: LCGFT: Detective and mystery fiction | Novels | Fiction
Classification: LCC PT2721.W36 T6313 2026
LC record available at https://lccn.loc.gov/2025040867

Interior illustrations by Dina Ruzha
Interior design by Janine Agro

Printed in the United States of America

10 9 8 7 6 5 4 3 2 1

EU Responsible Person (for authorities only)
eucomply OÜ
Pärnu mnt 139b-14
11317 Tallinn, Estonia
hello@eucompliancepartner.com
www.eucompliancepartner.com

AGNES SHARP *and the* WEDDING *to* DIE FOR

DRAMATIS

THE RESIDENTS OF SUNSET HALL

Agnes—ex-police, founder of the house share, and skilled butterfly wrangler

Marshall—ex-military, fan of firearms and of Agnes

Edwina—ex-Secret Service, reptile fanatic, mad as a box of frogs

Charlie—vlogger of Charlie's Wacky World of Wonders fame; fabulous, brings a touch of glamour to the house share

Winston—uses a wheelchair; the house share's rock

Bernadette—the bride, blind and in love, but not blinded by love

Jack—former contract killer; currently Bernadette's fiancé

Lillith—dead and in a tin, but still an important member of the house share

Hettie—the house tortoise; fresh out of the fridge

Oberon—a boa constrictor, pursuing higher things

Brexit—Sunset Hall's scruffy wolfhound

THE OTHERS

Christopher—good-looking man from the internet, Charlie's beau

Richard the Lizard—not-very-good-looking man from the internet, houseplant nut, Agnes's date

The Verger—Dominic: murder victim and paper hoarder

PERSONAE

Reverend Barnes—the Vicar of Duck End; rather fond of the sound of his own voice

Benjamin Stout—private detective

Countess Constance Purr—aristocratic owner of Foxglove Manor, blue-blooded flamingo

Dorothea Gretchen—bookworm and unwanted houseguest

Moira, Norma and Gilda/Hilda—members of the knitting circle the Knitwits

Mia—a complicated young girl

James—stripper for the more mature lady

The Sweet Potatoes—a swing band: four men and a female lead singer

MORE WEDDING GUESTS

Sylvie—the home help

Sylvie's Husband

The New Gardener

Charlie's Grandson and His Partner

Marshall's Daughter and Her Boyfriend

Nathan—Marshall's grandson

Sparrow—opportunistic burglar and friend to the house share

Sparrow's Plus-One

The Photographer

PROLOGUE

Agnes felt strangely empty after the wedding. She placed her peculiar fascinator on the kitchen table, made some tea and manoeuvred a generous slice of wedding cake onto a plate.

Then she arranged the cup of tea, the piece of cake and a cake fork on a tray with a jug of milk and was about to get herself a sugar cube but decided against it in the end. The truth was: she was sick of the sight of sugar cubes. Finally, she glided up to the first floor with the aid of the stairlift, not to her room, but to the sunroom, which was of course deserted and completely devoid of sun at this time of day. It smelled a bit musty too.

Agnes clicked on a reading lamp and watched for a moment as the light cast ominous shadows onto the walls. The chair—a gravestone; the spider plant—a spider, no less. Even her own shadow appeared shifty and strange. She sighed, shaking off the bad mood like raindrops. She poured some milk into her tea and shovelled the first forkful of wedding cake into her mouth. Delicious. She realised she'd left the teaspoon in the kitchen, so she stirred her tea with the cake fork, then took some paper and a pencil out of the games drawer.

She spent a long time staring at the empty sheet of paper, which seemed to glow in the light of the reading lamp. She had the urge to chew the end of the pencil, but that didn't seem wise, what with her fragile false teeth and all.

During her long life, Agnes Sharp had spent an inordinate amount of time dealing with murders—first in a professional capacity with the police, later privately in her spare time.

But she'd never planned a murder before.

It was no easy task.

She allowed herself another bite of cake and put her remaining grey cells to work. Eventually, she put the blunt pencil to paper and began to write.

1
KETCHUP

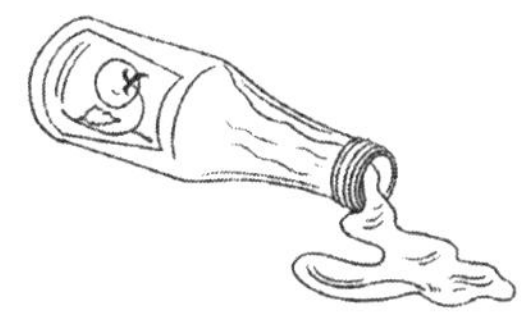

The anaemic afternoon sun streamed into the room at an awkward angle, forming pale puddles of light on the stone tiles. Outside, a few birds tentatively attempted their spring songs, but in Sunset Hall's utility room it was still quiet and wintery. One lone fly had prematurely taken to the cool air and was stubbornly launching itself at a windowpane, presumably in search of a little warmth.

Edwina lay lifeless on the floor, her face small and scrunched up, as if she'd just sucked a lemon, her hands contorted like claws. A red fluid oozed out of the corner of her mouth, and the same fluid was already forming an impressive puddle on the tiles.

Not far from her, next to two balled-up socks meant for the washing machine, lay the murder weapon, a pair of equally blood-smeared garden shears.

Charlie, who had dropped the washing basket in fright, stared at the horrific sight in astonishment.

"Edwina?"

Being so unaccustomedly lifeless made her housemate look smaller than usual, more fragile and, for the first time that Charlie could remember, really old. A haggard little old lady in a lilac tracksuit, her hair short and hedgehog-like, her sheep slippers too big and ridiculous. NO TIME TO DIE was emblazoned on her sweatshirt.

The fly abandoned the window and inspected the red puddle.

Charlie surveyed the scene for a while, then she crouched down next to her friend and stuck her finger in the pool of blood.

Thick and tomato-red.

Charlie sniffed it.

"So, that's where the ketchup went," she murmured.

The fly buzzed, clearly experiencing a sugar rush, but Edwina didn't move an inch and looked even deader than before, if that was possible.

Charlie continued mercilessly. "It's hamburgers today, Edwina. Have you forgotten already? Hamburgers and chips. And you know what we all think of chips without ketchup, don't you? Not a lot!"

The meals in their retirement house share might be monotonous, but there were a few things you could usually rely on. One of those things was ketchup.

Edwina opened one eye; it was alert and alarmingly blue.

"Go away!" she hissed. "It's a surprise!"

"I was surprised," said Charlie.

"It's not for you," muttered Edwina. "It's for Agnes! To cheer her up!"

The blue eye shut again.

"Cheer her up . . ." Charlie shook her head and started to pick up the laundry scattered around the utility room.

"Agnes likes murders," said Edwina stubbornly.

"But not yours!" Charlie hissed. "Now I've got ketchup stains on my blouse, and they're a bugger to get out!"

Dead Edwina shrugged.

Charlie tipped the laundry into the drum and started the machine. It was true that Agnes had been acting a bit strangely recently. *More strangely than usual*, that is. Stressed. Absent-minded. Unusually confused. An interesting murder might provide a remedy, but it wasn't as simple as Edwina imagined.

"Could you call Agnes?" Edwina was sticking to her guns.

Charlie put her hands on her hips. "Fine then. But it's the last time!"

"Agreed!" Edwina crowed with delight and licked a bit of ketchup from her lips.

THE REMAINING residents of Sunset Hall were sitting in the lounge together: Agnes, Winston, Marshall, Brexit the wolfhound, and Oberon, the house boa constrictor. They were all trying to get cosy despite the smoky fire in the hearth—with varying degrees of success.

Marshall, who was in an unusually good mood even though he had his left arm in plaster, was single-handedly cleaning one of his many firearms. It was a bit of a slog. Winston had manoeuvred his wheelchair underneath one of the reading lamps and was attempting a crossword. Agnes, the founder of the house share and owner of Sunset Hall, was knitting something shapeless in a dubious swampy green, swearing like a sailor every now and then. Brexit was dreaming, his paws twitching.

Oberon was the only one who seemed to be approaching the business of relaxing in a professional manner, basking contentedly beneath his heat lamp in the terrarium.

Charlie pushed open the door and dramatically placed her hand on her forehead, managing, despite the unkempt hair and ketchup on her blouse, to look fabulous as always.

"Edwina's dead!" she announced.

"Again!" Agnes put down her knitting, clearly annoyed.

"She means well," said Winston, without looking up from his crossword.

"What is it this time?" asked Marshall, with feigned interest. "Hanged in the loft? Drowned in the bath?"

"I hope it's not 'drowned in the bath' again!" Winston muttered. That scenario caused quite a flood last time, largely because Edwina had kept topping up the warm water post mortem.

"Stabbed in the utility room!" Charlie rolled her eyes. "With some garden shears. And you can all forget about ketchup on your chips now!"

Agnes struggled out of her chair. Her stiff joints and cantankerous hip made it a rather difficult undertaking.

"I think I should see for myself."

In a fit of vanity, she ignored her walking stick and padded along the hall towards the utility room, haunted by a cloud of grim and rather fundamental thoughts.

Had the pensioner house-share thing really been a good idea? In theory, it was about supporting one another, sharing their sunset years with like-minded people in a dignified manner, and easing one another's passing if necessary. In practice, there were snakes, ketchup-smeared housemates and unimaginative pseudo-murders to grapple with. And a real murder thrown in every now and then for good measure.

It was far from dignified!

But, as is so often the case, the realisation came a couple of years too late. The house was already full of pensioners and creatures great and small, and if Agnes didn't get a move on, Edwina was going to catch a cold into the bargain.

She pushed the door to the utility room open and groaned. Edwina really had gone to town with the ketchup. Agnes stepped closer and felt Edwina's pulse happily beating away. Then she took the garden shears in hand.

"Stabbed," she said loudly. "Puncture wound between the ribs, straight through her heart. Murder weapon: garden shears. Why the victim is bleeding from her mouth is therefore unclear."

Edwina sat up, beaming. "I thought it looked better that way."

"Hm," said Agnes.

"And who was it?" asked Edwina hopefully.

"How should I know?" Agnes muttered. She knew exactly what Edwina was getting at, but she didn't want to play along.

Edwina spread her ketchup-splodged arms. "Brexit!"

The wolfhound! Again! It looked like everything was Brexit's fault, in the house share and in life.

"Brexit's snoozing in the lounge!" said Agnes sternly. "He's got an alibi."

"But . . ." Edwina broke off and lowered her hands. "You're not happy at all!"

"I . . ." Agnes groped for words. "I'm a bit down, that's all. It's got nothing to do with murders."

Well, almost nothing.

"But it's spring!" cried Edwina, nimbly jumping up. "How can you be down when it's spring?"

Agnes looked at her enviously. If only she were as agile. Or at least half as agile. Even a tenth of her agility would have done Agnes some good. Was it too late to start yoga at her ripe old age? Probably.

"Someone should tell the weather!" she muttered, disgruntled.

"I tell the weather every day," Edwina reassured her, wiping ketchup from her mouth with a cloth. "The weather promised to improve. But what about you? You're not improving."

That was the strange thing about Edwina. On the whole, she was what less-informed people might call "confused." Nothing but nonsense and hundreds of hare-brained schemes in her head, and an unhealthy obsession with reptiles to boot. But sometimes she hit the nail on the head. It was most annoying.

"What's wrong with me?" snorted Agnes. It was meant to sound assertive, but came out as a strangely pathetic whine.

Edwina patted the back of Agnes's hands with her sticky fingers.

"Well, it's the verger, isn't it? He was murdered and you still don't know who did it. Nobody knows. But it's not so bad, Agnes. You don't always have to know everything." She nodded wisely.

A few months back, Agnes had discovered the verger hanging in the church bell tower. Not a pleasant sight on the way home on a Friday afternoon. Murder, Agnes had quickly realised, but instead of getting stuck in as she usually would have, she had packed her bag, overwhelmed, and gone on holiday. It was no secret that it was playing on her mind. Yet the dead verger was the least of her worries at the moment.

She lowered herself onto a stool, sighing.

"It's not the verger," she admitted. "It's this stupid wedding."

2
HOUSE MEETING

The merry month of May was fast approaching and this year it was shaping up to be especially merry, because as well as sunshine and lily of the valley, they had their housemate Bernadette's wedding to look forward to; she was marrying her old flame, Jack. In Agnes's opinion, it was a holiday romance gone horribly wrong. Now Bernadette was about to squeeze herself into a wedding dress—at her age! Then haul herself down the aisle and disappear from the house share to start a new life in an idyllic house in the Cotswolds. And the other housemates had nothing better to do than encourage her in her madness. Why? What was wrong with Sunset Hall? They had everything they needed to live a comfortable life! Hot meals. Nice rooms. Reptiles. Company. A beautiful garden. Brexit. Independence. Even the boiler had now been fixed. What more could you want at their stage of life?

Bernadette obviously wanted more. Love! Happiness! Agnes couldn't get her head around it. Normally, the very presence of her housemates annoyed her—but it turned out that it was even worse when they left, be it through death, like their friend Lillith just last autumn, or like now, through an unexpected and tragic marriage.

Agnes, who always needed a bit of time to get used to any changes, was lagging behind recent developments. Once a member of Sunset Hall, always a member of Sunset Hall! That's what she'd imagined when she'd founded the house share. Death and marriage were inimical to the house share and must be defied!

"You still haven't got a present!" said Edwina critically.

"I haven't," Agnes admitted. "Not even an idea for a present. No idea what I should wear, either."

Agnes resisted the urge to tear her already-thinning hair out, and broke off in frustration.

"That's not a problem," Edwina cooed. "Ideas are everywhere." Her ketchup-hands made a wide arc that encompassed not just the utility room, but practically the whole world.

Agnes groaned. "You should get changed," she said, before Edwina could regale her with any ideas. "And the shears need cleaning too. They'll go rusty if not."

Edwina pouted, and Agnes instantly felt a tiny bit better. She was Agnes Sharp, the voice of sanity in a house that was otherwise rather lacking in the sanity department! She had two feet firmly on the ground, with a walking stick, if need be, and wasn't going to let something as trivial as a wedding upset her.

"At least it's not a big do," she muttered once Edwina had finally shuffled off towards the sink with the shears. "Registry office, then an intimate gathering. How bad could it be?"

BUT AT dinner, as they all grappled with their dried-out hamburgers, and unanimously bemoaned the absence of ketchup, things looked rather different.

Bernadette and her fiancé, Jack, had come back from their romantic afternoon walk even chirpier and more rosy-cheeked than usual and had immediately started banging on about so-called good news.

The best part of the news was apparently that the corner-shop owner's daughter had done a runner with her riding instructor. Good for the daughter, good for the riding instructor, and it was presumably also pretty good for a load of horses, who could now relax a bit, but the real relevance of all this was that it meant that a certain wedding, namely the one between the corner-shop owner's daughter and the local bank manager would no longer be going ahead.

"Backed out and did a runner." Bernadette grinned and lovingly placed her hand on Jack's arm. Bernadette was blind as a bat, but she found Jack's arm as unerringly as a whole squadron of carrier pigeons. Agnes looked down.

"These things happen," said Charlie, gnawing on a burnt chip.

"But not very often," Bernadette countered. "It's perfect! Fate!"

"It means that Foxglove Manor had a date free at short notice," Jack explained, protectively placing his hand over Bernadette's. "We had to strike while the iron was hot."

Fate. Strike. Agnes narrowed her eyes suspiciously. Had Jack had something to do with the riding-instructor saga? It was no secret that Foxglove Manor was the best place around for weddings. Stately home, landscaped gardens, locally sourced fine dining. Apparently, they had a champagne fountain too. It was difficult to imagine anywhere more romantic and it was usually booked up years in advance.

And now, just like that, there was suddenly a date free? Jack seemed a little too pleased with himself for Agnes's liking. He might look like a lovable geriatric penguin on the outside, but he had a long and successful career as a hitman behind him.

The kind of guy who was used to efficiently removing any obstacles that stood in his way. Mind you, he hadn't made the other groom disappear, as would have been customary in his line of work.

"When?" Agnes looked a bit enviously at Bernadette's hand, so safe and sound in its Jack sandwich, and pulled out a pen to note the new wedding date on the house calendar.

When Bernadette warbled the date, she went rather pale.

"Two weeks? How on earth are you going to arrange—"

Bernadette interrupted her. "It's not a problem. The good thing about it is that the vicar is available as well. The vicar, the registrar, Foxglove Manor, the caterers, even a band. The whole shebang! All we have to do is turn up and invite twenty guests."

Twenty guests?

That was the fly in the ointment!

LATER THAT evening, after Brexit had polished off the rejected remains of the burgers and Edwina had switched off the light in the terrarium, the residents of Sunset Hall held a full meeting in the lounge by candlelight. The full meeting got its name because it usually involved a full complement of alcoholic beverages. Sherry, port, whisky, gin and tonic; whatever they fancied. Even Brexit was offered a brandy bean, but rather sensibly declined. Full attendance of all residents was, however, not necessary—quite the opposite, in fact. Bernadette and her groom had sneaked into their room like teenagers, and the rest of the gang used the opportunity to openly discuss the problematic subject of the wedding.

The date was resplendent on the calendar, thickly underlined, circled twice, with a little skull drawn by Edwina, and was getting menacingly closer with every passing second.

Fourteen days.

Twenty guests.

Five overwhelmed residents of Sunset Hall.

One tortoise, a boa constrictor and Brexit.

The numbers were not looking good and they all felt rather daunted by the planning. Jack and Bernadette deserved a wonderful day, there was no doubt about that. But what exactly constituted a wonderful day? That's where opinion was deeply divided.

"Tortoises!" said Edwina emphatically. "Loads of tortoises! We'll defrost Hettie. That's the first step!"

Hettie, the Sunset Hall tortoise, was currently busy hibernating in the salad crisper drawer in the fridge. Warming her up was an important seasonal event each year, but the others doubted the wedding preparations would end there.

"Foxglove Manor really is upmarket," Charlie pointed out. "I'll have to reconsider my entire outfit again. I'd initially thought smart-casual would do, but now it'll have to be super chic."

Charlie spent a disproportionate amount of her time looking fabulous and had even started a lifestyle vlog—at her age! *Charlie's Wacky World of Wonders.* It was wacky, all right.

Agnes let out a snort of discontent. The clothes issue was on her mind, too, and realistically, she had next to no chance of pulling a super chic outfit out of the bag. Charlie might be able to conjure a new, shimmering item of clothing from the depths of her wardrobe each day; Agnes, however, would be lucky if she could find some shoes with a semblance of a heel, stockings without ladders and a dress in a suitable colour. Not too light and not too dark—that was the key at weddings.

She realised that Marshall was looking at her dreamily

over the top of his whisky glass, and she almost choked on her drink.

"Could we maybe briefly discuss the elephant in the room?" she asked irritably.

Edwina looked up hopefully, but obviously there was no elephant.

"You mean the guest issue?" Winston nodded with concern.

"You're damn right that's what I mean!" Agnes responded.

Like everything in life, the unexpected date at Foxglove Manor had a catch. You couldn't just rock up with a groom, a tortoise and a boa constrictor, oh no, you had to invite an appropriate number of guests. The manor wouldn't even switch on the champagne fountain for fewer than twenty guests.

That might be no great shakes for the average couple, but it wasn't the case for Jack and Bernadette. The two of them had met years ago. Back then, Bernadette had hung around with a drug-dealing gang, and at some point, she'd decided to shop the gang leader to the police. After that she had been given a new identity, while Jack had stayed in the same line of business and could now look back on a successful career on the other side of the law.

Life had brought the two of them back together again, but their friendship groups—if you could even call them that—were clearly incompatible. And more than that: the wedding could only go off without a hitch if not a single one of their former acquaintances showed up. That made the guest list issue a bit tricky.

"We're going, of course!" said Marshall.

"We need fifteen more people," Agnes groaned, quickly adding: "and I don't think tortoises and snakes count at

Foxglove Manor" to head off Edwina. If Edwina was to be believed, practically anything could be solved with the help of reptiles. The reality was rather different.

"Well," said Charlie, "fifteen isn't a huge number, is it? If we put all of our friends together . . ."

Silence fell over the room as each of them sifted through potential friends in their heads. When you reached a certain age, your social circle shrank dramatically; for one, of course, because of unavoidable fatalities, but also because you got more and more cantankerous and quarrelsome. The sad truth was that even with five of them, they couldn't muster fifteen people whom they hadn't fallen out with.

Nevertheless, in the end they managed to cobble together a tentative list of sorts.

There was Sylvie, the cleaning lady, who only sporadically put in an appearance at Sunset Hall, and Marshall's daughter with her new beau, as well as her son Nathan, who was well-known to them all.

There was Sparrow, their burglar friend.

And Charlie had a grandson whom she got on well with, and Winston remembered a first cousin twice removed.

Then they ran out of steam.

The candles flickered; the residents of Sunset Hall drowned their sorrows. Silence lay over the table like a second tablecloth, until Marshall stood up and put the record player on. Soppy music oozed out of the speakers. Agnes fidgeted uneasily on her chair.

"It's not quite enough," Marshall muttered, briefly placing his hand on Agnes's shoulder on his way back from the record player.

The lovey-dovey lyrics made Agnes blush. "Where on earth are we going to find extra wedding guests?" she cried, possibly a bit too loudly. The others gazed at her, but Marshall had already moved on and was nursing his whisky again.

Charlie shrugged. "Where else, darling? The internet, of course!"

3

SUNNY SIDE UP

"You mean, you can order them online?" Agnes asked uncertainly, peering at the faces grinning back at her from Charlie's computer screen.

Charlie nodded encouragingly. "Sort of. This one here, for example: John, eighty-two, *wants to enjoy the finer things in life with you*."

"With me?" asked Agnes, aghast, staring at the photo of a man with a bulbous nose posing in front of a red car, his chest hair on display for all to see.

Charlie waved her hand dismissively. "*Enjoy the finer things in life* always means just one thing. You won't get him out of bed."

"Whose bed?" breathed Agnes. Hers? That was completely out of the question. She was prepared to put herself out for Bernadette's wedding, but putting herself out there was something else entirely. And anyway . . . She shook her head, but Charlie had already swiped John from the screen and was now pointing at Mark. Moustache. Dark circles under his eyes. Nice shirt.

"There. That's more like it: *looking for an elegant lady to accompany me on cultural adventures*. And he's only seventy-nine. Believe you me, every year counts!"

"Would you call Bernadette's wedding a cultural adventure?" Agnes asked, sipping her sherry. She felt a bit light-headed. Charlie had dragged her into her room after the house meeting, fired up the computer and then topped up her sherry glass far too many times.

Charlie grinned. "It's definitely an adventure. Here, how about this one: Richard. He's a bit pasty maybe, but he's looking for *company and good conversation*. That'd suit you, Agnes! You like conversation."

Agnes peered unenthusiastically at Richard, who was faintly reminiscent of a lizard.

"Then what? Would he really come to the wedding?"

Charlie swept a wisp of white hair from her face. "Absolutely! I tried it out for my vlog. If you contact five or six of them, there's usually at least one that takes the bait."

"Takes the bait," Agnes repeated, overwhelmed.

"And once he's taken the bait, you bring him to the wedding!" Charlie explained patiently. "And we'll find someone for Winston, Marshall and Edwina . . ."

"For Marshall?" muttered Agnes in disbelief, but Charlie wasn't listening.

"Edwina will be a tough nut to crack, admittedly, but I've got someone in my sights. A yoga fanatic. And hey presto: five more guests. Voilà!"

"Don't you think it's a bit . . ." Agnes faltered. Well, what? Dishonest? Immoral? Shallow? In principle, she didn't actually have anything against people meeting online. She just didn't want to go to the wedding with a lizard; that was the simple truth.

Charlie was wielding the sherry bottle again and shooing away Agnes's misgivings like pesky flies.

"Oh, Agnes! Modern women don't just throw in the towel

when they get to seventy. They're in the prime of their lives. And online dating is part and parcel of it."

Agnes didn't want to be in the prime of her life; she wanted to be in bed, especially at this late hour, preferably without John, Mark or Richard. It really wasn't too much to ask!

"Isn't it a bit risky?" she asked sheepishly.

"I don't see why." Charlie had her hands on her shoulders and was circling her elbows like little wings, presumably to loosen up the tight muscles from all her vlogging. "Look at them. Do you really think there's a killer lurking amongst them? Really, Agnes! Do you always have to have such a one-track mind?"

"I'm not thinking about murder," Agnes said defensively. "And if I was, it'd be Richard's murder. Or Mark's. I mean the risk . . ." She put her hand to her heart, which was beating away beneath her thin cardigan. She was three sheets to the wind and felt dazed and almost a bit guilty. ". . . the risk to my heart."

Charlie lowered her elbow wings and eyed Agnes critically.

"You old romantic, you! Who would have thought? But let's be honest, Agnes: When you're young, yes, it's a big decision. When you're thirty-five you could be stuck with the guy for fifty years or more. And your heart . . ." Charlie placed her hand on her heart like Agnes, but the gesture looked uncertain, more like she was checking whether there was still a heart inside there at all. "But at our age . . . so what? Till death do us part . . . ha!" She grinned mischievously at Agnes.

"But isn't it a bit late?" Agnes peered surreptitiously at her watch and downed the contents of her sherry glass. She wanted to get to bed!

Charlie, who seemed to have found her heart, stood up, swaying a bit.

"It's never too late for love!" she explained in the *Wacky World of Wonders* voice otherwise reserved for her followers. "We might *look* a bit shrivelled, but we're all twenty-five on the inside. We just want to be recognised and seen!"

Above all, Agnes wanted to hit the hay. With some difficulty, she heaved herself out of Charlie's desk chair and made for the landing.

"I was never twenty-five!" she muttered, pulling the door shut behind her.

"Then it's about time!" cried Charlie, clicking in a green box to send Richard the Lizard a message from Agnes.

AFTER BREAKFAST the following day, the residents of Sunset Hall set to drafting a wedding invitation, fuelled by toast and fried eggs. Time was of the essence.

Charlie, who had a few weddings under her belt, had told them how it worked:

Guests didn't just show up of their own accord; they wanted to be wooed and romanced, preferably with sickly sweet phrasing and the promise of a good spread. The invitation should look chic, sleek and, above all, normal, to lull the potential guests into a false sense of security.

They really couldn't afford for anybody to decline the invitation.

Winston, who had the most legible handwriting of all of them, sat at the dining table ready to write, while the others searched for the right words.

They searched and searched.

"*Dear friends*," Bernadette tried tentatively.

Jack gently touched her shoulder. "Most of them aren't really our friends."

"Thank God," said Bernadette, grinning. Her dark

sunglasses sat on her nose at a jaunty angle, her cheeks were rosy and glowing, and instead of her usual clashing colour combinations, she was wearing a practical but elegant suit in a deep-sea blue. Jack might have a shady career behind him, but he was good for her. There was no doubt about that.

"*Dear friends and non-friends*," Edwina suggested diplomatically, but Charlie firmly shook her head.

"*Hi, folks!*" said Marshall.

"Too casual," Charlie advised.

"*Dearly beloved wedding guests*," Winston attempted.

"Not casual enough," said Charlie.

"How about: *Dear guests*?" asked Agnes. "Any guest that's coming is a dear guest, simple as that."

Nobody seemed to have anything against *Dear guests*, so Winston put pen to paper for the first time.

Emboldened by her success, Agnes continued. "*We're hitching ourselves*, err, *getting tied up* . . ." Agnes was briefly reminded of the verger hanging in the belfry. Why was it haunting her like this? Dammit! Now she was all of a dither.

"*We're taking the plunge. Care to join us?*" said Bernadette, with a smirk on her face and a twinkle in her eye. Jack chuckled. The harmony between the two of them flowed over and spilled across the breakfast table. Agnes indignantly stabbed her spurned fried egg and watched the yolk run out. Sunny side up. Ha!

"Sometimes the heart can see what the eye can't," Winston mused.

"The heart can't see a damn thing!" Agnes hissed. "It doesn't have eyes, for goodness' sake."

The others looked at her in surprise.

"It's a quote, or something along those lines, anyway," Winston said, trying to placate her. "It's from *The Little Prince* by Antoine de Saint-Exupéry. A nice saying. The heart sees things invisible to the eye."

"Then you need glasses!" cried Agnes. Even she didn't know why she was in such a foul mood all of a sudden. After all, it was just about Bernadette having a lovely day at Foxglove Manor, ideally with some guests present.

Ashamed of her outburst, Agnes looked at her plate. "Winston, read out what we've got already," she said.

"*Dear guests*," read Winston.

It wasn't much.

Even Charlie seemed to be slowly running out of patience. "The guests don't care who can see or how well," she explained. "And with what. They want to know what they're going to get; it's got to leap out at them."

"Frogs," Edwina suggested. "Frogs for everyone! *Come and celebrate our nuptials with us at Foxglove Manor. There will be frogs!*"

"That's it!" Bernadette cried. "Just without the frogs!"

While Edwina sulked and Winston wrote the sentence down minus the frogs, Charlie studied the email that Jack and Bernadette had received from Foxglove Manor. "We should explain a bit about the order of the day. It's nice to know what to expect, particularly at a wedding. Champagne reception at ten, marriage service in the private chapel at eleven, followed by signing the register, a sumptuous wedding feast and dancing into the small hours. And Foxglove Manor's famous pot-au-feu to keep them going."

"Dancing?" Agnes almost fell off her chair. Into the small hours? There were precisely two activities that Agnes liked doing into the small hours. One of which was hunting murderers. The other: sleeping soundly, and preferably dreamlessly.

She tried to imagine the dancing: Bernadette and Jack, in a close embrace, in a world of their own, surrounded by a motley crew of wedding guests: Sylvie the cleaner and Nathan the Grandson. Sparrow and Richard the Lizard. Charlie, swathed in colourful marabou feathers; Marshall in his uniform draped in medals, jingling like a Christmas tree; Edwina with Oberon wrapped around her neck like an exotic snake dancer. All shuffling and swaying in an awful circle, with Agnes somewhere amongst them in a sensible silk dress.

It didn't bear thinking about!

Charlie seemed to read her mind and frowned.

"Maybe it's best not to mention the dancing. The band is called the Sweet Potatoes. I'm not expecting much, to be honest."

They got the rest of the order of the day down, then looked proudly at the impressive amount of writing on Winston's sheet of paper.

"Maybe we should say something positive to round it off." Charlie pondered. "Something that will encourage them to come?"

"*Come, or you'll regret it!*" Edwina suggested, drawing one of her skulls next to the order of the day.

"Come *and* you'll regret it," Agnes muttered, but Marshall heard her and raised an eyebrow.

Agnes blushed. "Well. I'm just saying it how it is."

The eyebrow lowered in disappointment, it seemed to Agnes.

4
BUTTERFLIES

The next day an official-looking bundle of white envelopes left Sunset Hall. Some of them travelled by post to far-flung corners of the United Kingdom—most notably Dartmoor, where Winston's cousin lived. Some were delivered by hand accompanied by empty promises and less-empty threats.

Agnes fixed a new note to the fridge. *Confirmed* was written at the top, followed by absolutely nothing else for the time being.

The waiting had begun. The day with the skull on the calendar was creeping unstoppably closer, and they were racking their brains about where on earth they were going to get the remaining guests from.

Then Agnes had an epiphany in the shower.

That wasn't anything unusual in itself. When the water was flowing and the shampoo was frothing, her thoughts flowed and frothed too. But unfortunately, she didn't often manage to remember her shower epiphanies for long enough until she was dry again and had the opportunity to immortalise them on paper. All sorts of good ideas had gone down the drain with the soap suds and shampoo residue.

But not this one.

As it tried to slip away, Agnes clung to it until she was dry and wrapped in her dressing gown.

Agnes decided to forgo the pen and paper, and instead put her slippers on so she could present the idea to her housemates in person.

She found Winston, Marshall and Edwina in the lounge. Edwina was feeding the fire with old newspaper; Winston and Marshall were in the process of organising the food and grocery shopping for the coming week.

They looked up in surprise as Agnes breezed in wrapped in her dressing gown, her hair dripping wet.

"We don't need to invite any more guests!" she cried, dripping on Winston's meal plan. "We'll just hire them!"

While Winston patted his plan dry—Agnes gleaned *bangers and mash*, *casserole*, *cauliflower cheese*—and Marshall drew up a chair for her, she explained that there were obviously people who didn't have a choice, people who had to show up at weddings because of their jobs. Photographers. Florists. And suchlike.

You could just hire them. The sky was the limit!

"Maybe Winston could do with somebody to help him with his wheelchair," said Agnes, grinning. Marshall grinned back.

"Why does it have to be me?" Winston moaned.

"And maybe a nurse as well?" Agnes was trying to be creative. "At our age, a nurse is never a bad idea! The people at Foxglove Manor don't care if the guests are there for work or pleasure, as long as they sit at the table and eat the wedding feast!"

"What about a private detective?" Edwina asked suddenly, holding a crumpled scrap of newspaper with small ads on it up towards them. It read:

Benjamin Stout
Private Detective
No case too difficult

"We'll see about that!" Agnes cried, and the next minute she, Winston, Marshall and Edwina were busy concocting a case for Benjamin Stout. A case that could only be solved at Foxglove Manor.

Agnes was finally starting to enjoy the wedding preparations after all.

THE FEELING quickly vanished once she was left alone in the lounge to wrangle with her knitting again. Marshall and Winston were doing an online grocery order, and Edwina was outside interviewing a new contender for the post of gardener. After the passing of their friend Lillith, they urgently needed somebody to tend the hydrangeas and dahlias. Edwina was taking her role very seriously and even had the urn containing Lillith's ashes under her arm, in order to instil a sense of respect in the current candidate and apply a bit of pressure. He seemed to be holding his own. By the skin of his teeth. What teeth he had left, that is. Agnes peered critically out of the window. The man was at least eighty and had a big bushy white beard, but generally made a pretty solid impression. He even nodded politely towards the urn when Edwina introduced Lillith to him.

Agnes tried to concentrate on her knitting. It was supposed to be a hat, a green hat. *Military green.* She irritably pushed the thought to the back of her mind and glared at her knitting project. At the moment it looked more like something you could store onions in, or maybe potatoes. Misshapen was the only word to describe it.

Just recently, a group of knitting-mad women had started making long colourful covers for tree trunks. Nobody knew why, but more and more trees with knitted accessories were popping up all over the village. What a waste of time!

Agnes was so lost in thought that she gave a start when somebody cleared their throat next to her.

"Bernadette!" she cried, half relieved, half disappointed. Whom had she expected it to be? And what did Bernadette want? Wasn't she busy being engaged?

"Hi," said Bernadette, sitting down next to Agnes on the sofa. Was Agnes mistaken, or did she look a bit sheepish beneath her glasses? What was going on? Had the lovebirds had a tiff? Was the wedding off?

"Where's Jack?" Agnes asked semi-hopefully. "Has something happened?"

"He's having a nap," said Bernadette drily. "At our age you need a nap every now and then, even if you're in love. *Especially* if you're in love. And it suits me just fine. I have a favour to ask of you, Agnes."

Agnes put her knitting away and braced herself for Bernadette's request, but her friend didn't say anything to begin with and seemed to be listening instead.

"Life works in mysterious ways sometimes," Bernadette finally muttered.

You couldn't really argue with that, so Agnes didn't say anything. Bernadette was somebody who appreciated a good shared silence. Agnes, however, felt uneasy after a while. The unspoken request hung a bit menacingly in the air.

"Are you having doubts?" she asked.

Bernadette chuckled. "Of course I'm having doubts, Agnes. Doubts abound! Me? Getting married! What a ridiculous idea! I never would have thought . . . I never expected . . . I don't think much of marriage in actual fact. When you can't see, you hear even more, and the things you hear . . ."

She fell silent again, and Agnes readied herself to have to laboriously drag it out of her.

"But?" she asked warily.

"It doesn't matter," Bernadette explained. "I know I'm too old for all of this. I know Jack's difficult and has led a morally questionable life, and that old habits die hard. I know that we barely know each other and we'll probably be at each other's throats after a while. Yet"—she reached out her hand towards the warmth of the fire, a gesture that seemed full of hope somehow—"none of that matters. In here"—she patted the centre of her body—"it feels completely different. Butterflies, do you know what I mean, Agnes?"

"Butterflies," Agnes repeated, at a bit of a loss, trying to imagine the fluttering creatures throwing themselves against Bernadette's rib cage. With limited success.

"If you get them, you have to give it a go," Bernadette continued. "Because if you don't, you're already a bit dead inside—and you'll be dead soon enough."

"Far too soon!" They could agree on that.

"I'd really like you to be my . . . how should I put it . . . bridesmaid doesn't sound quite right, but you know what I mean." Bernadette broke off and looked a bit embarrassed.

Bridesmaid did indeed sound a bit odd; it conjured up the image in Agnes's mind of a nimble figure in pastels desperately trying to catch the bouquet. All very far removed from Agnes.

"The butterflies get to me a bit sometimes," Bernadette explained. "I'd like to have somebody clear-headed by my side. Somebody who's not being driven to distraction."

Agnes stared down at her knitting bag and thought for a moment.

Agnes Sharp, butterfly wrangler. It was an honour—and an imposition.

"Okay," she said finally, and Bernadette squeezed her hand tightly, before returning to Jack, presumably driven back by the butterflies.

RSVP HAD been written haughtily on the invitations, and indeed a few confirmed guests could be added to the list on the fridge.

Charlie's grandson had promised to come, and he was even bringing his partner.

Marshall's daughter wanted to be there, complete with boyfriend and son, Nathan, a.k.a. the Grandson.

Winston's cousin declined the invitation, but Sylvie the cleaner wanted to come with her husband.

The new gardener had been appointed, and some of his first jobs were getting the brambles under control and attending the wedding.

They'd hired a photographer, and, with Marshall's help, Agnes had sent the private detective an email.

Charlie added a mysterious "Christopher" to the list, and Agnes was secretly afraid Richard the Lizard would be next.

Then an RSVP arrived that none of them had expected. One morning, Edwina found the letter on the hall table. At first glance it appeared rather promising: a pink envelope could only be a good thing!

But after Edwina had torn it open, things looked rather different.

"Somebody's really put a lot of effort into this," she cried as she presented the letter to the others at breakfast, and indeed: somebody had painstakingly assembled, then glued together a message from newspaper cuttings, letter by letter.

It read:

Something old,
Something red,
Something stolen,
Something dead.
I'll be there to make sure your big day goes off with a bang.
X.

"XAVIER?" EDWINA asked, glancing quizzically at the *X*. "We didn't even invite anybody called Xavier!"

"That's no Xavier," Marshall said gloomily after he'd found his reading glasses and studied the handcrafted letter in detail. "That's a coward! An anonymous poison-pen letter! Not nice at all!"

"What's the *X* about, then?" asked Winston.

"It's about ruining Bernadette and Jack's big day!" Agnes explained, taking the letter out of Marshall's hand. "It's designed to invoke fear. But whoever's behind this shoddy piece of craftsmanship is sorely mistaken! We're not scared! And Bernadette definitely isn't! We're not even going to tell her anything about it!"

She had got used to her new role as bridesmaid and guardian of the wedding, and took the nasty letter as a personal affront. With nothing but blind faith, Bernadette, spurred on by her butterflies, had decided to take a step into the unknown. And, inspired by their bridesmaid chat, Agnes had concluded it was more than just a personal decision—it gave them all hope. The huge gesture showed that you could decide for yourself when your life was over.

Nothing and nobody had the right to cast a shadow over her brave step!

"You really want to . . ." Charlie began to ask, but Agnes quickly put her finger to her lips and stuffed the letter and its envelope up her cardigan. Was something stirring on the first floor? Bernadette and Jack were notorious for their lie-ins, but once Bernadette was awake, she heard practically everything that went on.

Yes. Something creaked above them. Somebody was on their way to the bathroom.

"What if it's not just an empty threat?" Charlie hissed into her ear. "What if this Xavier means business? We can't just let Bernadette unsuspectingly stumble into a dangerous situation!"

Somebody flushed the loo on the first floor, and Agnes was in a rush to kick the subject of the wretched letter into the long grass.

"We'll keep an eye out for the signs," she whispered. "For something old, something red, something stolen and something dead. If we see any of them, we can start to worry. Until then . . . would somebody pass me the toast, please?"

5
SPORTY LITTLE NUMBER

Despite her outward show of bravery, Agnes was secretly worried.

She'd stuffed the poison-pen letter into the bottom drawer of her desk, where instruction manuals for long-gone household appliances and invoices from the eighties eked out their existence. But, even through the wood and paper, she could still sense it: a malicious, ominous presence. A few times she even had to fight the urge to retrieve the letter and examine it for clues with her reading glasses. What sort of clues was she expecting to find? The basic premise was blatantly obvious, and anybody who had enough patience to painstakingly glue individual letters onto the paper had probably thought about gloves too. Besides, by now almost all of the residents of Sunset Hall had handled the thing—they could forget about fingerprints.

What Agnes found most unsettling wasn't the stupid rhyme, but the envelope it had come in: rosy and untouched, with no address or stamp. It hadn't arrived in the post.

So, how had it ended up on their hall table?

Had the letter-crafter brazenly ventured into Sunset Hall, despite Brexit, boa constrictor, and seven fairly sprightly pensioners? And if not: Who had deposited the letter in their hallway? And how did X even know that there was a wedding on the horizon? Jack and Bernadette hadn't exactly been shouting it from the rooftops.

Had X been invited?

And what sort of idiot wrote a blind woman a poison-pen letter anyway?

Questions upon questions. Agnes was determined to pursue the matter, but she wanted to tread carefully.

"AGNES, ARE you ready? Agnes?"

Somebody was hammering on her bedroom door, and it made Agnes jump. Had she fallen asleep? Had the poison-pen letter been a dream? And what time was it? Afternoon, and by a long margin, she realised after looking at the clock.

The door flew open and there stood Charlie dressed to the nines, wearing a silk jacket, fox stole and even a hat, complete with three pheasant feathers.

"What's going on?" Agnes levered herself out of her wingback chair. "Are we going hunting?"

"Kind of." Charlie had a twinkle in her eye. "We were going to speak to the vicar and take a look around Foxglove Manor. You haven't forgotten, have you?"

Agnes, who genuinely didn't remember a thing, looked suspiciously at Charlie and her strange feathers. Had she really forgotten, or maybe not heard properly in the first place, or was Charlie trying to rope her into an unpleasant task?

"The vicar? How come? Isn't that Bernadette's job?"

Charlie waved her hand impatiently. "Bernadette and Jack are far too busy being engaged. I'm taking over the logistics—this wedding's not going to plan itself!"

Agnes realised that she wasn't going to get rid of Charlie that easily and went to look for her coat.

Coat. Scarf. Woolly hat.

Not a feather in sight.

"You're going dressed like *that*?" Charlie eyed Agnes with an expression of mild horror.

Agnes checked the mirror and shrugged. She thought she looked pretty respectable. "And why not? Believe you me: the vicar has seen worse."

"The vicar maybe . . ." There it was again: a twinkle in Charlie's eye.

Agnes wrapped her scarf around her neck, half wary and half curious, then bundled herself onto the stairlift, and into Charlie's sports car, resigned to her fate.

"Believe me, Agnes," Charlie nattered as she turned towards the entrance, spraying gravel everywhere in the process, "I've done it enough times. You can either organise a wedding or enjoy it. Not both."

Agnes sat awkwardly concertinaed up in the passenger seat and was pushed back into the seat as Charlie accelerated away. The car was a new acquisition. Did Charlie even have a valid driving license?

But it was too late for questions like that; her friend was already heading for the gate, where Marshall was standing holding a daffodil, looking confused and lost. Agnes waved to him, and her heart retracted a little, like a snail whose feelers had found something unexpected as it was crawling along.

Just then, Charlie turned onto the lane and put her foot on the gas, and from then on Agnes's heart was primarily preoccupied with beating, faster and faster, as they raced towards the village at record speed.

As they hurtled through the countryside, where an abundance of apple trees and hawthorn bushes were carefully considering blossoming, Agnes could feel the impending spring for the first time this year. It might still be cold, too rainy and inhospitable, but the way the light lay over everything—soft but stubborn, sticky as honey—was unmistakable, as was the smell. Green and earthy: the smell of plants dreaming of growing. It hovered in the cold air like a promise.

Agnes closed her eyes so she had to witness as little of Charlie's driving skills as possible, and tried to gather her thoughts. While Charlie was organising things, harassing the staff and poring over a seating plan, she would take a closer look at Foxglove Manor. How easy was it to gain access? How many staff worked on site? Was there anything that posed a potential risk? Animals? Machines? Trip hazards?

Agnes had no intention of making things easy for the letter crafter.

"First the vicar, yeah? We've got an appointment," Charlie said after a particularly tight bend in the road. "I mean, how long could it take?"

She obviously didn't know Duck End's vicar very well.

THE VILLAGE hall was just as lacking in charm as Agnes remembered from their visit to the coffee morning. On that occasion it had been teeming with bigoted pensioners; this time it was dead. Agnes eyed the considerable number of chairs that somebody had stacked into little towers, then Charlie spotted a sign that said PARISH OFFICE and dragged her along a corridor.

In the corridor, the verger awaited her.

Of course, he wasn't there in the flesh; after all the man had been dead and buried for several months, but Agnes still felt like she had seen a ghost.

"Come on, Agnes!" Charlie tugged at her sleeve, but Agnes was rooted to the spot in front of the notice board, where somebody had pinned a black-bordered photo of the verger. *Requiescat in pace* was written above it, but Agnes got the feeling that the verger seemed rather stressed peering out of the picture, as if his slightly protruding eyes were looking at her, overwhelmed and almost pleading.

"Is that the . . . ?" Finally, Charlie understood why Agnes wouldn't budge from the spot. "He wasn't exactly a looker, was he?"

"But he was a bloody good organist!" That was about the only thing that Agnes really knew about the verger, but she decided there and then that that was going to change. Fate had brought them face-to-face, so to speak, and the least she could do was ask a couple of awkward questions and find out more about the man himself. She didn't for one second believe the official verdict of suicide.

She had been the first to discover his body, presumably just minutes after his death. Nobody else had seen the expression of infinite surprise on his face. Somebody who had voluntarily put their head into the loop definitely wouldn't have looked as nonplussed as he had. As she was staring at the photo, a door opened at the end of the hallway. The vicar looked impatiently at his watch and cleared his throat, and Charlie finally managed to drag Agnes away. A few moments later they were sitting on uncomfortable chairs and were busy reassuring the rather bewildered vicar that they weren't the happy couple.

As soon as that had been cleared up, the cleric launched into his spiel. Although there was a lot of talk of love, grace and kindness, it quickly became apparent that he would rather be marrying the corner-shop daughter and the bank manager. None of Charlie's ideas gained his approval: not the funny house-share anecdotes, nor the loud rock music that

Bernadette liked to listen to in her room, nor the rice, glitter or petals that Charlie wanted to throw over the newlyweds.

"Unorthodox" was his favourite word. It was shaping up to be a rather boring day.

"Do you have any requests for the sermon?" he asked as he realised that his ideas weren't going down very well.

"As long as it's short," said Charlie quickly. "Short and sweet."

The vicar had leaned forward to write something down but stopped short and frowned. "Anything else? Any Bible readings? A favourite psalm, perhaps?"

Agnes and Charlie looked at each other in disbelief. Wasn't that his job?

"Nothing to do with blind people," said Charlie finally. "I know there's a lot of blind people in the Bible—none of that! Bernadette is blind. She doesn't need anybody else to explain it to her, the old blind worm."

The vicar's half-bald head turned pink. He wrote something down and then crossed it out

"And the ring bearer?" he asked, in a rather strained manner. "Have you had any thoughts about that?"

Charlie and Agnes looked at each other.

Charlie batted her eyelashes; Agnes grinned as broadly as her false teeth would allow.

"Hettie!" they said in unison. If the vicar was going to be such a spoilsport, at least it would be fun to lure the Sunset Hall tortoise down the aisle with a lettuce leaf.

"Excellent!" The vicar looked impatiently at his piece of paper, which had precisely one word written on it.

"Any other requests?" The cleric wasn't his usual talkative self and seemed like he was trying to get rid of them.

Agnes cleared her throat. "What about the music?" she asked. "I know the verger sadly . . ." She faltered and noticed the vicar's bald head turning a deeper shade of red. "But I'm sure there's a replacement by now, isn't there? Somebody who can play the organ?"

"We've got a new youth worker who's taken on most of his jobs," said the reverend finally. "But to be honest . . . We've now got a harpist for weddings."

"What a loss," Agnes continued mercilessly, not letting the vicar out of her sight.

"Dominic was . . . he had . . . nobody ever would have thought . . ." The vicar was struggling.

"Did he have any relatives?" Agnes asked quickly. "Were there any *signs*? Had anybody *expected* it?"

The bald head changed direction and went paler again, from red to pink to deathly pale.

"There were no signs." The vicar vehemently shook his head. "Dominic was a very private person. Cheerful, I thought. Now I'm obviously wondering if I could have done more."

Agnes had a funny feeling that he didn't fully believe the suicide verdict either.

6
PASTA PRIMAVERA

"The verger thing is really getting to you, isn't it?" Charlie said as she helped Agnes fold herself back into the sports car. "You shouldn't blame yourself for forgetting to call the police. It could have happened to anyone! And let's be honest: What exactly have the police done? Sod all. They've been about as much use as a chocolate teapot."

Agnes groaned, managed to swing her foot inside the car, felt a pang in her hip and painfully pulled the other foot in. "It took two days for somebody to finally find him. Two days! He was hanging there the whole time while we were busy finding our passports and looking forward to our holiday. Did you know that? If they'd found him earlier, they might have noticed something. The look on his face, for example."

"Maybe," said Charlie. "But then again, maybe not. We know from experience that the police around here aren't exactly observant, and, well, the look on his face . . . ?"

"It's not that I blame myself," Agnes explained as Charlie jumped in next to her and turned the key in the ignition. "The more I think about it, the more convinced I am that he was murdered, and in a pretty sneaky way. And where there's a murder, there must be a murderer. Do you really think he travelled from somewhere else, committed the murder, then disappeared again? Not likely. The murderer is here in Duck End—close by! Who knows—maybe he's even coming to the wedding!"

That put the big day in an exciting new light.

"THAT VICAR can talk for England," Charlie groaned and put her foot down. Raindrops chased across the windscreen. "Now we need to get a shuffle on, Agnes."

Agnes looked up, where fat angry rain clouds were gathering in the dark sky. "I really don't think we should go to Foxglove Manor now . . . and look at the weather! I'm not even wearing the right shoes . . ."

Charlie searched for, and found, the windscreen wipers, almost coming off the road in the process before managing to steer the car back on course at the very last moment. "Oh, the Manor isn't going anywhere. Let's go into town. I've booked us a lovely table at the Italian restaurant."

Ah, so that was the real reason Charlie had dragged her along. Agnes felt she should make a stand.

"But we can't just go to the Italian restaurant!" she cried. "What about dinner?! The others . . . Today it's . . ." She tried to remember what they were having for dinner this evening.

"Sausage casserole," said Charlie drily. "Edwina's cooking."

They bombed along country lanes from which the light had long since drained away. There was no sign of spring. The outlook was dismal for Agnes's argument too. She pursed her lips. Edwina's idea of haute cuisine consisted of combining tinned soup with tinned sausages and warming them up. It was the culinary low point of the week. Objectively speaking there was very little reason to argue against Charlie's Italian idea. Subjectively speaking, Agnes baulked at being blindsided and told what to do.

"Don't be a bore, Agnes!" Charlie cried, finally switching the sports car's lights on and putting her foot down again. "We've got a date!"

A double date, as it turned out.

ONCE THEY got to the restaurant, Charlie made a beeline for a tall gentleman with lovely silver hair and a bow tie.

Awaiting Agnes, however, was Richard the Lizard.

Although up to now she'd only seen one photo of him, she recognised him instantly by the lethargic way he was sitting and gazing down at the menu. On spotting Agnes, he struggled to his feet. Hip problems, Agnes could tell.

"Hi, I'm Richard."

Agnes nodded sceptically.

"You're actually a bit far out of my radius," Richard explained, offering her a limp hand. "But you wrote so beautifully about your travels and your houseplants that I just couldn't help but . . ."

"Err," said Agnes.

Next to her, Charlie was busy greeting the silver fox. A peck to the left. A peck to the right. Another peck to the left. She glanced over at Agnes and winked.

Agnes let go of Richard's clammy hand. She could well imagine who had really written to Richard. Travels and houseplants? Did Charlie really think that Agnes had so little going on in her life? Inwardly she was simmering with rage, but outwardly she faltered. "I don't think . . ."

"Agnes, darling, this is Christopher. Christopher, Agnes."

Unlike Richard, Christopher had a nice firm handshake, a steady gaze and a chin.

Agnes looked reproachfully at Charlie, but obviously she ignored her. “Be a darling, Christopher, and pick a wine for us!”

Christopher really was darling; Richard, however, fixed his reptilian gaze on Agnes and licked his lips.

“What a lovely hat,” he said finally.

Agnes tore the woollen hat off her head, knowing from bitter experience that her hair now resembled a bird’s nest. See what the Lizard had to say about that! But her date was sitting at the table again, looking earnestly at the menu.

“I might try the risotto. What do you think, Agnes?”

“I need an aperitif,” Agnes croaked. “At least one!”

“Hear, hear!” cried Charlie next to her, elbowing Agnes in the ribs.

When the waiter turned up and muttered something in Italian, she ordered a Campari and orange followed by a portion of pasta with asparagus and peas. Primavera. She wasn’t expecting much of the evening, but at the very least wanted a hearty meal that she could get her false teeth into.

After a few minutes it became abundantly clear to her that the Lizard wasn’t really looking for conversation as he’d claimed on the internet—never mind good conversation. What he was looking for was a silent partner, whom he could rant monologues at.

Agnes didn’t mind.

While Richard’s lips continued relentlessly moving, telling her about his three-bedroom house, his hiking trips and his beloved *ficus benjamina*, Agnes was busy observing what was going on between Charlie and Christopher. They were all over each other. If this was their first date, she’d eat her—well, more than just her pasta primavera, anyway.

It dawned on Agnes a little late that he must be the

Christopher she had seen on the guest list. Charlie's plus-one for the wedding. Had Charlie found him online too? And if she had, why had Agnes ended up with the Lizard?

The food arrived and interrupted Richard's flow for a while. Agnes tried the pasta—fresh, tasty and false-teeth friendly. She indulged in the rather exquisite wine that Christopher had picked out and came to a few conclusions.

Firstly: no matter how blasé Charlie might be acting, she obviously had a bit of a thing for him. Secondly: Agnes wasn't quite sure if Christopher was that into Charlie. Oh, he was doing and saying all the right things and had a smile on his face, but . . . maybe it was his smile that was ringing alarm bells for Agnes (she was reminded of the dead verger for the third time that day). Somebody who was really in love stepped into puddles of doubts and feelings every now and then, went all serious and soft and silent, even if only for a few seconds. It showed when Charlie sipped her wine.

Christopher, though, was smiling as if he were being paid to.

Thirdly—more a question than a conclusion: If Christopher wasn't there for Charlie, what *was* he there for?

"HE LIKES you," said Charlie once the two of them were back in the car after plenty of pecks on the cheek (Charlie) and a second limp handshake (Agnes). "A little nudge and he'll come to the wedding with you. Well done, Agnes!"

Agnes had said next to nothing the whole evening; that was what had left such a lasting impression on the Lizard. Now she felt overwhelmed; full and empty at the same time.

"I'm *not* going to Bernadette's wedding with Richard!" she said—emphatically, she hoped.

Charlie shook her head and put the car into the wrong gear. The engine screeched. "Don't be so narrow-minded, Agnes.

A little flirtation never did anybody any harm, not even you. You don't have to see him again after the wedding."

Agnes sank deeper into the passenger seat and didn't say another word.

The awkward truth was that it was a bit late for a little flirtation.

At least a week too late.

She was engaged.

Secretly.

To Marshall.

To a certain extent, it had been an accident.

7
RUNAWAY TRAIN

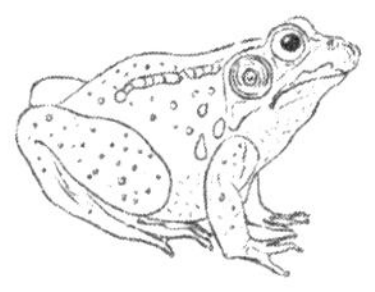

Marshall was sitting in an armchair watching the daylight casually take its leave of the sky. Outside, a bird was singing. A blackbird or a nightingale? Marshall wasn't sure but secretly hoped it was a nightingale.

Still not back yet. Shadows wandered. His toes were cold; the arm in the sling was making itself felt: a gently throbbing, almost affable pain. He would have liked to lie down, but that obviously wasn't an option. This wasn't his room after all.

Meanwhile, the sky was as dark as slate, and rain was throwing itself against the windowpane. It sounded like gravel.

Marshall had thrown gravel at windows in his time, and they had run out of their rooms, their hair loose and their eyes sleepy, questions and promises written all over their faces.

That was . . . quite some time ago.

Now he was the one looking out of the window, waiting for something. For spring, for example, but it was a long time coming, a bit longer each year.

What was he waiting for?

He looked down at his good hand; it was holding something, something small and appalling. This was the reason he was here. One of the reasons. A good reason. Marshall clung to it as if he were drowning.

It was so late already.

And it was still raining.

LAST WEEK Agnes had been sitting in her room unsuspectingly reading a murder mystery and nibbling on brandy beans when, thanks to her not-so-new hearing aid, she heard a loud crash.

She had paused, listened and waited for one of her more mobile housemates to investigate. Then she'd remembered that Bernadette and Jack had gone into town. Despite the steady rain, Charlie, Edwina and Brexit had gone for a less-romantic and welly-clad walk. And since Marshall wasn't moving either, and Agnes's murder mystery wasn't progressing very well—nobody was even dead yet—she had struggled out of her chair to see if everything was all right.

Outside in the hallway lay Marshall, quite clearly unconscious, in a sea of baubles. Agnes immediately realised what must have happened: Marshall had finally brought himself to put the box of Christmas decorations back in the loft—rather belatedly. He must have slipped on the steep steps and taken a tumble along with the baubles.

She had dropped the book in shock, kneeled down painfully next to Marshall and started to shake his arm.

To this day, Agnes wasn't sure that the whole thing wasn't a ploy, but the arm she had shaken quickly turned out to be broken, and later, while they were spending far too long waiting for a doctor in a narrow grey hospital corridor, Marshall had recovered from the shock and shamelessly exploited the unexpected tête-à-tête.

He was pale and looked the worse for wear, but also

somehow daring, and Agnes could still feel the shock deep in her bones. Aside from that, she felt guilty because she had been nagging him for months about the Christmas decorations.

One thing led to another. Marshall had looked at her feverishly, and she, haunted by a guilty conscience, had meekly said yes to everything.

Now she was engaged.

It was like a runaway train.

At first, she had hoped that he would forget the whole thing—Marshall forgot quite a few things these days—but that hadn't been the case. Marshall might forget breakfast, the washing-up and the Christmas decorations, but every time he saw Agnes he got this wet puppy-eyed look on his face, not unlike Brexit when he spied some meat on the table.

Engaged.

Her!

At her age!

Was she in love?

At least she wasn't married yet. Agnes wanted to very closely observe how things went for Jack and Bernadette before even thinking about taking the plunge.

She didn't want to move to the Cotswolds with Marshall. She wanted to stay here, at Sunset Hall!

She just wanted a bit of . . . well, she couldn't put her finger on quite what she wanted.

And what did Marshall want? In all the excitement at the hospital Agnes had forgotten to ask him, and since then she'd been avoiding him at all costs. Now she had to somehow tell him about Richard the Lizard!

SUNSET HALL stood dark and silent as Charlie parked her red sports car in front of the house. Nothing stirred, not even Brexit. Rain pelted the windscreen and Charlie groaned.

"Bloody weather! If it doesn't change soon, Jack and Bernadette are going to be getting married in the mud."

"With frogs!" said Agnes, and suddenly they were giggling like a pair of teenagers, until Agnes remembered she was supposed to be offended about the surprise attack and Richard the Lizard. The only person around here who liked surprises and reptiles was Edwina, after all.

She watched as Charlie got out of the car, glancing angrily at the heavens before rather unsteadily making her way over to the passenger door to help her out.

"Don't be all huffy with me, Agnes. I only organised a little date for you . . . Sometimes we have to get out of our comfort zones a little bit. If you stay in your comfort zone all the time, you're already dead."

More wisdom from the *World of Wonders*. Charlie grabbed Agnes's forearm and heaved. Her pheasant feathers were dripping. Agnes could feel the rain creeping down her neck despite her coat and scarf. Water always found its way. Water—and feelings. She looked up at Marshall's window, where muted light was seeping through a curtain. He was still awake. *Dammit.* Charlie had absolutely no idea how far out of her comfort zone Agnes currently was.

Miles out.

And obviously Charlie was wrong with her truisms. If you stay in your comfort zone, you're comfortable, that's all. The only people that are dead are dead people.

They parted ways in the hall because Charlie wanted to treat herself to a nightcap. Agnes made a beeline for her bed, trying to make as little noise as possible.

She took the stairlift upstairs, crept past Marshall's door, where a strip of light was pouring through the slightly open door, got to her room and shut the door behind her. She'd made it! Relieved, she pulled her hat off and shook the rain from her coat.

Then she put the light on.

"Agnes!"

Marshall leapt out of her chair as if he'd been bitten by a tarantula.

Agnes stifled a scream.

Marshall! In her chair! At this ungodly hour! What on earth did he want? Agnes felt a sense of guilt and fury at the same time. What a nightmare!

She opened her mouth to air her grievances, but Marshall held something out towards her, as if in defence.

A slip of paper.

Agnes looked for and found her reading glasses, and read the slip of paper.

Then she had to sit down.

"Do you think it could be a coincidence?"

"It'd be a pretty big coincidence!"

Once they had recovered from their respective shock, they both studied the newspaper article that Marshall had been holding in his hands when Agnes had walked in.

TRAGEDY AT THE ALTAR.

DOUBLE MURDER IN DUCK END.

EXTRA EDITION.

8
BRISTLY

It was old news. Practically pre-historic. Agnes could only vaguely remember the story; after all, it had been over forty years ago and she hadn't been in Duck End at the time. She'd been living in London and hadn't had anything to do with the case, either professionally or privately. But obviously the village rumour mill had got to work, and over the years the details of the case had been repeatedly hashed and rehashed.

It was a pretty straightforward story, really.

Myrtle Simpson and Johnny Grimes. Seconds before they were due to say "I do" in Duck End church, they were shot dead by the soldier Walter Taylor. A crime of passion, most people thought. To this day, the topic could pep up dull coffee mornings and boring parish socials.

But this wasn't about the bygone murder. It was about the newspaper article itself, neatly cut out and slightly yellowed. Where on earth had Marshall found it?

"Downstairs on the doormat," said Marshall, as if he'd read her mind. (Agnes dearly hoped he *wasn't* reading her mind.)

"So, somebody put it through the letterbox," she deduced.

Not exactly an investigative masterstroke, but the facts had to be ascertained. "Just like that?"

"In an envelope." Marshall had dropped the article onto Agnes's desk like a hot potato and was waving a pink envelope in front of her face.

X was back! No doubt about it!

"When?"

"Well, let me think, it was about . . ." Marshall furrowed his brow, and Agnes could tell that he had absolutely no idea when he had made his find. "It was already dark and I went downstairs again . . ." He faltered.

She could well imagine what had happened. Marshall had missed her at dinner, had been waiting for her return and had traipsed restlessly through the house while she was busy eating pasta primavera with Richard the Lizard.

She irritably pushed her guilty conscience away. It wasn't her fault that Charlie had lured her to a secret rendezvous! And the engagement wasn't exactly her fault either!

"And you didn't see anybody?"

Marshall rubbed his temples. "I think I maybe saw someone at the gate. A figure in white. Or maybe not. And then there was the rattling sound."

Rattling? A figure in white? Things were getting more and more . . . well . . . *colourful* probably wasn't the right word.

"Maybe?" asked Agnes. "What's that supposed to mean?"

"It means I was lost in thought," cried Marshall testily. "I've got other things on my mind right now!"

Presumably Agnes and the blasted engagement. Agnes felt a wave of solidarity with Marshall well up inside of her. They had the same things on their minds! That was something!

She quickly changed the topic before things got soppy.

"It's pretty obvious what's going on here."

Marshall nodded. "*Something old.*"

"X." Agnes sighed. "You know, I was wondering how he was going to manage it. *Something old.* I mean practically everything in this house is old. You'd think it wouldn't be that easy to find something that would stand out. But this . . . it's perfect! It even has a date on it!"

Marshall looked more closely and whistled through his teeth. "That really is a long time ago. Do you remember . . . ?"

Agnes shook her head. "Not really. The case obviously caused a big stir back then. The brutality of it. The tragedy, so soon before their . . ." She stopped herself from saying the problematic word. "But the truly mysterious thing was that nobody ever worked out what this Walter Taylor had against the bride and groom. The police couldn't make a single connection between the murderer and his victims. Obviously, there were the craziest rumours, but in reality . . . As soon as they took the gun from his hand he was as meek as a lamb. Let them take him away without putting up a fight and, as far as I know, never said a single word on the topic."

"A crime of passion!" said Marshall with utter conviction. "What else could it be?"

"But Taylor was a good ten years older than the bride and groom. He was stationed on the coast, and in all likelihood the three of them had never even . . ." Agnes fell silent and thought for a moment. "You mean, it tells us something about X? About *his* motive?"

Marshall was right—it wasn't really about what might have been going through Walter Taylor's head forty years ago. The question was what was going through X's head. Was he jealous? Of Bernadette? Of Jack? Or about the wedding itself?

"One of Jack's exes," Marshall presumed, almost looking

a bit wistful. Did he wish that Agnes would show a bit more interest and threaten past and future lovers with newspaper articles?

"Or Bernadette's," Agnes added. But it wasn't very likely. There were a lot of scoffed fondant creams in Bernadette's past, but as far as Agnes knew there hadn't been much romance. On the other hand, a former lover had just come out of the woodwork. If there was one, there might be more. Perhaps, in her role as bridesmaid, Agnes should have a heart-to-heart with her friend.

"In any case, it's the last thing you want to see when you're just about to get married," she continued.

Marshall didn't seem to hear her. He had the Brexit-staring-longingly-at-a-sausage look on his face again and was gazing at her intently, but silently. Agnes got up from the desk chair to put a bit of space between her and the look. Her face was glowing. She had drunk too much wine at dinner and her thought process was more sluggish than usual. Where to next? To the left, where her bed was awaiting her? That might give the poor man the wrong idea. To the right, to the wardrobe? Or onwards, to the loo? She could hardly barricade herself in the ensuite!

She stood in the middle of the Persian rug, at a complete loss. She was trapped! In her own room. And it was all because of that stupid newspaper article. She was absolutely furious.

"What on earth does he want?" she cried. "To scare them? But why?"

She went back to the desk and tapped the yellowed clipping reproachfully with her index finger. "What is it trying to *tell* us?"

Her fury seemed to hit Marshall, and all of a sudden, he looked tired rather than soppy. "Presumably that getting married in Duck End is a rather dangerous undertaking," he said drily.

"But they're not even getting married in Duck End. They're getting married at Foxglove Manor!"

There it was again—that funny feeling that something wasn't quite right. Obviously, something wasn't quite right if you were getting handcrafted poison-pen letters and ominous articles shoved through your letterbox, but it was something else that was unsettling Agnes.

A murder without a motive.

In the wrong church.

A letter to a blind woman.

A stupid poem.

Something was off about the whole thing. Close, but still slightly wide of the mark. It was as if the letter writer didn't quite know who their actual target was.

Marshall ran his fingers through his military buzz cut. "If there wasn't a motive forty years ago . . ."

"Of course there was a motive," Agnes interrupted. "Just because you can't see something, doesn't mean it's not there, not by a long chalk."

Her thoughts wandered involuntarily back to the verger. The motive there was unclear too. Agnes thought back to the photo on the noticeboard, then she looked at the yellowed newspaper article again.

All of a sudden, the two things seemed to bear a vague similarity.

The picture of the verger was a newspaper cutting, too, and had then—with a distinct lack of care—been stuck onto the noticeboard with a drawing pin. It was far from a respectful tribute. Usually, you'd expect a little table and a proper picture frame, and ideally a little vase of flowers.

Definitely not a drawing pin.

The article had been sent to intimidate them—maybe the picture of the verger on the parish noticeboard was there to serve the same purpose? A warning? But from whom? And for whom?

Who had pinned the verger onto the noticeboard?

And who saw it?

"Agnes! Agnes!" Marshall's face was suddenly hovering unsettlingly close to her face. Had she drifted off? While standing up? Agnes gathered herself.

"I'm thinking!" she cried in annoyance.

Marshall took a step back and tried to cross his arms. It didn't really work because one of his arms was in plaster. "About what?" he asked.

"About . . . about . . . X, of course," Agnes cried. The business with the verger would just unnecessarily overcomplicate her nocturnal rendezvous with Marshall. "We've got something old. Now we just have to brace ourselves for something red and something stolen. He'll have to deliver them, won't he? And ideally, we need to stop him before he can present us with something dead! We'll . . . we'll set a trap for when he tries to post something through the letterbox. That would be my suggestion!"

Marshall was still just standing there with his arms (sort of) crossed. There was a hint of a smile beneath his moustache. Was he laughing at her? Agnes wanted to say something biting to wipe the smile off his face, but next moment the smile and the moustache were making their way towards her and the words stuck in her throat.

Marshall took her hand and planted the hint of a kiss on the cool skin. She felt his breath and bristly whiskers. The smile remained there, too, warm and tickly. Marshall looked at her for a moment with a serious expression and then took a surprisingly gallant little bow.

"It's late," he said. "Good night."

Agnes just stood there, her mouth agape, watching Marshall as he made his way towards the door and, without turning around, disappeared into the hallway.

She still wasn't sure if it had been a good idea to get engaged—but she was suddenly very sure that being engaged to Marshall was better than being engaged to anybody else.

DESPITE THE wine and tiredness, Agnes found it really difficult to settle. She tossed and turned, tried counting sheep, goats, at a pinch, or if need be, lizards.

One.

One lizard. One lizard was more than enough. She knew Charlie too well to hope that the whole thing was over and done with after just one dinner. No, once Charlie got something in her head . . .

As if the stupid wedding wasn't already complicated enough, what with the guests and poison-pen letters! She slipped out from beneath the covers in annoyance, wrapped herself in her dressing gown and went to look for her slippers.

Then she took the stairlift downstairs and just stood in the hallway for a little while, at a loss. There was the doormat, above it the letterbox, through which the stupid article had made its way to them. Agnes peered outside through the stained-glass window in the front door, but thanks to the dark, she could only make out a little bit of veranda and gravel path. She doubted that it had been much different for Marshall—unless whoever delivered the article really had done their shady dealings wearing brilliant white. In that case, you probably would have been able to spot them from a bit farther away. But who wore white when they were trying to trespass on someone else's property to deliver an anonymous letter? A bride? A deranged Miss Havisham, who, loosely based on a Dickens character, goes around threatening happy brides? Now her imagination really was running away with her!

Agnes discontentedly made her way into the kitchen to calm her nerves with a glass of hot milk. While the milk unflinchingly headed towards its boiling point and was probably already burning on the bottom a little, Agnes examined the growing list on the fridge.

She saw that Charlie had already added Richard, presumably spurred on by her nightcap. She was very much mistaken!

Sylvie. The gardener. The photographer. Christopher. Sparrow.

Was one of them X?

It wasn't very likely.

She poured the hot milk into a glass and sipped it. Too hot! But it didn't matter. Agnes had long thought that the calming effect of hot milk lay not in the milk itself, but in the time you had to wait for it to cool down to a bearable temperature. There! She felt sleepy already!

Suddenly, she heard a noise behind her.

A dragging and scratching and rustling sound.

Here in the kitchen.

Really close by.

Next moment she was certain that the noise was coming from the fridge.

9

SPRING AWAKENING

The big day had finally arrived. The best day of their lives for some of them, or one of the best at least.

Specifically for Edwina.

The big day had nothing to do with the wedding. It was the day that Hettie the tortoise was woken from her cold slumber.

Everything was ready: a shallow dish filled with lukewarm water, a fluffy towel, a heap of fresh dandelion leaves that Edwina had tracked down somewhere in the still very bare garden, and of course the residents of Sunset Hall, every single one of them in a celebratory and slightly giddy mood.

Charlie was wearing her red kimono, Brexit his going-out collar, Winston a colourful striped jumper and Bernadette her best sunglasses. Agnes had managed to locate a presentable lace blouse in her wardrobe, and Marshall was draped in an appropriate number of medals. Even Lillith's urn was ready; Edwina had decorated it with a ribbon. Jack, for whom the house customs were still new, was the only one who stuck out a bit with his unkempt hair and dressing gown, but they appreciated the fact that he had struggled out of bed, unusually early for his standards, in order to witness the ceremony.

Edwina earnestly opened the salad crisper and fished

out a still very sleepy Hettie from amongst dry leaves and scrunched-up newspaper, then held her up in the air so that everybody could see her. Hettie indignantly flailed her legs, and relief spread through the kitchen; the residents of Sunset Hall were delighted.

Hettie might be scowling, but she was there, alive, ready to throw her scaly self into another summer of life. It was nothing short of a miracle and it gave them all hope. If Hettie could manage to escape the cold embrace of the fridge and give spring another chance, then it wasn't too late, not for anybody. Life could go on.

"Hettie!" Edwina announced, presenting the tortoise to them as if she were her firstborn. They all felt a little lighter, despite the wedding, vergers, poison-pen letters and engagements. They were mere details—the main thing was life itself!

"Hear! Hear!" cried Winston, although there was actually nothing to hear.

Charlie, who had been filming the whole affair, lowered her phone and blew the tortoise a kiss.

A puzzled grin spread across Jack's penguin face, Bernadette smiled and Marshall gently placed his hand on Agnes's back. In that moment, she didn't mind at all.

That wrapped up the formal proceedings. While the other residents of Sunset Hall scattered and went about their more or less everyday business, Agnes and Charlie remained sitting in the kitchen, drinking tea and watching Edwina devotedly swish the tortoise around in the warm water. It was an edifying and strangely moving sight.

Charlie shifted closer to Agnes and nudged her in the ribs. "Still angry with me?" she whispered.

Agnes stirred her tea to play for time. She wasn't quite sure how angry she was. On the one hand, the surprise-attack-rendezvous with Richard had been a bit much; on the other hand . . . Charlie meant well, and she really did seem rather remorseful.

That decided it.

"The pasta was good," Agnes said, offering an olive branch. "And so was the wine!"

Charlie grinned. "I knew it! He won't be any trouble at the wedding, I promise. The truth is: every head counts. I'll send him a message right away!"

Agnes's peaceful mood instantly went up in smoke. "I didn't mean . . ."

She followed Hettie's example and resigned herself to her fate. She might just be worrying over nothing. Maybe Richard wouldn't even come because the wedding was too far out of his radius. Or he might catch a cold or get lost or find somebody else to bore silly with his walking holidays.

Meanwhile, Hettie was staring peaceably out of her shell, sampling the bath water every now and then.

Edwina looked at her proudly. "I've got the best present," she said confidently.

"What is it?" asked Charlie absent-mindedly.

"A cake," Edwina explained. "The best cake!"

Agnes, who up to now had only experienced Edwina's baking skills in biscuit form, groaned.

"What about you, Agnes?" Edwina challenged. "What are you getting them?"

"A lizard," grumbled Agnes, shooting Charlie a venomous look.

Edwina, who had geared herself up to say something disparaging about Agnes's wedding gift, stared at her wide-eyed and even forgot to scoop water over Hettie's shell for a moment.

"Can I get married too?" she asked after a while.

"In principle." Agnes fell silent. She would rather not think about anything as ridiculous as Edwina's wedding.

"I'm getting married," Edwina announced. "I'm marrying Hettie!"

"Traditionally, it's preferable to marry humans," said Charlie. "Not that that's always a good idea either." She looked up from her phone, grinning, and winked at Agnes. "He's thinking about it!"

Agnes got up without saying a word. She had rather a lot to do and was determined to not give Charlie and Edwina's nonsense another thought.

She needed to have a sniff around in the village hall for information about the verger, and to explain the mission to the private detective they had invited to the wedding. A pretty hefty workload, even for someone who, unlike her, didn't require a nap every three hours. For Agnes it would be a real challenge.

IN A burst of dynamism Agnes got a taxi to the village hall and immediately regretted it. She had a plan, an excuse, and even a handbag—what she didn't have was a key. Agnes rattled the locked door to the village hall in frustration. There was nothing to be done. As she turned around, she saw the taxi disappear around the corner. A cold wind blew around her ears.

There was still no sign of spring.

Agnes pressed her nose against the glass door. There was nothing and nobody to be seen. Where on earth were they all? In her urge to escape the domestic issues, she'd rushed off like a headless chicken.

She had no desire to throw in the towel straight away, so she went along the side of the building and peered in through a window. A long room, filled mainly with chairs; children's drawings on the walls. A washroom. The vicar's office.

All empty.

Agnes spotted a mop and bucket in the middle of the next room. That was more like it. Where there was a mop, there was usually somebody doing the mopping, and maybe they could help her. Agnes shuffled farther along the building.

The back door was locked too, the window at the back too high to look through. She'd almost made a circuit of the whole building when she suddenly had the feeling she was being watched. A tingling sensation in her neck. She warily turned around, but all she was faced with was a neglected little garden filled with spiky shrubs.

And in it, a shabby little cottage. Blank windows like eyes, the door a tormented-looking mouth. The paint was peeling from the window frames. The brickwork was crumbling. Somebody had dropped a bottle on the veranda tiles and the broken pieces had never been tidied up.

Agnes was suddenly acutely aware that it was the house that had caused the tingling sensation in her neck.

"It's a bit creepy, isn't it?"

Agnes spun around and lighted upon a woman wearing a headscarf who was leaning out of one of the village hall windows above her.

"Hello," said Agnes.

"Hello," replied the woman.

They silently gave each other the once-over. Agnes tried to think up a reason for squeezing herself along the side of the village hall like a thief. She looked around. The house caught her eye again.

"Why 'creepy'?" she asked. Sometimes distraction was the best defence.

"Well, to be honest, it didn't look much different when he was alive," said the woman with the headscarf. "But now it seems to *fit* somehow. It creeps me out every time I look at it."

Agnes racked her brains. When he was alive—did that mean . . .

"You mean"—she looked over at the tragic little building again, and it really did fit—"that's the verger's house?"

The woman nodded. The wind tugged at her headscarf. "May he rest in peace. The poor sod."

"But he died months ago."

Properties in Duck End sold like hot cakes. Normally, after a death, a house was sold and renovated in next to no time, and then a family of five with a pug would move in.

The cleaning lady shrugged. "As far as I know, some aunt inherited the house, and I presume it's all a bit much for the old bird." She looked over her shoulder into the room she was currently cleaning. "I'd best get on; the knitting group's coming at three. They're not to be messed with."

She shook out her duster—luckily not in Agnes's direction—and retreated from the window. Not a second too soon; Agnes had already got a crook in her neck from all that looking up.

She peeked over the fence at the sad garden next door. The verger's house—on a silver platter, so to speak! She couldn't squander this opportunity!

10
PAPERWORK

Agnes followed the fence until she reached a crooked little door. The latch was rusted through, so she had no problem gaining access to the forgotten garden. She carefully picked her way past a climbing rose that had long since given up on climbing and was just wildly trailing all over the place. Then she found herself standing at the door watching the paint peel.

The door was locked.

Of course it was. Agnes hadn't expected anything else. She continued along the house, to peer through the windows using her by now tried-and-tested technique. She didn't really know what she hoped to achieve, apart from perhaps a glimpse into the verger's life. Who he had been as a man—and what had motivated somebody to put a noose around his neck. The police would obviously already have had a poke around, and she was far too late to find any real clues, but a little peek couldn't hurt.

The first window had newspaper stuck to it, but not the next one on the narrow side of the house. Agnes had to squeeze past a dried-out dwarf conifer, then she pressed her nose to the glass and peered inside.

At first, she thought there must be some kind of mistake.

Nobody could have lived in there. Not for years.

What she saw on the other side of the glass looked more like a waste paper dump than a living space. Books and magazines were piled up in stacks of differing heights, side by side. Some stacks reached from floor to ceiling; others would only have reached Agnes's hip—theoretically speaking. Practically speaking, there was no space between the stacks. A skyscraper landscape of the printed word! A ghost town made of paper!

Then Agnes spotted a cup perched a bit forlornly on a medium-sized stack of magazines. *House Beautiful.* Ha!

It was a completely normal teacup with a red handle and an unimaginative floral pattern, but it helped bring Agnes back to reality. The verger really had inhabited this space; he'd drunk tea, slept and, somehow, moved back and forth between the stacks of paper. He was an obsessive paper hoarder.

Agnes moved away from the window and leaned on the wall. Her heart was pounding like mad. Then she scurried on, from window to window. Paper dominated the interior of every room. In one, Agnes also discovered a chair; in another a standard lamp soared above thousands and thousands of newspapers, lonely and somehow heartrending. Nowhere did the home furnishings win out against the deluge of paper.

Agnes had made her way to the back of the house and placed her hand on the glazed back door so that she could see better.

The door yielded, and in front of Agnes was a narrow path, just wide enough for one person if they put one foot directly in front of the other. The path led straight into the verger's paper fortress.

Should she . . . ?

Something had become apparent to Agnes: the police

hadn't done a very thorough search of the house. How could they have? They must have taken one look at the yellowed paper landscape, labelled him mentally disturbed and blindly accepted the suicide theory.

That meant that maybe there were still one or two clues to be found, if an intrepid investigator like Agnes were to venture inside.

She sniffed the air inside the house. It smelled a little musty, but not entirely unpleasant. Agnes took one step forward, then another. Paper rustled under foot, but none of the stacks budged. She looked down at a tower of cookbooks from the eighties—*Cooking with Eggs*—then back at the door. Outside, she could make out a sprawling juniper bush that blocked the view into the neighbouring garden. It was pretty unlikely that anybody could see her, and if she was caught, she could roll out the confused-old-lady routine; nobody ever questioned it.

So, she followed the path, past gardening books and junk mail, and arrived in a gloomy hallway, which was really more of a gully between stacks of mail-order catalogues and telephone books. Aside from the deluge of paper, the house seemed pretty organised to her, orderly almost. What had prompted the verger to obsessively hoard printed matter? Could a question like that ever have a rational answer?

By now, Agnes had moved a fair way from the back door and could hardly see her hand in front of her face. It was so gloomy. She only now realised how cold it was in the house. She shuddered. Her biggest fear was falling over and being buried under a mound of paper.

It occurred to her that she was on edge after all. It wasn't a very good idea to be stumbling around deserted houses all on her own at her age, never mind a house like this. Marshall would not have approved. But what did it have to do with

Marshall, anyway? She was here because she felt like she'd left the verger in the lurch, and because she had a hunch that something sinister was going on in the village, right under their noses. She took a deep breath and waited for the fear to shuffle back to where it belonged—in the pit of her stomach. It had no business being in her head.

It gradually got lighter again. Agnes pluckily plodded on and arrived at two more doors. The one on the left led to the room with the teacup; the one on the right to the room with the window obscured by newspaper. The kitchen, Agnes ascertained on sight of a microwave, a kettle and three more teacups. Everything was strategically, but solidly placed on stacks of newspapers. And then there were the cranes. Somebody had taken advantage of the paper glut and folded magazine pages, newspapers and junk mail into paper cranes, not expertly, but meticulously. The beaky little sculptures made the room feel strangely playful.

DESPITE THE cranes, the kitchen exuded a touch of normality. There was a sink, two hob rings, a table and chair, and even a few square yards of empty floorspace. Agnes decided to have a little rest on the chair to get her thoughts in order and then beat a hasty retreat.

The chair was more comfortable than she had expected, and the kitchen suddenly felt rather cosy. A cave, a tent, a hideaway, lined with paper, guarded by cranes. The newspaper on the window let just enough light through, but the outside world stayed exactly where it should be: outside.

It dawned on Agnes that she was doing exactly what she had planned: seeing the world through the verger's eyes. She looked around with renewed curiosity. This is where he sat, drank tea and ate his meals, planned concerts, and presumably sorted through an unholy amount of paper. Unlike in the other rooms, there was a shelf or two. They probably held the things the verger had cherished most.

18th Century English Organ Music.

Managing Modern Youthwork.

Bell-Ringing: The English Art of Change-Ringing.

She frowned. It was that very English art that had been the verger's undoing—but why? After everything she'd seen, he seemed like nothing more than a lonely paper sprite who had spent a large proportion of his free time sorting and stacking printed matter. Obsessive, but harmless. Somebody who was only hurting himself.

Agnes stood up and stepped closer to the shelf with the books on it. Something was poking out from between them, a small yellowed volume that had something vaguely familiar about it. She grabbed it, pulled and the next moment she was holding a small-format newspaper that she knew very well. *The Sunday Post*, the unimaginatively named weekly newspaper from the just as unimaginative nearby county town. She'd held this publication in her hand countless times before, but had rarely opened it because she had a limited interest in cake recipes, car accidents and charity galas.

But now a funny feeling came over her. It wasn't a current edition, far from it. The typeface was different to what Agnes knew, the paper thinner and yellower.

She opened the newspaper, and a deluge of single letters of the alphabet poured out onto the kitchen table. Big letters and small letters. Colourful and black-and-white, but all neatly cut out. Next, the side of the newspaper caught Agnes's eye; someone had cut an article and the date from the top edge.

Agnes was slowly beginning to take fright. Her eyes wandered through the room, past the siege of paper cranes, whose beaks seemed to be curled into sinister expressions, and landed on one of the strategically placed teacups. In it was a dark liquid, complete with greasy streaks. Tea in a teacup wasn't usually a shocking discovery, but Agnes got goosebumps. The house had been empty for months; any leftover tea should be long dry.

X!

He was *here*!

It suddenly felt even colder in the kitchen.

11
CHEESECAKE

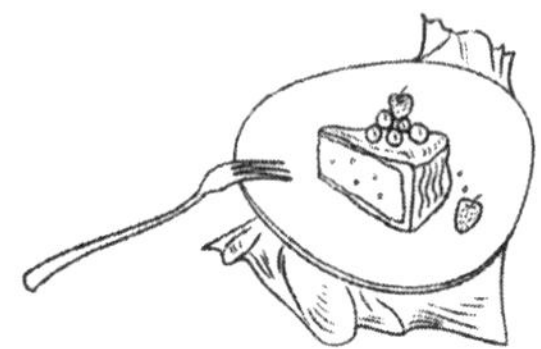

Private Detective Benjamin Stout was a surprisingly lanky man.

He had quick, clever eyes, a striking moustache and the knack of dressing appropriately, but completely inconspicuously. Agnes was sitting directly opposite him and even she would have been hard-pressed to describe his clothes. Shirt. Tank top. Trousers were presumably part of the ensemble. But was his overcoat grey or green? Was the shirt beige or brown or even yellowish? His lower body was covered by the marble tabletop, and Agnes couldn't for the life of her remember his trousers or his shoes.

All in all, the man didn't seem like a complete idiot. Agnes was pleasantly surprised.

She had taken a taxi to Foxglove Manor, a few miles outside the village, to meet the detective in the café as arranged. Now they were getting stuck into some coffee and cheesecake, while Agnes had the chance to give the manor, as well as the private eye the once-over. Killing two birds with one stone, although that turn of phrase didn't really seem appropriate in this elegant setting. She poured milk into her cup, stirred and felt very sophisticated in the process.

The café was the kind of place that surreptitiously patted you on the back. *Welcome. Well done. I'm chic. You're chic. We belong together!* The floor consisted of polished stone with a marbled, swirling pattern, as if somebody had poured ink into milk. The table didn't wobble. Agnes's cake fork had a good weight to it and lay in her hand like a samurai sword.

"Hmm," the detective murmured his approval after a forkful of cake had disappeared beneath his moustache. "Delicious. Thank you, Miss Sharp. How can I be of service?"

With the help of Winston and Marshall, Agnes had concocted an absurd story of a stolen diamond to lure Benjamin Stout to the wedding, but it suddenly seemed like a bit of a waste to give the detective a made-up mystery when so many real ones were buzzing around in her head.

"Well," she said to play for time. "It's a bit of a delicate situation, to be honest."

"It usually is." Benjamin Stout smiled warmly, and Agnes couldn't help but smile back.

"It's about my friend Charlie," she said. "We live together, in my house, I mean we're housemates . . ." She almost lost the thread before she'd even begun, but the private eye's smile brought her back on track. "She's started seeing this guy. Christopher. I think she only just found him online and . . . well, I don't really know. Something's not right about it. I'd feel a bit more comfortable if somebody was looking over his shoulder a bit."

Benjamin Stout tapped his moustache with his index finger. It was obviously his thinking pose.

"Have you met this Christopher in person?"

"Just the once," Agnes admitted. "At the local Italian restaurant."

The detective nodded as if it was a crucial piece of

information. "And what exactly is it about Christopher that makes you suspicious?"

"His smile," said Agnes without thinking. "He smiles too much. There's something fake about his smile."

"Smiling isn't a crime." He forked up another bite of cake and raised his eyebrows. Rather flimsy, is what the eyebrows said. A flimsy suspicion.

"It's just a gut feeling," Agnes admitted. "But my gut's usually . . . And she's just the type as well. Charlie, I mean. She's the type who always falls for the wrong kind of men." Whereas Agnes was more the type who didn't even fall for the right kind of men.

Benjamin Stout looked at her sternly, seemingly a bit puzzled. How old was he? Fifty? Sixty? A spring chicken, that was for sure. Was he not taking her seriously? Did he think romantic dramas on the other side of seventy were a waste of time? Agnes clutched her reassuringly heavy cake fork. She was here. At Foxglove Manor. With the detective. Everything was going according to plan. In principle, it didn't really matter if he believed her or not, just as long as he came to the stupid wedding.

She gathered herself and carried on talking. "There's a wedding coming up. Here at Foxglove Manor, in fact. Not Charlie's—thank God. My friend Bernadette and her fiancé, Jack. But Charlie's going to be there and she's bringing Christopher. I'd like to obtain an invite for you"—she acted as if the invites were highly coveted—"then you can see for yourself. If I'm wrong, I'm wrong. But if I'm not wrong . . . well, it's better to be safe than sorry."

The detective looked at her like she'd lost her marbles. There was an amused twinkle in his eye.

"And do you think it might be a good idea for me to use

the opportunity to keep a little eye on Jack as well?" he asked casually.

"No," Agnes squeaked in horror. Definitely not!

She was beginning to wonder if it was a good idea to invite a private detective to the wedding of a former contract killer. When you really thought about it, there was a lot that could go wrong! But it was a bit late for doubts. And apart from anything else, they needed Stout—maybe not as a private detective, but definitely as a guest. She realised that he thought she was jealous of her friend's happiness. He couldn't be more wrong. She was worried, that was all.

"I've got nothing against Bernadette getting married!" she blurted out. "She's . . . they're . . . they suit each other, and I've got nothing against love per se. I'm engaged myself, in fact! It's just this Christopher that worries me!"

"Congratulations," said Stout.

Agnes blushed. He'd managed to wheedle her top-secret engagement out of her by just staying quiet! He was better than she'd expected.

"The engagement's a secret," she snapped. "But it's not about that. It's about this guy. Have a look into him. Try to get some information on him. And enjoy a slap-up meal into the bargain. That's the job. Nothing more. Aren't you going to take any notes?"

Benjamin Stout shrugged. "Up to now you've only given me two relevant pieces of information. Christopher and the wedding. If I needed a notepad for that, you shouldn't even consider hiring me."

He had a sip of his coffee and then returned to the cheesecake as he outlined his fee, which consisted of an hourly rate and expenses. Calculated in fifteen-minute increments. Nightwork was extra.

Agnes was barely listening.

There was a sea of daffodils outside the picture window. Bumble bees busily bustled between them, glossy blackbirds patrolled the lawn, a magnolia's pinkish petals defied the cold wind. She tried to imagine Bernadette beneath the cherry trees, a bride with a flowing veil, head to toe in white.

She couldn't imagine it. Instead, the verger appeared in her mind's eye, a baleful figure in black, bald on top with a thin strip of hair reaching from one ear to the other, eyes bulging accusatorily out of his head. She had recovered from the initial shock she'd felt in the kitchen of the paper house, but she couldn't stop thinking about him.

Obviously, the verger wasn't, as she'd thought in the first throes of panic, the one who was drinking tea in there and sending them painstakingly handcrafted poison-pen letters from the other side. How could he be? The man had been dead and buried for months. Still, he must have had something to do with X—or X with him. She couldn't make head nor tail of it all. It scared her.

After her discovery, Agnes had staggered out of the house, completely stunned, and wandered back to the village hall, where she got the taxi she'd booked. On the way to Foxglove Manor, she'd racked her brains about what someone rattling around in the verger's house might have against Bernadette's wedding. Or was it even the verger's murderer sending them poison-pen letters? And why? Agnes had spent the whole time wantonly neglecting the case. Was that what this was about? Had somebody seen her in the belfry and been bothered that she hadn't called the police? But then why hadn't they reported it themselves?

No matter how she spun it, it didn't make any sense.

". . . and after the background checks, I can give you a

better idea of the price, if you would like. Would you like to proceed?" Benjamin Stout smiled at her. His cheesecake had disappeared.

"Yes, yes," said Agnes, "that's fine." In all honesty, the detective's fee was coming out of the wedding fund, and, as far as she knew, it was well-stocked. Jack had bought a house in the Cotswolds without batting an eyelid and didn't seem bothered that Foxglove Manor was costing them an arm and a leg.

Crime did pay after all, if you played your cards right.

Agnes attacked her cheesecake with renewed zeal. It really was very good indeed. If this was a taste of what was to come, then maybe there was a reason or two to look forward to the wedding.

"Have you been doing this long?" she asked between bites of cake. "The job, I mean?"

She already knew the answer; after all, she, Winston and Marshall had had a poke around his website. He had an interesting and pretty varied CV. Hairdresser. Travelling salesman. Security guard, prison officer, sales rep for hygiene products and finally, private detective. Agnes acted like she was eagerly awaiting his response.

"Quite a while. If you'd like any references, feel free to take a look at my website."

Agnes waved dismissively. "I'm sure you know your stuff. But can you make a living at it around here?"

"You'd be surprised." The detective grinned and Agnes, who had herself been involved in four murders in the last six months alone, wasn't surprised at all. Not really.

"Have you ever investigated a murder?" she asked out of curiosity.

"If I had, I wouldn't be able to tell you about it. Why? Have you got a murder case for me?"

"Me?" Agnes recoiled. "No. Of course not."

Not yet, added a pessimistic inner voice.

Stout now had a notepad and was making notes in a jagged, precise scrawl.

"I'm prepared to take your case on. I'll send you the contract by email, and if you're happy with everything, it'd be helpful if you could give me the following information." He pointed to his notepad. "The full name of this Christopher, his profession, place of residence, and anything else you can find out about him. How long your friend has known him. Anything you can tell me speeds up the process. As soon as I've got all that, I can get cracking."

Agnes gulped. She was going to have to snoop on Charlie; that's what it boiled down to! Was it right to set a private detective on your friend's beau behind her back? Charlie would be livid if she found out. On the other hand, the private eye was needed at the wedding and had to have something to do so that he didn't get any silly ideas and start looking over Jack's shoulder. At any rate, Stout would have seen straight through the stupid diamond ruse.

All the same, the cheesecake was suddenly weighing very heavily on her stomach.

While Stout excused himself and disappeared towards the loo, Agnes tried to convince herself that it was all right to suss Christopher out a bit. After all, Charlie had foisted Richard the Lizard on her. That wasn't very nice either.

"Can I get you anything else?"

Agnes was jolted from her thoughts. A waitress was clearing the plates from the table and smiling down at her. She was very young. Practically preschool age. Agnes noticed how chic her uniform was. A white shirt. Black trousers. A white apron almost down to the ground. Simple, but impactful. Tasteful to the nth degree; you had to give Foxglove Manor that. It was only the girl's smile that seemed a bit odd somehow. Painted on. More of a gymnastic routine for the face muscles than something that radiated from within.

"No, thank you. Just the bill, please. And I've got an appointment. With a Ms. Purr? Constance Purr?" Agnes looked questioningly up at the abortive smile. She could see it get even stiffer, as if it had been frozen in place on the girl's face. Agnes sighed gently. In the past, she wouldn't have given much thought to the quality of a smile. These days, however, she seemed to find fault with practically every friendly facial expression. Too nice. Too much. Too tormented. Was it her age? Did you just get cantankerous and crotchety as you got older? And what about her own facial expressions? There wasn't a lot going on with her face anymore. *A smile is the most beautiful thing a woman can wear*, her mother always used to say. Agnes tried to set her mouth in motion and looked expectantly at the morose waitress.

Suddenly, she heard a woman's voice behind her; it was strikingly deep. "Thank you, Mia. I'll take it from here."

12
FLAMINGOS

Agnes turned around and, thanks to the photo that Marshall had shown her on the manor's website, she knew who the woman was immediately.

Constance Purr didn't walk, she glided. One moment she was standing by the imposing indoor palm at the cake counter, the next she was right beside Agnes, clearing the last coffee cup from the table.

The girl in the white apron scurried away and Agnes looked up at an extraordinary apparition. Like her employee, Constance Purr was also wearing black trousers and a white shirt, but with a black velvet blazer over it, tailored like a riding jacket. Agnes, who spent the majority of her time in baggy cardigans, didn't understand much about fashion but she knew something made-to-measure when she saw it. An expressive face smiled down at her from the other side of the jacket collar.

Not young. Not pretty. Yet, there was something appealing about her. Dark sensual eyes, framed by even darker lashes. Bold red lips. A large, elegantly curved nose that gave her the air of a well-dressed flamingo.

"Constance Purr," she boomed, holding out a well-manicured hand towards Agnes. "We have an appointment? Miss Brown?"

Brown was Bernadette's—well, future maiden name. Agnes vigorously shook her head.

"Agnes Sharp. Bernadette—Miss Brown—asked me to take care of some of the organisation for her. As you know, time is of the essence."

Purr nodded curtly. "I should say it is! The most spontaneous wedding we've ever had! But obviously a stroke of luck for the couple—and the house! Please don't worry, Mrs. Sharp. Everything will be to our usual high standard, no matter how tight the time frame is."

"Bravo!" said somebody behind them, before Agnes could say anything, and the Lady of Foxglove Manor turned her long neck in surprise. Benjamin Stout was finally back from the toilet and was blending in with the dove-grey tapestry behind him.

"Your son?" Purr had reached out her hand in greeting again and Agnes almost fell off her chair. A son? Her?

"Nephew," said the detective flatly. "Unfortunately, I can't stay. Wonderful cheesecake, by the way. See you later, Aunty Aggy!"

He nodded politely and marched purposefully out of the café. Agnes thought that he really did seem to be an extraordinarily good detective; he was very quick on his feet.

"Well, I'll begin by giving you a tour," said the manager cheerily and offered Agnes her arm. Agnes, who otherwise would have flatly refused a stranger's offer of help, compliantly allowed herself to be helped out of the chair. Constance Purr wasn't somebody who took no for an answer.

THEY MADE a funny pair leaving the café arm in arm. Ms. Purr was tall, long-legged and full of energy. Agnes was not.

They turned down a corridor. "This leads to the old part

of the house; the riding arena is over there—probably not that relevant for your purposes. But the view over the gardens is beautiful, isn't it? It'll all obviously look a bit different shortly."

Agnes looked out at the gardens, which seemed as if they were being crushed by the leaden sky. It had started to rain again and the daffodils deferentially bowed their heads.

"Hopefully," she murmured, but Ms. Purr was already leading her up a ramp—*ideal for people with limited mobility*—through a lobby and into the ballroom.

"When I inherited the place, it was practically in ruins," Ms. Purr blabbered. *Countess* Constance Purr, actually, Agnes had read online. She wasn't just the manager—Foxglove Manor was her ancestral home.

". . . squirrels in the orangery, pigeons in the ballroom. And the maze was completely overgrown . . ." She was going all out to explain to Agnes just how awful and run-down everything had been before she had turned the tide with her strong sense of discipline and entrepreneurial spirit.

"Were there tortoises anywhere?" Agnes asked absent-mindedly as they crossed the claret carpets together.

"No tortoises," said the countess emphatically.

"What about frogs?" Agnes probed. Maybe Edwina would be in luck.

The countess frowned. "We might have a few toads in the vegetable garden. We grow all our own produce, you know. Local, fresh and of the highest quality."

"Excellent," said Agnes.

They had arrived in the middle of the ballroom. The countess let go of Agnes's arm, took a step back and awaited her reaction. Agnes looked first to the left, at a row of gracefully curved French doors that led out to a sweeping terrace, then to the right, at a corresponding set of mirrors. Above her, chandeliers floated beneath a ceiling fresco of clouds, angels and feathered creatures; beautiful old parquet stretched out for miles beneath her. Right in front of her stood a long dark-wood table, expectant somehow, as if it were a ship ready to set sail. So, this is where the wedding feast would be served.

She realised that the countess was still looking at her expectantly.

"Nice table," she said uneasily.

The countess looked a bit peeved. "Then perhaps it's best I show you our chapel, the sculpture garden, where we'll hold the reception if the weather's nice, and the Red Room, where the happy couple will sign the register."

Red Room? Sculpture garden? Agnes was struggling to concentrate.

"This is the cloakroom; we'll put the champagne fountain out there . . ." The countess was head over heels with excitement.

A flamboyance of ancestral flamingos stared down at Agnes from the walls. Some were wearing starched white ruffles as big as cartwheels; some were holding rebellious-looking lapdogs or brightly polished shotguns in their hands, but all of them had the same distinctive nose. Agnes wondered what it might be like to have dozens of disapproving forebears watching your every move.

"Would it be possible to see the champagne fountain, please?" she asked. Charlie would never forgive her if she returned home without a detailed description of the legendary fountain!

"The what? Oh, I see." For a moment the countess seemed not just perplexed, but also rather disappointed, then she put her head back and laughed. Her white teeth sparkled.

"Of course, our famous champagne fountain. This way.

I must say, Mrs. Sharp, I've never had a client quite like you before."

"Miss Sharp. And I'm not the client," Agnes reminded her. "I'm just . . ."

The countess wasn't listening. She led Agnes through another corridor into an ultramodern kitchen. Knives flashed, stainless steel gleamed wanly; the floor and tiles were as clean as you would hope an operating theatre to be. Two or three whippersnappers wearing ridiculous hairnets were busy cleaning potatoes and vegetables. Again, it dawned on Agnes how young the staff here were. Shouldn't they still be in school? Or was she now so ossified that anyone under twenty seemed like a baby to her?

She must have said something out loud—or did the countess have a knack for mind-reading? In any case, she turned to Agnes and beamed at her. Mia the waitress could learn a thing or two from that heart-warming smile!

"Many of our apprentices come to us through a charitable youth project. Hand in Hand. Young people who have had a rough ride get the chance to start over. We work with the council, the church and local youth leaders to effect real social change. And here it is!" She pointed proudly at the champagne fountain, but Agnes wasn't really with it again.

Youth work.

There it was, a thread that connected the verger with Foxglove Manor and, by extension, the wedding, thin as spider silk—but spider silk packed a punch!

The champagne fountain, however, was a bit of a disappointment. Without the associated champagne it was just a big, boring lump of crystal.

The manager showed her where you had to hold your glass to get it filled with bubbly.

Agnes feigned interest.

"Did you by any chance know the Duck End verger? Dominic?" she asked abruptly.

For a moment the countess looked like she was about to deny any knowledge, then she sighed. "What a tragedy! Dominic was *very* committed to the cause. It's so sad that he decided to do what he did."

She really did look sad, so Agnes asked a few more questions about the champagne fountain to distract her. She secretly felt giddy, a bit tipsy almost, like a hound who had just picked up a weak, but definite scent.

13

CUPCAKE

Hettie the tortoise was freshly washed and sitting in a wooden box, mourning the good old days.

The good old days were full of sunlight, warm stones and grass. A blue sky stretched out above her, endless and perfect. But what really made the old days so good was not being watched at every turn by two lemon-yellow snake eyes.

Hettie had lived a long and exciting life. She'd hatched from her egg under the burning-hot Greek sun and had almost been scorched by the blistering sand in the process. In her earlier years, she had escaped lizards, crows and cats; she'd survived floods and droughts.

She had been within an inch of dying of thirst in a little box, and in the depressing months that followed in the pet shop, she almost died of longing for the sun, the sky and the wind.

That was followed by an unpleasant time in a kindergarten, where she was continuously poked by little fingers, turned over onto her back and was even dunked into a pot of smelly paint. Hettie quickly realised that the kindergarten didn't have much to do with gardens, and she'd finally escaped through a hole in the fence, had crossed roads, outsmarted lawnmowers, escaped dogs and outfoxed foxes.

The tortoise had defied thousands of dangers, but seldom had she felt as threatened as she did now, beneath the unrelenting gaze of the snake. The split snake tongue tasted the air, retreated, tasted the air again. Back and forth. Over and over.

Hettie forgot to nibble on her dandelion, and tried pulling her head inside her shell.

First her head.

Then her legs.

She doubted that it would help her much should the worst come to the worst.

The good old days were over, that was for sure.

"SHE'S NOT eating much. She's lethargic. She keeps pulling her head in!"

Edwina pointed accusatorily at the tortoise, her finger sticky with cake mix. She'd taken Hettie out of her box and put her in the kitchen, where Edwina was busy pre-heating the oven and mixing together unholy amounts of flour, eggs and dried fruit.

The tortoise was there to act as a muse and a model while Edwina, ably assisted by Charlie, baked the cake to end all cakes.

Agnes had actually only come down for a cup of tea and found the two of them up to their elbows in cake mix.

"She only just woke up," Agnes said, leaping to Hettie's defence. Regrettably, the same couldn't be said of her. After the trip to Foxglove Manor, she'd put her head down for a while, but the eagerly anticipated sleep hadn't arrived. Instead, an endless procession of people, including the verger, Constance Purr, Christopher, Richard the Lizard, Benjamin Stout and an unfamiliar figure in white traipsed past her mind's eye. It was exhausting and soon got boring. She'd finally given up on sleep and made her way to the kitchen just in time to witness the creation of Edwina's bizarre cake. Now she was covered in a thin layer of flour dust, just like Charlie, Edwina, Hettie and the rest of the kitchen. It wasn't a good look.

"No," said Edwina rubbing flour out of her eyes with the back of her hand. "That's not it. Hettie's sulking!"

"Shouldn't we add a bit of sugar . . . ?" asked Charlie, trying in vain to rub cake mix off her forearms. "It is a cake, after all."

Edwina shook her head firmly. "Sugar's unhealthy."

"But it tastes good!" Charlie gave up on her arms and tried to remove a raisin from her hair. "You eat sugar. Tons of the stuff!"

"But I don't gift it to other people! That's"—Edwina searched for the right word—"murder!"

Agnes looked up. "It's only murder if someone's diabetic!"

Edwina crossed her arms stubbornly. Her main objective was to make a stable cake in the shape of a tortoise. Taste and texture were neither here nor there.

"So, I think you should . . ." Charlie found the raisin and threw it into the sink. "Dammit!"

Something hummed and beeped, then a tinny-sounding tune started up. *Somewhere over the rainbow* . . . Charlie patted her hip and finally fished her phone out of her apron pocket with the tips of her fingers.

The phone lit up and started up a second rendition of "Over the Rainbow."

"Gosh, it's Christopher!" Charlie looked frantically from her cake-mix covered hands to her phone and back again. "Agnes! You'll have to answer it!"

"Me?" Agnes hesitated. Christopher was just about the last person she wanted to talk to right now, but then again, she had promised Benjamin Stout she'd gather some information, and this provided the ideal opportunity. "What should I do?"

Charlie groaned. "Push the button. Not the red one. The green one!"

Luckily Agnes had her reading glasses on and managed to differentiate between the green and red buttons.

"Hello?" She listened uncertainly into the phone.

"Well, how's my little sweet cheeks today?" Christopher's voice oozed like warm treacle out of the phone, and Agnes almost dropped it in the mixing bowl.

"I, err . . ."

"Put it to my ear!" Charlie hissed, pointing at the relevant body part. Agnes got up from her chair with a sigh and muttered: "Just a moment, please," and went to circumnavigate the table.

Sweet cheeks. The things they had to listen to at their age. If Marshall ever tried using *sweet cheeks* with her, the engagement would be over in a heartbeat. And what had Edwina said before? Sugar was practically murder—and Christopher was sickly sweet poison!

Charlie was still pointing like mad at her ear; pet names were gushing out of the phone. "Darling. Sweetie pie. My petal. Is that you?"

Agnes sighed and finally held the phone up towards Charlie's ear so that she could hear some of the sweet nothings as well.

Charlie listened into the phone. "Darling?"

She pushed hair out of her face with her forearms, presumably so that she could look prettier for her phone call with Christopher.

"No, of course it's not a bad time. It's never a bad time for you to call, darling. That was Agnes. You remember Agnes? I'm at hers now; we're baking."

She went silent while Christopher probably said something calorific on the other end of the line.

Charlie chuckled and blushed.

"Of course I want to see you too. I've just got my hands full at the moment."

"Of cake mix!" screeched Edwina helpfully.

"Tomorrow?" asked Charlie. "Tomorrow would be wonderful! Your place? Or shall we go out? Perfect! Perfect! Perfect! See you then, darling! Can't wait!"

She signalled for Agnes to remove the phone from her ear. "Red button," she mouthed, and Agnes rushed to follow her instructions, not without first falling prey to one or two *buttercups* and *cupcakes*.

"Cupcake?" she asked disapprovingly. Charlie was many things. A bird of paradise, a prima donna, maybe even a fire lily. She definitely wasn't a cupcake. It was as if Christopher was randomly trying out all of the pet names he had collected in his life on Charlie. Agnes didn't like it one bit.

"He's very affectionate!" Charlie's cheeks were flushed, and Agnes reminded herself that she didn't have to like it; Charlie did, and she didn't seem to take umbrage at Christopher's sickly sweetness.

"Where did you meet him?" Agnes asked as casually as possible. "Online as well? And does he live nearby? What did he used to do?" A better opportunity to pump Charlie for information would not present itself.

"Oh, he was a surgeon." Charlie waved her cake-mix covered hands about. "I actually said I'd never date a doctor again, but since we're both retired . . . Christopher's got a super chic house. It's on the coast. You'd be amazed, Agnes!"

Agnes was determined to never set foot in Christopher's

super chic house, unless it was to free Charlie from his sugar-coated clutches. "And you met online?"

Charlie nodded. "Silverback Dating Agency. *For the more discerning woman.* I was only really doing research for my vlog. You know, Agnes. For Charlie Tries Stuff."

Agnes could remember all too well. Charlie had already been on a coach trip to Canterbury, had her hair coloured, and tried out a scantily clad male cleaner that almost brought on Winston's second heart attack—all in the name of trying stuff out. Next, Charlie was planning a tattoo. Maybe Agnes should be grateful—unlike a tattoo, Christopher definitely wouldn't last forever.

"But when he sat opposite me like that, with a rose in his buttonhole . . ." Charlie gushed. "I suddenly thought that I could do a hell of a lot worse. And now I'm trying him out for a bit longer." She grinned mischievously. "You know, Agnes, if you got yourself a mobile phone you could call Richard too."

Agnes had never been happier that she had avoided getting a mobile phone. Dealing with the house phone was difficult enough, and the thought of getting regular houseplant updates from Richard via mobile phone made her feel slightly nauseated.

"Hm," she said loudly. "And what . . . I mean, how . . . ?" Now she had completely forgotten everything she was supposed to find out for the private detective. Richard the stupid Lizard put her off her stride even when he didn't call!

Edwina had now stirred a whole host of dried fruit into the mix and created a claggy yellow-grey lump. "Done!" she cried. "Now for the cake tins!"

There would be five tins in all: two round ones of differing sizes for the shell, and three rectangular loaf tins that would make the head, legs and tortoise tail.

For Hettie as she looked now, the loaf tins wouldn't have been necessary. The tortoise was still sitting stubbornly in a corner and had her legs and head pulled in: a round, compact bad-tempered shell of a creature.

"Have you considered the fact that Bernadette can't see the cake?" Charlie asked as she helped Edwina pour the mix into the tins.

"I have," said Edwina. "It doesn't matter. The cake won't just look like a big tortoise; it'll *feel* like one too."

"Hard and rough," said Charlie.

"Exactly. Hard and rough!" Edwina had thought of everything. She was grinning from ear to ear.

After she'd successfully transferred the cake tins into the oven, Edwina lifted Hettie onto the kitchen table, drew a heart in the dusting of flour coating her shell and gave her a floury kiss. "Stop sulking, my petal!"

Agnes rolled her eyes. Only in Edwina's world was love that simple.

14
FLOUR

While Edwina sauntered out of the kitchen with Hettie under her arm, and Charlie rushed back to her room—presumably to have more of Christopher's sweet nothings rammed down her throat—Agnes sat at the kitchen table for a little while.

The oven was on full blast and was making the room unusually warm and cosy. A delicate, sweet smell filled the air, like singed fruit. Not unpleasant at all.

Agnes drew things in the dusting of flour on the kitchen table.

First a question mark.

Then a C. She had a bad feeling about this Christopher. A retired surgeon, huh? House by the sea? The sea was quite far away. He obviously had a wide radius, unlike Richard. Agnes wondered how easy it would be to rent a house by the sea for a few months. What did Charlie actually know about the man who called her *sweetie pie*? Did she really want to know anything about him? Or was it enough to be compared to sweet confections and smiled at? Thanks to her reading glasses, Agnes had been able to make out the caller's name. Christopher W. It wasn't much, but she might be one letter closer to the truth. That's if Christopher the surgeon was operating under his real name.

And something else was troubling Agnes. *I'm at hers now; we're baking*, is what Charlie had said. *At* Agnes's. Not *at home*. Agnes got the impression that Charlie hadn't told her beau anything about the house share and Sunset Hall. That was a bit of a gut punch. There it was again: the uneasy feeling she'd secretly been carrying around for quite a while now. It couldn't be avoided any longer. She was worried. Their house share was drifting apart like ice floes in the spring. Lillith. Bernadette. Now Charlie. What if she wanted to move to the coast with Christopher?

Was Benjamin Stout right? Was Agnes jealous of the new men in her friends' lives?

No, there was more to it than that. Just recently a "them" and an "us" had developed in Sunset Hall. "Us" was her, Edwina, Winston, Marshall, Charlie (for how much longer?), Hettie, Oberon and Brexit; them was Bernadette and Jack. And the "us" was keeping a secret from the "them."

X.

With that, Agnes had arrived at the second floury question mark of the evening.

She drew a triangle beneath it. One corner of the triangle was them at Sunset Hall, the second was the verger, the third Foxglove Manor. Somewhere within the triangle was the anonymous letter-crafter. But where? And why? It was a mystery to Agnes—a mystery that had to be solved as quickly as possible if Bernadette was going to enjoy her big day without the appearance of anything red or dead.

She needed a plan. And she needed allies.

She pensively scrawled an *M* on the tabletop and stared at it for ages, going a bit red in the process. Then she stood up, more quickly than was advisable at her age, wiped the letters from the table and stalked out of the room.

OBERON THE constrictor was full of the joys of spring. It didn't matter that rain was thrumming on the windowpane from outside and he was still sitting under his heat lamps. No, spring was a matter of the heart, and Oberon's snake heart was beating strong and proud and steady, and as of late it was beating for *her*. She was sitting in a box not two snakes' lengths away from him, and there were still obstacles in his way, but Oberon knew that it was only a matter of time before his forked tongue would be flickering across her shell.

She seemed to know it, too, because she lay there motionless and timidly pulled her head in.

It warmed Oberon's snake heart, and that had absolutely nothing to do with the heat lamps. After a long, dull winter, life was finally worth living again. Sure, he'd been well fed, with plump rats that landed lifelessly in his little kingdom, ready to be devoured. But no matter how long the woman on the end of the stick waggled it about, they weren't particularly interesting.

In marked contrast to *her*.

She was living and breathing.

She was prey, not sustenance.

That was an important distinction.

She was really getting under Oberon's skin: it felt tight around his middle, dry around his eyes and tickly under his scales. It wouldn't be long before he was wriggling out of himself, newly born, rejuvenated, beautiful and strong.

Then he would be ready for her. He possessively hissed over the side of his glass terrarium towards the shelled creature.

~

LATER THAT day, as five charred cakes were cooling in the kitchen and the whole house stubbornly reeked of burnt raisins despite repeated attempts to air it out, Agnes called another full meeting. Bernadette was out with Jack again and was probably frantically trying on wedding dresses. It was the perfect time.

In her impatience, Agnes was the first person in the dining room. She put glasses out and located a bowl of nuts for anyone whose false teeth were still up to the challenge.

Then she opened the drinks cabinet. Whisky for Marshall, whisky for her too, port for Winston, sherry for Charlie and fruit juice for Edwina.

Just as she was wondering whether she should test a little whisky just to be on the safe side, Marshall suddenly appeared in the doorway.

"You look positively grey, Agnes," he said in concern.

Grey? Her? Agnes glared at him. While other men made use of half a cake shop to give a compliment, Marshall couldn't think of anything better than "grey"? Yet she'd just been annoyed about the hollow sweet nothings, and unlike Christopher, Marshall didn't permanently have a meaningless grin plastered across his face; he actually seemed genuinely concerned. Was he right? Hopefully she wasn't coming down with something—getting ill was the last thing she needed. She raised her hand to feel her forehead, but Marshall beat her to it.

His hand was warm, dry and surprisingly big. And if his hand felt warm, her forehead was cool and . . . well then. No fever, at least. Marshall seemed to have reached the same conclusion and removed his hand and rubbed his fingers together.

"Dust," he said.

Grey *and* dusty! That was the final straw for Agnes! She

felt her forehead to check, puzzled at first, then amused, then she started laughing. It was a laugh that had been eluding her the whole exhausting day, and here it was, written right across her forehead.

"Agnes?" Marshall looked at her with even more concern.

"Flour." She grinned. "Not dust. Flour! You think *I* look grey? You should see Edwina! And Hettie! And the kitchen! Flour power!" Agnes had to sit down. She could feel tears of laughter running down her cheeks, presumably trailing flour down her face.

As if in confirmation, Edwina trotted into the room, dusty as a pantry moth who'd got a bit carried away.

"Another full meeting," she said disapprovingly, as she padded to the table and poured herself a glass of fruit juice. With every step a little white dust cloud billowed from her clothes.

"Have you seen my cake?" she asked, taking a sip of her juice.

"I wouldn't call it cake." Unlike Agnes and Edwina, Charlie had somehow managed to rid herself of all the flour dust. She was wearing an aubergine-coloured kaftan, a red scarf and orange leather slippers. Fabulous.

Winston was the last one to roll from the lounge into the dining room and take his usual place at the table. Everyone was there. Agnes felt warm all over. They might be about to lose one of the members of their house share, but the spirit of Sunset Hall lived on.

While the others focused on their drinks or daringly tried the nuts, Agnes started reeling off the day's investigative successes. She didn't get very far.

She was dramatically describing the verger's house—the piles of paper, the cold, the strange little islands of humanity in a sea of paper—when Marshall banged his good hand on the table so hard that the glasses shook. They all looked up at him in surprise. It wasn't like Marshall.

Charlie raised her eyebrows. "Marshall?"

"She should never have gone in there!" cried Marshall, scowling at Agnes. "You should never have gone in there. It was too . . . dangerous!"

It dawned on him that the others were staring at him. With some difficulty, he managed to get his hand under control and hid it under the table. Clouds of disapproval billowed out of him, like the clouds of flour from Edwina before.

"It wasn't dangerous," said Agnes in an attempt to reassure him. "It was just paper."

"Paper is dangerous," cried Marshall. "Paper is the most dangerous thing of all!"

"Do you think that's why they killed him?" asked Edwina. "Because of paper?"

It wasn't such a stupid idea. What if, in his hoarding hysteria, he'd got hold of an important piece of paper? One that somebody was willing to kill for?

"In any case, he's dead." Edwina downed her glass of fruit juice in one. "Still."

"But that's not everything!" cried Agnes, realising that she wasn't drumming up any interest in the verger's case.

Winston choked on a nut and coughed. While the rest of the household well-meaningly, but unsuccessfully slapped him on the back, Agnes explained about the hole in the old newspaper and the matching article that X had stealthily slipped them. She kept Marshall's nocturnal visit to her room to herself.

"Theory one"—Agnes held out a finger towards the dining table—"X has something to do with the verger's death.

Theory two: the verger had something to do with Foxglove Manor. Theory three . . ." She fell silent. The truth was: there was no theory three. Not yet. There was just a funny feeling in the pit of her stomach.

"It's all still a bit vague," she admitted. "But it's *there*."

"That changes everything!" said Charlie. "It would mean that X isn't just some harmless nutcase, but that he's capable of anything. Shouldn't we tell Bernadette?"

Agnes, who had already asked herself the same question, shook her head. "It's not Bernadette I'm worried about."

It took a while for the others to understand what she was getting at.

"Jack," said Winston wisely.

Agnes nodded. They might know the groom as their friend's admirer and their likeable housemate, but the truth was that they knew hardly anything about him. Jack had spent his whole life working for organised crime. His methods would inevitably differ from theirs. How far would he go to protect his long-awaited marriage to Bernadette?

"Maybe there's a killer behind it all," she said finally. "Or maybe it's just a stupid, tasteless prank. Somehow, I don't think Jack would make a distinction. And we want to try to prevent murders, not contribute to them!"

They could all agree on that.

"What now?" asked Edwina, a little impatiently.

Agnes grinned. "We're going to set a trap. For X!"

15

RATS

Over the next few days, they came to realise that the trap for X had something in common with umbrellas: If you had one, you didn't need it. As soon as the contraption was in position, they didn't hear a peep from the letter crafter. It was all quiet at Sunset Hall—only if you strained and used a bit of imagination, could you hear a menacing, shuffling sound: the slow, but inexorable approach of the wedding.

But then, one lovely afternoon, Agnes was startled by a blood-curdling scream. She leapt out of her chair and looked around in all directions, disoriented. There was nobody in her room, anyway. The high-pitched scream had come from downstairs. The kitchen or the dining room. Thanks to her hearing aid, Agnes could now locate sounds quite accurately.

The hallway came to life. A door was flung open. Agnes heard Winston's wheelchair roll across the threshold. Somebody was hammering on her bedroom door; next moment Marshall was standing in her room.

"Everything all right, Agnes?"

"Never better," she said. "That came from downstairs. I think it was Charlie."

She marched past Marshall towards the stairs. She had

to wait a while at the top of the staircase because the stairlift was already in use; Winston, armed with a poker, was floating downstairs to rush to Charlie's aid.

Edwina padded out of her room barefoot with a limp balloon in her hand.

"Do you think it's another burglar?" she asked hopefully. Their last burglar, Sparrow, had been a roaring success. They were still in touch and he'd even promised to come to the wedding.

"I don't know," said Agnes. "I think it's something else this time."

While she waited for the stairlift to work its way back up to her, Agnes tried to imagine what might have happened to Charlie in the kitchen. Had she slipped? Had a fall? Had an exceptionally large spider sidled up to her, an unwelcome harbinger of spring? Or was it the mobile phone's fault? Had Christopher compared her to the wrong sweet confection or done something unkind? Or was one of her surprisingly engaged internet followers making life difficult for her? People online could be pretty crass.

Once the lift was finally back upstairs, Agnes heaved herself onto the seat and pushed the green button.

CHARLIE WAS sitting at the kitchen table looking pale, but calm and apparently unharmed. Brexit was broadly wagging his tail while his damp nose hopefully sniffed a pile of post that was lying on the table. Winston had put the poker to one side and was patting Charlie's shoulder; Marshall was standing to attention, as was his habit; and Edwina was blowing up her balloon.

"Don't worry, kids," said Charlie, fondly stroking Brexit's long back. "It was just a shock, that's all."

Agnes looked everywhere, but couldn't see anything that could have caused the shock. An empty teacup was sitting on the edge of the sink—not properly rinsed out, but there was nothing particularly shocking about it—and there were the letters on the table. And a little parcel that Brexit seemed particularly interested in.

Agnes went cold. She was suddenly absolutely certain that whatever caused the shock was in that parcel.

Charlie saw her looking and nodded. "Something dead!" she whispered.

Agnes stepped closer and peeked inside the parcel, unfazed. In the box lay three rats, neatly wrapped in plastic, cushioned in bubble wrap and covered in stickers. Definitely dead. *Rat* was written on the labels. *Medium.*

"Yuck," said Winston.

"Whatever next!" Marshall muttered.

"Oh, there they are!" cried Edwina, letting go of her balloon. It purred through the room, shrivelling as it went and finally landed in the unrinsed teacup. "They're my rats! And they need to go in the fridge!"

"Not in our fridge," Marshall grumbled.

"Why is somebody sending you rats?" asked Charlie weakly.

"I ordered them!" Edwina explained proudly. "From a catalogue!" She found the corresponding catalogue, which was also lying on the kitchen table, and waved it at them. *Reptile World.*

"You ordered dead rats from a catalogue?" Agnes asked. It was an alarming development. Now that Edwina had discovered the realm of mail order catalogues, the floodgates had opened.

"They're for Oberon," Edwina explained. "They do live ones as well . . ."

"Dead rats were definitely the right call," Marshall said quickly. "But they shouldn't just turn up on the kitchen table and put the fear of God into Charlie. You can pop them away now!"

Edwina disappeared happily with her rats, presumably to treat Oberon to a snack. The others stayed awkwardly where they were.

"I thought . . ." Charlie was still a bit green around the gills.

They all knew what Charlie had thought. They had been waiting for a new message from the mystery letter writer for days. No news would usually be good news, but in this case the opposite was true. The closer the wedding got, the more ominous X's silence seemed.

Agnes was now afraid that the *something dead* wasn't over with a few rats, but she didn't really want to think about it. She turned around and stepped into the already rather dusky hall. It was about time they put a few lights on so that none of them tripped in the dark and injured themselves, resulting in more wasted hours waiting around at the hospital. Experience had taught her that it could lead to all sorts of unexpected complications.

Her finger was already hovering over the light switch when she suddenly heard a bell chime. It was an unfamiliar sound. Agnes knew the sounds of her house inside out. She couldn't possibly be mistaken, especially with her hearing aid in. She was hearing this sound for the first time.

Then everything happened at once.

A dark shadow appeared in the stained-glass window of the front door.

The door handle turned.

It dawned on Agnes what the sound was: it was the warning signal of their newly installed trap for X. Marshall had ordered a nifty little gadget online that they had all installed together, something with a light barrier and a camera that was supposed to detect and record anybody who approached the front door. The device would then give a warning signal and a light would flash.

Only, this particular somebody hadn't just approached the letterbox; he was already standing in the hallway. Agnes could make out a tall black figure, framed by the dwindling light from the garden.

X! He was here! And this time he wasn't just delivering a letter!

Agnes looked around frantically, spotted her handbag on the hall table, grabbed the familiar bamboo handle, took aim and swung. Thanks to the darkness in the hallway, the figure realised too late and the bag hit his ear. Something flew through the air. The figure let out a surprisingly high-pitched scream, staggered and supported himself on the wall.

Brexit was barking.

Marshall was calling Agnes's name.

Somebody finally put the light on.

Suddenly, the situation was far less dramatic. A darkly dressed older woman with her hair in a bun was leaning against the wall clutching her ear. She looked bad-tempered, but not dangerous, like a librarian outraged at people whispering too loudly, but unable to do anything other than glare. In front of her stood Brexit, an imposing figure with wild grey fur and flashing teeth, barking like mad.

Maybe Agnes had overreacted a little? She sheepishly put her handbag back on the side table.

Edwina appeared in the doorway to the lounge, holding a long stick with a dead rat on the end of it.

"A burglar!" She beamed.

The woman with the bun blinked in confusion. "I'm not a burglar! I rang the bell. Three times. And nobody answered, so . . ." She took her hand off her red ear, bent down and fumbled around on the floor for something. "The door was open!"

"That doesn't mean everybody and his dog can just walk on in here," said Agnes sternly. "We've got Brexit, after all!"

The woman looked up, presumably surprised that politics were being discussed all of a sudden, then she carried on fumbling around on the floor. Charlie dragged an excitable Brexit back into the kitchen; Edwina shrugged disappointedly and went back to the lounge with her rat. Winston discreetly hid the poker under his blanket and rolled closer to the strange visitor. "Can I help? Are you looking for something?"

"My glasses," the woman snapped. It almost sounded like a sob.

Now that they all looked at the floor, the lady's glasses were hard to miss. Thick things with wide black frames and lenses like magnifying glasses. The woman carried on haplessly feeling for them.

Marshall, who still retained a degree of flexibility, stooped and pushed the glasses towards the searching hands. The woman snatched them, stood up and put the spectacles on her nose, then she glared at the residents of Sunset Hall.

As a child, Agnes had often been told a fairy tale with three dogs in it. One with eyes as big as teacups; one with eyes as big as mill wheels and a third with eyes as big as a tower. She'd always thought it was an overexaggeration, but after the visitor had her glasses on again and was looking at them with her massively magnified grey eyes, she could better imagine it.

"I'm not a burglar," the visitor repeated. "I'm Dorothea Gretchen. When's the wedding?"

16
A NICE CUP OF TEA

They led the visitor into the lounge, deposited her in an armchair and opened a fresh packet of biscuits to mark the occasion. Charlie had managed to calm Brexit and disappeared into the kitchen for a second time to make some tea.

Winston shoved the poker into the stand by the fireplace, and Marshall crossed his arms, or rather his arm. Unlike other people, Marshall crossed his arms when he was relaxing.

"Well," said Agnes a bit awkwardly. "A nice cup of tea and everything's right with the world again, isn't it?" It was a platitude, and it was untrue to boot. No matter how many cups of tea you guzzled, it unfortunately had very little influence on the world, and Dorothea's injured ear wouldn't directly benefit from the tea either. Agnes looked down at her biscuit. It wasn't the first time she'd physically attacked a visitor. How embarrassing. But what did the woman expect, creeping into their house in the dark like that? Wasn't that a bit suspicious, no matter how many times she claimed she'd rung the bell and was called Dorothea Gretchen? Anybody could say that. Was the bell broken, or had they just not noticed the ringing because of all the excitement about the rat?

"Tea with a tot of brandy!" Charlie breezed into the room carrying a tray. Charlie always served things with a tot of something if the mood needed lightening a little. While the residents of Sunset Hall slurped their tea, Dorothea ignored her cup, and instead politely nibbled the biscuit Winston had pressed into her hand.

She seemed to feel a bit better once she had finished the biscuit.

"I'm sorry for just turning up unannounced like this. I didn't mean to . . . I just wanted to . . ." Her hands fiddled with her glasses. "Samantha is one of my oldest friends. We went to school together, but then we lost touch. But when I heard about her wedding—well, I thought I'd pop by. It's never too late to catch up, is it?"

She fumbled around on the coffee table for a second biscuit.

Agnes and her housemates cast meaningful glances at one another. Samantha. That's what Bernadette had been called before she had been given a new identity. There were definitely a few holes in Dorothea's story. For one, she was clearly much younger than Bernadette. Went to school together? Unlikely. And if you wanted to get in contact with an old friend again, weren't there better ways than just standing in their hallway one evening completely unannounced? A letter, for example, a phone call—or at least a postcard?

But, fraud or not, as soon as Bernadette and Jack were back, everything would be cleared up fairly quickly. Until then, they could allow Dorothea a few biscuits and make polite conversation. In all honesty, they were a little curious as far as Bernadette's past was concerned. All they knew was that in her younger years she had brought down some kind of mafia guy—but exactly how it had all played out and how she had met Jack remained a mystery.

Sunset Hall had a simple rule: the past was like a suitcase. You could unpack it or just put it in the loft. Either way was acceptable. What was important was the here and now.

It was a good rule, but it meant that there were now quite a few imaginary past-stuffed suitcases up in their loft. Winston was an introvert; Marshall kept things close to his chest; Edwina didn't really remember much; and Agnes had better things to do than wallow in sentiment. The only one who regaled the house share with endless anecdotes about her many husbands was Charlie. Bernadette's suitcase, however, was the most well-guarded of all.

Edwina suddenly let out a triumphant scream. Agnes looked up and just managed to make out Oberon transforming lightning-fast into a sinuous, muscular bundle, not dissimilar to a ball of yarn. Somewhere in the middle of the ball, was the medium-sized rat from the internet. Edwina contentedly put the stick aside and closed the terrarium lid.

"Bon appétit!" she said.

Agnes sipped her tea. More brandy than tea, actually. No wonder Winston looked a bit red in the face. "Old friendships are so important," she said, to bring the conversation back to Bernadette. Another platitude.

Dorothea nodded and her hand made its way to her ear again. Agnes saw that she'd got a nasty graze on her temple too. Her guilty conscience stirred; better late than never. She downed her tea in one and got up unsteadily.

"I'll get a plaster!" she announced.

As she left the room to look for the first-aid box in the bathroom, she passed Oberon, who really had bitten off more than he could chew with the medium-sized rat. The first-aid box was like Sunset Hall's Holy Grail and was usually missing, but with a bit of luck . . . Her foot bumped into something hard and she very nearly collided with the wall. Through some kind of miracle, she caught herself in time and looked down.

There stood a little black leather suitcase with metal clasps and worn handles, a suitcase that in its way bore a striking resemblance to Dorothea Gretchen.

Agnes tapped her foot against it and wondered what memories might be stuffed inside.

AGNES RUMMAGED around in the bathroom cabinet for ages, not so much because she really hoped she'd find the first-aid kit, but more to gather her thoughts and escape the tense atmosphere in the lounge.

So, this Dorothea Gretchen knew Bernadette from before, under another name. She'd somehow heard about the wedding (how on earth was that possible?), but she wasn't on the invite list. Yet she'd just rocked up, far too early and with a suitcase in tow.

The suitcase was the thing that most unsettled Agnes. A suitcase meant that you couldn't get rid of the suitcase-owner that easily—and there was almost a whole week until the wedding! It was the first time that the blasted festivities felt too far off rather than too close.

She realised that she was staring blankly at the contents of the bathroom cabinet. Antiseptic, cotton balls, tissues, eraser, ear plugs (as if anybody here needed them—these days you just switched off your hearing aid), a triple pack of soap in a box and behind that . . . she reached in and managed to unearth a single lonely plaster. There you go—sometimes persistence paid off!

When Agnes returned to the lounge, the situation had changed drastically. Bernadette and Jack were back. They must have only just arrived; Bernadette was still in her coat and raindrops glistened on Jack's hat.

Charlie poured tea and brandy into two fresh cups; Dorothea Gretchen blinked towards the new arrivals; Winston and Marshall looked on keenly. Oberon, cheered on by Edwina, had almost finished swallowing his rat. Only the tail was left peeking out of his mouth.

For a moment, it was completely silent in the room, then Dorothea managed to locate Bernadette—seemingly with the help of a kind of sonar rather than her eyes—and reached out her thin arm towards her.

"Blindworm!"

"Bookworm?"

ONCE BERNADETTE had recognised the visitor and hesitantly, but politely, greeted her, there was nothing left for the residents of Sunset Hall to do but make up a guest bed for her.

Agnes aired, Charlie made the bed, and Marshall carried the ominous suitcase up to the first floor with his good hand, while Dorothea and Bernadette sat on the sofa arm in arm, calling each other "Blindworm" and "Bookworm" respectively. They obviously had a lot to tell each other.

"Now we're in for it," said Charlie to Agnes while they spread the sheet across the bed.

Agnes nodded. "Just creeping into the hallway like that—it's not normal. There's something fishy about it. I don't trust her." In her annoyance, the sheet slipped from her grasp and they had to start from scratch.

Charlie laughed. "You don't trust anyone, Agnes. Apart from Marshall, maybe."

Agnes blushed a little. "Maybe I'd be a bit more trusting if people didn't blindside me with blind dates."

Her friend shrugged. She didn't seem the slightest bit guilty. "It's all for a good cause. You don't always have to trust everyone straight away, Agnes; sometimes you can just have a bit of fun. But this Dorothea seems like a total bore. Just imagine her sitting at the table with us every day. Imagine—the . . . the hen night!"

She dropped the bed linen in horror, and the sheet crumpled into a heap for the second time.

Agnes knew how the sheet felt.

Charlie was a big fan of hen dos in general, and this hen do in particular, and had put a lot into planning it. They were all going to a favourite pub. Charlie had booked two rooms—one for the gents, who could avail themselves of a little Dutch courage with some expensive whisky; and one for Bernadette, Edwina, Agnes and herself. There would be music, nibbles and, of course, champagne. And she'd organised a surprise as well.

"And now we're stuck with Dorothea Gretchen!" she groaned.

It wasn't a very attractive proposition. Dorothea Gretchen didn't seem like the kind of person to be shaken off that easily. She had somehow managed, within an hour, to go from near-burglar to an official houseguest with her own room and freshly laundered sheets—almost without saying a word; just by steadfastly sitting there. Agnes had to admit that she didn't like the visitor—hadn't liked her from the off. Beneath her veil of helpless short-sightedness there lurked something aggressive, maybe even hostile. Agnes didn't generally see herself as an anxious person, and she wasn't in the habit of smacking every unexpected guest around the head with her handbag. But something about the way Dorothea had crept into the hall . . . Agnes's subconscious had instantly reached a conclusion and had acted on it.

Agnes trusted her subconscious. More than she trusted Dorothea Gretchen, anyway.

Why had Bernadette welcomed her so readily? Was it one of those friendships where you forgave each other's character flaws for old time's sake? And if the two of them really were such fast friends, why had nobody invited Dorothea to the wedding, especially when they'd all been desperately racking their brains for guests? Was Bernadette indebted to the Bookworm in some way? Or—even more worryingly—did Dorothea have something on Bernadette? On Bernadette—or *Jack*?

While Agnes stood there lost in thought, Charlie had made the bed on her own. She plumped the pillow and placed a reassuring hand on Agnes's shoulder. "Don't fret, Agnes. Let's make the best of things."

Agnes had a gloomy feeling that the best of things wouldn't be particularly good. Her eye was drawn to the little black suitcase next to the bed, ominous as ever.

Charlie stood next to her and looked down at the suitcase as well. "How someone can travel with so little luggage is a mystery to me."

Their eyes met.

"And that's not all that's a mystery to me," said Agnes quietly. "Why don't we have a quick peek inside?"

Charlie raised an eyebrow. "Agnes, Agnes . . ." she tutted.

"Bernadette deserves to have a wonderful day," said Agnes stubbornly. "If there's something in the suitcase that could make her big day less wonderful, then I'd like to know about it."

She bent over the little suitcase and got to work on the old-fashioned buckle. It was stiff and awkward, especially when your dexterity wasn't what it once was. The first buckle opened; the second put up a fight. Charlie shook her head, half disapproving, half amused, then she disappeared into the bathroom, presumably to check there was enough loo roll. The loo roll supply was a recurring issue in their house share.

The second buckle unfastened, too, and the suitcase opened a crack.

Then Bernadette and Dorothea were suddenly standing in the doorway, arm in arm.

Agnes froze.

Charlie, realising Agnes's predicament, made a big song and dance as she came out of the bathroom. "So, the room is ready," she cried, leading Dorothea away from the suitcase and through the room as noisily as possible while Agnes frantically tried to do the buckles up again.

". . . and over here is the ensuite. Careful with the warm tap, the water gets very hot . . ." She glanced over her shoulder.

Agnes had done up the second buckle and gave her the thumbs-up. Just as she had struggled to her feet again, Dorothea turned towards her. The mill-wheel eyes seemed to be looking straight at Agnes.

Agnes felt herself getting hot. Dorothea was so short-sighted that she had had to feel for the biscuits on the coffee table. It was impossible for her to have seen from the other side of the room—wasn't it?

She took a few steps away from the suitcase, towards the door, and cleared her throat. "Right, so this is your room," she said superfluously. "Dinner's in an hour. Stew or something."

As the official hostess, she probably should have said something welcoming. *I hope you have a comfortable stay* for example, or: *Make yourself at home*, or at least: *Welcome*. But none of it wanted to leave her mouth. She was all out of platitudes.

She was shaken to her very core.

Before Bernadette and Dorothea had turned up, she had indeed been able to take a quick peek inside the dubious black suitcase. And what she'd spotted looked very much like a gun.

17
SOUP

Agnes fled to her room and slammed the door behind her. Her heart pounding, she sat down in her beloved wingback, but today even her trusty old chair didn't help her relax.

The annoying thing about it was that Agnes couldn't be completely sure. There had only been a few seconds between her unfastening the second buckle and their guest turning up. And she hadn't been wearing her reading glasses either, so the contents of the suitcase had been a bit of a blur. But the blur had borne an uncanny resemblance to the stock of a gun. After all, she had worked in the police for long enough and set eyes on plenty of firearms in her time. But weren't there other things that looked a bit like guns? Curling tongs maybe? The only problem with that theory was that Dorothea Gretchen didn't have a single curl on her head. Her straight grey hair was scraped back so severely that it hurt to even look at it.

But the fact that whatever it was looked exactly like a gun didn't mean that it really was a gun. Didn't they make lighters that were modelled on guns? But why would Dorothea, who was clearly travelling light, pack an oversized lighter? Agnes tried to imagine her smoking out of the window. To no avail.

Dorothea didn't seem the type to smoke. She didn't drink. If Agnes hadn't seen her with a biscuit, she would even have doubted that she ate. Austere. That was the word.

But, suppose . . .

Suppose . . .

If the thing in the suitcase actually was a gun, then that raised a whole raft of new questions: Why? What for? And how well—or badly—could Dorothea Gretchen really see? Firearms were traditionally meant for people with eyes that more or less worked. Was their visitor just pretending to be partially sighted? If she was, then she was doing a sterling job of it. And if she wasn't . . . Agnes wasn't sure what scared her more: a Dorothea who could see what she was aiming at, or a Dorothea shooting blind. Both options were pretty unappealing.

But maybe Bernadette's friend was just the anxious sort?

Maybe the firearm was just for self-defence?

Maybe.

But then again, maybe not.

"AGNES! DINNER time! Grub's up!"

Agnes opened her eyes wide and found herself staring into Edwina's happy face.

She'd fallen asleep! Again! And in the middle of a crisis situation!

"Where's . . . ?" Agnes began to ask, not sure who, or what, she meant. Dorothea? The gun? Bernadette, maybe? The next logical step would be to have a serious chat with Bernadette and find out as much as possible about Dorothea.

Edwina had hold of her hand and was pulling. "Dinner time," she repeated patiently. "It's vegetable soup. From the freezer."

Agnes blinked.

"Marshall warmed it up. It's on the table already," Edwina said.

"And"—Agnes tried to find the words—"our guest? Is she at the table as well?"

"Everyone's at the table," said Edwina. "You're the only one missing."

Agnes sighed. Everyone. That meant that for now she'd missed the chance to discuss the ominous guest with Bernadette in confidence.

"What do you think of her?" she asked quietly.

Edwina usually only had cold-blooded creatures on her mind, but every now and then she could be rather insightful. She shrugged. "She calls herself Bookworm, but she's not a worm," she said regretfully. "With a worm, you can tell when they've eaten something. You can't tell with her. And I haven't seen her reading any books, either."

Agnes nodded. It wasn't a bad analysis of the situation. She stood up. "I'm coming. I'll be there in five minutes. Feel free to start without me."

Agnes washed her face, then popped a cardigan on and made her way towards the stairlift as promised. She passed the guest room on the way.

Before she could really think about it, her hand was on the doorknob. She warily pushed the door open. If everyone was down at dinner, the coast was clear up here. A perfect opportunity!

She peered into the room. It looked exactly as it had when she'd left it. Even the suitcase was in the same place. Excellent! She rushed over and got to work on unfastening the stubborn buckles.

First one. Then the other. It wasn't very nice to rummage

around in a guest's private things, but this was too important to just be ignored. Agnes needed to be certain. As soon as she had found the gun, she could take it downstairs with her and challenge Dorothea, not to a duel or anything like that, but to discuss the fact that it was the height of rudeness to bring a gun into someone else's house . . .

Only, there was no gun.

Some grey fabric.

Some checked pyjamas.

Black felt slippers.

Underwear.

Socks.

A tiny washbag.

An enormous glasses case.

Absolutely nothing that remotely resembled a gun.

Had Agnes been mistaken? Could she have been *that* mistaken?

Or had Dorothea already hidden the gun somewhere? Agnes looked around. The guest room was rather homely; there were cushions, books, shelves and nick-nacks galore.

Plenty of hiding places for something gun-sized. Agnes would have liked to start the search there and then, but she knew she didn't have the time. At any moment, Dorothea could excuse herself from the table, and apart from that, they'd notice Agnes was missing.

She longingly surveyed the room, but reason prevailed. Agnes shoved the contents of the suitcase back inside as best she could and did the buckles up tightly. She felt like she'd been fooled. Outfoxed.

She gloomily left the room and waited impatiently for the stairlift. At least one thing was now certain: either she had completely imagined the whole thing, or the gun was now hidden. Hiding something that wasn't a gun didn't make any sense. The more Agnes thought about it, the surer she was that she couldn't just dream up something as dramatic as that from thin air. Being mistaken was one thing, but seeing things that weren't there? She hoped she wasn't that far gone yet.

The stairlift had made it up to her and was beeping encouragingly. Agnes was just about to slide herself onto the seat when something made her stop.

Somebody was standing downstairs, right next to the bathroom door on the ground floor. Somebody with mill-wheel eyes. Agnes gave a start. Dorothea Gretchen! How long had she been standing there? And why was she standing so still?

Agnes suddenly didn't feel like pushing the button and being transported downstairs into the lap of their strange, and possibly armed, houseguest—not even for warm vegetable soup. She crossed her arms and waited.

Dorothea stayed where she was, too, turning her head back and forth. Was she looking or listening? Had she heard Agnes come out of her room? Or was it just the beeping of the stairlift that had grabbed her attention?

Agnes could hear her housemates' muffled voices coming from the dining room—much too far away. She suddenly wanted nothing more than to be sitting at the table with them, soup spoon in hand.

18
BISCUITS WITH CREAM

Agnes waited with bated breath as Dorothea Gretchen lurked at the bottom of the stairs, slowly turning her head back and forth. A bit like in one of those films, where the heroes have to go up against short-sighted, but perilous monsters, dinosaurs or aliens.

But unlike most dinosaurs, Dorothea obviously had the sniffles. She sneezed once and then a second time, then she pulled a tissue from her skirt pocket and blew her nose. Agnes wondered how big the pocket was—big enough for a gun? She had no desire to find out.

Luckily, at that moment the door to the dining room opened. Her housemates' voices didn't in fact get louder, but quieter—a sure sign that they had been talking about something that shouldn't leave the room, probably about their unexpected visitor.

She heard footsteps in the hallway.

"Agnes?"

Marshall! Agnes slumped down onto the stairlift with relief. Together with Marshall, she could find a way to deal with Dorothea.

"Ag—" Marshall appeared at the foot of the stairs and

came across Dorothea, who was in the process of putting her tissue away. "I . . . huh . . ."

Typical Marshall! Despite how tense she was, Agnes had to smile. Too polite to ask the guest straight out why she was lurking in the hallway, but not polite enough to let it slide.

Now Marshall had spotted Agnes on the stairlift and quizzically raised his eyebrows. Agnes waved at him and then put her finger to her lips. Marshall nodded briefly, turned to the guest and cleared his throat, making a sound somewhere between a question and a threat.

Dorothea had been faffing with her tissue for far longer than was necessary, and now she searchingly reached out her hand.

"Marshall? I think I'm a bit lost. Is this the way to the dining room?"

Lost! A likely story! If she'd really got lost on the way to the loo, she could have called for help, couldn't she? She had been lying in wait for Agnes while her soup was getting cold in the dining room—that was the truth of it! And how come she was calling Marshall "Marshall"? Agnes was suddenly absolutely furious.

"This way." Marshall side-stepped her outstretched hand. Dorothea had no other choice but to follow his voice past the bottom of the stairs towards the dining-room door. Agnes heard voices and then a door closing. She breathed a sigh of relief and pushed the stairlift button, and realised that her hand was shaking.

"Agnes? Everything all right? Your soup's getting cold."

Marshall was back, waiting at the foot of the stairs as Agnes hurtled towards him at a fairly respectable speed. She couldn't currently care less about the temperature of her soup—as long as she wasn't on her own with Dorothea in the hallway anymore.

Marshall helped her out of the stairlift.

"You look pale," he said.

Grey. Dusty. Pale. Couldn't he say something nice for a change? They were engaged, after all! Agnes didn't want to be compared to a muffin, but a teeny-tiny compliment on her eyes, hair or clothes every now and then wouldn't go amiss. She looked down at what she was wearing and found she had her oldest grey skirt on again—the one with the big, practical pockets. Her jumper was straight out of the ark. In that sense, poor Marshall didn't really have much to go on. She decided to have a chat with Charlie about fashion—preferably before she found out that Agnes had a private detective looking into Christopher.

She realised Marshall was holding her hand and still looked worried.

"I think she's got a gun," she said to distract him.

Marshall's mood brightened.

"A gun?" he asked with interest. "What sort of gun? You mean Dorothea Gretchen?"

"It's not a collector's piece," Agnes snapped. "It's a problem." For a moment she'd forgotten how much of a firearms enthusiast Marshall was.

"And why is that?" Marshall looked surprised. The presence of guns was never a problem for him. It was more their absence that had caused problems in the past.

"Because it's not in her suitcase anymore!" said Agnes sharply. "That's why. We have to be careful, Marshall."

Marshall struck a military pose just to be on the safe side. Agnes strode past him, half annoyed, half relieved.

"Come on," she said. "My soup's getting cold."

IT TURNED out that Agnes's soup had been cold for quite some time.

She apathetically spooned the liquid into her mouth, then pushed her bowl away.

There wasn't much else going on at the table either.

Most of the others had already finished eating and Charlie was rummaging around in the fridge for some afters.

Bernadette was talking rather unenthusiastically about the wedding preparations; her guest nodded every now and then; Edwina was telling Winston in great detail about Oberon swallowing the rat; and Marshall was watching Dorothea, the potential gun owner, with renewed interest.

Jack, usually a master of light-hearted conversation at the table, refused to say a word.

Did he think that short-sighted Dorothea would forget all about him if he laid low? He was probably very much mistaken.

"The medium-sized rat is actually quite big," Edwina explained. "Especially with Oberon still being so young."

Winston nodded and smiled.

". . . at first we wanted a simple ceremony at the registry office, but then a date came up short-notice at Foxglove Manor and we thought . . . some things are a once-in-a-lifetime thing," Bernadette blabbered.

Especially at our age, thought Agnes.

Now or never. That was the reality of the situation.

Dorothea nodded and didn't smile. She stared stonily at Bernadette with her enormous eyes, not dissimilar to how Oberon had looked at the rat earlier.

". . . and then it was just the tail hanging out," Edwina added, beaming, indicating how long the aforementioned tail had been. "Dead as a dormouse."

"Bravo!" said Winston.

An awkward silence descended upon the table. Agnes racked her brains for a few innocuous words, but nothing came to her. Only now did she realise how deeply this had shaken her. Their guest might not be a guest at all, but an enemy! Something like that was always unpleasant, but now, so close to the wedding, it seemed particularly inconvenient.

Charlie returned from the kitchen with a tray full of dessert plates.

"Biscuits with squirty cream!" Edwina was delighted.

The others were a little less enthusiastic. "Biscuits with squirty cream," was more of a regular occurrence at Sunset Hall than Agnes would have liked. With its iceberg of cream and dusting of cocoa, it really did look like a dessert, but in truth it was just a glorified biscuit, and it wasn't very easy to eat either, especially when false teeth were in play.

The residents of Sunset Hall had developed a variety of strategies to deal with this particular pudding.

Edwina licked the cream off the biscuit; Charlie smashed it to pieces with her spoon and then ate the crumbs with said spoon; Winston pushed the cream onto his plate and dunked the biscuit in it.

Marshall just heroically bit into it, which usually led to him acquiring a cream-moustache over his real one.

Agnes preferred to first eat the cream with her spoon and then tackle the bare, thankfully soggy biscuit.

And suddenly it occurred to her that that's exactly how they should maybe approach their visitor. Dorothea Gretchen had turned up at theirs as a guest, as an alleged acquaintance who didn't want to miss her dear old friend's wedding. That was the cream iceberg. What was hidden beneath it couldn't yet be said with any degree of certainty. Best-case scenario: some kind of hard biscuit—worst-case scenario . . . who knew? They could tackle the biscuit later—first they had to get rid of the cream!

Agnes licked her spoon clean and glared at Dorothea, who was focused on her plate and was peering doubtfully at the biscuit, her face up close to it.

"It really is an astonishing coincidence that you heard about the wedding, Dorothea," she said.

Dorothea abandoned her biscuit and looked vaguely in Agnes's direction.

"Not really," she said.

"But of course!" cried Agnes. "We're here racking our brains for people to invite, and then you suddenly turn up, even though you haven't been in touch for donkey's years! If that's not a coincidence . . ."

"What are you trying to say exactly?" asked Dorothea sniffily. She clearly didn't like where the conversation was going.

"Well," Agnes responded, "you weren't in contact; otherwise, surely you would have called or written, instead of just turning up here. And yet here you are. It's like some kind of miracle, Dorothea."

"Hear! Hear!" cried Winston, who had obviously understood what Agnes was getting at.

The cream had to go, no matter how hard Dorothea Gretchen tried to stubbornly play the innocent Bookworm.

"It was online," said Dorothea, unmoved.

"Online? The wedding?" Jack had forgotten to remain invisible and looked at Dorothea in alarm.

"Well, not the wedding exactly. But . . ." Was there really a hint of red colouring Dorothea's face all of a sudden? Undoubtedly. Two feverish patches appeared on her cheeks. It didn't suit her.

"But?" Agnes probed.

19
WORLD OF WONDERS

Dorothea's scrawny hand pointed vaguely in Charlie's direction. "They were all over each other on her video. And then she started banging on about all this wedding stuff. What should I wear? The best wedding presents. Fascinators: Yay or nay? Things like that. It wasn't difficult to put two and two together."

Dorothea allowed herself a smug little smile.

Agnes realised she was gawping. Dorothea followed *Charlie's Wacky World of Wonders*! Dorothea Gretchen of all people, the blandest creature for miles around! It was pretty tragic, really—for Dorothea, but also in some respects, for Charlie. She probably imagined that her audience consisted of unconventional, creative women with painted fingernails. In truth, it was creatures like Dorothea, listening to her makeup tips and pearls of wisdom only to ignore them!

Charlie seemed to be thinking the same thing. She put her spoon to one side and held onto her napkin like it was a lifebuoy.

"My *Wacky World of Wonders*? But I didn't even . . ."

"You said enough," said Dorothea in satisfaction, eating a spoon tip's worth of cream and then pushing her plate away.

The others had lost their appetite as well. The wedding was online? This was not good!

Jack leapt up and stormed out of the room without saying a word.

Bernadette turned her head back and forth a bit helplessly, from Dorothea to the door. She finally stood up and followed Jack. She seemed worried.

"Well then," said Winston to smooth the waters. "Wonders never cease. Funny thing, the internet, huh?"

Agnes drew a question mark in her cream with her spoon. Was Dorothea telling the truth? Could someone who could see as little as her really go online? But the short distance to the screen was probably one of the few visual things she could actually manage with her glasses. And there was something about the look on Dorothea's face, something bashful . . . It had been embarrassing for her to admit to the *Wacky World of Wonders* thing. And because she found it embarrassing, it was probably true.

Agnes sighed. One of those stupid coincidences with unintended—and in this case, unpleasant—consequences. But if you thought about it, the thing with Charlie's vlog didn't really explain much.

So, Dorothea recognised Bernadette in a video. Then she'd deduced from Charlie's comments that there was a wedding coming up. Couldn't she just have contacted Charlie? Sent an email or a text message, or any of the many other almost miraculous methods of communication that were available these days? But she hadn't. Instead, she'd found out where Charlie lived and had just rocked up with her stupid little suitcase.

Dorothea Gretchen had wanted to *surprise* them.

That required a healthy dose of energy and bottle, and a downright obsessive interest in the wedding. It wasn't normal!

"That's that, then." Charlie sighed. It wasn't clear if she meant dinner, the rejected biscuits or the vlog thing. "Who's loading the dishwasher?"

Edwina, still energised by the successful snake feeding, offered without being asked. While she rushed back and forth between the kitchen and the dining room, the others sat at the table, stunned. Agnes wished Dorothea would finally disappear, preferably into the ground, or at least to her room so that she could discuss the situation with her housemates. But the guest just sat there mutely, seemingly listening for something as Charlie did her best to make conversation. A rather wonky half smile hung below Dorothea's huge glasses.

Agnes finally gave up. She was dog-tired—probably much more tired than Brexit who had been snoring on the shag-pile carpet for hours. She wanted to go to bed, to fall into a deep sleep with no vergers, letters or Bookworms.

She got up. "I'll be going, then." Dorothea was making no attempt to act like a polite houseguest, so why should she play the perfect hostess and sit tight at the table?

Her housemates were far from pleased that Agnes was making herself scarce, but she couldn't muster the energy to feel worried about any of it, not even the gun thing. Dorothea wasn't about to start firing off shots straight away. They could deal with her in the morning. It had been a busy day, full of shocks, big and small, and Agnes just wanted it to be over.

THE DESIRED deep sleep did indeed come as soon as Agnes had pulled the bedcovers up to her nose: a sleep black, heavenly and completely devoid of dreams. But then, what felt like mere seconds later, it was gone.

She opened her eyes. Apart from the gentle green glimmer of her radio's electronic digits, everything was dark. She could see the bedpost, a dark tower, and behind it, only just visible, her bedroom door. Somewhere on the other side of that door a madwoman with a gun was fast asleep. That's if she was asleep.

Agnes screwed up her eyes and tried to entice the deep sleep back: first with promises, then with threats. To no avail. A veritable crowd of problems had gathered in her mind and were staging some kind of midnight ball. The wedding. The verger. Marshall and Richard the Lizard. Handcrafted letters and stacks of paper. Christopher and his sweet nothings. And now, the cherry on top, so to speak: a houseguest with unclear motives and a gun. All problems she hadn't had a month ago!

Where on earth had all of these problems come from all of a sudden? And more importantly: How was she going to get rid of them? And if she couldn't get rid of them, then could she at least combine them? Maybe some of the problems were in fact one and the same? Could Dorothea be the mysterious letter-crafter? Had she turned up to personally take care of the something red and dead with her gun? It wasn't difficult to imagine her painstakingly arranging snippet after snippet and dissecting magazines at very close range. On the other hand . . .

Agnes threw the bedcovers off. She had to make some enquiries—before Dorothea was sitting in their midst bringing the more or less normal operation of Sunset Hall to a standstill.

She wrapped her dressing gown around her and off she went.

A few moments later she was knocking softly on Marshall's door.

Nothing.

Agnes knocked harder. Marshall's hearing was actually still pretty good, but maybe the early hours of the morning weren't . . .

The door opened, and Marshall, also wearing his dressing gown, stared back at her.

"Marshall?"

Nothing. Marshall carried on sullenly staring half past her. Agnes peered over his shoulder and noticed that the bed was undisturbed and the whole room was filled with blue light from the computer screen, not dissimilar to an aquarium.

Did the man never sleep?

"Marshall?" she asked a bit more loudly and tapped his chest with her finger. The staring was becoming unsettling.

The physical contact seemed to have an effect. Marshall opened his eyes wide and then really looked at her.

"Agnes? Has something happened?"

That was better. "I need to go online!" Agnes declared.

"Right now?" Marshall looked around frantically.

"Right now!" Agnes shoved past him. Why was he acting so strangely? They were engaged, after all!

"Okay."

Marshall closed the door and looked at her doubtfully.

"I'd like to take a peek at *Charlie's Wacky World of Wonders*," Agnes explained. "I want to know exactly when Dorothea could have found out about the wedding. Think about it, Marshall: she might be the one who wrote the poison-pen letter!"

"Okay," Marshall repeated without a great deal of enthusiasm for her theory, it seemed to Agnes. He leaned over and started pushing the computer mouse back and forth.

Agnes normally didn't give two figs about computers and up to now she'd given Charlie's vlog a wide berth. It was quite enough to experience Charlie and her hippy happy ideas in real life. She could definitely do without the *Wacky World of Wonders*.

But after she'd watched a few of the short videos, she had to admit that they were actually rather entertaining. In front of the camera, Charlie didn't just look fashionable; she came across as rather knowledgeable, and her tips . . . well, when you saw it in a little box like that, even the craziest of ideas seemed perfectly reasonable. A handmade feather headpiece? Why not? Online dating on the other side of eighty? Charlie's introduction would have enthused Agnes, if she hadn't known from bitter personal experience what online dating could lead to.

Even their house share somehow looked more attractive on the screen. A group of like-minded people inspiring and encouraging one another—not like the reality of a group of like-minded people constantly reminding one another to put used cups in the dishwasher and separate the lights from the darks.

"There!" Marshall interrupted her thoughts. Agnes had been so fascinated by the *Wacky World of Wonders* that she'd almost forgotten about him. "There they are!"

He was right. Charlie had largely been careful not to share too much about her housemates. A blurry Edwina in the lotus position in the background, a pan shot of Winston drying up, the back of Agnes's head at the kitchen table (she was shocked by how flat her hair looked from that angle)—that was all. But in the very first video Charlie introduced everyone, and Bernadette and Jack had been sitting beside each other on the sofa. Bernadette's hand had been resting on Jack's knee; Jack had his arm around her waist. Clearly a couple—but no sign of the wedding as yet. The first wedding comments came much later, only about four weeks ago. Agnes looked absent-mindedly at the screen, where Charlie was waxing lyrical about wedding outfits.

Something suddenly dawned on her: whatever reason Dorothea Gretchen had for being here, she had no intention of coming to the wedding. Gun or no gun, one thing had definitely been missing from her suitcase: a wedding outfit.

20
WOOLLY

The next day, Agnes found herself in the village hall again. Marshall at her side, two knitting needles in her hands and opposite her, three women with perms and garish ill-fitting knitted jumpers, who beamed with joy as they held balls of yarn out towards her. Moira, Norma and Gilda—or was it Hilda?

"A man!" said Norma approvingly. "We've never had a man here before."

"We don't get many new people at all," Moira added.

"Until today, that is. Two at once! Welcome, welcome. Tea or coffee? Red, yellow or orange?"

The last question was referring to the yarn selection.

"Hm." Marshall was sitting to attention on his chair—or maybe stock-still was a better description—and looking imploringly at Agnes.

"Red," said Agnes, reaching out her hand for the red ball of yarn. "And tea, please."

Grinning, she passed the ball of yarn to Marshall. He only had himself to blame for the awkward situation he currently found himself in at the local knitting group. Morale had been low ever since Dorothea had infiltrated Sunset Hall. It was as if somebody had put blankets over their heads, as if all they could do was fumble around, speaking in hushed tones, their minds like cotton wool; just as long as they didn't do anything that would attract the attention of the Bookworm. Dorothea had the unpleasant habit of appearing out of nowhere without a sound, and the thought that she might have a gun on her didn't exactly help.

So, Agnes had decided to beat a hasty retreat and investigate outside of the house. The verger would lead them to X somehow, she hoped, and as soon as X was unmasked, they could get the wedding out of the way without any worries and finally get rid of Dorothea. That was the plan that had led her and Marshall to their undercover operation at the Knitwits knitting group.

She hadn't managed to give Marshall the slip, presumably because he couldn't stand it at home with Dorothea either. He'd muttered something about having "an interest in handicrafts" and got behind the wheel of Charlie's sports car despite having his arm in plaster to chauffeur Agnes to the village hall.

Now he was sitting there holding a ball of yarn in his good hand, looking uncertainly over at her.

Agnes curiously turned her attention to the knitting project. The plan was to make the oak tree in the village square a colourful little coat or, rather, a skin-tight jumpsuit. It wasn't clear what the village oak was supposed to do with clothing, nor what exactly the knitting group were hoping to get out of it. But that was by the by—the important thing was to talk to the knitters and somehow steer the conversation towards the topic of the verger.

In any case, the three women were far too interested in Marshall for Agnes's liking.

Moira rushed over with a cup of tea; Norma passed him

some knitting needles; and Hilda/Gilda curled her hair around her finger as if it were some kind of craft project in its own right.

Marshall stared in horror at the knitting needles, then he bravely reached out his hand towards them.

"What a modern man!" Moira gushed.

Marshall's ears went red. He sat there holding the knitting needles in his clenched fist, even more upright than before, and didn't move a muscle. That was the thing about Marshall. While most people crumpled up when they were put under pressure, he got stiffer and stiffer. They probably taught you that in the military.

Agnes examined the shapeless patchwork that the group had knitted together at previous meetings—it was a kind of giant multicoloured rag. An inordinate amount of time must have been put into the aforementioned rag; it would be rather odd if the knitters hadn't heard or seen something interesting at some point during one of their many gatherings. It just had to be teased out of them.

"Lovely project!" she said, hoping she sounded appropriately enthused. "You must have been working on this for ages!"

"Since the summer," said Hilda/Gilda proudly.

"Since the summer," Norma repeated.

Well then! More than enough time to have noticed something about the verger's comings and goings!

Meanwhile, the Knitwits had got to work. Knitting needles were clattering; it was a convivial, strangely homely sound. Agnes took the red yarn from Marshall's hand and started casting on.

"There are lots of lovely projects going on here in the village hall," she unflinchingly continued. "I've heard good things about the youth work."

The convivial clattering ceased, and the three ladies stared stonily at her.

"Really?" Moira asked.

"That would surprise me," said Norma.

"Well," muttered Agnes. "Maybe not anymore. But before." She left a meaningful pause in the hope that one of the three Knitwits would fill it with the verger's name.

"You mean, before . . . ?" Gilda/Hilda drew an invisible line across her throat with her flat hand. She didn't look particularly sad about it.

Agnes gulped.

"It was *even worse* before!" said Moira with disdain. Her double chin trembled.

It turned out that the youth group was the Knitwits' natural sworn enemy. The youths stuck chewing gum under tables, left dirty mugs all over the place, listened to loud music and smoked out of open windows. ("Better than at closed windows," muttered Marshall, but only Agnes heard him.) Once—Moira, the head knitter, conspiratorially lowered her voice—they'd even found a spliff on the windowsill.

"Good-for-nothings, the lot of them," Norma grumbled.

"At least the new guy's got a better grip on them," Gilda/Hilda rejoiced.

"But we still always lock our things up so that nothing disappears," Moira said.

Agnes wondered what kind of reprobate youths would have their sights on oversized multicoloured rags. She couldn't imagine. Admittedly, youth crime was a problem, but surely not to that extent!

It seemed that the Knitwits didn't have very much to say about the verger. They were only worried about their rag—on the other hand: if the music disturbed them . . .

Agnes looked up from her knitting. "Does that mean that there's a youth group on *right now*?"

"In the back room." Moira sighed.

"We've already made a complaint," Norma added. "But does it make any difference? Not a jot!"

Agnes waited for the three of them to be engrossed in their handiwork, then she leaned over to Marshall and hissed into his ear: "I'm going to take a look at the youth group. Distract them."

She pushed her knitting into his hand and got up.

"I'm just popping to the loo," she said. "Could you maybe give Marshall a bit of a hand? He's only a beginner."

The three enthusiastic helpers were immediately falling all over each other, and Marshall and his ball of yarn, while Agnes slipped out of the room practically unnoticed. Maybe it had been a good idea to take him with her after all—who would have thought?

Out in the hallway, Agnes looked left, then right. There were lots of doors and very little to go on in terms of which one led to the back room. As far as Agnes could tell, there wasn't even a back and a front in the village hall, unless of course you were the Knitwits and you thought you were at the centre of the universe. She listened for loud music, but couldn't hear anything. Just as she had decided to try one of the many doors, another one flew open.

Agnes spotted four or five young people in the room behind the door, all seemingly sitting around doing not very much. And then she found herself eye to eye with a sixth youth, the one who had flung the door open.

"I'm looking for the toi—" Agnes started to defend herself, but the young girl had already rushed past her towards the exit.

Her eyes were watery.

Black mascara was smudged down her face.

And she'd already disappeared—a streak of a girl.

On the spur of the moment, Agnes followed the sobbing girl, first outside, then along the side of the building. She obviously hadn't given chase to a teenager for quite some time, but thankfully the girl didn't run very far. Once she had reached the back of the village hall, she slipped through a gate that was familiar to Agnes, and into a neglected garden.

Agnes's heart was pounding. The young girl was trying to get into the verger's house! If that wasn't a lead, then she didn't know what was!

A big drop of rain brushed her cheek; a second landed on the tip of her nose. Within a few seconds it was rather a lot of raindrops.

She glared up at the sky, but she didn't hesitate. There was something about the way the girl ran through the garden, straight through bushes and brambles, that seemed haunted. Something desperate. Now was not the time to be a sissy.

She followed the young woman through the gate. Where was she going? Agnes rushed along the weed-strewn path. The rain was working its way through her cardigan and trickling coldly down her back.

She turned the corner and found herself ankle-deep in a puddle. Water seeped into her practical trainers, which up to now had heroically fended off the wet. Agnes briefly toyed with the idea of giving up and going back to the warm knitting-group room, but then she had a word with herself. Her cardigan was soaked through, her hair was sopping wet, her shoes were drenched—she couldn't get much wetter. What did she have to lose?

There was no trace of the girl behind the house. Had she slipped inside through the patio door, just like Agnes had a few days before? That wouldn't be ideal: Hadn't Agnes faithfully promised Marshall to not go it alone anymore . . . ? On the other hand, how would he find out? After all, he was tied up with the knitting group.

Agnes was just about to try the patio door when she caught sight of a cigarette butt, which, lashed by the rain, was merrily floating in a puddle by the house. Fresh, not yet wet enough to sink. A cigarette butt with a trace of lipstick visible on it.

Agnes abandoned the patio door and carried on.

After a few steps, she spotted a second path and then, behind a prickly bush that stretched its rather tangled thorny fingers every which way, an old well.

The young woman was sitting on the edge, dangling her feet into the well shaft. She had lit a second cigarette (goodness knows how with all this rain!). She was cupping a protective hand around the glowing tip and staring through the smoke into the depths below.

When she noticed Agnes, she looked up and dropped the cigarette.

They stared at each other for a few moments; the girl hostile, Agnes concerned. The way she was sitting on the well—almost in the well! How deep was it? And she didn't seem to care that she was drenched. Most people seemed to curl up a bit when it rained, to reduce the surface area exposed to the elements. Agnes herself had her shoulders raised and had wrapped her arms around her middle, but the teenage girl was just sitting there as if the rain couldn't touch her. There was something hopeless about it; it unsettled Agnes. She raised her hand, she hoped in a friendly and generation-crossing gesture of greeting, but the young woman just glared at her.

Then she jumped—thankfully not into the well, but off the edge of the well, smirked and ran off.

Something tugged vaguely at Agnes's memory.

21
STEAMY

Agnes returned to her knitting group soaking wet and empty-handed, to find Marshall in the middle of a scrum: confused, tangled up, and practically tied to the chair with red yarn. The three Knitwits surrounded him excitedly giving well-meaning but useless advice and trying to release him from the web of yarn.

It was only her sneezing that drew their attention.

"Agnes!" cried Marshall, half relieved, half horrified. "You're completely soaked!"

Still observant in extreme situations. Must be the military training.

"There's something wrong with the tap," Agnes explained nonchalantly. A little puddle had formed at her feet and was starting to send offshoots towards the knitting group.

"But . . ."

"No buts." Agnes had no desire to discuss her current situation with anybody, especially not here, especially not with Marshall.

"Did you learn anything?" she asked.

"Well." Marshall looked at the floor in shame. He was still holding a knitting needle in his fist like an ice pick; the other one had gone astray.

"The first step is always the hardest," Moira said, defending him. "We had a few teething problems, but he actually shows great promise."

Marshall's face went as red as his ball of yarn. He made another valiant attempt to free himself. His chair wobbled. Gilda/Hilda patted him soothingly on the back.

Teething problems! Good grief! The Knitwits weren't just very average knitters with doubtful taste and narrow-minded ideas; they were completely deluded. Agnes now understood why they only knitted things for trees: trees didn't complain. Trees just stood there, stoically waiting for the nightmare to be over—a bit like Marshall, who was sitting there in resignation after his latest attempt to free himself had failed. Nitwits indeed.

"I think we should go," he said meekly.

"Already?" cried Norma.

"So soon?" Moira complained.

Complete entanglement and being dripping wet were obviously not good enough reasons to prematurely turn your back on the knitting group. Agnes tried to stifle a second sneeze. She grabbed a little pair of scissors lying on one of the tables and cut Marshall free amid loud shrieks of protest from the Knitwits.

Marshall didn't miss a beat. He leapt out of his chair, grabbed Agnes's arm, took her coat from the hook and dragged her towards the door to the hallway. He only stopped at the front door. It was still torrential out there, and a veritable lake had spontaneously appeared in the car park.

"It's raining," Marshall muttered.

"I know." Agnes sighed.

The Knitwits were moaning behind them. Hilda/Gilda poked her permed head into the hallway and waved. That decided it. Marshall took a manly step forward, out into the rain.

"I'll get a brolly," he called, rushing towards Charlie's car.

Agnes sighed for a second time, then she set about following Marshall. What use was an umbrella when you were already soaked to the skin? The man meant well; he just wasn't thinking straight. She waded through the car-park lake, got to Marshall, who was rummaging about in the boot, and tapped him on the shoulder.

Marshall, who by now looked like a sea lion with his dripping moustache, slammed the boot shut and waited damply but gallantly until Agnes had successfully folded herself into the car. Then, in a surprising display of agility, he jumped behind the wheel, closed the door and turned the key in the ignition. The little car purred.

Marshall started pressing buttons.

Headlights.

Blowers.

Ugh, cold.

"Heating?" Agnes suggested. She realised her hands were shaking. Her false teeth were moving independently and chattering away to themselves. Marshall pressed another button and the radio started up. *And now the weather with Heart Radio.*

Agnes groaned. She didn't need Heart Radio to tell her what the weather was like. The weather was blithely throwing itself against the car windows. Through wet streaks, she saw that Moira had appeared in the doorway and was waving goodbye with a yellow ball of yarn.

"See you next time!" she called.

Marshall put his foot down and Charlie's sport scar lurched forward while Heart Radio told them about an extensive area of low pressure. They got to the High Street, which had transformed into a shallow, but ambitious river. Little streams trickled down the windscreen.

"Wipers?" Agnes suggested.

Marshall found the necessary lever. It didn't make much difference.

As soon as they were out of the village, Marshall stopped on the side of the road.

He turned the heating up and pointed the little blowers at Agnes. Then he suddenly magicked a woollen blanket from somewhere and wrapped her up until only the tip of her nose and her wet hair were left poking out.

Agnes tried to resist, but to no avail. "You're wet too!"

"But not as wet as you!" huffed Marshall. "And not for as long as you! Something wrong with the tap, huh?"

"Well, you know," Agnes muttered feebly.

"Do you know what I think?" said Marshall. "I think you left the village hall and went over to the verger's house again, while I was tied up with those women . . . almost literally! Even though you expressly promised me . . ."

Agnes looked sheepishly out of the window, or rather she tried to look out of the window, but there was nothing to see.

Milky nothingness.

All the moisture in the car had steamed up the windows and made the outside world disappear.

But the heating had finally remembered what it was for and was blowing hot air at them. The climate inside the car was almost tropical. It was only a matter of time before orchids would take root, and humming birds would flit by, or maybe even those tiny little extremely poisonous frogs. Edwina would be in her element.

Agnes tried to free herself from the woollen blanket, but didn't stand a chance. Marshall had wrapped her up really well. There was no escape. There they were, sitting together in a little, warm bubble. The outside world had disappeared. Rain was pattering on the roof, a strangely mocking, strangely intimate sound. Heart Radio was crooning away: *I've got my love to keep me warm . . .*

Agnes sighed again. Love wasn't enough. Not to keep you warm, and not in general either. "Sometimes I really do wonder . . ." Marshall angrily ran his hand through his wet hair. Thankfully he was far too upset to notice the potential romance of the situation, but to Agnes everything suddenly felt a bit too close for comfort. And she had a funny feeling in the pit of her stomach; every now and then she thought she could feel a kind of trembling in her tummy—or was it more of a fluttering?

Were these the butterflies Bernadette had spoken about? She hoped not!

Butterflies were just about the last thing Agnes needed right now.

Everything was suddenly too much for her. The verger. Dorothea. The heat. The cold. The wet. The stupid letters and the stupid wedding. Marshall, the closeness and the rain, but above all the look in the eye of the girl at the well, so young and old and hopeless.

She realised there were tears running down her cheeks, although God knows there was quite enough moisture in the car already.

"I think she was going to kill herself," she said quietly.

22
STRIPPER

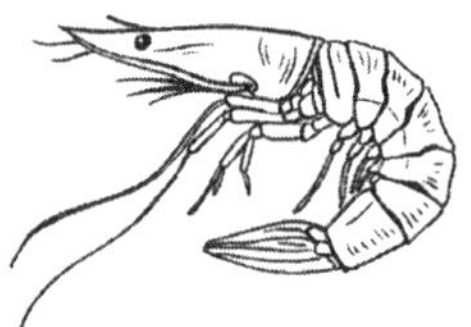

Over the next few days, far from lifting, the fog surrounding Dorothea Gretchen seemed to be getting thicker and fuggier.

The guest had infiltrated their house like dry rot. She drifted mutely from room to room, sat with them at the dining table or in front of the fire, or in the sunroom, not dissimilar to a haggard dark cloud. That was all she did. The gun stayed out of sight and various attempts to draw Dorothea from her reserve came to nothing. They had all tried to build a connection with her somehow; even Hettie had bitten her ankle. Dorothea had just withdrawn her ankle. She answered questions briefly and politely, blinked a lot and didn't give anything away.

It was nerve-jangling. Agnes was even beginning to wish the guest would start merrily firing away—at least then they would know what they were dealing with.

Bernadette and Jack weren't giving much away either. Jack was a changed man since the guest had arrived. All he did was scowl, eat his meals in silence and vanish into thin air whenever he could. That annoyed Agnes. There wasn't long until the wedding and the bride and groom should have been spending their time loved up, giddy with anticipation.

Instead, the atmosphere was gloomy—no sign of butterflies anywhere. In her role as bridesmaid and butterfly wrangler, Agnes felt that she should have a word with Bernadette, to steer things back towards pre-wedded bliss and—ideally—get rid of Dorothea. Why didn't Bernadette just throw her out on her ear? Agnes had a thousand questions and at least a dozen good pieces of advice, but Bernadette dodged any private conversation. She seemed resigned to her fate, sitting next to Dorothea knitting on the sofa or walking arm in arm with the Bookworm through the garden. It didn't look particularly amicable, not even loyal—more like they were shackled together with invisible handcuffs.

The mood at Sunset Hall reached a new low. They were all stressed and bad-tempered and bit each other's heads off at every opportunity. They would rather have bitten Dorothea's head off, but they choked on their words when she looked at them with her mill-wheel eyes.

THEN CAME the day that, in Agnes's opinion, deserved at least as many skulls on the calendar as the wedding itself—the blasted hen do.

Charlie made a big song and dance of piling them all into a cab, then off they went to the much-vaunted gastropub, where a boozy adventure awaited them.

Only, Dorothea was sitting right next to Agnes and while she took up virtually no space, she nevertheless managed to effortlessly fill the whole taxi with a feeling of trepidation. Yet again she was wearing the same grey dress and smelled rather stale. Agnes, who had thrown herself into a violet silk blouse and put on perfume to mark the occasion, tried to move away from her—to no avail.

"Who's excited then, kids?" Charlie was wearing a colourful

patterned ensemble with a risqué neckline and was desperately trying to create a party atmosphere.

"I'm not!" Edwina was wearing her NO TIME TO DIE sweatshirt again, and jogging bottoms with sparkly stripes. She was sulking because she hadn't been allowed to bring the snake, the tortoise or Lillith to the party.

"Come on, Edwina." Charlie grinned. "There's going to be snakes—or rather a snake dancer!"

"Hear! Hear!" muttered Winston rather doubtfully.

Agnes, plagued by a feeling of foreboding, sank deeper into her seat.

Once at the pub, they split into two groups. Jack, Winston and Marshall disappeared into a room on the ground floor to do a whisky tasting. Agnes would have liked to join them, but Charlie had linked arms with her and Bernadette, and led them slowly but surely up the stairs. Edwina and Dorothea followed with sceptical looks on their faces.

The party room was so pretty that Agnes forgot her unease for a while. There was an oval table with a fine white tablecloth laden with grapes, canapés, sweet treats and a cheeseboard. The table and chairs were strewn with paper hearts; an arrangement of roses was in the middle of the table. Bottles awaited them in a cooler, candles flickered; the aroma of orange blossom and cinnamon filled the air. Charlie really had gone to town. She proudly led Bernadette around, explaining everything to her. "Not bad, huh? Your last taste of freedom. We've got to celebrate that!"

Was Agnes mistaken, or did Bernadette make a funny face at the mention of the word *freedom*? She involuntarily glanced over at Dorothea, but she was sitting straight-backed at the table, eyeing the canapés with a look of contempt that would be hard to beat.

A waiter came and took their drinks order. Agnes reminded herself that the main aim of a hen do was to get drunk and forget the impending wedding for at least a few hours. She ordered a glass of red wine.

Edwina had spotted a stuffed stag's head on the wall and was soothingly stroking its beard.

"Let's make a toast!" Charlie opened the bottles of champagne. Agnes hoped the cork would hit Dorothea's head and put her out of action for a few hours, but Charlie was an experienced champagne-opener and everything went off far too smoothly.

They poured the champagne and toasted.

To the bride!

To young love!

May they live a long . . .

Agnes's feelings of foreboding were back. She sipped her champagne until her nose fizzed. Then she noticed the elegantly dressed man sitting in an armchair near the door. Had he been there before?

She discreetly scooted closer to Charlie and tugged her sleeve. "There's a man," she whispered. "Back there! In the armchair!"

"I should hope so!" cried Charlie. "May I introduce James. James is the surprise."

The man stood up and introduced himself to each of them by way of a very chivalrous kiss on the hand.

He looked like people often look in films, but hardly ever in real life: fine features and flawless skin, with narrow hips and broad shoulders, a characterful nose and shiny, salt-and-pepper hair. The way he moved was manly and graceful, and even Christopher could have taken a leaf out of his book as far as his smile was concerned.

Agnes realised she had been staring at him for far too long.

"James is a stripper for the more mature lady," Charlie explained. "And he'll be entertaining us with his skills tonight."

James took an elegant little bow and beamed at them all.

"Canapés first," said Agnes, to gloss over her embarrassment. A stripper? Really? Had Charlie completely lost her . . .

She reached for a prawn, then another. James seemed to take the hint and retreated to his armchair.

Agnes stared reproachfully at Charlie and hissed: "I can't believe you booked a stripper . . . The man isn't even fifty! It's such a bloody cliché, Charlie. And for *Bernadette* . . . Have you considered that she can't even *see* him?"

"She's allowed to touch him," said Charlie impassively.

"Maybe she doesn't even *want* to touch him!" Agnes spat.

"Oh, she wants to touch him, all right." Bernadette grinned.

Agnes tried to calm herself down. If her housemates could hardly wait for that youngster to rip his clothes off . . . She realised she hadn't seen Bernadette grinning that happily for days. Since Dorothea had arrived, to be precise.

"I thought he was a snake dancer," Edwina huffed.

"He *is* a snake dancer," Charlie responded, smiling. "In a certain sense."

"So, where's the snake then?" Edwina would not be fobbed off with vague promises.

"The snake comes later," Charlie divined, and Agnes rolled her eyes. Disappointment was on the cards, above all for Edwina, but probably for the rest of the gang too.

She grabbed a second glass of champagne and accepted the inevitable.

23

BUS STOP

The rest of the evening went by in a bit of a blur for Agnes. She ate prawns and strawberries and cheese, all jumbled up; she tried a lot of drinks and attempted to ignore James's muscular and very bare torso as best she could. All in all, it was a surprisingly successful party. Charlie was sophisticated; Bernadette laughed until she cried; Edwina got over her disappointment about the snake thing and had a serious conversation with the now very scantily clad James about yoga.

Only towards the end, when the canapés had been demolished and most of the bottles were empty and James, complete with clothes, had toddled off, did they notice that Dorothea had disappeared. So, that's why morale was suddenly so high!

She wasn't in their room and she wasn't in the boys' room. She wasn't down in the pub or in the restaurant, and she wasn't in the toilet either. Marshall, Winston and Jack hadn't seen her the entire evening and were showing an indecent degree of enthusiasm as far as the disappearance of their houseguest was concerned. It couldn't be said that the three of them were entirely sober anymore—the whisky tasting had obviously gone well. The household and the happy couple made another toast, this time with whisky. Nevertheless, Agnes had an uneasy feeling in the pit of her stomach. The arrival of their guest hadn't boded well, and her disappearance probably didn't bode well either.

But she was just . . . Or was she? Agnes had to admit that she couldn't remember exactly when she had last seen Dorothea. They had clinked glasses during the toast, yes. But after that? Agnes had been far too preoccupied with not looking at the stripper to pay any heed to Dorothea. And apart from that, the last few days had taught her that you didn't need to worry about Dorothea—she clung to you like a limpet anyway.

Only: now she was gone.

"Well," said Charlie tipsily. "Maybe she's not feeling well. Did she drink a lot, Agnes?"

"Just because somebody has drunk a lot, doesn't mean that they just disappear into thin air." Agnes was currently living proof of that. "As far as I can remember, she didn't have anything to drink. Just a glass of orange juice."

"Party pooper," said Charlie ungraciously.

Agnes suddenly wished she'd followed Dorothea's example. Everything was spinning and rocking, as if the pub weren't a pub, but a galley being rowed by half-naked strippers on a stormy sea. She knew very well that champagne always turned her head into some kind of roller coaster, and yet she let them twist her arm every single time . . . Air! Fresh air! They could look for Dorothea later, and let's face it, even if they didn't find her, it wasn't such a great loss.

She must have said the thing about air out loud because all of a sudden Marshall had grabbed her by the arm and slowly but surely steered her towards the door.

There was indeed a lot of fresh air outside. Fresh and

damp. It had started to rain again, and Agnes and Marshall stood next to each other under the thatched eaves and stared out into the pub's front garden.

"Did you have a stripper as well?" Agnes asked after the first wonderfully cool breaths.

"A stripper?" Marshall asked in alarm.

That was a no, then. Agnes's alcohol-fuelled thoughts had already wandered back to Dorothea. "We bring her along and she sneaks off," she blabbered. "She really is a piece of work. I hope we nev—"

Next moment, Marshall had wrapped both his arms around her, and it took Agnes's breath away for a while. It wasn't that hugs were so completely alien to her—Charlie was a generous hugger when she was in the right mood, and even Bernadette allowed the odd physical display of affection every now and then.

But this hug was different. It was as if more than just her bony body was being embraced. This hug was for all of Agnes, and for a blissful moment she felt calm, held together, whole. Then, over Marshall's shoulder, her gaze wandered across the rain-drenched road and towards the other side, where somebody was sitting at the bus stop staring over at them with mill-wheel eyes.

Agnes's knee-jerk reaction was annoyance. It was her first proper hug for ages and probably the most romantic thing to have happened to her in the last thirty years—and Dorothea couldn't just leave them to it, could she? She had to creep up behind them and ruin the mood with her stupid humungous eyes!

Then it occurred to her that something wasn't quite right. Dorothea was staring far too fixedly—and nobody sat at a bus stop as stoically as that in the pouring rain.

Marshall seemed to notice that her enthusiasm for the hug had waned somewhat and took a step back.

"Sorry," he said. "I didn't mean to . . . I just wanted to . . ."

Agnes batted away his apology. "It's not that, Marshall. It's just that Dorothea's sitting over there. And I think something's wrong."

Only once they had crossed the rain-drenched road hand in hand, did it become clear quite how much was wrong with Dorothea: Practically everything. Her pupils were fixed and dilated; she didn't have a pulse; she wasn't breathing; and her fingertips were like blocks of ice.

"She's dead," said Marshall, having tested her pupils with the torch on his mobile phone. Agnes, who was searching Dorothea's wrist for a pulse, came to the same conclusion.

"It's so sudden," she said, shocked.

She had spent the last few days wishing that Dorothea and her sketchy gun would go to hell, but now that it had happened, she felt bad—possibly worse than if she'd actually liked her.

"Too sudden," said Marshall soberly.

Agnes knew straight away what he was trying to say. "You mean there's something fishy about it?"

Marshall ran his fingers through his wet hair. "I mean: What's she doing out here on her own at the bus stop in the middle of the night? It's not normal—not even for Dorothea."

"You mean she was . . ." Agnes cast a critical eye over dead Dorothea. Murdered? At first glance, there were no visible injuries, but it was dark, the street lamps didn't give off much light and Dorothea was wearing her stupid dress, which was soaked with rain and even darker than usual. It would be all too easy to miss an injury under her clothes. Or maybe she was poisoned? Did somebody poison her orange juice?

Agnes's head was spinning. "Oh dear," she said. "Oh dear, oh dear!"

The alcohol had faded away. Instead, panic was taking hold. Agnes looked over at the pub, then down the road. Nothing.

"I think we should . . ." Marshall started to say, but Agnes resolutely shook her head.

"Let's just think!" she said, and dragged Marshall back towards the pub by his elbow. "Thinking should always come first!" Were there any cameras around here? She couldn't see any.

Back in the pub, she frog-marched her housemates into the whisky room and told them about the latest developments.

It was very sobering.

"And she's really dead?" Bernadette asked over and over.

"Completely dead?" asked Edwina just to be sure.

"Dead as a doornail," Agnes confirmed.

"Well, every cloud . . ." said Winston.

"Maybe," responded Agnes. "But then again, maybe not. Here's the thing: What was she doing out at the bus stop? It just doesn't make any sense!"

"Maybe she was waiting for a bus?" Edwina suggested. "Maybe she didn't fancy the snake dancer?"

"We're in the middle of nowhere," said Agnes. "There are no buses, especially not at night. No, I think she was meeting someone. And now she's dead. That can't be a coincidence, can it?"

"You think she was murdered?" asked Charlie, looking a bit pale. Their household had had dealings with a few murders before, but Charlie still had a hard time coming to terms with things like that.

Agnes shrugged noncommittally.

"It wasn't me!" Jack blurted out.

All eyes turned to the groom, and he blushed. "Well," he muttered, "I know how it looks, and . . . it wouldn't have been difficult . . ." He looked sheepishly over at Bernadette. "But I *didn't* do it . . . That's the point."

"And we were all together," Winston corroborated.

"And we all went to the loo at least once," added Marshall.

He had a point. If alcohol went in one way, it had to come out the other.

Consequently, they'd all taken a trip or two to the toilet. It wouldn't be difficult to slip out of the back door and . . . But how? And had she really died a violent death?

"It's not about who was in the loo when," said Agnes irritably. "The question is: What are we going to do now? Assuming Dorothea really was . . . Then you all know what that means!"

The others nodded earnestly. Their house would be overrun with incompetent police officers questioning them and sticking their noses where they weren't wanted. Worst-case scenario, the wedding would be called off. Best-case scenario, they would lose valuable time.

Jack chuckled. "Bloody Dotty . . . If the police start poking around in my affairs, things could get . . . complicated."

None of them wanted "complicated." What they needed at their age was "simple." Simple, yet effective.

"Let's just leave her here!" suggested Edwina. "Let's just go home and forget about her!"

"Someone will find her," said Winston. "And the people in the pub will know that she came with us. That's not a solution! It doesn't help at all!"

"Shame," said Edwina.

"I . . . I could make her disappear," said Jack after a while. "If nobody finds her, nobody will ask any difficult questions."

At first, there was resistance. Most of them assumed that you couldn't sweep corpses under the carpet that easily, no matter how awkward they happened to be. On the other hand . . . On the other hand, it did seem like a rather attractive solution. And they were all a bit tipsy.

Jack disappeared and came back a few minutes later, soaked to the bone.

"Stab wound," he said. "Between the ribs, straight through the heart. Very clean. Exactly what I would have done."

The mood sank even lower. Up to now they had still secretly been hoping that Dorothea had suffered a heart attack at an awkward time. But now things looked rather different. Not only had it become clear that their unbeloved houseguest had been murdered, but on top of that, the groom was now the prime suspect. They could forget about a worry-free wedding now.

Unless . . .

24

CHERRY JAM

Hellish warbling roused Agnes from her slumber. She opened one eye, then the other. Sunlight pierced her skull.

She quickly closed her eyes again and tried to go back to sleep. Sleep was so important, especially now. Go to sleep, go to sleep, just don't think! Her head hurt.

Thinking should always come first—that's the bold statement she'd made yesterday. Things were rather different today. Just don't think, especially not about yesterday.

Agnes could tell from the red shimmer behind her eyelids that the sun was still lurking out there somewhere. Typical. They'd had bad weather for ages, and today of all days, just when she could have done with a dull rainy day . . .

No, it was best she didn't think about rain either.

The hellish warbling started up again.

Agnes squinted and faced the daylight. There was nothing for it. Sleep had got away from her; she had a piercing pain between her temples, and her head was so full of unthought thoughts that it was near bursting point. The thoughts had to get out, one after the other, but not right now.

Better at the breakfast table, accompanied by coffee and aspirin.

And she really had to do something about that incessant warbling.

It took a while for Agnes to identify what was disturbing the peace. Right in front of the half-open window a blackbird was sitting on a branch, singing his little blackbird heart out. And because Agnes had obviously forgotten to take her hearing aid out before going to bed, the feathery creature's full-of-the-joys-of-spring song was being conveyed straight into her already-addled brain. Stupid bird! It was spring: So what? What was there to sing about?

Agnes managed to get to the window and glared at the blackbird.

"Get lost!" she muttered.

The blackbird stared back at her, clearly offended, then he took to the air and fluttered away to regale someone else with his singing skills.

Well, that was that! Agnes peered longingly back at her bed, then she caught sight of her sleeve. She was still wearing the same silk blouse she had been wearing yesterday. And the same skirt. They were completely rumpled. They had obviously got wet and were in a pretty bad state. They needed to be washed! Right now!

Agnes suddenly had an overwhelming urge to wash everything: her clothes, herself, preferably the whole world! The world had to be clean! She made it to her bathroom, liberated herself from the crumpled clothes and turned the shower on.

She did feel a tiny bit better beneath the warm jet of water, but only a bit. Her headache abated, but her chest felt tight and heavy. Something terrible had happened yesterday evening, hadn't it? And it was only a matter of time before she would remember exactly what it was.

She dried herself and picked out some comfortable clothes

that would help her through the coming day: a soft plum-coloured jumper and a dark-blue knitted skirt. Just nothing grey! She was sick of the sight of grey clothes.

Dressed and her hair done, Agnes ventured downstairs.

Charlie, Winston, Marshall and Bernadette were already sitting at the kitchen table. It smelled of coffee and toast. A rather large pack of aspirin was at the ready too.

Agnes's heart sank even more.

Her housemates looked exactly how she felt: Shattered. Stunned.

She sat down at the table and Marshall poured her a coffee.

"Well then," she said. It sounded like a squawk.

"Toast?" asked Marshall.

Agnes shook her head mutely. Her gaze wandered over to the chair that had been occupied by Dorothea yesterday. She would have given anything to see her sitting there right now: mill-wheel eyes, a disapproving expression and a grey dress.

All just a dream. A terrible, tawdry dream.

Charlie peered at the empty chair, too, then she lowered her gaze.

"Did we really . . ."

Winston stirred his Alka-Seltzer like mad.

Agnes clung to the tabletop and tried to manage all of the memories suddenly flooding her brain.

Yes. Yesterday, they really had . . .

. . . booked a taxi.

. . . removed dead Dorothea's glasses and combed her hair over her forehead—it was probably the first (and last) time that her hair had had free rein.

. . . picked the dead woman up between them and used all of their combined strength to somehow manoeuvre her into the car.

. . . told the taxi driver that their friend couldn't hold her drink.

. . . hoped to God that Dorothea wouldn't leave any blood on the taxi seats.

. . . given the driver a generous tip.

. . . deposited Dorothea in the boot of Charlie's red sports car.

. . . stood in the drive in a bit of a daze while Jack took Dorothea for her final spin.

Agnes groaned. "Have we completely lost our minds?"

"Well," said Bernadette defensively. "Gone is gone."

It wasn't clear if she meant Dorothea or their minds.

"It's not that simple," hissed Agnes. "We weren't in full command of our mental faculties, were we? We might have made some kind of mistake . . ."

Yesterday, fuelled by alcohol and panic, it had suddenly seemed like a brilliant idea to make Dorothea's awkward and unwieldy body disappear off the face of the earth. Now, sober, and in the glaringly cold light of day, things looked rather different.

How could they just . . . It was mad, not to mention immoral. Agnes used to be in the police; she knew exactly how things like this went. The more you tried to cover something up, the easier it was to find evidence later on.

She wrung her hands. "What do you think's going to happen when they find her?"

"They won't find her."

Jack stood in the doorway. He was fresh from the shower, wearing a dapper blazer and seemed positively rosy compared to the rest of the household, albeit a bit bleary-eyed.

And in such high spirits. Such very high spirits.

Hands in his pockets, he strolled over to the breakfast table, gave Bernadette a peck on the cheek and sat down.

"Jam?"

Until then, nobody had thought about jam. Charlie pointed towards the fridge.

While Jack hunted down something to spread on his toast, making little sounds of delight every now and then, Agnes tried to gather her thoughts. Bernadette's fiancé was so—together. Maybe he didn't have a hangover. Had he reined himself in a little at the bloody stag do? And if he had—did that make him even more suspicious than he already was?

Jack noticed the look in her eye and his friendly penguin gaze cooled a little. He closed the fridge door and returned to the breakfast table with a jar of cherry jam.

"It wasn't me, Agnes," he said plainly. "You can suspect me until the cows come home, but it doesn't change the facts. You're all like family to Bernadette—would I lie to you? Would I be capable? Of killing Dorothea? Absolutely. With pleasure. Of lying to all of you? No."

Obviously offended, he started buttering his toast more forcefully than was strictly necessary.

"And let's be honest—from a professional point of view . . . Stabbing her to death at the bus stop like that, right next to the pub where I spent the whole night with a load of witnesses—that would be pretty amateurish. If I'd killed her, you wouldn't even know she was dead yet."

He bit into his toast with a confident smile. Bernadette laid a reassuring hand on his arm.

Agnes believed him—what else could she do? She was in this far too deep—and the impending doom of the wedding was hovering over them like a menacing pink cloud.

The wedding. That's right. That's what she needed to concentrate on. They had to somehow get the blasted wedding over and done with; then this nightmare would be over. The wedding was a crossroads of sorts. X. The verger. Dorothea's demise. In a mysterious way, all roads seemed to lead to the wedding. Hopefully things would calm down afterwards.

Bernadette and Jack would merrily disappear off to the Cotswolds; Agnes and Marshall would . . . Agnes didn't want to think about what she and Marshall would do in the future. Yesterday's hug hadn't been bad, but they'd had dead Dorothea to deal with straight after—it marred the memory somewhat.

Agnes sighed and wondered if she might manage a slice of toast after all.

"And she really is . . . gone?" Charlie asked, her head in her hands.

"She couldn't be more gone," Jack reassured her. "Believe me, Charlie, this isn't my first rodeo."

"No." Charlie gulped and forced a smile.

"No body, no problem." Jack grabbed a second slice of toast and piled jam onto it. "At least, that's my motto."

In the absence of butter, the red jam seeped into the toast like . . . Agnes felt a bit queasy; she didn't want to think the comparison to its conclusion.

"Well," she said after a while, "we should at least come up with some sort of plan. I mean—what if someone misses her? What if somebody knows that she was staying with us?"

Jack shrugged. "Then she was staying with us and now she isn't."

"Hear! Hear!" said Winston. He was a bit green around the gills, too, but was obviously trying to look on the bright side.

"I don't think anybody will miss her," offered Marshall.

Agnes looked at him in surprise. "Well, we should at least

get our stories straight just in case, shouldn't we? And get rid of the evidence in her room."

"What evidence?" asked Jack, a hint of a smile playing on his lips. "What room?"

Agnes nodded. You could say what you liked, but it was good having a professional on board. "So, there's probably only one other person who knows what happened to Dorothea."

"The murderer." Jack nodded. "And he's hardly going to go to the police now, is he?"

"Maybe not to the police, but . . ." Agnes broke off. If Jack was really as good at making bodies disappear as he said he was, the police would never investigate this murder. And that meant that Agnes was stuck with this case. Disagreeable as she may have been, Dorothea deserved for her murder to be solved.

25
LIMPET

Agnes allowed herself a second aspirin, then she made her way upstairs to take a look at Dorothea's former room. Trust was good, control was better. At least, that was true in Sunset Hall. Marshall made as if to follow her, but Agnes signalled for him to keep his distance. In her old age, she was turning into somebody who perverted the course of justice, destroyed evidence and concealed crimes. Clearly a grey area. She had to think things through properly—feelings were the last thing she needed right now.

The guest room seemed very quiet to Agnes. Obviously, that was to be expected after Dorothea's departure in the boot of Charlie's sports car, but it seemed like the room was holding its breath in anticipation of the Bookworm's return.

"She's not coming back," Agnes muttered, and she felt the room relax—or maybe it was just her finally taking a breath. No matter how unpleasant Dorothea's death had been, there was no denying that there was something invigorating about her absence.

Agnes looked around. Jack's work was clean. The bed was freshly made, the wardrobe empty, the bathroom spotless.

Nothing in the room betrayed that up to yesterday it had housed a Bookworm.

Agnes sat on the sofa and tried to think. Easier said than done. Her headache might well have abated, but instead she felt slightly dazed. That wasn't very good for solving a houseguest's murder—or covering it up.

Bernadette stuck her head around the door.

"Agnes? Are you in here? Everything all right?"

"Yeah," said Agnes doubtfully.

Bernadette stepped closer and joined her on the sofa. She seemed crestfallen.

"Jack didn't do it," she said. "I'm sorry that everything has got so out of hand. I shouldn't have . . . I should have . . ."

"It's not your fault," said Agnes.

"Not completely. But some of it is." A sparkling tear trailed down her cheek from beneath her sunglasses.

"Were you really friends?" asked Agnes. Straight-talking Bernadette and sneaky Dorothea didn't exactly seem like a match made in heaven.

"Back in the day," said Bernadette, "maybe. She wanted to be my friend; I know that much. And I never said no. To be honest, I didn't dare."

Bernadette not daring to do something—it was almost inconceivable.

Agnes didn't say a word and tried to turn her silence into a question mark.

"I should probably tell you the whole story," said Bernadette.

"I think that would be a good idea."

"I met Dorothea at school," Bernadette explained. "Only, it wasn't a normal school; it was a school to help visually impaired people manage better in the world. Dorothea could see a little bit, but still not much, and she started helping me. She brought me little presents. She wanted to meet up in the afternoons. Things like that. She was younger than me, and I thought, well, what harm could it do for me to take her under my wing a bit—but to be honest she was a bit of a limpet even then."

Agnes nodded. That came as no surprise to her.

"It was around the time that my brother got mixed up in drugs. Just a little dealing to start with. Nothing earth-shattering, and I started hanging around with him and his friends. I didn't want to leave him alone with the gang, you know. And Dorothea—well, I don't think she cared what we were doing, just as long as she could come along. She got on surprisingly well with all of the guys. But then I met Jack. She didn't like that. Not at all. She tried to warn me, but she was on a hiding to nothing. To be honest, getting a new identity was an appealing proposition if only because of her."

"And you never saw her after that?"

Bernadette shook her head.

"It must have given you a fright to have her suddenly turn up at the house like that," said Agnes.

"Not straight away. I was just surprised. I thought that maybe she really did just want to come to the wedding. But then . . ."

"She was trying to stop the wedding?" Agnes guessed. You didn't need to be Sherlock Holmes to work that out.

"At first, she just tried to talk me out of it. Then she tried to blackmail us. She said she had something on Jack. From his past. She said she had proof of all sorts of things that he'd done. And if we didn't split up . . . She even had a gun . . ."

So, she did have a gun! Agnes gasped for air. She'd been right! "Tell me more about the gun!"

"Dorothea claimed it was a murder weapon that implicated Jack. He said it was nonsense. That he'd never used that gun. He didn't like that model. Didn't even like pistols. They were too loud. And even if he had used it . . . After all these years, any evidence would be long gone. We should have thrown her out straight away, but for some reason . . . Keep your enemies close, I thought. Jack thought so too."

Agnes didn't say a word. The question mark still hung heavily in the air.

So, Jack not only had the opportunity and the technical skill to stab Dorothea to death; he also had a plausible motive. The police officer in her was ready with the handcuffs. But the police officer wasn't the only person in her head and hadn't been for a long time. There was also Bernadette's good friend, bridesmaid, butterfly wrangler. And there was somebody, who, over the course of many years, had learned that things were seldom as simple as they seemed.

"I know what it looks like," said Bernadette defensively. "But . . ."

"You trust him," said Agnes plainly. How could you trust somebody like that? It was a mystery to her. "Completely?"

"Either you trust someone completely or not at all," said Bernadette. "There's nothing in between. I should have trusted him from the very start. He would have understood why I went to the police. But I kept everything to myself and left him in the lurch. I've been carrying that around with me my whole life, like a"—she searched for the right words, but didn't have much success—"like some kind of stupid baggage. And now I've got a second chance. It's like a miracle, Agnes. This time I'm going to believe in him, no matter what."

"I understand," said Agnes. But did she really? "It's just that he's in such a good mood."

"He's in a good mood because he was able to do something for us all. For Sunset Hall. Make a contribution. Do something he's good at."

You could look at it that way.

Edwina took care of the reptiles.

Winston did the meal planning.

Marshall ordered stuff on the internet.

Charlie had hare-brained ideas.

And Jack made inconvenient corpses disappear.

Division of labour at its finest.

"If it wasn't Jack, who was it?"

It was an important question. Who else would have known that Dorothea was going to be in that very pub on that very night? Who else had an interest in planting a knife between her ribs?

"Dorothea's things . . . ?" she asked.

"Gone," said Bernadette.

"And did Jack make sure he . . . ?"

"Of course he did. He knows what he's doing."

Agnes sighed. Of course Jack knew what he was doing. "Any clues?"

Bernadette shook her head. "Nothing. Just underwear and blood-pressure tablets and a spare pair of glasses and eye drops. Things like that. More conspicuous was what he didn't find."

"What's that?" asked Agnes, an uneasy feeling in the pit of her stomach, where a cup of coffee and two aspirin tablets were currently convening.

"No mobile phone," said Bernadette. "And no gun, and her stupid little handbag wasn't there either."

The coffee in Agnes's stomach was churning.

"Jack thinks she had them with her," said Bernadette, "and the murderer took them."

"Great," said Agnes. It never rains but it pours. "Does that mean the murderer now has something on Jack?"

"We don't think so." Bernadette combatively craned her neck. "She was a fantasist, Agnes. She made a mountain out of every molehill. A few months together at school, getting ice cream together a couple of times, two cinema trips and a scarf that I gave her because it made me itch—and we were bosom buddies, forever and eternity. She made stuff up, Agnes. I have no idea where she got the gun from, but we're absolutely certain that it has nothing to do with Jack."

"But does the murderer know that?" Agnes asked quietly. Not for the first time, she was wondering if Dorothea might have been behind the poison-pen letters. She could hardly ask Bernadette because the other residents of Sunset Hall had agreed to keep the letters a secret from the lovebirds. What a stupid idea. The stupid ideas were rapidly stacking up. Was it their age?

Downstairs, the doorbell rang. It went right through Agnes. Was it the police? Already?

Harsh sunlight filled the room and traced a pattern of quivering leaves on the wooden floor. Bernadette seemed rather unhappy.

Nobody should look that unhappy, Agnes thought, especially not Bernadette, especially not so soon before what was supposed to be the best day of her life. For now, Agnes decided to sweep the wretched Dorothea problem under one of their many Berber rugs.

"Gone is gone," she chirped. "Let's focus on the wedding. We can worry about everything else later."

Bernadette squeezed her hand and already looked a bit better.

"How are the butterflies?" asked Agnes.

Her friend grinned. "Not bad."

Just then, Charlie stuck her head around the door. She looked fresher than before; her cheeks were slightly flushed.

"Agnes?" she trilled. "Would you come downstairs, please? Your beau is here. He's got flowers. And he'd like to see you."

26
TULIPS

Agnes was in such a panic, she almost fell off the stairlift on the way downstairs.

Richard the Lizard!

Here!

Now!

She didn't want to see him—much less with flowers, much less in Marshall's presence.

She wished the stairlift would sink down into the depths, ideally all the way to Australia, but obviously that was too much to ask. Instead, the stairlift dutifully delivered her to the ground floor.

She could hear voices coming from the lounge.

"And that's Lillith," Edwina was saying. "She's in a tin. And this is Hettie. And she lives in a kind of tin too."

"I see," said the Lizard uneasily. "I'd actually rather like to see Agnes . . ."

"Agnes doesn't live in a tin," Edwina lectured him.

"Not yet." Agnes stepped into the room, her heart pounding. If things carried on like this, the tin wouldn't be that far off.

Damn. Winston and Marshall were there too. Winston

just seemed curious; Marshall looked like a volcano that was about to erupt.

"Agnes!" Richard the Lizard rushed towards her, a huge bunch of tacky yellow tulips in his hands. "How lovely to see you."

Agnes was planning on letting him down gently, but nothing came to mind.

"Tulips," she said finally.

"Tulips for a tulip!" Richard beamed at her.

Agnes stared at him, completely speechless. Was that supposed to be some kind of joke?

Richard squinted. "Just a token of my gratitude. I was so happy, Agnes. The wedding invite—I was so touched. I don't often get invited to things, you see."

That came as no great surprise to Agnes.

"I just wanted to . . ."

Marshall slammed his cup down and stormed out of the lounge like some kind of rhinoceros.

Agnes sighed. "I think there must have been a misunderstanding."

"Misunderstanding?" Richard looked down at his tulips, red-faced. "You mean you don't want me to come to the wedding?"

"Of course I do, but . . ." Agnes suddenly felt sorry for him. *But not with me!* is what she'd actually wanted to say, but she couldn't bring herself to say it. "It's just that . . ."

"Our first date went really well, didn't it?!" said the Lizard combatively.

Date! Agnes hoped against hope that Marshall was out of earshot.

"I'll get a vase!" she muttered, rushing towards the kitchen. Edwina followed her.

"Is that your boyfriend?" she asked, in an unusual show of interest.

"He is not my boyfriend!" cried Agnes, randomly ripping open kitchen cupboards, not so much in search of a vase, but of a suitable hiding place. "He's an acquaintance. A *distant* acquaintance!"

Not distant enough, sadly.

"He looks pretty good," said Edwina thoughtfully. "He looks a bit like Hettie!"

Agnes paused. Thinking about it, Richard did look a bit like Hettie: wrinkly neck, small eyes, grumpy face.

"Charlie set me up with him," she said. "He's from the internet."

"Like the heat lamps!" Edwina beamed.

"Just like the heat lamps. We need him to make up the numbers for the wedding. But I don't want to go to the wedding with him. He goes on and on about his walking holidays!" Agnes suddenly had tears in her eyes. First Dorothea, and now Richard had turned up and unnecessarily upset Marshall.

"Walking holidays? That's nothing!" Edwina had conjured up a vase from somewhere and rushed back to the lounge with it.

Agnes poured herself a glass of water. Keeping one's fluids up was so important in old age. She should probably offer Richard something too. Tea and biscuits? But the longer he stayed, the more awkward the situation might become. Maybe just a cup of tea? The advantage of tea was that you had to brew it first, which gave Agnes the opportunity to spend a precious few minutes in the kitchen before she would have to return to the lounge. She put the kettle on, listened to the water boiling and closed her eyes. What a day!

Marshall had almost blown a gasket. How dare he get so upset just because somebody had brought a few tulips over. Agnes suddenly felt angry. The cheek of the man to slam his cup down like that just because they were ever so slightly engaged! After all, she could receive as many tulips as she liked!

She opened her eyes and realised that the kettle had long since boiled. She quickly poured the hot water into a cup and half-heartedly dunked a tea bag into it. Milk? Sugar? How was she supposed to know how the Lizard took his tea? After all, they barely knew each other. And she'd like to keep it that way!

"Black. Seven sugars!" Edwina was back, without the vase, but with a smile on her face. She took the cup from Agnes's hand, chucked a handful of sugar cubes in and merrily stirred the tea. "I wonder if he'd like a bit of lettuce with it?"

"No lettuce," said Agnes decisively. Then she had an epiphany. "But maybe he'd like one of your biscuits." Edwina's biscuits were harder than concrete and could be relied upon to send unwanted guests packing.

"Do you think so? Nobody likes my biscuits!" cried Edwina, in a rare moment of self-reflection.

"Richard's not like other people," Agnes responded truthfully.

Edwina beamed. She dug out one of her bomb-proof biscuits, placed it onto the saucer and bounded into the lounge.

Agnes felt hopeful. Maybe she didn't have to get rid of Richard after all—maybe he could just be *redirected*!

"Agnes?" Charlie had managed to track her down in the kitchen and reproachfully put her hands on her hips. "What are you doing in here? Richard's in the lounge. Shouldn't you be looking after him?"

"I . . ." Agnes tried to find the right words. "I think Edwina's taken him off my hands!" She grinned optimistically.

"Edwina?" Charlie stared at her open-mouthed. Even that looked good on her, much to Agnes's annoyance.

"We're just doing the biscuit test!" Agnes grinned even more broadly.

27
SHORT CIRCUIT

Agnes grabbed Charlie by the sleeve and pulled her to the other side of the kitchen. Sunset Hall was an old house, so there was a hatch with sliding doors between the kitchen and the lounge. It was there so that food and drink could be served as quickly and easily as possible, ideally by an invisible kitchen fairy.

Unfortunately, there hadn't been a kitchen fairy in Sunset Hall for a long while, invisible or otherwise, and they ate in the dining room, not in the lounge. The hatch was a crackpot idea—but now it seemed to Agnes like it was heaven-sent.

She put her finger to her lips and slid the first little door open, followed by the second. They stared into the lounge through the opening, spellbound. Richard and Edwina were sitting opposite each other at the table in the bay window, separated only by an enormous bouquet of yellow tulips.

". . . whereas *monstera deliciosa* obviously prefers more light . . ." Richard droned on, absent-mindedly dunking Edwina's biscuit into his tea. Edwina was hanging on his every word. Winston, who was still sitting unnoticed in his corner, looked as if he were watching a fascinating, but experimental piece of theatre.

Richard bit down into the biscuit, completely lost in thought. He chewed and swallowed the biscuit, which the dunking had obviously softened somewhat. "*Tradescantia*, however, can be put almost anywhere."

"You see?" Agnes whispered to Charlie. "He's eating the biscuit! If that isn't love at first sight, I don't know what is."

"At first bite!" Charlie giggled. "Unbelievable!"

The two of them watched as Richard brought the dreaded biscuit to his lips a second time.

"Men!" Charlie remembered that Richard was Agnes's date and glared. "Oh, Agnes. I'm so sorry. If I'd known that he was so fickle, I would never have . . ."

Agnes batted her apology away. "It's really not a problem, Charlie. As long as Edwina's happy."

Edwina was happy. She craned her neck so that she could see as much of Richard as possible over the tulips.

"*Monstera deliciosa*," she repeated dreamily. Then something seemed to occur to her. She clapped her hands together and rushed past a flabbergasted Winston towards the terrarium.

"Oh no," groaned Charlie. "She's going to introduce him to Oberon!" As far as Edwina was concerned, that was a sign of affection, but if Richard were to get a ruddy great boa constrictor shoved in his face without warning, it could irreparably damage the delicate bonds that seemed to be developing between the two of them.

"Not Oberon." Agnes was watching the goings-on in the lounge like a hawk. Edwina got hold of one of Oberon's heat lamps and carried it over to the table. Then she plugged it in again and directed the warm beam of light at Richard.

"Is that all right?" she asked.

"Yes, yes. Thank you." Richard nodded vacantly.

Meanwhile, he had almost finished his biscuit. "*Dracaenas* like dry heat too."

"Just like Oberon. And Hettie!" Edwina smiled encouragingly at Richard. Her love interest dabbed biscuit crumbs from the saucer with his fingertip.

"He really doesn't have any taste at all," Charlie whispered into Agnes's ear. Agnes nodded, clearly impressed.

Richard was eating Edwina's biscuits.

Edwina had sacrificed one of her prized reptile lamps.

The signs were undeniably there.

"What's Winston still doing in the lounge?" grumbled Charlie. She had already forgiven Richard his flightiness and was now hell-bent on defending love's young dream. "The two of them need some time alone!"

Winston was sitting with his empty cup, looking a bit lost.

Charlie waved her hands to get his attention.

Winston spotted her in the hatch and raised his eyebrows.

"Get out of there!" Charlie mouthed, gesticulating towards the door.

Winston got the picture. He put his cup down—much more gently than Marshall—and rolled towards the lounge door.

Meanwhile, Richard had arrived at shade-loving plants; Edwina looked at him in wonder. In the reddish light of the heat lamp, he really did have something strikingly reptilian about him.

Winston rolled into the kitchen. "Another stroke of luck, Agnes," he said. "Did he really eat one of Edwina's biscuits?"

Agnes nodded in delight and discreetly shut the sliding doors to the hatch. The Lizard problem seemed to have been solved for the time being—Winston was right: a stroke of luck, indeed!

Obviously, there was no future in it. Sooner or later,

Edwina would discover that Richard didn't hibernate. And Richard would find out that Edwina was only interested in plants if she could feed them to tortoises. But what did it matter if Edwina's little infatuation wasn't forever? After all, it only had to last until the wedding, and that was just a few days away. That was doable, as long as Richard and Edwina didn't have too much of a chance to get to know each other.

"Stupid, isn't it? The thing with Dorothea . . ." Winston sighed.

Yes, Dorothea. In her relief, Agnes had forgotten all about her for a moment. Winston really could be a bit of a party pooper sometimes.

"Gone is gone!" Charlie repeated. It had become Sunset Hall's mantra as far as Dorothea was concerned.

"It's not really about Dorothea as such," Winston admitted. "It's more about how she died."

"It wasn't Jack!" Agnes might well harbour a private doubt or two, but in her role as bridesmaid she was prepared to defend the bridegroom—maybe not to the death, but a little way, at least. No bridegroom, no wedding: those were the facts.

"Then it must have been somebody who knows Jack."

Now that Winston had said it, it was suddenly clear as day. The way that Dorothea had been eliminated so cleanly and professionally—it was more than just a strange coincidence. It was a sign. A message. But what exactly was it saying?

"A . . . colleague from back in the day?" asked Charlie hesitantly.

"Someone from his past. That could be problematic for us," said Winston with concern.

If there was one rule for the approaching nuptials, it was that the past be left in the past. After all, the bridegroom was a professional hitman and the bride was the one who had shopped the drug gang to the police.

Something like that would be frowned upon in certain circles.

So frowned upon that somebody would wage a vendetta all these years later? But what sort of revenge would target Dorothea, who seemed to be only marginally connected to events, rather than Jack and Bernadette themselves?

Before Agnes could get to grips with this idea, she heard high-pitched shrieks coming from the lounge.

"Richard's on fire!" screeched Edwina. "Richard's on fire!"

Then something hissed. And the light went out in the kitchen.

Agnes groaned. Couldn't Edwina keep a man in check for more than five minutes without there being some kind of catastrophe? Clearly not.

It quickly transpired that Richard's polyester shirt had caught fire under the heat lamp. Edwina had reacted lightning-quick and put Richard out with the water from Oberon's drinking bowl. In the process, some of the liquid must have got into the electrical socket and caused a short circuit. But it wasn't as bad as Agnes had first thought. Edwina was already busily patting Richard dry with the sleeve of her jumper. By all appearances, the fiery interlude had barely interrupted the blossoming relationship.

"Even cyclamen get sunburned every now and then," Richard murmured.

"It's because you're wearing a shirt," Edwina explained. "Hettie doesn't wear shirts."

Now that the Lizard had a hole in his clothes, the visit was brought to a gratifyingly abrupt end. Richard completely ignored Agnes, but took his leave of Edwina with a great deal of chivalry. Charlie promised to link the two of them up online.

Winston was already at the fuse box in the hallway.

The lights went on. It wasn't really necessary because the sun was out for a change. Agnes felt almost warm, or was that just the knowledge that she'd escaped another catastrophe by the skin of her false teeth? She turned the light off and stood aimlessly in the hall for a while. The Lizard was gone. What now?

Winston rolled back into the lounge, skilfully balancing a fresh cup of tea on his lap.

"Marshall's in the sunroom," he said under his breath as he rolled past.

Agnes nodded. Winston might look like an egg on wheels, but there were no flies on him.

The sunroom. Agnes decided to avoid the sunroom at all costs for now. She knew that having a little word with her fiancé would clear the air. But she had no desire to have a word with him, little or otherwise. What she really wanted was to hide under her duvet until all of this had blown over. But she knew that wasn't the answer.

She grabbed a random book from the shelf and decided to sit in the garden and read in the sun for a while. That's how people her age should be spending their time—on sun and books, not murders and romantic dramas.

She passed Edwina in the doorway, still standing there waving, even though Richard and his ancient Audi had long since disappeared from the drive.

"*Monstera deliciosa.*" Edwina sighed.

28

BREAK-UP

Unlike most snakes, Oberon knew there was a heaven.

He'd been there more than once.

Lots of times, in fact.

Heaven was on the other side of the glass lid on his terrarium.

Anything was possible there.

Arms could twine their way towards you like branches; shoulders could carry you aloft. It went a long way in all directions: forwards, backwards, downwards and especially upwards. The sun was upwards. The sun in heaven moved, unlike the one in the terrarium. It was fatter, warmer, bigger. The trip was worth it just for the sun.

The only thing that kept Oberon from spending more time in heaven was the glass lid. But something critical had happened. Hands had appeared and taken his water bowl. Since then, the lid hadn't been on properly and the way to heaven was open to him.

Oberon didn't hesitate for long. It was all about seizing the moment. Hesitation wasn't snake-like.

He tensed his muscles and started to slither through the gap towards heaven's countless temptations. There were a thousand reasons to reach for heaven, but the best one was of course her: his shelled beauty, his one and only living prey.

Oberon felt the warmth inside of him. It didn't come from one of the many suns. It was a warmth that he carried within himself like a round, healthy egg.

He was made to hunt her.

It was his purpose and his passion, the deepest and most beautiful reason for his existence.

And she was made for him.

They belonged together. There was no doubt about it.

Oberon's snake heart was beating quickly, bursting with love and joy. He had made it out of the terrarium and onto the wooden floor, and her scent already lay in the air, tender as a promise. He happily wound his way towards his love, following his forked tongue all the way.

ONLY ONCE she'd sat down in the dappled light under the wisteria, did Agnes realise that she'd forgotten her reading glasses—they were probably in the kitchen or in her room. Had she even had them on today?

In any case, the glasses weren't here, and so her simple plan to sit and read was up the spout. So, she would just sit and enjoy the sunshine, listen to the wind, breathe in the scent of the wisteria.

That seemed age-appropriate too.

Unfortunately, it was a little on the cool side.

Obnoxious flies circled like miniature vultures.

Her headache was back.

Agnes didn't manage more than five minutes of the age-appropriate sitting-in-the-sun before she started fidgeting around on the bench.

She thought about Dorothea, damp and dead, also on

a bench. Sitting on a bench was clearly a step in the wrong direction. Agnes got up.

Her thoughts wandered to Marshall, who had hugged her in the rain yesterday and was now sitting in the sunroom, seething.

That's how quickly things could change.

She sighed. She had to talk to him; there was no getting around it.

Agnes stood up, cast a final glare at the bench and walked towards the house clutching her book.

Stairlift.

Sunroom door.

Agnes placed her hand on the doorknob and listened. She could hear Charlie's voice coming from somewhere inside the house. Probably on the phone with Christopher again. A lost bumblebee angrily buzzed away at the landing window. The washing machine rattled downstairs. You really did hear a lot with a hearing aid in. The sunroom was the only place that was quiet. That came as no great surprise—Marshall was the master of silent rage.

She plucked up courage and went in.

Marshall was standing at the window looking out at the garden. He didn't turn around.

Agnes stepped hesitantly into the room and made her way towards the sofa.

"Edwina set Richard on fire," she said, just to have something to say.

"Good." Marshall continued to look out of the window.

"There really is no need to get so worked up." Agnes sank down onto the sofa. Was a sofa better than a bench? It was softer at least.

Marshall spun around and marched towards her. Agnes

braced herself for some kind of stupid accusation, but he just gingerly sat down next to her: not too close, but not too far away either.

Now that it was time for a big talk, nothing came to mind. She tried age-appropriate sitting again. The silence between them seemed to expand until it filled the whole room.

Marshall sat silently next to her for several minutes, vividly reminiscent of a small, but active volcano.

He finally blew.

"I'd imagined being engaged slightly differently!"

"Me too!" Agnes snapped back without thinking. An argument! She felt hopeful. They argued a lot. They knew how to argue better than they knew how to be engaged.

"Do you think that just because we're engaged I can't talk to other men?" she boldly surged on. "Do you really think I'd fall for this Richard just like that? With his stupid tulips and his houseplants and his wrinkly neck? Don't you think I have any standards at all?" Strictly speaking, Marshall had a wrinkly neck too, but that wasn't the point. "It was Charlie. She set me up with him. Do you think I'd go for any random old twit from the internet just because he brings me a few flowers?"

"No," said Marshall quietly. "Of course I don't."

It took the wind out of Agnes's sails a bit. How was she supposed to have a proper argument if he was just going to agree with everything she said? It was very unsporting of him!

"Then . . ." Agnes looked askance at him. "You're not jealous of Richard?"

Marshall snorted. "I couldn't care less about Richard."

"So, what's the problem then?" cried Agnes, who felt the anticipated argument fizzling out. Even as she said it, she knew it was a mistake.

Marshall looked at her intently.

"I'm not worried that you're going to run off with this Richard chap," he said. "I'm disappointed that you didn't think it necessary to tell Charlie about our engagement, even when she organised a date for you. It's not fair—not even on that bloody clown."

Agnes gulped. To her surprise, Marshall had hit the nail on the head.

"But . . ."

"I know we decided not to say anything yet," Marshall continued. "So as not to steal Bernadette's thunder. But there's a big difference between saying nothing and going on dates with other people to keep it secret. An engagement that absolutely nobody is allowed to know about is no engagement at all. *That's* the problem!"

He stood up without looking at Agnes and stared out of the window again. Agnes looked at his back and gasped for air like a fish out of water.

But . . . she wanted to say. *But* . . . There was no but. Marshall was absolutely right. She could have just taken Charlie to one side and explained things, instead of playing along with the stupid Richard shenanigans. But she hadn't. She'd been embarrassed. But why? What was so embarrassing about being engaged? People got engaged every now and then, didn't they? She had to make a mountain out of a molehill. Marshall had every right to be angry.

But how angry was he?

Silent-treatment-at-dinner angry?

Sulking-in-the-sunroom-for-a-whole-day angry?

Calling-it-a-day-on-the-engagement angry? Agnes's heart skipped a beat. Even though she'd spent a lot of time thinking about how she could elegantly manoeuvre herself out of this bloody engagement, she suddenly realised that it wasn't what she wanted. Not now. Not like this.

And maybe it's not what she wanted full stop.

"Marshall . . ." she said gently.

It seemed like a small eternity until he turned around. He didn't look furious anymore, just fragile.

Fragile and sad.

He sat down next to her again, a bit closer this time, and took one of her hands in his good hand. Agnes peered down at her fingers, which looked at home there. She could feel her heart in her mouth.

"I've been really happy these last few weeks," said Marshall. Agnes looked at him in surprise and wanted to say something, but he carried on talking: "I know it probably wasn't very obvious, but . . . It's not that easy to be happy at our age. But I *was* happy. *Am* happy. Nothing you do could change that."

Agnes opened her mouth to say something, but then closed it again. She suddenly had an uneasy feeling that everything was going in the wrong direction, slowly but steadily, like a leisurely landslide. She groped for words that would stop the landslide, but nothing came to her. Why did nothing come to her when she most needed it?

Marshall realised she was upset and shook his head with a smile. "But I'm no idiot. I know where things are headed for me. It's not so bad. It really isn't that bad, Agnes."

She couldn't look him in the face, so concentrated on her fingers. They looked really rather cheerful and content in Marshall's hand. Things *were* bad. Worse than she'd thought.

"I know that one day in the not-too-distant future, I'll wake up and I won't know what day it is. Or what year. What decade. Who the chap in the mirror is, or the people sitting at the breakfast table with me." Marshall chuckled. "You don't want to put yourself through that. *I* don't want to put you through that. It's all right. Don't be sad, Agnes."

Agnes wasn't sad. She was incandescent with rage. So that's what he thought of her—that she was a coward. That she was going to leave him in the lurch just like that!

While she was still groping around for words, Marshall let go of her hand and stood up. Agnes's fingers suddenly felt lonely.

"That's not . . ." she cried. "How . . ."

But Marshall didn't let her finish. He smiled at her, a smile that was brave and somehow encouraging, and marched out of the sunroom, down the stairs, presumably out into the garden. For a walk across the fields, maybe. It was spring after all, and the sun was finally out.

Agnes would have liked to run after him, but running obviously wasn't on the cards these days. So, she made do with sitting there, thunderstruck.

He had completely misunderstood her.

Worse still: she'd misunderstood herself.

She'd spent the whole time thinking that their engagement was an inconvenience. A kind of accident. Something that she had to age-appropriately sit out.

That was it. Agnes, who had always been so proud of avoiding age-appropriate things like the plague, had been held back by a stupid limit in her own head. Love was something for young people. Younger than her, at any rate. Anything else was embarrassing (Bernadette) or downright suspicious (Charlie). It wasn't for Agnes. It was too risky. It had always been too risky. Charlie had been absolutely right: it was now or never! And wasn't everything at her age a risk?

Agnes sat there and felt grottier than she'd felt in a long while. Wounded and disappointed, above all in herself. Like a balloon after a party, hanging forgotten from the ceiling, getting limper and wrinklier with every passing minute.

She'd ruined everything.

She'd fallen in love, got engaged and then ruined it all. That was the truth of the matter.

Her thoughts did what they usually did when faced with the emotional nitty-gritty: they turned to murder. Compared to what was going on in her head, murder had something comfortingly objective about it.

A mystery.

Something that could be solved.

29
STORM CLOUDS

Agnes might not be any great shakes as a fiancée, but she could solve mysteries. The Richard thing had knocked her off her stride for a while, but the fact of the matter was that Winston was absolutely right. Dead Dorothea was a huge problem, no matter how careful Jack had been afterwards. Why had the Bookworm been sitting on that bench yesterday? Whom had she been waiting for? And who had set a trap for her?

She suddenly felt the need to talk to someone about the case. Cases. Somebody whose head wasn't filled with butterflies and wedding bells.

Winston! Winston had never shown the slightest interest in the world of women and was pleasingly immune to butterflies.

Agnes heaved herself off the sofa and peered out of the door to the sunroom. No sign of Marshall. The coast was clear. Her heart sank a little at the absence of Marshall, but her head had everything under control and steered her decisively towards the stairlift.

Just as she'd got comfortable on the seat, another scream resounded through the house. There was an above-average amount of screaming going on in their house share. She was almost certain that the scream had come from Winston. Even his cries of dismay had something sedate about them.

Once downstairs, Agnes armed herself with her close-combat-tested handbag and flung the door to the lounge open. There was Winston, astonishingly red in the face, and on his lap was something that looked like an oversized, angry Chelsea bun.

It was twisting and turning.

And hissing.

"Agnes," Winston gasped in relief. "I'm glad you're here. The little tinker got out. Gave me quite a fright, I can tell you. But I've got him now."

As if he'd understood, Oberon reared up and hissed venomously. He'd grown rather a lot in the last few months, presumably because of all the dead rats that Edwina had ordered online.

Agnes lowered her handbag and inched closer.

Winston groaned. "He almost got into Hettie's box. I caught him just in time. Would you put him back in his terrarium? I can't propel myself and hold him at the same time. That's the problem."

"I, err . . ." Agnes frowned. Oberon's pugnacity had saved her life last winter. It was one thing admiring the snake behind glass, but quite another wrangling a disgruntled mass of muscle from A to B. "Where's Edwina?" she asked.

"Not here!" Winston held the snake towards her, sweating. "I don't think he likes men."

"Who does?" said Agnes, instantly regretting it. Winston seemed a bit taken aback, and it was unfair of her to take her bad mood out on him. After all, Winston didn't have anything to do with her current situation. And hadn't she just wished for a distraction? A task that would take her mind off things?

She grabbed the snake and made her way towards the terrarium. Oberon stopped struggling and triumphantly slithered up her arm. Next moment he was around her shoulders like a wilful, but not inelegant stole.

He had no intention of going back into the terrarium, no matter how forcefully Agnes pulled his snake tail. If it was even his tail. Where exactly did a snake's body end and the tail begin? She couldn't make head nor tail of it.

Oberon masterfully ignored her. Was she going mad, or was he getting heavier with every passing minute?

"He . . . he doesn't want to," she groaned.

Winston just looked relieved to be rid of the snake. "Give him a little time," he advised.

"I don't have time!" hissed Agnes, glaring down into Oberon's lemon-yellow snake eyes. "I don't have time for this!"

Oberon didn't respond. Of course he didn't. He was a snake.

Agnes, however, now spoke to reptiles.

First Richard. Now Oberon. Soon she would start discussing things with Hettie, and from there she was just one step away from losing all of her marbles. Maybe life was better that way. Easier. You only had to look at Edwina: happy as Larry, even with Richard the Lizard.

Winston seemed to have recovered from the shock. "Sit down for a minute," he suggested. "You look stressed, Agnes!"

"I am stressed!"

She gave up trying to shake Oberon off and sank into a chair next to Winston.

"I'm worried," she sighed.

"About Marshall?"

Agnes blushed. "That too. It's not that simple. *Nothing* is simple!"

Winston nodded sympathetically, and Agnes felt a little less heavy-hearted. A problem shared was . . . well, a problem shared.

"Did you never have any problems?" she asked. "With, well, you know, I mean . . ."

"With love?" Winston shook his head. "With everything else, maybe. But not love itself. Love is the best thing in life; I hope I don't have to tell you that, Agnes."

"I . . ." Agnes sensed herself becoming pig-headed again. Who did Winston think he was, lecturing her on love? He hadn't exactly shown himself to be an expert in affairs of the heart. Quite the opposite, in fact.

"So, what happened?"

"To my love? Long dead." Winston smiled, not sadly, but tenderly somehow, as if that love was something that still warmed him from afar.

"I'm, err, I'm sorry to hear that," Agnes stammered. What was wrong with her today? Why was she blundering from one clanger to the next?

"You don't need to be sorry," said Winston. "I had love in my life; that's the main thing. Everything else"—he fumbled around frustratedly with the wheel of his wheelchair—"is manageable."

Dorothea suddenly popped into Agnes's head. She had been in their lives too—and now it was causing them nothing but trouble.

Agnes decided to steer Winston away from the thorny subject of love, and towards the case.

"I'm worried about this murder too," she said. "It's all connected to the wedding. I just don't know how."

Winston had a faraway look in his eye.

"It just doesn't make sense," Agnes carried on. "The verger

was already dead when Bernadette met Jack again. Yet there seems to be some kind of connection between him and the wedding. How is that possible?"

"It's not possible," said Winston plainly. "If it seems like that, then maybe it's just because they both have a connection to a third thing. What's the third thing?"

He took a piece of paper out of one of the pockets on his wheelchair, placed it on the table in the bay window and drew a long line on it.

"That's time." Winston smiled. He had a weakness for timelines.

Then he drew a cross. "That's the death of the verger. This is when we were on holiday; this is when Jack and Bernadette met. This is when they were on Charlie's video online. This is when the first poison-pen letter arrived. This is when Dorothea turned up, and this," he drew a final cross, "is when she was murdered. And this"—he drew an asterisk—"is when the date at Foxglove Manor became available, which might not be entirely insignificant."

Agnes and Oberon peered at Winston's sketch with interest.

"You mean, that's not a coincidence either?" She pointed to the asterisk with *Foxglove Manor* written next to it.

"It's a pretty big coincidence," said Winston. "If you're romantically inclined, you could call it fate. If not . . . it could be something else entirely."

"I suspected Jack at first," Agnes admitted. "But now I'm not so sure." She slammed her flat palm to her forehead, a bit more forcefully than she had intended. "We should check the story out. About the riding instructor and the bank manager. To see if a wedding really was called off. Why didn't we think of that sooner?"

"I checked it out," said Winston matter-of-factly.

Agnes looked at him in surprise. "Really? How?"

"Sylvie." Winston looked rather smug. The home help was a dependable source of all sorts of gossip and tittle-tattle.

"And?" asked Agnes keenly.

"The wedding fell through," said Winston. "But the bride-to-be didn't do a runner. She had an affair with her riding instructor; it was leaked and so the husband-to-be called off the wedding. You might well ask yourself why it was leaked when it was."

Agnes understood the crux of it. The affair might have come to light through some kind of coincidence or carelessness—or someone might have very deliberately blown their cover.

Winston drew an ominous cloud above his timeline. Little dashes came out of it, like rain. "I can't make sense of it at the moment. Because we don't have all of the facts. There might be something else at play. Something that connects all of these events."

Agnes glanced out of the window to make sure real storm clouds weren't gathering. The new gardener was in the process of cutting back their roses, rather too late in the season and, it seemed to Agnes, with more enthusiasm than expertise. Next moment she leapt up, but lost her balance a bit because of the heavy snake. She faltered and steadied herself on the table, almost knocking over Winston's neat stacks of paper.

"Careful, Agnes!"

Agnes ignored him and was already at the door. Out there, near the fence, something was hanging in the birch tree.

Something big.

She rushed out of the door onto the veranda, along the side of the house, past the gardener, who was intently hacking away at the roses, towards a beautiful birch.

Something was hanging in one of the lower branches—someone!

"Edwina!"

Edwina, who was sitting on a branch, motionless and seemingly lost in thought, turned around and waved at Agnes. "Hello, Agnes."

"We agreed no more murders," said Agnes sternly. "Especially not out in the open."

Edwina shook her head and slid down the trunk. It wasn't a long way down, but Agnes's heart almost stopped. What on earth was Edwina doing up a tree at her age?

"This isn't a murder," Edwina explained, "but I can't get it down." She pointed accusatorily at the thing that was disfiguring the birch, some kind of gigantic, brightly coloured piece of material that seemed very familiar to Agnes. It was the village oak's little coat that the three Knitwits had been obsessively beavering away on since last summer. Now it was unceremoniously wrapped around the trunk of the birch tree and looked like something a toddler had made.

"Lovely." Winston had caught up with her and was staring up at the tree. "What is it?"

"It's not lovely," Agnes hissed. "It's something *stolen*. And we've got to get it down as quickly as we can."

One thing was clear: if anybody got wind of the fact that the knitting group's pride and joy was hanging in their birch tree, Agnes and Marshall would quickly become the main suspects, and she had no desire to grapple with three angry knitting-needle-wielding Knitwits. She rushed back into the house in search of a pair of scissors, only then realising that she still had Oberon around her shoulders. Never mind. The snake seemed happy, and Agnes had got used to the weight. There was even something empowering about it—if she could carry a snake on her shoulders, she could do anything!

But first the knitted monstrosity had to be taken down. Agnes located a pair of scissors for Edwina, then they both wrangled with the fabric, Agnes at the bottom and Edwina farther up. Oberon ogled the birch and his tongue darted hopefully upwards. Winston was shouting well-meaning, but completely useless words of advice from the veranda.

They finally managed to release the tree, mainly thanks to Edwina's climbing skills. The oversized blanket flopped down onto Agnes, completely covering her and Oberon for a moment. Oberon's tongue furiously flicked into her ear. Agnes sniffed. The smell reminded her of . . .

"Oberon!" Edwina pulled the blanket from Agnes's head, not to help her, but to get to the snake. Edwina grabbed Oberon, who had a dreamy look in his eye and suddenly allowed himself to be removed from Agnes's shoulders, meek as a lamb. With the snake under one arm and the knitted monstrosity under the other, Edwina trotted back into the house. Agnes and Winston followed.

In the lounge, Oberon was banished to his terrarium again. Agnes spread the blanket out on the coffee table.

"You think it's the *something stolen* from the letter?" asked Winston. Agnes had completely forgotten about him for a moment.

"No doubt about it," she said. "This is the knitting group's main project, and they guard it with their lives. Well, they did. Something obviously went awry with the guarding." She stroked the disintegrating woollen creation, deep in thought. It was completely useless as tree attire, but it was perfect as a warning from X. You couldn't miss it and it was definitely stolen. That meant . . . a lot of things.

For one, Dorothea could unfortunately be ruled out as the potential letter-writer. The blanket had only just turned up at Sunset Hall, whereas Dorothea had already left Duck End for good. It was a shame, but you couldn't have it all.

There had to be someone behind it, and whoever it might be was very well informed. How else could they have known that she and Marshall had been to the knitting group and would recognise the monstrosity? Somebody was going to an awful lot of trouble. No matter what one might think of the letter-crafter's verse, the things that X was presenting them with were well chosen. Conspicuous. Unambiguous. The newspaper clipping. The blanket. But where were the red and the dead? Agnes wondered if Dorothea might have been the dead, but something about it didn't feel right. The letter-writer's offerings were symbolic. Dorothea's dead body was the thing itself.

OBERON WAS sitting under his fake sun again, but the glass walls surrounding him did not detract from his meditative mood. He had overcome them before, and he would overcome them again. It wasn't about that right now.

Far more important were the things he had tasted today: the prey, the tree and, above all, the sun.

He had always assumed that the little suns that illuminated his world weren't everything that there was. There must be something bigger somewhere, something higher, more beautiful, more important. Now he had seen it with his own yellow snake eyes: his world was just a pale imitation. While he had to make do with dead rats, outside there was living, breathing prey, beautiful and lovable.

While he was winding himself around pathetic branches or reluctant shoulders, in the real world a tree was reaching up into the sky, tall and dauntless and rustling, longer than every snake put together. There were bound to be more.

And instead of the little, inconsistent suns in here, there was a big light out there, from which all warmth radiated.

It was a profound realisation that needed to be digested—in this sense rats and realisations were not dissimilar, but snakes could digest just about anything.

Why was he in here and not up a tree?

Why was the sun outside and not in here?

Was it right?

Again and again, he pressed his nose to the glass. His life was too cramped for him now. The old Oberon had to go!

Finally, the skin at the tip of his nose split. It was tickly, cool, sensitive. A little pain, a lot of hope.

How beautiful the world was. So sharp and bright.

He wormed his way between two branches, and his old skin peeled off like the skin of a fruit. It pulled a bit. What did it matter?

Snakes could shed their skin; that was one of the attractions of being a snake. Beneath every current Oberon there was always a new one waiting: bigger, shinier and more beautiful than the one before.

Oberon allowed himself a nap and, with fresh longing, steered his dreams towards his armoured prey.

30
GLAD RAGS

"He looks good!"

Agnes, Charlie and Edwina stared down at Oberon somewhat enviously. His white skin was shimmering even more beautifully than the trunk of the silver birch; the pale-yellow snake pattern on his body looked freshly painted; and his eyes were gleaming like two ripe lemons.

They, on the other hand, had gathered in the lounge to finally—better late than never—discuss the tiresome topic of wedding outfits.

It was easy for the men. Marshall would throw on one of his full dress uniforms and affix a few more medals to his chest than usual, Winston owned precisely one suitable suit and Jack, as the groom, was definitely well prepared. Jack was always well prepared, they now knew.

The same couldn't be said for them. Edwina spent the vast majority of her time almost exclusively in brightly coloured track suits, Agnes's wardrobe was full of clothes from the eighties and Charlie was spoilt for choice.

"I've got a skirt," said Edwina, proudly placing said item of clothing onto the coffee table. Charlie and Agnes stared at it. Where on earth had Edwina got hold of a skirt that in colour and texture was practically indistinguishable from a pair of jogging bottoms?

"No way," said Agnes. "You're wearing the blue dress." The blue dress was just about the only respectable piece of clothing in Edwina's wardrobe.

Edwina stuck out her bottom lip. "The blue dress is stupid. It hasn't got any pockets, and I can't climb in it either."

"You won't have to climb at the wedding," Agnes assured her.

"But I could," said Edwina. "Just not if I've got that stupid dress on."

"I think Richard would like it," said Charlie, winking at Agnes.

Edwina's bottom lip retreated. "Do you think so?"

"Definitely," said Agnes. "I know him well, after all. Blue is his favourite colour, you know?" That was a lie. Agnes had no idea what colour the Lizard preferred. It didn't matter right now. What was important was that Edwina didn't turn up to the festivities looking like a sack of potatoes.

"But it's boring," Edwina moaned.

"Richard's boring too," Agnes said, placating her.

"And it doesn't have to stay boring!" Charlie, who had dragged a whole bagful of fabric downstairs, conjured up a huge, deep sea-blue silk scarf with fish, jellyfish and sea snakes splashing about all over it.

Edwina, in a rare fit of speechlessness, quickly grabbed it.

"I'll lend it to you," Charlie offered. "If you wear the blue dress."

"I'll wear the blue dress," Edwina promised. "I'll wear it every day!" She wrapped the scarf around her shoulders like a superhero cape.

"Once is enough," Agnes assured her.

"What about shoes?" asked Charlie.

"I've got some glitzy trainers!" Edwina declared.

"They'll do," Charlie decided, with the authority of her *World of Wonders* experience.

With that, Edwina was fully kitted out. Agnes envied her. Edwina couldn't care less what she looked like. As long as it was glitzy, comfy and had something to do with snakes.

Surprisingly, Agnes cared rather too much about what she was going to wear. Despite many irritating years of bitter experience that suggested it would be nigh on impossible, Agnes wanted to look good at the wedding. After all, Marshall was going to be there.

She sighed. She didn't believe that things could be remedied with a pretty scarf and a bit of lipstick, and yet . . . It was going to be a big day: for the happy couple and for the case. She wanted to have a clear head and not spend the whole day worrying about what she was wearing.

"I thought this, this or this." She spread two dresses across the coffee table: one apple-green, one apricot-coloured, then a lilac silk suit. Now that all of the clothes were lying in front of her like that, they seemed rather ridiculous: over-the-top and old-fashioned. Where had they come from? Had she ever even worn them?

"Hmmm." Charlie fell into an ominous silence, then she gingerly picked up the silk. "Perhaps we could do something with the blouse."

"What about on the bottom half?" Agnes gestured doubtfully down at herself.

"Hold your horses!" Charlie reached into her bag of tricks again and conjured up some midnight-blue fabric that also looked like silk. "A wrap skirt," she said. "It goes with everything."

The deep blue of the skirt really did bring out the lilac tones in the blouse. Agnes felt hopeful.

"Try it on!" Charlie pressed the skirt and blouse into her hand, and Agnes made her way upstairs on the stairlift.

Try it on! That was easier said than done. Back in her room, it took Agnes a while to peel herself out of her skirt and cardigan. The blouse wasn't a problem: It buttoned up at the front, but the skirt was another story . . . She wrapped it round herself quite a few times, and finally it was on. She hesitantly stood in front of the mirror. It wasn't bad. She was shorter than Charlie, and the skirt reached the floor, but that meant she wouldn't have to worry too much about what to put on her feet. The blue and the lilac looked like they were made for each other, and with the addition of a pretty brooch and a string of pearls she would look presentable. Good, even. Charlie knew her stuff; you had to give her that. Agnes felt a sense of relief, but then she realised that her heart was pounding like mad.

Where had the time gone? There was still so much to do, so much to think about. Could she really make sure Bernadette's big day went off without a hitch and hunt down a murderer? It was a lot of hats to wear!

Hats: Yes! She needed something on her head. She flung open her wardrobe. A black trilby. A black woollen cap. A black wide-brimmed hat. All perfectly suited to a funeral and used multiple times in recent years. But they didn't seem like the right choice for a wedding. Well, maybe Charlie would come up with something. Agnes opened her bedroom door to show her friend the outfit and found herself nose to nose with Marshall, who was obviously also making his way towards the stairs.

She could do without that right now.

"Marshall!" Agnes gazed at him open-mouthed; he stared back rather reproachfully.

"I . . ." he said, beating a hasty retreat back to his room. Marshall was a military type, so retreating was something he usually liked to avoid. Agnes felt a bit bad.

Luckily, Charlie came upstairs at just the right moment.

"So, Agnes? How do you feel in it?"

Agnes stood there looking downcast and let Charlie admire her outfit.

"Beautiful!" Charlie beamed. "Doesn't she look beautiful, Marshall?"

Marshall grunted noncommittally and disappeared into his room.

Charlie was far too busy with outfits and wedding stuff to have noticed the strained atmosphere. "Would you come with me a minute, Agnes? You're the bridesmaid, after all, aren't you?"

Agnes nodded glumly. Never in her life had she felt less like a bridesmaid. And that was saying something.

But Charlie linked arms with her and led her resolutely towards the stairs. "Could we quickly go through the running order again?" Charlie waved a piece of paper in her face. "I don't want to panic anyone, but . . ."

Agnes sighed. Of course Charlie wanted everyone to panic. Like so many other things, panic suited Charlie. She revelled in it.

31
CLOVER

The running order for the wedding actually looked pretty civilised on paper. Harmless. Considered. As if chaos wouldn't be lurking round every corner.

7:30 A.M.: Breakfast at Sunset Hall.

8 A.M.: The bride to get ready.

9 A.M.: Departure. Charlie to drive Bernadette. Everyone else to get taxis.

9:30 A.M.: Arrival at Foxglove Manor. Welcome drinks in the rose garden. Mingling with the other guests.

PAPER WAS notoriously patient, but reality wasn't quite as cooperative. Once the big day had arrived, time lurched forwards in fits and starts. Agnes had just been sitting with a giddy Charlie and an Edwina so smartly dressed that she was barely recognisable, then she had helped a nervous Bernadette into her wedding dress, and suddenly she was standing in front of Foxglove Manor in her skirt and blouse, one of Charlie's borrowed fascinators on her head, and a diamond brooch pinned to her chest.

She shook hands and tried to remember people's names. The man in the dark suit was their new gardener, wasn't he?

He looked like a different person in a white shirt and tie! And what on earth was he called? There was Charlie's good-looking grandson with his exceedingly handsome partner; over there was Sparrow, their burglar friend, wearing a velvet blazer from the seventies, with a disgruntled-looking plus-one. Christopher appeared in an immaculate tailcoat and immediately placed his hand on Charlie's hip. Charlie planted a smacker on his cheek, and Agnes averted her eyes. Over there was Benjamin Stout, so inconspicuous that he almost blended into the hedge. Hopefully he had the Christopher situation in his sights. Agnes gave him a little wave, but the detective ignored her, a clear sign of his professionalism.

In the background she spotted Constance Purr, who was in the process of supervising a little band of white-aproned staff as they put up the champagne fountain. Was Agnes imagining it or did she look rather stressed? You would expect a little more decorum from someone who was used to dealing with weddings day in and day out, wouldn't you?

Agnes resolved not to have any champagne. The situation was overwhelming enough sober.

A hand gripped her forearm, vice-like.

"Agnes, I'm so nervous!" In her beautiful dress with her sunglasses on, Bernadette didn't look the least bit nervous, more like the coolest bride for miles around. But her voice was shaking.

"There's no reason to be nervous," Agnes reasoned with her. Apart from X, Dorothea's murderer and the dead verger of course, but she wasn't going to tell her friend that. After all, this was her big day.

"Of course there's a reason," hissed Bernadette. "It's my wedding: the one I've been waiting more than fifty years for! If I can't be nervous today, when can I be?"

Agnes couldn't really argue with that. She patted Bernadette's hand to reassure her.

"Everything's all right," she said. "You should enjoy your day. You look great. The sun is shining. What more could you want?"

"All these people . . ." Bernadette complained. "I mean, I hardly know them . . ."

"Twenty guests," Agnes explained. "They wouldn't do it for any fewer."

"I know." Bernadette sighed. "But . . ."

"You know me," said Agnes. "You know Jack. That's the main thing. You don't have to know everyone."

Bernadette didn't seem convinced. "Jack isn't here yet." She sighed a second time.

"He'll be here soon," Agnes promised. "Marshall is with him—he won't let him out of his sight."

"It's not about that," spat Bernadette, tapping her cane irritably on the ground. That was better! An irritated Bernadette was preferable to a nervous Bernadette.

"I'll introduce you to a few people," Agnes suggested. "Then you'll know them! For example, Edwina and Richard are now coming. Richard is Edwina's plus-one. Richard, this is Bernadette. The bride," she added just in case, although the white dress was probably a bit of a giveaway.

Richard gave a little bow, chivalrously offered Bernadette his hand and muttered something about oleanders. He had his glad rags on, too, although it made him look no less lizard-like. After the handshaking he merrily jabbered on about a trip through the Abruzzi, as reptile expert Edwina skilfully steered him through the crowd towards the champagne fountain. Agnes decided to intervene—experience had taught her that it wasn't a good idea to bring Edwina into contact with alcohol.

She left Bernadette in Winston's charge—Winston was just the person when nerves needed calming—and rushed after the Lizard and Edwina.

Edwina saw her coming, stopped Richard and turned to Agnes.

Agnes bowled up to the two of them, words of warning about champagne on the tip of her tongue, but Edwina took the wind right out of her sails.

"We're just looking," she promised. "We're just looking at the fountain fizzing, that's all. Isn't that right, Richard?"

Agnes blinked in disbelief. Who was this sensible person in the dress, silk scarf and fascinator, and what had they done with Edwina?

Edwina let go of Richard for a moment and conspiratorially held a little basket up towards Agnes. In the basket, on red velvet, were two things: Lillith's tin decorated with a bow, and a highly polished Hettie. The tortoise seemed ill-tempered. And there was little wonder—Edwina had tied a little cushion onto her shell with the rings on it. Such things were frowned upon in tortoise circles.

Agnes gazed incredulously down at the furious-looking reptilian ring bearer. A few weeks ago, this had all seemed like fun and games; now all she could see were problems.

"What if she doesn't want to?"

"She will," Edwina declared. "Hettie's hungry. And Richard's got some iceberg lettuce—her favourite!"

Richard obediently pulled a little transparent bag of lettuce out of his suit pocket.

"Later!" Edwina admonished, before the two of them headed towards the champagne fountain again. The white-aproned elves of Foxglove Manor had just got it working and a little queue had already formed. At the front stood

Christopher, holding two glasses, having a serious discussion with Constance Purr. The man really knew the way to Charlie's heart!

Something clicked next to Agnes, and she spun around.

There was a young woman with a chic blond pixie cut taking rather obtrusive pictures of her. *Click. Click. Click.* Agnes was just about to give her a piece of her mind when she remembered: she was probably the photographer they had booked. Agnes attempted a smile.

"Agnes, don't just stand there! It's starting! You can have photos taken later!"

Charlie linked arms with her. She had put her hair up, was wearing a tiny little blue hat with a veil and a dress that floated around her like an orange, semi-transparent cloud. Unconventional, but magnificent. She looked like somebody who rode elephants, ate gilded grapes and went hunting with silky greyhounds—not like somebody who was making sure a wedding went to plan. But appearances could be deceptive.

"I'm not having my . . ." Agnes shooed the photographer away. "I was just . . . Already?"

Charlie took out her list. "Ten o'clock: Short wedding service. Hopefully it really is short. Help me, Agnes. We've got to get them all into the chapel. Where the hell is Christopher?"

Agnes pointed towards the champagne fountain, but Christopher wasn't there anymore. She obediently started directing guests to the chapel. Was Jack here yet? Who was the woman in pink? Why did people even get married? It was like hell on earth!

AGNES WAS finally sitting down again—in the chapel, right next to Bernadette. Bernadette had to sit at the back to start with so that Marshall could lead her to the front when the time was right and give her away to Jack.

That was all right by Agnes.

She took the opportunity to sit back and observe the other guests from a distance. There really were a lot of them. At the front in the second row sat Richard and Edwina, Charlie and, off to the side, Winston in his wheelchair. He noticed Agnes looking and gave her the thumbs-up. That bolstered her. Everything would be all right. But where were Jack and Marshall? The vicar was already doing something at the altar. To the side of him sat a harpist with long hair, plucking her strings in readiness.

Agnes thought about the verger and his organ music. Did he used to play at weddings here? Was that the connection to Foxglove Manor that she had been searching for?

"They're here," Bernadette said, interrupting her musings, and sure enough, Jack and Marshall were suddenly standing next to them. Jack gently placed his hand on Bernadette's shoulder as he passed, then he made his way to the front. Bernadette beamed and she really did look like a bride all of a sudden: fresh and glowing, from the inside out. Agnes felt warm all over. It had arrived: Bernadette's big day—and anybody who tried to spoil it would have her to deal with!

Marshall sat down next to her and Bernadette, while Jack took his rather lonely place in the front row. Well, at least the loneliness wouldn't last long.

The harpist started up. A solemn, yet cheerful melody rang out, glistening like dew. Christopher turned up and rushed less cheerfully down the aisle and squeezed into the second row next to Charlie, not a second too soon. The vicar was already talking; he greeted them all, started on the parable of the mustard seed, got a bit bogged down, then tried to get them all to sing. The little congregation made a rather half-hearted attempt.

"*The lord is my shepherd . . .*"

Agnes just opened her mouth every now and then; next to her, however, Marshall sang with great gusto, in a surprisingly beautiful baritone. Agnes suddenly had a lump in her throat.

After the song, the vicar regaled them with an anecdote from his uneventful parish life and once again blessed everyone present just to be on the safe side.

Then things got serious. The harpist reached for the strings again, and Mendelssohn's renowned "Wedding March" filled the room. Everyone stood up; even Winston sat up straighter. Marshall offered Bernadette his arm, then they both slowly made their way to the altar, where Jack and the vicar were waiting. Jack's blank penguin eyes looked a bit damp, and tears were suddenly rolling down Agnes's cheeks. Had she brought any tissues? Of course she hadn't. Dammit. Schoolboy error. With a bit of luck, you could get through a funeral without tears, but there generally wasn't a dry eye in the house at weddings. Still, Agnes's display of emotion had taken her a bit by surprise.

Her old friend Bernadette, the most stoical and sarcastic of all the housemates, was boldly embarking on a grand adventure, white and fearless as a sailboat. Agnes was happy for her, but it was the kind of happiness that stung a bit too.

She had never worn all white and walked down an aisle at a snail's pace. Had she missed out? Where was the problem? What was wrong with her? The tears flowed more quickly, and Agnes still had no idea where she was going to get a tissue from. She cursed the decision to let Charlie talk her into loaning her a silly silk clutch that might match the colour scheme but was full to capacity with just a coin purse and blood-pressure pills in it. To hell with vanity! What use was looking good if you could barely see anything through a veil of tears?

Marshall and Bernadette finally reached the altar, and Bernadette was given away to Jack as planned, then Agnes leaned forward and let her tears drip onto the floor—that is, until somebody held out a clean handkerchief towards her.

Agnes grabbed it gratefully, dabbed her eyes and loudly blew her nose before turning to the donor of the handkerchief. Marshall, of course—who else still used proper handkerchiefs? Fresh tears rolled down her cheeks.

Marshall sat down next to her.

"Something's happening at the front," he said soberly.

Agnes dabbed her eyes again and saw that he was right. In the second row, where Charlie, Christopher, Edwina and Richard were sitting, there seemed to be some kind of a muffled commotion. Heads were disappearing under the pew, Charlie was hissing something, and Edwina had a worried look on her face. Then Christopher leapt up and rushed out of the chapel, closely followed by Edwina.

Richard wavered for a moment, then scurried after Edwina. Charlie whispered something to Winston, then she came up the aisle, too, a fabulous orange cloud trying to be inconspicuous, and failing. The other guests looked round.

Charlie bent down to Agnes and Marshall.

"She's gone!" she whispered.

Agnes knew whom she meant straight away.

HETTIE THE tortoise had had enough of all the attention. After all, she had a shell and all creatures with shells value their privacy. Being in your shell was good, not being noticed in the first place was even better. Everybody knew that.

Today, things weren't looking good as far as privacy was concerned. No matter how grumpy Hettie tried to be, no matter how crossly she hissed, hazy faces hovered over her like unwanted clouds blocking the sun. Voices hummed, rising and falling in unison like a flock of pigeons in a summer sky. The real sky, meanwhile, had disappeared for now, and the ground beneath her was unpleasantly cool despite the wicker and fabric she was sitting on. Somebody had had the audacity to tie a ribbon around her body and attach something to her shell. And to top it all, she was sharing the basket with a tin.

Nobody was offering her any lettuce.

What a cheek!

True tortoise, Hettie waited a while, then she started to hatch escape plans. Most tortoises are master escape planners. This is a little-known fact because sadly most tortoises aren't very good at putting their plans into action. But Hettie was ever the optimist.

She would climb onto the tin, stand on her back legs, reach for the edge of the basket with her front claws and pull herself up. Then . . . well, then she would have to improvise.

Hettie struggled for a while without even getting close to the edge of the basket, and was on the verge of getting even grumpier when her world started shaking.

The basket wobbled, then tipped over. Suddenly, she was sitting on the very edge that she'd been ineffectually striving for. Behind it was stone, down-to-earth and confidence-inspiring.

Freedom was so close she could taste it!

Hettie left the basket behind and stalked decisively past a host of glammed-up feet, towards where it seemed lighter and warmer. The ground beneath her was cold stone to begin with, then gravel and finally lovely green grass. The sun was shining. Insects were buzzing. Otherwise, it was quiet. Hettie rested for a while in the glorious tranquillity beneath three egg-yolk yellow daffodils, then she felt hungry again. She turned her back on the daffodils and marched off, looking for some dandelion, ideally some lettuce—at a pinch, clover would do. Unfortunately, the lawn here provided slim pickings. Hettie decided to ignore the grass and to look for something edible in the shade under the hedges. There were a lot of hedges with straight edges, but nothing that suited Hettie's sophisticated tortoise palate.

After she'd stalked back and forth for a while, Hettie realised that there was a foot disturbing the peaceful scene.

Actually, it was two feet.

That came as no great surprise as feet were almost always in pairs. These two specimens were pointing motionlessly at the sky, rather atypical behaviour, but Hettie had previous experience with feet pointing skywards. They didn't tend to make a fuss. Hettie warily stepped closer. As ill luck would have it, some appetising four-leaf clover was growing right between the two feet. Hettie examined the situation for a while. On the other side of the feet, things were as you'd traditionally expect: calves, knees, torso, arms and even a head.

Nothing moved, and it didn't seem like anything was going to spoil Hettie's meal. She pluckily stalked closer, aimed for the first clover leaf and took a bite.

32

MAZE

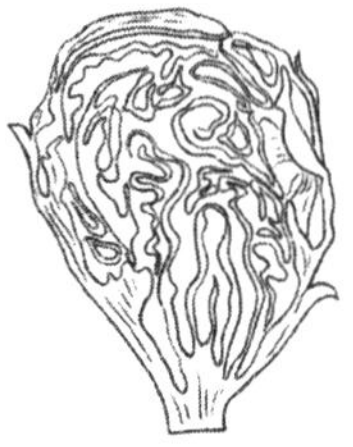

Agnes stepped out of the cool darkness of the chapel, into the sunshine and squinted. Daffodils swayed gracefully on the lawn as Edwina, the hem of her blue dress hitched up to her knees, ran through them less gracefully, calling for Hettie. Her glitzy trainers sparkled in the sunlight.

"Kids, we've had it now. Don't panic. Keep calm!" Charlie's orange cloud appeared next to Agnes. Charlie fanned herself with the piece of paper with the running order on it. The whole don't-panic thing obviously wasn't going particularly well.

"When do they need the rings?" Marshall had come outside, too, and was shading his eyes from the sun and peering across the lawn.

Charlie frantically looked at her little gold watch. "In a quarter of an hour, I'd say. Twenty minutes at the latest, depending on whether the vicar keeps it as short as he said he would. And I drilled it into him that he should make sure his sermon wasn't too long. But he does seem to like the sound of his own voice." She raised her hands to run her fingers through her hair, remembered her updo just in time and lowered her hands again.

Twenty minutes to find a little brown tortoise in over an acre of parkland! Things weren't looking good for the exchanging of rings.

"She can't have gone far," Marshall muttered, but he didn't sound convinced. They all knew how quick Hettie was when she was hungry.

"How do we know that she's not in the church anymore?" Agnes asked.

Edwina interrupted her search and stopped dead in the middle of the lawn, her cheeks red. Her fascinator was on the wonk. "She's not in the church. Hettie didn't like the church. It was too cold. Hettie likes the sun! And greenery!"

"And how . . . ?" Agnes fell silent. Remonstrating with Edwina was pointless. Their friend might normally be a walking catalogue of disasters, but when it came to tortoises, she knew what she was talking about.

"The basket tipped over." Edwina looked at the ground, shamefaced. "I had put it on the floor and then it tipped over somehow."

That's what must have happened. While Marshall and Bernadette were walking down the aisle at a snail's pace, Hettie was striding snappy tortoise steps in the opposite direction—the wedding rings with her.

"You think you've thought of everything . . . The bride or groom doing a runner—these things do happen from time to time. But the rings . . ." Charlie struggled again with the urge to run her fingers through her hair and shook her fists in frustration.

"It's not over until the fat lady sings," said Agnes decisively. "We'll look for Hettie. We'll find her. Bernadette will have a wonderful day. The end!"

"The end!" cried Edwina.

Agnes sent Edwina off to the left, towards the orangery, and Marshall to the right, towards the rose garden and champagne fountain. Charlie was going to look on the other side of the chapel, which apparently led to the vegetable garden—an attractive proposition for any hungry tortoise. Agnes took the area right in front of her, separated by a hedge, on the other side of the daffodil lawn. It was the closest and seemed straightforward enough.

She looked at her watch. "Let's meet back here in a quarter of an hour. If we haven't found her by then, we can start with the wailing and gnashing of teeth. Not before."

It was a good plan.

Or *a* plan, at least.

Sighing, Agnes made her way across the grass to the hedges. There was a rounded entrance cut into one of the hedges. Shadows lay beyond it, a sign above it. Only once she'd got closer could she read what it said.

MAZE.

Great. Agnes needed a maze like she needed a hole in the head. But a deal was a deal.

Resigned to her fate, she stepped through the opening and found herself in front of another wall of hedge. A narrow passageway led left and right. No tortoise as far as the eye could see, but that wasn't particularly far. There were more openings in the second hedge. Agnes cast a final wistful glance back at the chapel, where in not more than fifteen minutes two rings were needed, then she made her way into the maze, not exactly brimming with confidence.

SHE WAS the last one to return to the meeting point after almost twenty minutes—it wasn't called a maze for nothing!

But she did have Hettie, the reluctant ring bearer, under her arm complete with the rings.

Charlie cheered, and Edwina flung her arms around Agnes's neck. Marshall limited himself to looking relieved.

Despite her discovery, Agnes's mood was subdued. Because of her discovery, strictly speaking. Because of the *other* discovery. One problem had been solved and another much bigger one lay in the maze, toes pointing skywards.

But first they had to think about the wedding. After all, toes pointing skywards were a fairly common occurrence, especially in Duck End; Bernadette, on the other hand, had been waiting a lifetime for her big day. It would be rude to keep her waiting any longer.

Agnes went back to the chapel, Charlie, Edwina and Marshall in tow. The harpist was plucking her strings with her long fingers again; Jack and the vicar were looking rather quizzically in their direction. So, the sermon was over, something of a miracle if you knew their vicar. Now the rings were needed, but Agnes doubted that Hettie was up to the job. Richard and his supply of prime iceberg lettuce were back, but Hettie had a brisk walk behind her, as well as a tummy full of clover. Even Agnes didn't particularly want to move—how was the tortoise supposed to feel? She passed Hettie to Edwina, signalled towards the altar and sank down onto a pew in relief.

After all, there was nothing stopping the ring bearer herself from being carried down the aisle. Edwina strolled sedately down the aisle and held the ring bearer and rings up to the bride and groom. The vicar, who still looked rather irritated, remembered the running order and continued.

. . . for better, for worse . . .

. . . in sickness and in health . . .

. . . to love and to cherish . . .

. . . till death do us part . . .

It should have been the most moving part of the whole ceremony. Jack's penguin eyes were damp, a sparkling tear rolled out from beneath Bernadette's sunglasses, and even Richard the Lizard, who was uselessly holding out the lettuce towards Edwina, had an unusually rosy complexion for a lizard.

Under normal circumstances Agnes would have sobbed at least two hankies full, but her eyes were dry. Her brain, however, was working overtime. How? Why? And what now? Was it too much to ask to have a wonderful day without a dead body lying around somewhere?

She took a deep breath in and out, then in again.

Breathing was a good start, no matter what else was going on. Finding tortoises, marrying friends, covering up murders—everything started with a few deep breaths.

Marshall held another hanky towards her, but Agnes shook her head.

She turned to Charlie, who had sat down on the pew behind her, and was impatiently glancing at the door every now and then. "Where the hell is Christopher?" she whispered in a not-very-ladylike way.

"Forget Christopher for a moment," Agnes advised her. "Show me the plan instead."

She took the piece of paper from Charlie's hand and squinted. Nothing to be done. The running order was printed far too small, and obviously she hadn't been able to fit her reading glasses in the chic little clutch. She huffed in frustration.

"What I need to know is: Are we doing anything in the maze?"

"Of course we are." Charlie consulted the plan. "Straight after the signing of the register and before the wedding feast.

One-thirty: Walk through the maze. Photos. There's supposed to be a charming little garden with cherry blossoms and sculptures in the middle, you know?"

"I know." Agnes sighed. What Charlie didn't know was that the idyll was currently being severely disturbed by a less-than-charming body. As soon as it was found, someone would call the police, who would want to question them all, and before they knew where they were, they could forget the wedding feast, the tea dance and the pot-au-feu. And they'd be lucky if the bridegroom wasn't arrested into the bargain. The dead body in the maze dealt a large blow not just to the wedding, but to the rest of Bernadette's life too. The body had to go. And quickly. There was no doubt in Agnes's mind.

She was beginning to understand how people slipped into criminality. It didn't happen suddenly. It happened gradually, bit by bit. Making Dorothea's body disappear under the influence of alcohol had given them quite a headache and a generous dose of guilt, but now she was already used to the thought of perverting the course of justice. The question wasn't so much the *if* anymore, but the *how*. Stupidly, the person most au fait with such things was rather busy getting married, so it would fall to the rest of the Sunset Hall residents to navigate this delicate situation.

"You look funny." Charlie eyed her critically. "She looks funny, doesn't she?"

Marshall nodded.

Agnes shrugged. Looking funny was the least of her worries. They had roughly three-quarters of an hour to get a body out of the maze and hide it somewhere, without being seen or leaving any evidence behind. No easy task. Agnes was happy that she'd opted for flats.

Cheers erupted from the front rows. The vicar had just

given Jack permission to kiss the bride, and he was enthusiastically fulfilling his duty. Agnes allowed herself a moment of emotion, then she turned to her housemates again.

"We've got a problem," she whispered. "Quite a big one. And it's lying in the maze."

33
COMPOST

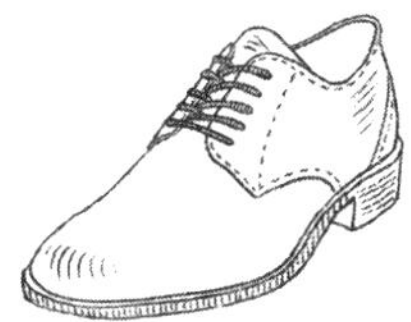

Agnes, Charlie and Marshall spent the rest of the ceremony feverishly hatching plans under their breath. They needed a means of transport, a hiding place and, ideally, some gloves, and pronto. It was a tricky one, but Charlie argued that if you could plan a wedding, you could plan practically anything. When Christopher finally turned up in the chapel again, red-faced and proudly holding out a bag towards them, Charlie impatiently waved him aside.

"I sent him to my car to get my jewellery box. In case we needed replacement rings," Charlie explained. The ring problem was now resigned to the past, and the current problem obviously wasn't one for Christopher. Such things were best dealt with by a small circle of people made up of trusted members of the house share.

By the time the vicar was finally finished and Jack and Bernadette were breezing up the aisle arm in arm as Edwina scattered lettuce leaves, they had a plan of sorts, which above all, required a lot of luck.

While Agnes hugged Bernadette and heartily shook Jack's hand in front of the chapel, Marshall disappeared off towards the rose garden and Charlie brought Winston and Edwina up to speed with the latest Sunset Hall plans. Edwina clapped her hands together with glee, whereas Winston went pale and looked horrified.

Agnes took Bernadette to one side. "There's a slight organisational hiccup," she whispered. "Unfortunately, it's a bit urgent, so we won't be able to make it to the signing of the register."

Bernadette beamed beneath her sunglasses. She looked like nothing in the world could get to her. "What will be, will be," she said. "Is it . . ."

"It's really not a biggie," Agnes lied quickly, "but we need to take care of it straight away."

"Is it a surprise?" Bernadette asked, grinning.

"More like the opposite of a surprise," Agnes explained.

She could see Marshall standing in the shade of the hedges trying to surreptitiously wave to her.

Edwina appeared next to Bernadette. She was beaming too. "I heard . . ."

"Have you already congratulated Bernadette?" Agnes interrupted her.

Edwina pulled a face. "Twice already."

"Then you should congratulate her a third time," said Agnes sternly. "And then we're going."

Edwina crowed her congratulations and scattered a few more lettuce leaves at Bernadette's feet, just to be sure.

"It's just the tip of the iceberg!" she quipped.

Agnes groaned. Edwina was right, as usual.

"THAT REALLY is . . ." Charlie's voice faltered and trembled, a bit like blancmange. Despite her lovely dress, she didn't look fabulous anymore. Her pink lipstick was now the only flash of colour on her face. The rest was pale, albeit not quite deathly pale.

The dead body at their feet was far paler.

Agnes nodded. "Why now? Why him?"

She nudged the lifeless corpse with the toe of her shoe. But no matter how much she nudged him, dead was dead.

"If I'd have known, I would never have suggested him," Edwina said guiltily.

"It's too late for that," spat Charlie. "You and your stupid ideas."

"It's not really Edwina's fault," Marshall said.

Benjamin Stout had made an excellent impression on Agnes too. Understated. Capable. Friendly. Why it had to be him lying lifelessly on the grass between the cherry trees and the sculptures jeopardising their wedding plans was a mystery to Agnes.

"He didn't have anything to do with it!" she huffed. The detective had been a coincidental guest, just making up numbers. Why would someone . . .

"Maybe he saw something he shouldn't have," said Edwina gloomily.

"Well, it definitely wasn't a heart attack." Marshall pointed at a small patch of blood on Stout's white shirt. "A knife between the ribs. Just like . . ."

". . . Dorothea!" Agnes added. For a moment she felt relieved. If Stout had fallen victim to the same killer as Dorothea, that at least meant one thing: Jack was officially in the clear. The bridegroom had been far too busy getting married; he definitely hadn't had time to wander through the maze stabbing people. That was something. But practically anyone else could have nipped to the maze and . . .

"Agnes," said Marshall gently next to her. "We don't need to solve his murder; we need to cover it up."

Agnes nodded. Marshall was right. Time was of the essence.

She distributed the gardening gloves that Marshall had found in the shed next to the rose garden.

"The maze has four exits," Marshall explained, pointing to a site map on his phone. In the absence of her reading glasses, however, Agnes could only make out a blurry patch of green. "One at every point of the compass. This is the one we came from. Right leads to the rose garden, left to the orangery and back there leads to"—Marshall paused for effect—"the car park. And next to the car park there are a few sheds behind a hedge. There's bound to be somewhere we can hide him for the time being."

Agnes nodded. Obviously, they couldn't make Stout disappear for evermore like a professional like Jack would have done. But if he was found in a few days' time instead of today, it would be a win. Then Bernadette would at least have her big day in the bag. What happened after that—who could say? That was one of the good things about getting old: you took each day as it came. And every day was a small victory.

"Agnes?"

Agnes realised that her housemates were looking at her expectantly and remembered the issue at hand.

"I thought Marshall could grab him under the arms," she explained. "Charlie and I can take a foot each. And Edwina can keep a lookout." Edwina stuck her bottom lip out.

"It's the most important job, Edwina," Agnes assured her.

And it was the truth. If anyone saw them moving the body, they'd had it. Dressed in silk, tulle and full dress uniform they were easily recognisable as wedding guests, never mind the gardening gloves, and in the blazing sun, Benjamin Stout unfortunately looked very dead indeed. It wasn't something you could talk your way out of. So, it was about making sure that nobody saw you in the first place.

"If someone comes, you shout and we'll quickly throw him in the bushes and act as if we're mucking around," Agnes reminded her. With a bit of luck, it wouldn't come to that. The guests should be busy with signing the register and the white-aproned Foxglove Manor elves with preparing the wedding feast.

That was the theory, at least—now it was time to try it in practice.

Things started surprisingly well. After all, they'd had some experience with Dorothea.

They stopped at every opening in the hedge so that Edwina could poke her head out. When she shouted "iceberg," the coast was clear.

But after a while, Charlie started to moan, and Agnes was gradually getting out of breath too. Stout was heavier than he looked.

At the next corner, Edwina's "iceberg" didn't happen. She flailed her arms mutely and dived sideways into the hedge. As agreed, they jettisoned Stout and leapt into the hedge too. Agnes pressed herself into the greenery and cursed the shimmering silk of her blouse. Branches pricked through the fabric. As usual, Marshall was suitably dressed in his green uniform jacket, but next to him Charlie's garish orange dress billowed. If someone so much as glanced in their direction, the game was up.

Four white-aproned Foxglove Manor elves with blankets, glasses, little tables and a wheelbarrow went past the opening in the hedge without looking in their direction. Agnes was pre-occupied with breathing again. In. Out. Just don't panic. Her heart was pounding like mad. After the initial fright, she started to peel herself out of the hedge. Together with Marshall, she helped Charlie to extricate the delicate fabric of her dress from the branches. Up ahead, Edwina whispered "iceberg," and they set to grabbing Stout under the arms again, or under the knees, whatever the case may be.

The rest of the transfer went without a hitch—if you could talk about dragging a dead body through a maze as going off without a hitch. Things like that normally only happened in nightmares—if at all. But here they were hiding a dead body again, without complaint and in perfect harmony. They had come a long way in the last few weeks.

They reached the maze entrance without further incident, and there, next to the car park, just as Marshall had promised, were a couple of practical-looking sheds.

Agnes allowed herself a moment of hope. Maybe everything was going to be all right after all. Why not? If as many things went wrong as at this wedding, then a few things had to go right every now and then—that was just probability.

The car park was dead, and Edwina crowed "iceberg" again.

The final push.

There was an impressive compost heap between the sheds. Agnes patted Stout's calf apologetically, then they lowered him into a little well in the heap. Marshall started shovelling leaf litter onto him with a spade that had been leaning against one of the sheds: first on his face and upper body, then along his legs.

Not the worst place to end up, Agnes thought. Natural. Organic. And it smelled pleasantly of leaves. Stout could manage here for a little while. Finally, his left foot disappeared beneath the leaf litter, then his right foot; then the compost heap looked like normal again.

Marshall put the spade aside and collected the gardening gloves so that he could put them back where he'd found them.

"Iceberg," Edwina squawked triumphantly.

"Didn't he have two shoes before?" Charlie wondered.

34

CUPID

Agnes, who was nothing if not scrupulous, wanted to go straight back into the maze to retrieve the missing shoe, but Marshall stopped her.

"After all, it's only a shoe," he said. "If somebody finds it, it might seem a bit odd, but it won't necessarily arouse suspicion. Not immediately, anyway."

Agnes opened her mouth to say something and then shut it again. Leaving evidence behind like that went against her better judgement, but Marshall was right. And apart from anything else, it wasn't their murder. There was no need to be too pedantic about eliminating all of the evidence.

Before, she had been far too preoccupied with the body, but now curiosity reared its head again. In practical terms, there were only two groups of people who had the time and opportunity to get near the detective with a knife: the staff and the guests. Had he been lured into the maze? How—and above all, why? Who might have something against Stout? After all, he didn't seem to have anything to do with anybody here. Or was it not about the man himself? Had the killer just wanted to stab *somebody* to death—and Stout was in the wrong place at the wrong time?

Was the detective the "dead" that the poison-pen letter had heralded? Was there really someone trying their utmost to stop Bernadette and Jack's wedding? If so, he was a bit late to the party. Was that a good thing? Or was it something that might push the killer to commit more acts of violence?

"Agnes? Shall we?"

She looked up. Marshall was impatiently holding his arm out towards her; the others were looking at her expectantly. Agnes absent-mindedly linked arms with Marshall and they followed Charlie, who was making her way towards the estate's main entrance with the determination of a drill sergeant.

"The signing of the register is happening in the Red Room," she announced. "Wherever that is."

Agnes gulped. "Red Room" had an ominous ring to it, especially in the context of the poison-pen letter. What was going on here?

When Agnes and her friends finally located the right room, the signing of the register was basically over. Jack and Bernadette were stepping out into the foyer, even more married than they had been before. Everyone was offering their congratulations, and luckily Edwina had run out of lettuce. Agnes allowed herself a little breather on a bench and watched from a distance. She was tired, hungry and worried. There really was a lot expected of bridesmaids these days.

Edwina rushed over to Richard and tore the basket carrying Hettie out of his hands. Agnes grinned. So, there was a hierarchy as far as the reptiles in Edwina's life were concerned, and Richard didn't seem to be particularly high up.

Marshall spotted his daughter, together with his grandson, Nathan. He let go of Agnes's arm and rushed over to them. Agnes always struggled to see Marshall in his nervous daughter, but the two of them seemed to have a good relationship—sometimes too good. After all, it meant that last year they'd had to look after the Grandson for a whole week. He'd eaten them out of house and home, and then almost fallen victim to a murderer, but he still seemed to have fond memories of his time at Sunset Hall. When he noticed Agnes, he rushed over to her, grinning.

"Hello," he said.

"Hello, Nathan," Agnes responded warily. He'd grown so much! The Grandson was at least a head taller than she remembered—and he'd thinned out too. Dark curls crowned his head again, but the way he was standing, the assertive, direct eye contact . . . For a fleeting moment, Agnes saw a hint of Marshall in him.

She smiled. "So, how are you enjoying the wedding?"

"It's a bit boring, to be honest," Nathan admitted.

Agnes blinked. The wedding did have rather a lot of drawbacks, but boredom wasn't something she had encountered as yet. "It's not about us," she said, "it's about the happy couple."

Charlie, who had been pepped up by a glass of champagne that Christopher had brought her, cleared her throat and tapped on her glass with one of her red fingernails. "Dear guests, we shall now continue outside for a stroll through the maze," she announced, "and some photos. And then we'll celebrate properly with a wonderful wedding feast. I can hardly wait."

Charlie didn't look like she could hardly wait, and the thought of having to return to the maze made Agnes feel a bit queasy. But it was on the plan, so it had to happen. Anything else would have looked suspicious.

Most of the other guests actually looked like they could hardly wait, presumably because the wedding was slowly but surely heading towards the food. They readily followed

Charlie as she led them outside towards the ominous dark hedges.

Agnes, however, stood in the doorway with mixed emotions as she observed the well-dressed guests optimistically making their way across the lawn. Did one of them have Stout on their conscience? And if so—who? And how would she find out?

Somebody held out their arm towards her, more a demand than a courtesy.

By now, they knew their way around the maze quite well, so Agnes and Marshall made it to the centre before most of the other guests. The clouds of pink cherry blossoms and the tasteful stone sculptures no longer stirred any romantic feeling in Agnes but brought on a dull feeling of dread. This is where they had found Stout, spattered with cherry-blossom petals, a munching Hettie between his feet. It hadn't even been two hours ago, yet it seemed far, far away, like a different lifetime. She saw that a few Foxglove Manor elves had set up tables and were pouring glasses of champagne and orange juice. The photographer was also poised, her camera in her hands ready to capture love's not-so-young dream. But maybe love, peace and harmony weren't the only things she'd caught in her photographs.

On the spur of the moment, Agnes tugged Marshall's sleeve.

"We need the photos," she whispered. "*All* of them."

Marshall understood immediately and nodded.

Meanwhile, a crowd of people was streaming into the little garden, Jack and Bernadette leading the way, happy and rosy, just like the cherry blossom petals. For a moment, Agnes felt a rush of emotion again. Bernadette and Jack had done it! They were married, despite all the obstacles and dead bodies in their way. For a brief moment, Agnes felt proud of her role as bridesmaid, then her thoughts turned to the guests again. All there, as far as she could tell—apart from Stout, that is.

Charlie's grandson was strolling around arm in arm with his partner, marvelling at the sculptures; Charlie was happily being dragged behind a cherry tree by Christopher; and Edwina was sprinkling petals over Hettie's basket. The gardener was looking at the hedges with an air of professional respect.

Nobody seemed surprised not to find a dead body in the maze. They drank champagne and posed beneath pink clouds of blossom for photos. It was like a fairy tale, at least it was if you didn't know about Stout, who was lying beneath old leaf litter just a hundred yards away, champagne a distant memory.

Marshall abruptly let go of Agnes's arm and marched off without so much as another word and made his way towards his grandson. Agnes was left a bit hurt. It's true that they weren't engaged anymore, and although Marshall had dutifully delivered her from A to B, he obviously had no desire to spend too much time with her under the blossoms—and who could blame him? She looked awkwardly at the ground—and saw the shoe. It was lying in the grass not far from the entrance and was partially covered by pink petals. But only partially. If she got a bit closer, she would be able to shove it under one of the hedges with her foot, then they would all have one less thing to worry about!

Off Agnes went, but since her balance wasn't what it once was, the nudging went rather more slowly than she'd expected.

Just then, somebody behind her shouted: "Cheese!" Agnes got a shock, leaned forward and picked up the shoe, to her great surprise, without falling over. In the given circumstances, it was just about the stupidest thing she could have done, but her nerves were strained, and it had happened before she could think things through properly.

Behind her stood the photographer, who was in the process of taking a photograph of Edwina and Richard beneath the cherry blossoms. Edwina was holding the basket at an angle so that Lillith and Hettie were in the photo too; Richard looked a bit annoyed.

Nobody noticed Agnes, thank goodness, but now she was standing there holding the shoe.

She had to get rid of it before anybody started asking stupid questions. That was how it differed to a fairy tale. In fairy tales, it was about whom the shoe fit; in the real world it was about making the shoe disappear before it connected someone to a murder victim. Agnes frantically looked around. White-aproned elves were running around everywhere carrying bottles, glasses or plates of canapés. There were more elves than guests, truth be told; it was a bit ridiculous. It wasn't easy to find a quiet moment to throw the shoe into the hedge. And if one of the helpful white aprons saw her drop something, they would probably pick it up and then there would be the awkward question of what she was doing with a worn-out gent's shoe.

At the same time, Agnes could see the photographer stalking through the cherry-tree branches like a voyeuristic panther, her lens constantly to her eye. If she took a photograph of Agnes with the shoe, sooner or later there would be trouble. She had to do something, and quickly!

At the back was a little fountain with three stone Cupids. One of them was holding a rose, one of them was aiming an arrow at Agnes, and the third—well, he was the reason the fountain was gurgling and filled with water. Somebody had placed some white gravel on the edge of the fountain. It looked pretty. It was quieter around the fountain because the grass was a bit muddy there. Agnes stepped closer. As she'd hoped, the water wasn't clear, but green and murky. It was covered in duckweed. If a shoe sank in the fountain . . . But did shoes sink? It depended on the individual shoe, and Agnes didn't want to take any chances. She grabbed a few stones and shoved them inside the shoe. Was that enough? It was a big shoe, with the potential to be very buoyant.

Agnes thoughtfully shoved a second handful of gravel into the shoe, then chucked it into the water. It turned a little, and sank into the green depths as she'd hoped. A silvery bubble glugged to the surface, then a second and finally, after a short pause, a third.

That was that.

Sunk.

Bye bye, shoe!

Agnes was just about to breathe a sigh of relief when she realised that somebody had been watching her from the other side of the fountain, partially obscured by cherry blossoms.

An elf.

A girl.

Watching her—and realising that there was something amiss with the shoe.

Maybe it was the combination of dark eyes, a haunted look and the water feature, but all of a sudden, Agnes's brain made some connections: the girl in the verger's garden, the young woman with the forced smile who had served her cheesecake at Foxglove Manor, a stack of paper and—hazy and barely tangible—a white figure.

Agnes raised her hand imploringly: in surprise, and so that the elf didn't get the wrong idea about her.

The shoe isn't really anything to do with me, said the hand.

I was so blind!

Above all, it said: *Wait! Don't go!*

Don't run away!

We need to talk . . .

The young woman didn't believe a word the hand had to say. She cast a final, inscrutable look at Agnes, then she disappeared between the cherry trees.

For a moment, Agnes stood there as if she'd been struck by lightning. Dammit! Her mouth was dry. A thousand thoughts were rushing through her head.

The verger in the belfry.

The girl in the apron.

A house full of paper.

Benjamin Stout's dead body.

Agnes was on the brink of understanding something important. She tried to spin around. What came out was more of a lurch. Hopeless undertaking or not, she had to try to talk to the girl.

And it was at that very moment that her foot slipped on the muddy grass.

She flew towards the fountain.

And then she wasn't flying anymore.

Marshall had grabbed her hand at the very last moment.

Petals fluttered in front of her eyes.

Agnes flailed. She pointed towards where the girl had disappeared.

"There . . . back there . . . I was wrong!" she huffed. "It's not a threat, Marshall! It's a warning!"

Then she ran out of puff. Marshall wasn't just holding her arm, but was supporting her waist too. They looked at each other for a few moments, eye to eye, while the fountain carried on obliviously burbling away and the stone Cupid stubbornly pointed his stone arrow at the two of them. A gentle breeze swirled more and more petals into the air.

Then Agnes heard a *click*.

"Beautiful!" the photographer gushed.

35
THE SEATING PLAN

The magic moment only lasted three seconds before Marshall helped her onto her feet again. Then he hastily put her down and took an annoyed step back. Despite the pink petals sitting mischievously on his epaulettes, he didn't seem to be in the mood for romance. He seemed more like somebody who had just accidentally sat on an ant's nest.

They were no longer engaged.

Agnes shooed away a few rebellious butterflies that were fluttering away in her tummy, and focused on her mission.

"We've got to find one of the white aprons," she quickly explained. "About so high"—she raised her hand to indicate the girl's height—"dark hair, dark eyes, sharp features . . ." Even as she was describing the girl, she realised how ridiculous the whole situation was. There were at least twenty Foxglove Manor elves running around all over the place. Most of them were female; lots of them had dark hair. Why were there so many of them here, to keep a few guests in drink? Agnes now had a theory of sorts for that too.

"Forget it." She sighed and waved her hand dismissively. All these elves were so similar. A description alone wasn't going to cut it. No, she would have to keep her eyes peeled and find the girl herself.

Just then, a clear, brittle sound rang out in the little garden.

Charlie had tapped her glass with her fingernail again. Expectant faces turned towards her.

"Kids," she cried, although strictly speaking there was only one child present, "it's time! I have just been informed that our fantastic wedding feast is ready. Please empty your glasses and follow me into the ballroom."

She had visibly recovered; she was no longer pale and the corners of her mouth gracefully curled into a real smile. Christopher and the champagne therapy seemed to be working wonders.

Agnes, however, groaned inwardly. Following her again! Marshall dutifully held his arm out for Agnes, but she shook her head and made for the gap in the hedge on her own. She didn't want to get on Marshall's nerves with her aches and pains anymore. He was a gentleman, but he obviously didn't want to have any more to do with her than was absolutely necessary. If need be, she'd manage to get to the ballroom under her own steam.

Marshall stared at her blankly for a moment, almost a little hostilely, then he gave a brief nod and walked past her.

It's for the best! Agnes explained to her furious butterflies.

She marched resolutely across the lawn towards the manor. It was interesting watching the brightly coloured ragtag wedding party on migration. Richard, for example, seemed rather stressed and tried to shake off Edwina's arm more than once. He didn't get very far. Edwina spent her days grappling with a boa constrictor; a lightweight like Richard didn't stand a chance. Agnes watched Charlie and Christopher, who were holding hands and visually made a very good couple. She considered the fact that Stout's task had been to suss out the slick charmer. She could forget about that now, of course. Did the task have anything to do with the detective's demise? Should she put Christopher at the top of her list of suspects? Why not!

Bernadette and Jack, clearly on cloud nine, floated across the lawn arm in arm. Agnes's bridesmaid-heart did a little joyful skip. They were so happy! It had all been worth it, all the effort for the wedding and even the trouble with Stout, Dorothea and the poison-pen letter. Where were the "red" and the "dead" that the letter had promised? There was only one person who could answer that question: the girl from the well, cheesecake server and elf on duty. Agnes had now finally remembered her name: Mia.

Agnes's thoughts leapt ahead to the impending wedding feast. It would be an elaborate affair with multiple courses, matching wines and lots of back and forth. A slew of elves would be needed to keep everything on track, and, if Agnes was lucky, Mia would be amongst them. Agnes wouldn't let her escape a third time.

As the first guests made their way into the manor, chattering away, a lonely cloud covered the sun and all of a sudden, the grounds looked gloomy. Still a fairy-tale castle, no doubt about it, but the kind inhabited by dragons with lots of teeth or toothless witches hatching sinister schemes.

Agnes shuddered, then plucked up the courage to follow the others into the ballroom.

CHARLIE HAD spent days wrangling with the seating plan, but Agnes wasn't convinced by the fruit of her labours. Agnes was sitting near the head of the table between the photographer and Sylvie, the home help. At least she was a safe distance from the loquacious vicar. Seated opposite her, partially hidden by a grand floral arrangement, was Charlie's grandson. He was rather easy on the eye, but Agnes had no idea what to say to someone that age. Maybe the enormous floral arrangement would mean it wouldn't come to a conversation, but what if it did? At first, she was at a loss, but then a topic came to her: Brexit! Charlie's grandson would definitely be interested in the wolfhound.

Agnes requested a glass of wine and let out a deep sigh.

She looked along the table and spotted Marshall. Their eyes met briefly, then Agnes quickly looked away. At the end of the table, there was a gaping empty place setting where Stout should have been sitting. Obviously, nobody could expect him to be at the table given the circumstances.

Most of the guests seemed to be grappling with similar problems to Agnes: What on earth should they say to the person next to them? Charlie's idea had been to *break down walls* and *make new connections*, but most of the guests seemed to be struggling with new connections and preferred to crane their necks towards their far-flung friends and partners. Richard was the only one who seemed pleased with the arrangement as he was no longer at Edwina's beck and call, and he fled to the toilets looking relieved. Agnes enviously watched him walk away. A loo visit wouldn't hurt—but standing up again, crossing all of the rugs, making her way along the corridor? She'd be better off sitting tight for a bit.

She looked up, where sparkling chandeliers played with the light, then to the side at a wall full of gilt-framed oil paintings. More of the castle owner's flamingo ancestors in white cloud-like wigs or pompous armour, with or without weapons, but all with almost-identical cold avian eyes.

Sunlight stretched through the windows towards the table,

but couldn't quite reach it. There were flowers everywhere. A thick botanical aroma lay in the air. It reminded Agnes rather unpleasantly of the compost heap. The light was swallowed by the dark parquet, and suddenly the uneasy feeling that had gripped Agnes out on the lawn was back. There was something amiss in Foxglove Manor. But what was it?

Charlie stood up, imposing and very orange, and tapped her dessert spoon on her glass. A high, clear ring. Agnes realised that Charlie herself hadn't broken down any walls—Christopher was sitting right next to her and on the other side of her was her grandson's partner. Tim? Tom? Theo? Typical Charlie, surrounding herself with the event's most handsome men under the guise of a seating plan! And Agnes was stuck with Sylvie.

Charlie greeted the wedding guests and the happy couple for the umpteenth time, quickly recounted how the two lovebirds had got together again after a chance encounter on holiday—she avoided any mention of the murders in the hotel. Bernadette blushed; Jack looked like the happiest penguin in the world. On Charlie's signal, the elves poured champagne for all of the guests again—who in the world could drink all this champagne? Certainly not Agnes! She glared at the champagne bubbles fizzing in her glass. Champagne was the enemy of thought and a sure-fire way to get a headache! Nevertheless, she obediently raised her glass like the other guests and toasted to the bride and groom with Sylvie and the photographer, all while trying to keep an eye on the elves. A crowd of pale young faces passed by, but the one Agnes was looking for was not among them.

At least something substantial was finally being served. Well, maybe *substantial* wasn't the right word: Little round pastries floated on huge plates. Some kind of profiterole filled with herbs? Agnes stabbed it with her fork and it collapsed in on itself. But it smelled delicious. Charlie suddenly appeared next to Agnes as she was polishing off the profiterole.

Agnes braced herself for bad news.

"I hope you're ready?" Charlie whispered and then winked.

Agnes eyed her with concern. Ready for what? Was somebody else dead?

Charlie noticed her clueless expression. "For the *speech*!" she breathed.

36
SUGAR

That's right. The speech! It was the part of her bridesmaid duties Agnes was most dreading. Getting rid of dead bodies was an activity she could accept, but giving a speech under the watchful gaze of over twenty pairs of eyes? It didn't bear thinking about.

She had pushed the idea to the back of her mind as best she could and hoped for a miracle.

But as usual, no miracle had been forthcoming.

"Yes, yes," she mumbled, looking down at the table.

Charlie nodded happily. "Good! You're up after the soup!" And with that, she had ruined Agnes's appetite until further notice. The arrival of each new course was now watched with trepidation in case it turned out to be soup.

During her career with the police, Agnes had seen a raft of unpleasant things: kidnap victims with their mouths and eyes glued shut, badly decomposed bodies in the park, neglected children in squalid beds, overdosed drug addicts with flies crawling over their fixed eyeballs.

But none of those things appeared in her worst nightmares.

In her worst nightmares she found herself, dressed in either a dressing gown or a dreadful swimming costume, standing in front of an audience of cultured older people looking at her expectantly, whispering to one another and making notes every now and then. Agnes stood in front of them on a slightly raised platform and in a spotlight, knowing that everything would be all right just as long as she opened her mouth and said something. But her mouth stayed shut, as if it were secured with a padlock. Words wandered restlessly through her body and fizzled into thin air long before they reached her lips.

Bit by bit, the older people in front of her became more and more unhappy, started shaking their heads and exchanging disappointed looks while Agnes desperately tried to spit out any old word—at least one.

What finally came out of her mouth wasn't a word, but a scream, which never failed to wake her with a start. Then she had to build herself back up with a glass of warm milk or a double whisky before she could even think about going back to sleep.

Now that terrible dream was about to become reality.

And there was no whisky as far as the eye could see.

Agnes quickly drank her red wine, then the champagne, then she kept a nervous vigil for the soup.

She had prepared, hadn't she? She had spent several joyless evenings cobbling together something nice to say about Bernadette and Jack—and, as Charlie had insisted, without any mention of murder and mayhem, which wasn't exactly easy given how the couple had met. Even their romantic reunion in a luxury hotel had happened while a serial killer was on the loose. Not to mention Dorothea and Stout . . .

Agnes stared downheartedly at her plate—and gave a start.

This plate was deeper than its predecessors, almost bowl-like, and there was something runny in it, which, despite the artfully arranged petals, was plainly still soup.

"Are you feeling all right?" The photographer, who up to now had mainly only been interested in her camera, leaned over to her.

"I'm fine," Agnes regurgitated. What would happen if she just ignored the soup? If she didn't eat any, it didn't count, did it? The smooth, green surface of the soup looked as menacing as a deep pond with the unspeakable lurking in its depths.

She couldn't manage a single spoonful. Instead, she turned to the photographer.

"Could I trouble you for your champagne, please?"

Scrounging a drink from a complete stranger went against all table etiquette, but drastic times called for drastic measures.

"Huh?" A look of surprise crossed the woman's face, but when she saw Agnes's face, the colour of which likely rivalled the soup, she pushed her glass towards Agnes. "Of course you can. I don't drink when I'm working, anyway. Are you sure you're all right . . . ?"

Agnes drained the glass in one. "Not really. But much better now. Thank you!"

Then Charlie was beside her again and pulling her up by her elbow. Next moment Agnes was faced with an audience of expectant older people, all looking at her attentively.

Her neck felt damp and sweaty.

She took a deep breath. Just don't forget to breathe! She never breathed in her dreams; that was her first mistake. She stood up, swayed a bit and caught herself.

In.

Out.

Agnes glanced briefly down to make sure that she was still wearing her chic silk ensemble and not a dreadful swimming costume.

Then she started speaking.

~

ONLY ONCE hesitant applause was rippling around the room, did it dawn on Agnes that her speech must be over.

She really had said something. But what? She couldn't remember and didn't want to either. But maybe it hadn't been that bad. The faces around her didn't look as disappointed and unhappy as the ones in her dreams.

A bit surprised, maybe.

A bit confused.

The main thing was that the speech was over. Agnes raised her glass, which a diligent elf had since refilled with champagne, and toasted the bride and groom.

"To the butterflies!" she said, not quite sure what she meant by it.

"And the frogs!" Edwina shouted.

"The frogs!" cried Charlie, laughing. Christopher kissed her hand.

"Hear! Hear!" chimed Winston.

Bernadette smiled happily, and Jack had damp penguin eyes again. The speech really couldn't have been that bad.

Marshall stood up abruptly and stormed out of the room.

Whether the engagement was off or not, that made Agnes feel a bit sad.

She sank back into her chair and sipped her champagne.

"Wow," said the photographer next to her. "What a speech!"

Agnes looked at her in disbelief. "Really?"

"Really," said the woman. "I go to a lot of weddings, but it's not often you hear something like that . . ."

Was that a compliment? Whatever—just as long as Agnes had the speech behind her. She'd really done it! A sudden feeling of euphoria flooded her body, and she eagerly awaited the next course, her appetite restored. What was it? Craning her neck towards the happy couple, who had obviously been served first, she spotted some kind of croquette with salmon swirls. But then, there seemed to be a little mix-up and instead of the salmon, Jack had accidentally been served an empty plate. No big deal, you would have thought, but the sight of the plate caused something strange to happen to Jack's face. Any happiness seemed to flow out of him, as if some kind of floodgate had suddenly been opened, and an expression of horrified disbelief flashed across his face. It only lasted a moment, then he was wearing his stoical expression again, but his eyes remained cold and dull as stones. The friendly penguin had gone and now somebody else was sitting next to Bernadette. Somebody who was hard as nails.

Agnes blinked in surprise. What was going on? Or had she just drunk too many glasses of champagne too quickly? Was she tipsily making mountains out of molehills? Deep in thought, she scarfed down her salmon, then there was another problem to navigate: an expedition to the toilet. She really couldn't last much longer.

As she made her way along the table, she noticed that there were three empty places: Stout's, Richard's and Marshall's.

What were they playing at? A game of musical chairs?

Agnes left the ballroom and followed the promising toilet signs through a corridor with a vaulted ceiling. Poorly groomed stag heads gazed down at her with their glassy eyes. As she stepped into the corridor after her successful trip to the toilet, somebody was sitting far too rigidly on a bench.

Agnes gave a start. Her recent experiences with people on benches hadn't been good. But, as she stepped closer, she saw that it was Jack. Not dead at all, just a bit pale and unusually preoccupied.

She hesitated. Jack and Bernadette as a couple had become a common sight, but encountering Jack on his own was completely different: it made Agnes feel vaguely queasy, somewhere between shy and wary. Finally, curiosity won out.

Agnes sat down next to the bridegroom on the bench. "Is everything all right, Jack?" Obviously, everything wasn't all right; Agnes could see that from the get-go.

Jack looked up, almost a bit shocked. It was very unlike him. "I didn't really want to get married," he blurted out.

Agnes looked at him in surprise. Cold feet? Wasn't it a little late for that?

"I thought it was too dangerous," Jack hastily added. "For Bernadette. But, she's so ballsy. You know, Agnes. You really can't say no to her. 'Nobody's interested in the old fogeys,' she said. But now somebody *is* interested in the old fogeys, and I'm kicking myself."

"Hm," said Agnes noncommittally. Had Jack found out about the poison-pen letters? Or was he talking about something else? "Has it got something to do with the empty plate from before?" she asked warily.

"It wasn't empty," said Jack blankly. "There was sugar on the plate. Cubes of sugar."

Sugar cubes? As far as Agnes was aware, Jack wasn't even a diabetic. A few bits of sugar seemed completely harmless.

"It means he's here," whispered Jack. He sounded so horrified that Agnes felt the need to turn around to make sure there wasn't a terrifying third person sitting on the bench.

Here was the thing: as you would expect from somebody in his line of work, Jack was not easily fazed.

An enormous spider in the broom cupboard? Not a problem.

A gigantic delivery of loo rolls in the hall because Marshall made a mistake with the zeros online? Jack didn't bat an eyelid.

A dead body in the boot? Cool as a cucumber.

But something had really spooked him.

Agnes shuddered. "Who's here?" she whispered back.

Jack's response was so quiet that Agnes could only hear it thanks to her trusty hearing aid.

"The Sugar Man!"

37

A WOLF IN SHEEP'S CLOTHING

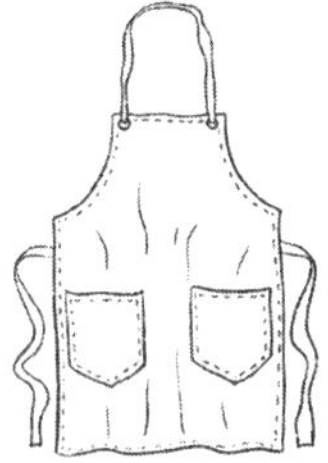

The Sugar Man? That didn't exactly sound very threatening.

"An old adversary?" asked Agnes.

Jack sighed. "Worse. An old colleague."

It took a few minutes for Jack to quietly explain the whole situation to her: Back when Jack worked for the organisation, he hadn't been the only contract killer on their books. For one thing, because there was an awful lot of work, and for another because organised crime was nowhere near as organised as you might think. Every underboss had his own preferences and his own people. One of them was the Sugar Man. His MO was that he didn't have one—nobody knew how, when or where death would strike. He was decried for his brutality and cold-heartedness, even in the business.

Thanks to Bernadette, the Sugar Man's career experienced a huge hiccup, because he was one of the gang members arrested during the raid. For a long while after that he went completely off the radar, and Jack lost track of him.

"And now he's here," groaned Jack. "And he's out for blood. Bernadette's! I wouldn't mind if it was just me. I could take certain measures. But my Bernadette . . . And the problem is: I have absolutely no idea what he looks like."

The fact of the matter was that Jack had only seen the man in person once or twice, always in big groups of people and he hadn't exactly been sober—and it had been over fifty years ago. You could hardly blame him for not remembering the man's face, height or build. But it didn't make things any easier.

Agnes's head was spinning. She had just been looking forward to the next course, and now her appetite had been completely ruined (again). She had so many questions.

Who was the Sugar Man?

How had he found Bernadette?

And above all: How were they going to get rid of him?

Or was the whole thing just some kind of misunderstanding?

There was no time to drag all of the necessary information out of Jack. There was a wedding happening in that ballroom over there, and any second now somebody would notice that the bridegroom was missing.

Jack seemed to come to a decision and leapt up. "He's not getting us. We're off. Right now. We'll get in a car and leave."

He turned to go, but Agnes caught hold of his sleeve just in time. "What if he *wants* you to leave?" she asked. "After all, he sent the sugar cubes. There must be a reason for it. I don't have a lot of experience in this area, but as far as I'm aware, it's rather unusual to warn your victims, isn't it? Unless you want them to do something. Like run away, for example."

Jack stopped in his tracks. He suddenly looked like a penguin again, a lonely one in a documentary, floating on an ice floe through Antarctic storms.

"Just breathe for a minute," Agnes advised. "In. Out. Think

about it: You're sitting at a table with umpteen servers and twenty guests. How's he going to get to you? Of course he wants you to leave."

"In. Out?" asked Jack.

Agnes nodded. The bridegroom sat back down on the bench with her and took a few deep breaths like she'd said. Something in his eyes changed—from panic to determination. "You're absolutely right," he said quietly. "I'll go back and talk things through with Bernadette—and you shouldn't sit around here all on your own."

BACK AT her seat, Agnes barely noticed what she was shovelling into her mouth. Her thoughts were spinning around the Sugar Man.

Was a now rather geriatric killer here to seek his revenge on Bernadette after decades in prison? It would answer some of the questions she had. Others . . . not so much.

Had somebody else put the sugar cubes on Jack's plate to rattle him? Whoever it was must know an awful lot about Jack and Bernadette.

Was the Sugar Man responsible for Stout too? It seemed rather likely. How many killers could there possibly be at a single wedding with only twenty guests? And what did he have against the detective? Had Stout seen something that he shouldn't have? Or had he somehow recognised the killer?

Agnes stared cluelessly at her plate. She had no idea what she'd just eaten. An elf appeared next to her to spirit away the empty plate, and her mind wandered to the other, seemingly empty plate that had put Jack into a spin. One of the Foxglove Manor aprons had brought it. Did that mean that whoever was behind it had allies amongst the staff? Or had he made an unsuspecting elf serve the sugar cubes under some kind of pretence? And which elf should she ask to find out? Not for the first time, Agnes found herself feeling annoyed at the stupid, chic uniform at Foxglove Manor. How was she supposed to find the right white apron amongst so many practically identical ones?

She looked over at Jack and Bernadette, who were whispering to each other, a picture of marital harmony. Bernadette seemed to be taking the latest news remarkably well. She was maybe a bit paler than before, but managed to keep a stiff upper lip. She nodded and smiled, holding Jack's hand. Agnes watched her friend sitting blind and brave at the table, determined to stand up to the world and the Sugar Man, and noticed her own fear slowly turning to fury. So, somebody was trying to ruin Bernadette's big day? Well, he hadn't bargained on Agnes and the other residents of Sunset Hall!

She stared along the table, from guest to guest. How hard could it be to spot the wolf in sheep's clothing? She wasn't born yesterday, after all.

She knew at least two things about the Sugar Man: he was—as the name suggested—a man, and he must be about seventy years old. On the face of it, there were three guests who matched these criteria. She got up quickly and whispered a question into first Charlie's ear, then Edwina's.

Armed with the answers, she returned to her seat and lost herself in her thoughts. She'd assumed she didn't have much to go on, but she'd been wrong. She had seen a lot—enough to have a strong suspicion as far as the identity of the killer was concerned. Obviously, there was no real guarantee that the Sugar Man was a guest, but where else would he be? In the kitchen? Amongst the elves? In one of the back rooms?

She stared slightly melancholically over at Benjamin Stout's untouched table setting. Then she realised that Marshall's seat was still empty too.

She suddenly felt worried.

Marshall had been in the loo for far too long.

It wasn't unusual for the man to be a bit away with the fairies every now and then, but in the current climate, Agnes couldn't just leave it at that. She stood up, slipped out of the room as inconspicuously as possible and made her way towards the toilets. It was less risky than you might have thought; after all, the three suspects were at the table. As long as she was quick, there shouldn't be any problems.

She peered up and down the corridor, then she knocked on the door with the relevant sign.

"Marshall?"

No answer.

Her heart pounding, Agnes pushed the door open a crack and peered into the gent's toilets.

"Marshall?"

There was nobody there. The space in front of the sinks was empty, the doors to all three cubicles were wide open.

Agnes's initial reaction was one of relief. She'd been afraid that . . . Nonsense! She hadn't been afraid of anything!

She closed the door and looked uncertainly along the row of dark oak doors. Maybe he'd just got a bit lost—easily conceivable in such a rambling place. As she rounded a corner, she saw a door closing to her right. Marshall? Agnes really hoped it was Marshall!

Some excited butterflies did somersaults in the pit of her stomach.

On the spur of the moment, she went through the door—and found herself in thick darkness.

In front of her: footsteps that suddenly stopped.

"Marshall?" Agnes's heart was in her mouth. "Marshall, we need to talk. There's so much going on. Please stop sulking, Marshall!"

"Agnes? Is that you?" She went weak at the knees when she heard Marshall's familiar voice. For a moment she'd been afraid that . . .

"Are you in there, Agnes?"

It took a few moments for Agnes to realise that Marshall's voice wasn't coming from inside the room, but from the other side of the door.

38
LIGHT BULB MOMENT

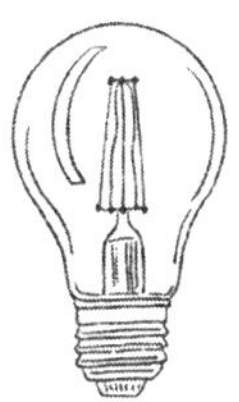

Agnes's breathing was suddenly quick and irregular, miles away from a healthy in-out. Her heart was pounding like mad. She felt something rush towards her in the darkness.

It went past her.

A draught. A clicking sound.

A scream. *Her* scream.

Footsteps hastily withdrawing, and then, farther away, a second *click*.

Somebody was rattling at the door.

"Agnes! My God, Agnes! Has something happened? Are you hurt?"

Agnes blinked. Was she hurt? She had screamed, no doubt about it. But as far as she could tell, it had just been the shock.

She felt a bit dizzy, and her heart was leaping about in her chest . . . But otherwise?

She wished Marshall would stop panicking.

"It's just a door, Marshall," she said and was surprised at how firm her voice sounded. "It was open just now. We'll get it open again somehow, don't fret."

In actual fact, she was relieved. Only now did she realise

how worried she had been about Marshall, but there he was, alive and well, taking his anger out on the door.

"I'm all right," cried Agnes, in an attempt to calm him down.

That, however, was a bit of a stretch. After all, she was still stuck in a darkened room with an unknown person who was quiet as a mouse. Not exactly ideal. Her hands found the door handle, which was bouncing madly up and down thanks to Marshall's efforts, and felt for a key or a bolt. Nothing. Whoever was in there with her and had just shoved past her must have taken the key out.

"Agnes!" cried Marshall. "Why did you lock the door? We can talk everything through, Agnes."

"I didn't lock it," Agnes explained. "It was somebody else."

"Somebody else? Who? Who's in there with you?"

"I don't know," she said more quietly.

"Is . . ." Marshall's voice cracked. "Has he done anything to you, Agnes?"

The door handle started moving again.

Agnes would have liked to have said or at least thought something, but Marshall was making a hell of a racket.

Light. Light made everything better. She warily moved away from the door, following the wall, in search of a light switch. As she did so, she realised she wasn't really afraid of the other person in the room. If they had wanted to do something to her, it probably would have happened by now. Apart from that, a vaguely familiar whiff of cigarette smoke lay in the air and she had a hunch. If she was right, this person wanted only one thing: not to be seen. But Agnes and the power of modern electricity were about to put pay to that.

Agnes's hands found a switch and clumsily fumbled with it.

Then it was suddenly bright in the room. The light flickered a few times, as if it couldn't really decide, but then it stayed on.

Agnes saw that she was in some kind of storage room.

Metal shelves.

A stone floor.

Dark eyes watching her through the open shelves.

"Hello," said Agnes, waving and smiling.

"Shit," said the girl from the well.

IT TOOK a few minutes for Agnes to sort the situation out, but they got there eventually.

The young woman had realised that barricading herself in with Agnes wasn't helping anyone, and after she'd been reassured that it was only Marshall on the other side of the door, not *them*, she had relinquished the key and let a rather het-up Marshall in. Marshall had hugged Agnes, thereby shocking her butterflies into flight.

Agnes had promised to let the young woman go once she had answered a few questions.

Now the three of them were sitting on a chest: Agnes and Marshall side by side, the girl a certain distance away, clutching a little backpack.

Mia, cheesecake server, elf and the very same girl who had been sitting on the well that day, swung her legs.

"And you really haven't got anything to do with *them*?" she asked, not for the first time. "I mean: What about the shoe?"

"The shoe was just a stupid coincidence," Agnes responded. "The only person I have anything to do with is Marshall—and the others from Sunset Hall."

Marshall beamed.

"Okay," said Mia, looking nervously at the door. "Is this going to be quick?"

"The more quickly you answer, the quicker it's going to be," Agnes said. "First question: Did you kill the verger?" It wasn't exactly a gentle starting question, but Agnes had never really believed in small talk.

Mia looked at her in shock, then lowered her head.

"Yes," she said quietly.

Now it was Agnes's turn to be shocked. It wasn't the response she'd expected. She had only asked the question because she was almost certain that Mia didn't have anything to do with the verger's death. She had just wanted to lure the girl out of her shell, and, in her experience, false allegations were perfect for that, just like lettuce.

"But . . . I got the impression that you liked him," Agnes blurted out.

"I liked him," said Mia. "He was my best friend. He . . . he used to lend me books. He was the only person who ever believed in me." Tears rolled down her cheeks, smudging her makeup.

"But . . ." Agnes didn't know quite what to say.

"I should have just left him in peace. Everything I do goes wrong. It's my fault he's dead," the girl affirmed.

Aha. That sounded a bit different.

"Did you put a rope around his neck?" Agnes was determined to make things crystal clear.

"No!" cried Mia. "Of course I didn't. But it's all my fault . . ."

A sob. Even more tears. Once again, Agnes found herself cursing her ridiculous mini-bag, but luckily Marshall seemed to have an almost inexhaustible supply of handkerchiefs. Was that why military uniforms had so many pockets? For hankies?

Agnes passed the handkerchief to Mia. "Whoever put the rope around his neck is to blame," she said patiently. "Not you. Do you know who it was?"

"Yes and no." The girl sobbed and blew her nose. Agnes cast a frustrated glance at Marshall. This was taking a while, and time was of the essence.

"I know *why* they killed him," Mia explained. "But I don't know exactly who it was. They bring people in for that. From outside."

After some toing and froing, Agnes had finally managed to tease a few facts out of the girl.

Just as she had suspected, this whole mess had all started with Foxglove Manor.

So much for discipline and entrepreneurial spirit. Constance Purr had refurbished her ancestral home with a criminal workforce and drug money—no wonder her flamingo ancestors were looking down on her with such disgust. The wedding business was just a cover. The real profit was in supplying the whole county with pills and white powder.

And the social enterprise Hand in Hand? It was the beating heart of the operation.

Young people who hadn't had an easy start didn't have it easy at Foxglove Manor either. They didn't learn the craft of cookery here; they were being exploited, intimidated and used as drug mules.

"It's crap," said Mia, "but it's still the best place I've ever lived. I've got my own bed and I can have a shower whenever I want."

Agnes gulped. "But then something happened with the verger," she guessed. "He found out that there was something amiss with the project."

"It's my fault," the girl repeated. "He saw all of my bruises and wanted to know what had happened. He wouldn't let it rest and I didn't want to lie to him. He was the only person who cared."

So, Mia had told him what was really going on at Foxglove Manor, in doing so, started a chain of events. The verger, who was in youth work for the right reasons, had been completely outraged. He might have been a bit of a fuddy-duddy, but he was no coward, so he had given Constance Purr a piece of his mind. And the only reason he hadn't gone to the police was because Mia had begged him not to.

"Three days later he was dead. I might as well have put the rope around his neck myself," whispered Mia. "What's the difference?"

"There's a huge difference," Agnes said and gently took the damp handkerchief.

She thought about Winston's timeline and the big cloud that he'd drawn above it. Now she finally knew what was in the bubble. Winston had been right; there was something that connected Foxglove Manor, the verger, Jack and Bernadette: Drug dealing. Organised crime. Now she just had to figure out the details.

She held the dripping hanky towards Marshall, but he mutely and rather confusedly shook his head. Agnes shoved it behind the chest and changed the subject.

"What do you know about the Sugar Man?" No matter how interesting the bigger picture might be, Agnes's main goal was to identify the killer who had infiltrated Bernadette's wedding.

Unfortunately, Mia didn't know anything about the Sugar Man. But she had overheard that something terrible was going to happen to the bride. The boss hadn't been very pleased about it, but she'd cooperated.

"Is that why you sent the letter?" asked Agnes.

For a moment, Mia looked like she was going to deny it, but then she nodded.

"I thought that if I wrote something creepy and sent the article about that freaky murder, they might not want to get married here anymore. I'm so sorry."

"You've got nothing to be sorry about," said Agnes. "It was very creative. An awful rhyme, but sent with the best of intentions."

She was secretly a bit annoyed with herself. She should have realised a bit sooner that there was only one person who saw her come out of the knitting group and knew that she would recognise the Knitwits' creation: the girl from the well. And the white figure that Marshall had seen? In her elf outfit with her blouse and her long apron, Mia was completely white, well, she was from the front.

The girl looked like she was about to start bawling her eyes out again, and Agnes didn't want to put an unnecessary strain on Marshall's supply of hankies. She quickly asked another question.

"Why nothing red? And nothing dead?" She'd been wondering for a while why the letter writer had put so much effort into crafting the letter, but had then taken a rather slapdash approach to carrying out the threats.

"I couldn't think of anything red," Mia admitted. "And I did catch a mouse . . . but then I couldn't bring myself to . . ."

The girl was squeamish, unlike Edwina, who took great delight in ordering dead rats online. "Can I go now?" asked Mia.

"Where are you going to go?" asked Agnes.

"Anywhere but here!"

"You can stay with us at Sunset Hall for a while if you like," Agnes rashly suggested. "We've got a lot of showers." Mia might not be in their age bracket, but Agnes couldn't let a young girl go it alone like that. And anyway, she still had so many questions that she didn't have time for at the moment. "The key to the back door is hanging in the apple tree."

Mia didn't acknowledge her, but stood up without saying a word and scurried towards the door.

"Brexit won't hurt you," Agnes shouted after her, just in case. "But I'd watch out for Oberon if I were you."

Something was lying on the chest. It must have fallen out of Mia's backpack. Agnes showed it to Marshall, then thoughtfully turned it over in her hands. It was a single, perfect, beaky paper crane.

39
THE SWEET POTATOES

Once Agnes was back at the table, it occurred to her that she hadn't asked Mia about the shoe. She grumbled her way through the sorbet, and the first and second dessert. Only once the cheese course was being served had she pulled herself together enough to begin to answer her own questions.

Mia had seen her with the shoe, had been scared and run away. Then she had assumed that Agnes was in cahoots with "them."

Why? The only logical explanation for Mia being scared of a simple gent's shoe was that she knew that the shoe belonged to somebody who had been murdered. She must have assumed that Agnes was in the process of destroying evidence (not entirely incorrect), and lumped her in with the murderer (she couldn't have been further from the truth). Had she witnessed the murder? That seemed rather unlikely to Agnes—if she'd seen something as violent as that with her own eyes, squeamish Mia would have run a mile. But what if . . . Agnes was reminded of the posse of elves they'd almost run into when they had been moving the body. It was possible that the girl from the well had been amongst them. Those elves had had glasses, bottles, but also blankets and some kind of wheelbarrow. In the moment, Agnes had been far too stressed to question it, but now she began to wonder. Why the blankets? They were rather rough and ready—not exactly suitable for a reception in the sculpture garden, but they were perfect for covering a dead body. Somebody had sent the elf posse to get rid of the body—but thanks to Agnes and her friends' efficient work, there had been no body to be found. That meant that the murderer and Constance Purr had to be in cahoots.

"May I take that?"

Agnes gave a start and looked up at an unfamiliar elf and then back down at her plate, where a French soft cheese was in the process of conquering new territories.

"Yes, I'm finished. Thank you."

And with that, the meal was finally over. Thank goodness! Agnes couldn't remember a single course—but she wasn't hungry anymore. That was something.

What was next? Hopefully something without a fixed seating plan—they had a lot to do. Their housemates had to be told about the Sugar Man, and then they would have to come up with a plan to keep themselves safe and catch the killer. Agnes really wished she had paid more attention to the finer details of the running order.

But luckily, Charlie was on it. As soon as the last plate had been collected and the guests started looking wearily back and forth, she leapt up, hovered at the top of the table and tapped her glass again.

"Dear friends. I'm sure we could all do with a bit of exercise after all that delicious food. Please follow us into the Garden Room for a tea dance with the Sweet Potatoes. I, for one, cannot wait."

In the run-up to the wedding, Agnes had been dreading the Sweet Potatoes, but now they seemed heaven-sent—perfect to inconspicuously speak to her housemates and bring them up to speed with the latest developments.

On entering the Garden Room, Agnes was spellbound for a moment, despite the tense situation and numerous problems. It wasn't called the Garden Room for nothing. The walls, and even the ceiling, were adorned with elegant frescoes. Painted ivy twined towards a watercolour sky, lifelike birds of paradise fluttered soundlessly amongst exotic ferns. The real garden stretched out on the other side of the window: blossoming trees and white daffodils. Palm leaves filtered the lazy afternoon sun.

It really was beautiful.

Then Agnes was reminded of how all this opulence was probably being funded: by a lot of suffering and the exploitation of children like Mia, who was allowed to have plenty of showers, but not much else.

She couldn't help but frown.

Next moment the music started up, and for the first time, Agnes caught sight of the Sweet Potatoes. There stood four elegant young men in white tuxedos and a curvaceous singer who was writhing in front of a microphone and bore more than just a passing resemblance to Oberon.

The band didn't play cheesy radio hits like at most weddings, but swing music from the thirties. They started with a snappy "Let's Fall in Love," and before she knew what was happening, Agnes's left foot was tapping along to the beat. It was a shame she had to catch a murderer, really—she wouldn't have minded sitting down for a while to listen. Jack, who wasn't letting Bernadette out of his sight, led his bride straight onto the dance floor. Agnes nodded favourably. There, in the middle of the room, all eyes on them, the murderer couldn't touch them. Charlie dragged an inattentive-looking Christopher into the room; her grandson and his partner were already performing an expert jitterbug on the gleaming dance floor.

Marshall appeared in front of her, his good hand behind his back, a bit red-faced.

Agnes looked at him impatiently. What was the matter now? They'd made up, hadn't they? And apart from anything else, they had other problems right now. There was no time to waste—after all, there was lots to discuss.

She held out her hand towards him.

"Come on, Marshall!"

Marshall looked at her sceptically for a moment, as if he was expecting some kind of trap, but when the hand stayed where it was, he hesitantly took hold of it and led Agnes to the dance floor. He supported her back with his good hand; Agnes, who didn't want to touch his plaster cast, gently placed her hands onto his shoulders.

Then they were in hold, and Agnes started talking. Surrounded by velvety saxophone, she briefly explained to Marshall all about the Sugar Man and her hunch that he was one of the wedding guests.

Let's fall in love . . . cooed the singer.

Agnes wouldn't normally have much time for dancing, but Marshall was moving her rather masterfully across the dance floor; she was just far too engrossed in her deliberations to notice.

"Agnes," said Marshall gently.

Agnes, who was in full flow, ignored him. "A man over seventy. There's not many of them around here. There's our new gardener, Charlie's Christopher and Richard. That's it."

Richard the Lizard was a sore point, and Agnes glanced up at Marshall to see how he was taking it.

"Hm," said Marshall, seeming rather pleased with himself.

Agnes was just about to carry on talking when he decided to say something else after all.

"I'm over seventy too. Winston's over seventy."

"Yes, I know, but . . ." She looked at him blankly. She would never have even considered . . . "That's ridiculous. Winston's lived with us for years. Why would someone spend years . . . And anyway, he's in a wheelchair. How would he have run through the maze and . . . And as for you . . ."

"It wasn't me," Marshall reassured her. "I was just being thorough."

He twirled Agnes around and led her past the windows. A faint aroma swirled around them, like dying daffodils.

"We've got three prime suspects," Agnes resolutely continued. "The question is one of likelihood. It's likely that the murderer took the initiative and made contact with us to get access to the wedding. Richard *did not* take the initiative. He, err, he was online and we . . . err, Charlie sought him out. So, it's . . . not particularly likely that . . ."

Let's—step—*fall*—step—*in*—step—*love* . . .

Why—step—*shouldn't*—step—*we* . . .

"Agnes," said Marshall a second time, but Agnes was so delighted to have the wretched Richard issue behind her that she merrily carried on talking. "Things look rather different with the gardener and Christopher. The gardener responded to an advert and was very keen to get the job. Even Edwina didn't scare him off. That was only a few weeks ago, and Jack and Bernadette were already online. So, the gardener is a suspect. And he knows how to use a pair of garden shears, well, kind of."

She looked expectantly up at Marshall. Obviously, the murderer wasn't always the gardener—but that didn't mean that the murderer couldn't be the gardener every now and then.

"Hm." Marshall didn't have anything more to say about the gardener. He looked like he was away with the fairies. Agnes sighed. Could the man not even concentrate when it was a matter of life and death?

"And then there's Christopher," she continued. "Lots of things point towards Christopher." All this dancing and thinking was tiring her out. Her cheeks were glowing. For many reasons, Christopher was her personal favourite.

"*He* made contact with Charlie," she explained. "Not the other way around. Charlie joined this dating agency and . . ."

"A dating agency?" Marshall was finally giving her his full attention. "Did you join the dating agency too?"

"No," Agnes reassured him. "Why would I . . . Well, not directly, anyway . . . The point is: If Dorothea somehow got in touch with the gangsters from back in the day to help sabotage the wedding . . . If she made them aware of Charlie's videos—then it wouldn't be hard for someone like the Sugar Man to work out that Charlie was looking for love. She made a video about it, do you remember? He could have just joined the dating agency too. And because he's good-looking . . ."

"You think he's good-looking?" Marshall interrupted.

"Of course he's good-looking," Agnes said. "But that's not the point . . ." She lowered her voice as Charlie and Christopher swished by. "The point is that he could have targeted Charlie in order to infiltrate Sunset Hall. Charlie's nuts about him, but he, on the other hand . . . I've had a bad feeling about him for a while. What does he want from Charlie?"

"Well, she's a very attractive woman," said Marshall.

Agnes looked at him in surprise. She knew that Charlie was

attractive—but for some reason it surprised her that Marshall had noticed too.

"Do you think so?" she asked quietly.

"Of course," said Marshall. The hint of a smile played on his lips.

40

IN THE SWING OF THINGS

"Hm," mumbled Agnes. "Whatever. Apparently, he's a plastic surgeon. That seems to fit, doesn't it?"

Let's fall in love . . .

"Hm." Marshall wasn't quite with it again.

Agnes shook his shoulders. "And if he's responsible for Stout . . . He had the opportunity at least. After all, he was really late coming into the chapel, wasn't he? He had to squeeze past Edwina to get to his seat. He could have knocked Hettie's basket over on purpose. And once Hettie was gone, he was the first to run outside. What if he was after Stout rather than Hettie? He lured him into the maze under some kind of pretence and stabbed him to death—and nobody noticed anything because we were all too busy looking for Hettie!"

Agnes looked enquiringly up at Marshall. It was the beating heart of her theory and she was proud of it.

"It's possible," Marshall conceded spinning her around. They danced on, through spears of golden afternoon light.

Make—step—*our*—step—*own*—step—*paradise . . .*

They were silent for a few bars. It was almost harmonious.

"And there's something else," said Agnes finally. "About Benjamin Stout. I asked him to keep an eye on Christopher . . ."

"You did *what* . . . ?"

Agnes blushed a little. "There was something off about him, that's all. Stout's a good detective. Was a good detective. Why send him on some wild goose chase for some stupid, made-up diamonds? And now he's dead. That's a bit suspicious, isn't it?"

"You're focusing too much on Christopher," said Marshall, a bit peeved.

"Because he might be the killer!" cried Agnes, a bit too loudly. Charlie's grandson, who was dancing by, looked over at her in surprise, and she felt herself blush even more.

"And just one more thing," she said quietly.

"What now?" asked Marshall gloomily.

"Well. They call him 'the Sugar Man.' It's a bit of an unusual name for a killer, isn't it? There must be more to it! And do you know what Christopher calls Charlie?"

"Sweet cheeks," said Agnes. "Cupcake. Things like that. He really is sickly sweet. If that's an old habit, it could be the reason he's called 'the Sugar Man,' couldn't it?"

"Cupcake," Marshall tried it out.

Agnes nodded earnestly.

"Cupcake," Marshall repeated softly.

Something about his voice made Agnes look up. She stopped nodding and was just about to say something, but the words got caught in her throat. She was on a dance floor! With Marshall! How on earth had that happened? Clouds of frantic butterflies fluttered in her stomach.

"I was going to let things lie," said Marshall after a while. "But after your speech . . . It really touched me, Agnes."

Agnes stared at him. What on earth had she said in the blasted speech?

"You're absolutely right," Marshall continued. "Happiness

isn't just a coincidence. It's a decision. It's for people who take a chance. And that's why I think we should . . ."

He broke off and looked at her expectantly.

Agnes was completely confused for a moment.

But then she understood and she wanted to run away or for the ground to swallow her up.

Instead, she closed her eyes and nodded.

THREE MINUTES later, Agnes and Marshall were engaged again.

Objectively speaking, it was a crazy decision. Subjectively the two of them actually felt rather good about it.

And being engaged didn't mean that you had to get married straight away.

An engagement was one thing.

A wedding quite another.

You didn't have to look far to see plenty of reasons not to have a wedding. Everyone at Sunset Hall had spent weeks trying to give Bernadette a day that she wouldn't forget, and what was the end result?

So far: two dead bodies and one killer who was in the process of infiltrating Sunset Hall.

The numbers weren't good.

And it was best to not even think about how much the whole thing must have cost. Murder and drugs or not, Foxglove Manor was an expensive venue.

Something suddenly dawned on Agnes: if the Sugar Man was in cahoots with Constance Purr—and a lot of things pointed in that direction—you could be almost certain that the killer would not strike at the wedding. A murder in the maze was probably just about acceptable if you tidied up afterwards, but a murdered bride or groom? You couldn't hush that up very easily and it wouldn't look very good in the brochure. After something like that, the countess could forget about her wedding business and her drug hub along with it.

No, Constance Purr had a strong vested interest in keeping the number of murders at her establishment to an absolute minimum.

Hopefully, that meant that they were safe during the wedding.

That's why the Sugar Man had sent Jack a warning. It was supposed to dampen the mood and make him leave the manor. And it had almost worked! Jack, who was normally as cool as a cucumber, was a bundle of nerves when it came to Bernadette.

It also meant that Stout's murder must have been a matter of extreme urgency. After all, it was still a huge risk for the countess and her dodgy dealings.

Agnes's conscience was piqued. If her assumptions were correct, she had set the private detective onto a contract killer. That wasn't good for your health.

She looked up at Marshall, who was now leading her across the dance floor to the sounds of "Begin the Beguine." Agnes was surprised at how easy it was to dance when you didn't fight it.

"We've got to get Charlie away from Christopher somehow," she said.

Marshall instantly agreed with her—but in his current state, he probably would have agreed if she'd suggested breeding slugs in Alaska.

"And we need a plan," she continued. "Several plans . . ."

Marshall nodded and listened to her with an enraptured look in his eye.

By the time the woman started singing the next song, her voice velvety, they were done—with dancing and the plan.

Agnes could do with a breather, and Marshall was currently completely content being engaged. He didn't seem to need anything else.

But he hadn't reckoned on Agnes.

There was so much to do.

Agnes had to speak to Winston, Jack and Bernadette, and then somehow prise Charlie away from Christopher. If need be, she would ambush her in the loos.

Marshall had to run the gauntlet of asking Edwina to dance and then steal a camera.

Finally, they all had to work together to make sure that the best day of Bernadette's life wasn't her last.

41

A SLIPPERY SLOPE

The afternoon flowed into the evening.

Somebody had turned on the chandeliers in the Garden Room. Warm light caught in the crystals and mirrors.

The Sweet Potatoes had worn themselves out and were having a drink on the little stage.

It was blue and dusky outside the windows. The outlines of the trees blurred; the sky absorbed the darkness like a big midnight-blue sponge. Only the white daffodils continued to glow in the half-light, like delicate candles.

It had been a beautiful day. Not a drop of rain. One lonely cloud in the sky.

Bernadette was married, Agnes engaged once again.

Hettie had been found.

But on the flip side . . .

Benjamin Stout was dead and had probably already begun to turn into compost.

Foxglove Manor was a hive of criminal activity.

And then there was the Sugar Man prowling around.

You can't have it all, thought Agnes philosophically.

After all, it wasn't over until the fat lady sang—that's if they were careful.

Most of the guests were standing around in small groups drinking tea, nibbling away at the official wedding cake—Edwina's rock-hard tortoise sculpture hadn't yet had any takers—or were sitting around exhaustedly in armchairs.

Nathan the Grandson had curled up asleep on a sofa like a donut.

Richard, who Edwina was constantly forcing to check on Hettie in the next room, looked rather green around the gills. And he hadn't even tried Edwina's cake yet.

Even the elves looked worn out.

Agnes was staring out of the window, into the dusk, while also observing all of the goings-on in the Garden Room behind her in the reflection. There wasn't much going on. She had been secretly watching Christopher all afternoon, but apart from still seeming like a slimeball, the man hadn't put a foot wrong. He smiled, he danced (not half badly, Agnes had to admit), and every now and then he brought Charlie refreshments. Strangely enough, that only strengthened Agnes's suspicions. The man was a professional. Of course there was no chink in his armour. What had she been expecting?

She tried to see the scene in the room through the Sugar Man's eyes.

A doll's house.

A playroom.

Something to entertain him.

The killer had found Bernadette after many years. Now all he had to do was sneak into Sunset Hall and get rid of her. Maybe not that easily, thanks to Jack, Edwina, Oberon and Brexit, but it wasn't exactly rocket science.

But he hadn't.

He'd waited for the wedding.

Why?

He didn't just want to do away with Bernadette.

Oh no.

He wanted to see her happy, rosy-cheeked and married.

He wanted to witness what he was destroying.

A cool draught snaked its way through the gaps around the windows and wafted around her shoulders. Badly insulated, just like Sunset Hall. Too badly insulated to keep the murderers out.

Agnes shuddered beneath her silk.

Jack had said that the Sugar Man used to have a bad reputation back in the day. A bad reputation amongst professional hitmen—that was saying something. It didn't bear thinking about what all those years of prison and grudge-holding might have done to him. Nothing good, that was for sure.

Nothing good at all.

Something suddenly dawned on Agnes. It wasn't enough to thwart his current plans as regards the wedding. The Sugar Man was calculating, patient, competent and probably hell-bent on revenge.

He had to go. For good. As long he was alive and at large, Bernadette and Jack could forget their rosy sunset years.

But how were they going to be sure to get rid of him?

The classic method would obviously have been to prove that he was responsible for Stout's murder, and ideally Dorothea's too, so that the police could arrest him and take him into custody again, but somehow Agnes didn't believe that would ever happen. For one thing, the man was a professional and likely hadn't left any evidence in his wake; for another thing, the residents of Sunset Hall had been dutifully tidying up dead bodies for him. And without the relevant body, it would be nigh on impossible to pin the slightest thing on slippery Christopher.

Agnes suddenly felt hot and penned in. She needed a bit of air, cool or otherwise. She hastily opened one of the double doors and staggered outside. She looked up at the stone nymphs lining the terrace, staring at her with their unsympathetic almond eyes.

Breathe.

In. Out.

The air smelled of grass and distant cherry blossoms.

That was better.

One thing had become clear to her: a higher body count was unavoidable. The killer would strike again, unless . . .

In. Out.

He had to go, didn't he?

If he couldn't be sent back to prison, then they'd have to . . .

In. Out.

It was the only logical solution.

It was a slippery slope. One minute you were hiding a dead body or two; the next you were planning . . .

For good reason, and that's what it came down to.

But how? Maybe it was best not to think too much about the "if." The "how" was complicated enough on its own. At least, in Jack, they did have an expert on board.

Before they put their money where their mouths were, they had to be absolutely certain that Christopher really was their target.

Suddenly an arm wound its way around Agnes's waist from behind. She gasped and instinctively grabbed her handbag. Unfortunately, her current handbag was a ridiculous silk affair that wouldn't even have made an impression on a hamster.

"Cupcake!"

A chin rested on her shoulder; a moustache tickled her ear.

"Marshall!" hissed Agnes. Her heart was in her mouth. "That's not funny!"

Marshall let her go and looked a bit embarrassed. "I know. It's just . . . I mean, who knows how long we'll be engaged for this time. I want to make the most of it, that's all."

"But no cupcakes!" Agnes warned him.

Marshall managed to look embarrassed and happy, all at once.

"And anyway . . ." Agnes wanted to tell him that she had no intention of calling off the engagement again, but she couldn't find the right words.

Marshall understood regardless and grinned.

"Have you got the camera?" asked Agnes, to change the subject.

"The camera's gone," he said. "The poor photographer is distraught."

"Damn," said Agnes. "He beat us to it. He must think she got something incriminating. Or maybe he's just thorough."

"But hasn't Christopher been here the whole time?" asked Marshall.

"He went to the loo," declared Agnes. "Supposedly. But he might not have stolen the camera himself. If he's in cahoots with Foxglove Manor, almost any of the staff could have done it for him."

They went back inside together. Marshall held her arm. Warm air sloshed around Agnes like soup.

"I tried to speak to Charlie," she said quietly. "But I don't really know how to. She's so crazy about Christopher, and what evidence do I have? The best I've got is Benjamin Stout's death, but if I tell her that I set the detective on her beau—it's not going to go down very well, is it?"

Marshall nodded. "Maybe it's best not to say anything to

Charlie for now. Knowing her, she might take him to task, and we could do without that."

"But I don't like her being in the dark," Agnes complained. "I mean, she trusts him. She would go anywhere with him. She's like a . . ."

She'd been about to say "rat cornered by a snake," but remembered just in time what Oberon had done to the medium-sized rat and held her tongue.

"If we can't get Charlie away from him, we need to get him away from her," said Marshall after a while. He let go of Agnes's arm and patted one of his uniform pockets. "Leave it to me."

42

POT-AU-FEU

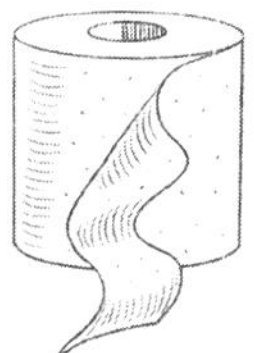

Marshall grinned at her, did an about-turn and marched towards the bar area. Agnes plopped down onto a sofa to calm her butterflies. What time was it, anyway? She was far too giddy to be tired but could feel the exhaustion in her bones. What was the plan after the Sweet Potatoes? The blasted wedding had to be over at some point! Agnes wanted nothing more than to discuss the current situation in peace with her housemates: in the lounge, in the kitchen or even in the sunroom—just not in snatches between dances and cake, or in the loo.

"It's an unusual event, isn't it?" Winston rolled next to her and smiled.

Agnes nodded and smiled back at him, putting on a brave face. She'd already told Winston about the Sugar Man over a piece of wedding cake. He'd actually taken the news quite well. Winston took most news quite well.

The Sweet Potatoes were playing again, and Charlie's grandson was whirling his partner around the dance floor. Oh, how it must feel to be that light-footed. And that young! Charlie had heroically asked Richard to dance. It wasn't going very well. Christopher and Marshall seemed to be deep in conversation at the bar.

"He's got to go," said Agnes after a while.

Winston immediately knew whom she meant. "That won't be an easy undertaking. After all, he knows what Jack used to do. He'll be on his guard."

"Against Jack," said Agnes quietly. "But maybe not against us."

Winston looked at her wide-eyed: surprised, but not really shocked. Just like Edwina, he'd been with the Secret Service back in the day but had somehow managed to keep his head. Nothing upset him. He turned his attention to the dance floor again. An unusually melancholic look crossed his face. After a while he shook his head and chuckled. Bitterly? Or had something tickled him? It was a surprising display of emotion for Winston, and Agnes wondered how many glasses of champagne her housemate had already guzzled today. Too many, arguably. They had been neglecting Winston a little—rightly or wrongly, his wheelchair hadn't exactly made him first choice for dancing and transporting bodies. Agnes felt a pang of conscience and immediately quashed it. It was a luxury she could ill afford right now.

She tried to imagine polished Christopher as a corpse. Even then he'd probably look good. But the thought that she might have to bring about this transformation was almost unthinkable. On the other hand, just sitting there and watching the Sugar Man shorten Bernadette and Jack's sunset years wasn't a very attractive prospect either.

Over at the bar, Marshall and Christopher seemed to be getting on like a house on fire: they were grinning and repeatedly chinking glasses. Agnes frowned. On the face of it, they just looked like two gents having a rather animated and genial conversation, but Agnes didn't like the fact that Marshall was drawing the Sugar Man's attention onto himself. What on earth was he thinking? The man was dangerous.

She clocked Charlie, who had finished dancing and was wandering back and forth, seemingly a bit lost without Christopher, like a lonely glow-worm. Then one of the elves approached her and said something. Charlie nodded in relief. Agnes noticed that she looked tired under the lipstick and rouge.

Once the elf had disappeared, Charlie stepped into the middle of the room and clapped her hands.

"Dear friends, bride and groom, guests. I hope you had a wonderful time with the Sweet Potatoes. I know I did. Please put your hands together for our talented musicians!"

They all gave a big round of applause. The men in the white tuxedos bowed, the singer graciously spread her arms. As all eyes were on the quintet, Agnes saw movement at the bar. Marshall seemed to have spotted something on the counter and was reaching his hand out towards it. It only took a moment, and anybody who hadn't been observing Marshall as closely as Agnes probably wouldn't have noticed, but she was certain that something had just happened.

She got palpitations.

Hopefully Marshall wasn't up to anything stupid.

When they'd shown enough appreciation to the Sweet Potatoes, Charlie clapped her hands again.

"All good things must come to an end, so I would like to invite you to the Billiard Room, where we will round off the celebrations with Foxglove Manor's famous pot-au-feu."

Agnes's stomach rumbled. Was she hungry again? After all the courses and the tea and cake she'd stuffed herself with, it seemed like a physical impossibility, but the truth was: the more you ate, the more you wanted to eat. She realised she was rather looking forward to the whatever this pot-au-feu turned out to be.

She nodded to Winston and got up a bit unsteadily from the sofa. Then she looked around for Marshall. Gone, as was Christopher. Agnes was seized with panic for a moment, then she spotted the two of them by the door making their way towards the food, still deep in conversation.

She quickly linked arms with Charlie, who was standing rather helplessly in the middle of the room, looking around.

"Come on," Agnes said. "You've done such a wonderful job of organising everything, Charlie."

Charlie laughed drily. "To be honest, I can't really remember anything that's happened today. Apart from . . . well, you know."

Agnes nodded. Moving Benjamin Stout's body had been the emotional zenith of the wedding for her too—that and dancing with Marshall. Now that she thought about it, the dance with Marshall had actually been even more unforgettable.

"What are you grinning about?" whispered Charlie. "I could definitely have done without that particular experience."

Not surprisingly, the Billiard Room proved to be extremely elegant and sumptuous. Pictures of dogs and horses hung in front of brocade wallpaper; leatherbound books showed their smooth spines, golden letters catching the light—and of course there was a gigantic billiard table in a rich green that looked a bit like a football pitch for gnomes.

The Foxglove Manor elves had set up their serving station in a corner and a little queue of guests had already formed, Marshall and Christopher right at the front. Agnes decided to wait until the queue had disappeared, and sank into a plush sofa. Richard and Edwina were bickering on the neighbouring sofa.

"I've already checked on her nine times already," Richard griped. "She's sitting in her basket and looking around. What else would she be doing? She's a tortoise."

That obviously didn't land very well with Edwina. "But *how* is she looking around?" she asked. "That's the point. I'll check on her myself . . ."

"Couldn't we just have five minutes . . ." Richard began, but then changed tack. "I saw them in the wild on my walking holiday in Greece, you know? That's what they do: they just sit and look around."

Edwina wouldn't be fobbed off with threadbare tortoise anecdotes and leapt up to check on Hettie's welfare with her own eyes.

Agnes could see the end of their funny little romance on the horizon. Edwina's heart belonged to cold-blooded creatures; Richard couldn't compete despite the obvious similarities. It was a miracle that he had lasted as long as he had.

Somebody sat down next to Agnes on the sofa. It was Marshall, and he'd brought her a little bowl of what looked like soup.

"Everything's all right," he said proudly.

"Good. Me too." Agnes took the bowl from his hand and started spooning the mixture into her mouth. Tasty. Tomorrow they'd be having corned beef again; it wouldn't do her any harm to get her fill now.

Suddenly, she heard a hard, clear sound coming from the other end of the room, like glass on glass. Christopher had banged his bowl down onto a marble table and was standing there with a strange expression on his face, slightly bent over.

For the first time since Agnes had met him, he didn't look very good. Pale. Shaken. Tense, somehow.

Charlie rushed to his side and the two of them exchanged a few whispered words as Christopher folded up like a jackknife. He tried to smile, but didn't quite manage it and finally stormed out of the room, still partially folded.

Charlie came over to Agnes and Marshall.

"Kids, heads up. There's something amiss with the food!"

Agnes stopped eating, alarmed. Poisoned? Was *that* the Sugar Man's plan? Wasn't that bad for business?

Once Charlie had walked away, Marshall leaned over to Agnes and whispered in her ear: "Don't worry, there's nothing wrong with the food."

Agnes raised her eyebrows, and Marshall opened one of his many uniform pockets and she got a peek of a packet of medication, a well-known laxative that everyone at Sunset Hall had used at one time or another. "Marshall!"

Marshall shrugged nonchalantly. "Well, we wanted to get him away from Charlie, didn't we? I know with relative certainty where Christopher will be spending the next twenty-four hours—not with Charlie, that's for sure."

Agnes was open-mouthed. Marshall had given Christopher laxatives. Simple, but effective. It was best not to think about why he had laxatives on him at a wedding.

You just didn't ask some things, even if you were engaged.

Especially if you were engaged.

Agnes was just about to dig into her food with renewed confidence when she heard a terrified scream behind her.

She spun around and saw that Bernadette had collapsed in a corner.

Jack was kneeling on the floor next to his bride, staring at her wide-eyed.

43

HETTIE III

The mood was rather sombre in the taxi on the way home. The image of Bernadette lying on the carpet in her white dress like a crumpled-up tissue and then lifelessly being carried out of the room on a stretcher, was etched on their minds.

Nobody had imagined that her big day would end like that.

"I never would have thought . . ." whispered Charlie.

Agnes nodded. Obviously, they had been prepared for it, and yet for a moment, they'd really believed that . . .

"Hats off to her," said Winston. "She's a much better actress than Edwina."

"Hey!" cried Edwina, who you couldn't see much of at the moment because she was holding her oversized tortoise cake on her lap. After the cake hadn't found any takers during the tea dance, Edwina hadn't hesitated to adopt it and had dubbed it Hettie III.

"She was very convincing," said Agnes. "She had to be."

That was the plan they had concocted under their breath during the tea dance: As long as the wedding was still going, Jack and Bernadette seemed to be relatively safe because Foxglove Manor's reputation was on the line. It would get dangerous as soon as the two of them left the premises. And since the Sugar Man seemed to be quite a versatile killer, it was hard to predict when and how he would strike. Had he tampered with Charlie's car? Did he have a connection at the local taxi firm? Was he going to lie in wait for them at Sunset Hall? If Christopher really was the killer, he was currently rather preoccupied in the toilet and wouldn't be lying in wait for anyone, but that couldn't be relied upon. Nothing had been proven as yet, and Agnes didn't want to take any chances.

Now Bernadette was under observation in the local hospital, and Jack, who was probably armed with a couple of scalpels by now, was by her side holding her hand. It was probably safe to say that it wasn't the wedding night they'd dreamed of, but it was the safest thing Agnes could think of on the fly. The killer couldn't be prepared for it—and if he tried to approach Bernadette at least he would be seen by lots of witnesses. Obviously, it wasn't a long-term solution, but it gave them a bit of breathing space to work out a proper plan.

"I hope Christopher's all right," Charlie fussed, checking her phone for the umpteenth time; it sat in her lap, black and silent. As yet nobody had told her that her beau was currently the prime suspect.

"He'll be all right," Marshall said. "He's probably just got an upset stomach. Maybe he ate too much."

He smiled at Agnes, and Agnes involuntarily smiled back. The wedding might not quite have gone to plan, but there had still been something romantic about it as far as she was concerned.

"How dramatic." Winston sighed, although he didn't exactly look unhappy. He had something on his lap too: Hettie, the original tortoise and ring bearer, in her basket, and Lillith in her urn.

By all appearances, Edwina had now had enough of her

lizard boyfriend. Richard might look like a reptile, but he didn't have many of the endearing qualities that Edwina admired in other cold-blooded creatures, and he cared far too little about Hettie for her liking. So, she had unceremoniously taken the tortoise basket out of his hand and entrusted it to Winston, and although Richard looked guilty and mumbled something about Greece, he had been forced to get into his ancient brown Audi alone and empty-handed. Served him right! That houseplant nut was just about the last person Agnes and the gang wanted to see right now.

The taxi lurched from pothole to pothole, throwing Agnes to and fro. As far as she could, she tried to tip towards Marshall as she was being thrown about. It was softer than the car door on the other side. Not by much, but still. Marshall didn't seem to mind. Being engaged had its perks.

When they finally rolled up Sunset Hall's gravel drive, Agnes felt a strange mix of relief and foreboding. Had they really only left here this morning, relatively fresh and chirpy? It seemed like an eternity ago. Two eternities. At least.

As the driver opened the taxi's sliding door, Agnes stared at her house. The automatic garden light was on the blink—again—and the shadows underneath the bushes and shrubs seemed bottomless. Deep pools of black ink. Anything could be hiding there. Absolutely anything.

A bat, obviously full of the joys of spring, turned a somersault in front of a crescent moon.

An owl hooted.

Marshall offered her his hand, and Agnes clambered out of the car while the taxi driver fleeced Charlie. Obviously. When it came to half-cut wedding guests with one real and one cake tortoise in tow, you could charge what you wanted. On Agnes's advice, Charlie hadn't rung the local taxi firm, but somebody from the next bigger town. It had come at a price, but it was better to be safe than sorry.

Despite the tension, Agnes couldn't suppress a yawn. They were all waiting at the front door while Marshall and Charlie rifled through their various pockets and bags looking for a house key. Excited barking came from inside the house. Brexit had spent the day with a dogsitter, but had been brought back this evening and was happy as a sandboy. Nobody got as excited as Brexit when Agnes came home—not even Marshall.

"Ha!" Charlie was the first to locate a key. She unlocked the front door. Brexit thundered out, spinning around and equitably distributing dog hair onto all of their glad rags. He sniffed Hettie III briefly and the original Hettie for a bit longer, then he dashed back into the house to bring them one of his soft toys.

"Kids, I'm shattered," said Charlie, stretching in a rather unladylike way. "I know we should plan something, but there's always tomorrow."

"Hopefully," said Agnes drily. But in principle, Charlie was right. They'd married off their friend, hidden a dead body, conducted a manhunt—it had been an eventful day, and they were all exhausted. Winston was already on the stairlift making his way upstairs; Edwina gave Hettie a good-night kiss and put her back in her usual box.

"Good work, Hettie," she praised the tortoise. You could say that again. Not only had Hettie successfully transported the rings, she had also found a dead body. She should be proud of herself.

"Good night, Oberon," cried Edwina, hitching her blue dress up to her knees and skipping up the stairs, likely also on her way to bed. Oberon excitedly stuck his tongue out towards the glass of the terrarium; Brexit, who had finally located a suitable toy, stood in the hallway optimistically wagging his tail. Nobody was playing with him, but Agnes patted his hairy head as she passed. Marshall carried Hettie III into the kitchen, then he stood loyally next to Agnes and suppressed a yawn, but Agnes could tell how tired he was. She smiled.

"Good night, Marshall." There was no sense in making any big plans when they could barely keep their eyes open. Marshall looked a bit embarrassed, then he planted a bristly kiss on her cheek and retreated from the kitchen.

Agnes got it. Romance was important. Not being murdered was also important. But, when you got to a certain age, sleep was the most important thing of all.

ODDLY ENOUGH, Agnes didn't go to bed herself. She was exhausted, yes, but she knew she wouldn't get a wink of sleep—not without having hashed out at least a tentative plan. She discovered that a kind elf had filled the space around Hettie III's feet with real pieces of cake. More food? Why not?

Agnes felt strangely empty after the wedding. She placed her peculiar fascinator on the kitchen table, made some tea and manoeuvred a generous slice of wedding cake onto a plate.

Then she arranged the cup of tea, the piece of cake and a cake fork on a tray with a jug of milk and was about to get herself a sugar cube, but decided against it in the end. The truth was: she was sick of the sight of sugar cubes. Finally, she glided up to the first floor with the aid of the stairlift, not to her room, but to the sunroom, which was of course deserted and completely devoid of sun at this time of day. It smelled a bit musty too.

Agnes clicked on a reading lamp and watched for a moment

as the light cast ominous shadows onto the walls. The chair—a gravestone; the spider plant—a spider, no less. Even her own shadow seemed shifty and strange. She sighed, shaking off the bad mood like raindrops. She poured some milk into her tea and shovelled the first forkful of wedding cake into her mouth. Delicious. She realised she'd left the teaspoon in the kitchen, so she stirred her tea with the cake fork, then took some paper and a pencil out of the games drawer.

She spent a long time staring at the empty sheet of paper, which seemed to glow in the light of the reading lamp. She had the urge to chew the end of the pencil, but that didn't seem wise, what with her fragile false teeth and all.

During her long life, Agnes Sharp had spent an inordinate amount of time dealing with murders—first in a professional capacity with the police, later privately in her spare time.

But she'd never planned a murder before.

It was no easy task.

She allowed herself another bite of cake and put her remaining grey cells to work. Eventually, she put the blunt pencil to paper and began to write.

There were a few particularly important things to consider.

For one, they had to be absolutely certain that the person they were getting rid of really was the Sugar Man. They couldn't allow themselves even the slightest mistake.

For another, Agnes—and presumably the rest of Sunset Hall too—wanted as little as possible to do with the Sugar Man's death. If he could just disappear, never to be seen again, like in a bog or something—that would be ideal. Unfortunately Agnes didn't have a bog at her disposal. But maybe something like a bog? They had to set some kind of trap for him. There was only one problem: the Sugar Man wasn't somebody who walked blindly into traps—he was somebody who set traps for other people. But maybe they could use that to their advantage?

Apart from that, his death mustn't look suspicious—Agnes had no desire to spend her remaining time on this earth in prison or being questioned about the Sugar Man. Life was short enough, and she had better things to be doing with her time—like being engaged, for example.

It was a rather tricky situation.

She realised that she'd polished off the piece of cake, and pensively sipped her tea.

If they wanted to have any prospect of succeeding, they had to understand the killer as well as they could. What made the man tick? What was going on in his head? And how exactly had he found Bernadette after all this time?

As far as Agnes was concerned, everything had started with dotty Dorothea. She had wanted to "save" Bernadette and stop the wedding—but she hadn't come straight to Sunset Hall. There was a gap between when she saw Charlie's video and the evening she turned up with her stupid suitcase. Why?

For one, Dorothea had to find out exactly where they lived—but with a bit of patience, if you watched all of the videos and paid close attention to Charlie's comments and the backdrops, it was possible to figure it out.

And Agnes suspected that Dorothea had done exactly what Agnes was doing now: She had planned something. Probably not a murder, but an intervention. She had obviously believed that she could exert some pressure on Jack. Where had the pistol come from? Had it been in Dorothea's possession for a long time? Agnes doubted that. The Bookworm clearly couldn't stand Jack—if she'd had "evidence" against him back then, she would have used it much sooner.

No: the gun could only have come into her possession very recently. Where had it come from?

Agnes had a strong suspicion: Dorothea must have somehow got in touch with someone from the gang to find out how she could get at Jack. Not directly probably, but maybe through one or two old acquaintances? Hadn't Bernadette said that the Bookworm had got on surprisingly well with the gang?

Now Dorothea might have been deluded, but she wasn't stupid—she would have known that any contact with the old gang could put Bernadette in danger. And she had liked Bernadette. So, she had probably just hinted and asked in vague terms—but obviously not vaguely enough. Somebody had drawn the right conclusions, and somehow it got back to the Sugar Man. The killer must have then gone looking for Bernadette, but he still didn't have any idea where she lived.

But somebody else had known: Dorothea.

That's where the pistol had come in.

He must have sent Dorothea the gun, along with the fictional backstory connecting it to Jack—and she had led him straight to Sunset Hall! It must have been something along those lines, anyway.

The pistol had been the trick the Sugar Man had used to track down Bernadette!

Only Dorothea had felt a pang of conscience when she realised that it wouldn't be that easy to break up Bernadette and Jack—and that's why she had ended up dead on a bench. The Sugar Man had probably lured her there with a text message, taken the telltale gun from her and stabbed her between the ribs.

Agnes swirled the remains of her tea in her cup and wished she could see into the future. If she was right, the Sugar Man's actions up to now showed great powers of observation and attention to detail, as well as a huge amount of patience and intelligence. Stopping him in his tracks was going to be no mean feat—unless they could use his professionalism for their own purposes. But, how?

She stared mercilessly at the piece of paper in front of her. There wasn't much on it.

How?

When?

Where?

Questions abound. Not a rational answer in sight.

Agnes put her cup back onto the tray, and in doing so she saw something flashing on the games table. The little white plastic box, the one that had come with the CCTV-thing they'd ordered online that had a stack of complicated instructions. Agnes hadn't really been listening when Winston and Marshall had installed it like excited schoolboys, but then she did remember one thing: The new equipment beeped and flashed. If it flashed, then the thing had recorded something.

She froze.

Listened.

Sniffed.

Was there a funny smell around here?

Was she imagining things, or could she hear somebody breathing, only just audibly?

The little box flashed persistently, and Agnes went cold. There was somebody here! Not just in the house, but in the sunroom! And if she hadn't been so intent on her stupid plotting, she would have realised ages ago.

She looked around for potential weapons to defend herself. There was her cake fork—always a solid choice, but it obviously wasn't the right calibre for dealing with the Sugar Man—and there was her rather blunt pencil. The little white box could also be used as a projectile. But that was it. Should she scream? But what? And for whom?

Why hadn't Brexit barked? He usually had such a good snout. Why was everything going wrong? Agnes allowed herself five seconds of self-pity, then she tried to calm herself down a bit.

In. Out.

Thinking should always come first. Bold words that she now had to put into practice.

So, he was here in the room. But, where?

The sunroom was actually pretty open. Most of the walls were lined with bookshelves, there was the games table, which she was sitting at, there were a few neglected houseplants—since Lillith's death, nobody looked after them anymore—and there was a decommissioned fireplace that served as a bit of a dumping ground for all sorts of bits and bobs. Only two hiding places came to mind: either lying on the sofa, which was positioned facing away from the room so that you had a nice view of the garden when you sat on it, or behind the door.

Agnes couldn't imagine the killer lying idle on the sofa.

She slowly turned around.

Seconds passed, stretching out like chewing gum. Was someone hiding back there?

Nothing.

Her heart was now working overtime. Was she just over-tired and overwrought? Was she imagining things? Hopefully! She lived in hope!

Nothing if not thorough, Agnes got up, armed with the cake fork, warily walked over to the sofa and peered over the back of it.

Next moment a figure launched towards her, hazy as a

ghost, and screamed at her. "Oh my fucking God! Fucking hell! What the hell? I fucking knew it!"

Agnes had instinctively raised the fork, but on recognising the voice, she lowered it, hid it behind her back and gestured with the other hand for the figure on the sofa to calm down.

But that was easier said than done. "You said I could come! You said it yourself, you old crow! What the fuck?"

"I . . ." Agnes felt a huge sense of relief but also felt rather guilty.

"You said I could come and have a shower!" Mia, the girl from the well, moaned.

44

A WARM SHOWER

Agnes quickly regained her composure. "Of course you can have a shower here," she said. "You just caught me by surprise, that's all. I just didn't think . . ."

"Neither did I," said Mia, slumping down, not unlike the herby profiteroles from the wedding feast. "But as I cycled away from the manor, I realised I didn't have anywhere else to go."

"Hm." Agnes had meant it when she'd invited her, but now the situation had fundamentally changed. Sunset Hall was readying itself for a killer. It was far too dangerous for a young waif like her, and she wanted to get rid of the girl, preferably right away. But a promise was a promise.

She looked Mia up and down. She was like a baby bird—ruffled, but full of potential. A few square meals, some nice people who genuinely cared about her, the odd piece of well-meaning advice and an education—and she'd blossom into a decent human being.

But there were a few things to sort out first.

Agnes sat down next to the girl on the sofa.

"Are you hungry?" she asked. "There's still loads of wedding cake in the kitchen. Go and get a piece. Make yourself a cup of tea. And then we'll have a little chat, yeah? Proper chilled."

That was how the youth of today spoke, wasn't it? Agnes glanced surreptitiously at the girl. "You're not scared of Brexit, are you?"

Mia shook her head. "He brought me a toy earlier on. Brexit's all right."

Agnes sighed. If only the same could be said of the other Brexit!

"I would leave the tortoise cake well alone!" Agnes warned her, but the girl was already on her way to the kitchen.

AFTER MIA had returned with three pieces of cake and a peppermint tea, they sat next to each other on the sofa.

Mia stuffed herself with wedding cake and Agnes tried to wheedle information out of her.

"How did you know that something bad was going to happen at the wedding?" she asked.

The girl chewed. Chewed and swallowed and talked with her mouth full. Had she been brought up in a barn?

"I was in the Green Lounge. Dusting. There's always dusting to be done, you know. It's an enormous house: when you think you've finished dusting you have to go back to where you started. People think that a life of drugs and gangs is exciting, but the truth is you spend the whole time doing crappy menial jobs. Washing cars. Dusting. Keeping watch. Digging the garden. More dusting."

She forked the next bite of cake into her mouth.

Agnes tried to be patient. The girl was obviously hungry.

"And then what happened?" she asked after a while.

"Then Madam came in all of a sudden. Madam's . . ."

Agnes impatiently waved her hand. She could work out who Madam was.

"Madam was on her phone. The Green Lounge is one of the best rooms for getting signal, you know? When I saw her, I hid behind a curtain. I hadn't reached my quota for the week—I didn't want her to tell me off. Anyway . . ."

"Anyway?" Agnes pressed. It wasn't easy getting anything sensible out of the youth of today.

"I could tell straight away that she was stressed. She was refusing to do something. She was going mental. But the guy on the phone must have been pretty persuasive. It must have been one of the bosses. He wanted Madam to have this couple's wedding at the manor. And then they wanted to send a 'man.' I know what that means. They sent a 'man' for Dominic too. When I heard that, something snapped . . . Something inside me . . . Not again—do you know what I mean?"

Agnes tried to work out what she meant. The Sugar Man had connections. And these connections meant that he could control the wedding.

Mia stuffed herself with even more cake and carried on talking with her mouth full.

"The very next day the stuff about the slapper and the riding instructor came out. Everyone at Foxglove Manor knew that something was going on between the two of them; he taught in our arena. Everyone kept it under wraps. But then Madam let the cat out of the bag. She had photos, I think. And suddenly the date was free. She was livid for the whole week. Well, actually, she's always livid because she has to deal with scum like us."

"And you found out that Jack and Bernadette were the couple they had set their sights on," Agnes deduced. "And decided to warn them with the handcrafted letter. That was brave of you."

The girl shook her head vigorously. "I was a coward. I'm always a coward, otherwise I wouldn't be here now. If I really was brave, I would have gone to the police ages ago. But I had to do something—or I would have burst."

The next piece of cake made its way to her mouth. As far as Agnes could see, Mia wasn't far off bursting now.

"Did you see him?" asked Agnes. "The man they sent? Do you know anything about him? Anything at all?"

"No. Just that Madam is afraid of him. She moaned and went ahead, and stressed about Foxglove Manor's reputation, but she did exactly what he wanted."

"Hm," said Agnes. "That man is now on his way over here, you know? I'm afraid you can't stay here. We should think about where you could go—after you've had a shower." She smiled at Mia, encouragingly, she hoped.

The young woman didn't look particularly surprised. She was probably used to being pushed from pillar to post and being fobbed off with empty promises.

She polished off the rest of the cake, then stood up.

"Where's the shower?" she asked.

Agnes led the girl into her room, got her a fluffy towel and a blue woolly jumper and pointed her in the direction of the ensuite.

As the water ran in the bathroom, Agnes sat in her favourite chair and racked her brains.

Mia couldn't go back to Foxglove Manor. It was far too dangerous. But it would be even better if Foxglove Manor itself would disappear off the face of the earth, maybe not the building, but the shady dealings that were happening there. It was astonishing what went on there under the guise of youth work and charity . . . It had riled up the verger, and the more she thought about it, the more it riled her up too.

If they could stop Purr and her cronies in their tracks—it might not be the same as officially solving the verger's murder, but it would be a step in the right direction.

They would probably never find out who had put the rope around his neck—but it was obvious who was responsible for the verger's death: the many-headed monster of Foxglove Manor.

Heads were going to roll; it was just a question of which ones.

Agnes tried to think of a colleague in the police who hadn't retired yet. That was no mean feat, but eventually a face appeared in her mind's eye. An enthusiastic youngster with dark hair and prominent ears. She had been his mentor. A nice man: conscientious, clever and decent. People like that did exist, even in the police. Agnes tried to remember his name. Andy, she knew that much. But his surname? Collard? Colin? Collins! Andy Collins! Commissioner Collins! Now she had it. Back in her day he'd been a young constable, but he'd risen up the ranks despite being a thoroughly decent bloke.

Agnes sat down at her desk and rummaged around in her neglected letter drawer until she found the right envelope. There! He had sent her a card for her eightieth. It had lady-birds and a stupid rhyme on it. Attaboy!

She noted down his address, then got out some paper and started to write.

BY THE time Mia returned from the bathroom, shrouded in plumes of steam, Agnes had finished writing the letter. She folded it and put it in an envelope, but she didn't seal it.

It looked like the shower had done Mia good. She had put the jumper on and didn't look like a Foxglove Manor elf anymore; she looked like a human being, rosy-cheeked and—for the first time since they had known each other—cheerful almost.

"Nice bathroom," she said appreciatively. "Sorry about all the effing before. I was just shocked, that's all. I didn't mean anything by it."

Agnes waved off her apology. "Don't worry. I say 'fuck' every now and then too. Especially when there's nobody around."

She smiled.

The girl smiled back uncertainly.

Agnes pointed at the chair next to her. "Sit down for a minute. I'd like to discuss something with you."

Mia's eyes immediately clouded with mistrust, and Agnes felt a pang of conscience. What she had in mind wasn't entirely without risk—but it was the best advice she could give Mia. She completely understood why the girl hadn't gone to the police yet, and why she had dissuaded the verger from doing so. Her word against that of an aristocratic businesswoman—no chance. But if Mia could find a police officer who believed her, ideally someone high up the food chain—then things might be different.

"You liked the verger, didn't you?" Agnes asked.

Mia nodded earnestly. "He was weird, what with all the paper, but he was all right. He told me stories. About kings and popes and old Greeks. Stuff like that. And his books . . . I'd never read a proper book before, you know? But Dominic told me that you're safe when you're reading. As long as you're in a book, nothing bad can happen to you. If it wasn't for him, I wouldn't be here anymore," she said plainly.

"And you want justice." This time Agnes didn't formulate it as a question.

"What's justice, anyway?" The old familiar look of hopelessness returned to Mia's eyes, and Agnes felt a bit mean.

"This!" she said. "This is justice!"

The girl hesitantly took the letter, read it, read it again. The towel turban slipped off her head, but she barely noticed.

"It's just paper," she said finally.

"Paper is important," Agnes countered. "Your friend the verger knew that. He probably overdid it a bit, but he took paper seriously, didn't he? And he was right. And apart from that, paper's not always patient. This paper's had enough."

"And this Collins, you reckon he'll believe me?"

Agnes nodded.

Mia put the letter into her little colourful rucksack and Agnes felt hopeful.

"What about my . . ." Mia struggled to find the right word. *Friends* wasn't quite right, nor was *colleagues*. ". . . the others? At the manor? The ones like me?"

"If they're young and were being exploited like you, not much will happen to them. What do you think will happen to them if you do nothing?" asked Agnes gently. "You said it yourself: They can have a shower whenever they want, but not much else. And in three or four years it'll be too late for them."

"But it's wrong! Snitching on them is wrong!" Mia looked imploringly at Agnes.

Agnes could sense that she wanted to blow Foxglove Manor's cover. She just needed a bit more encouragement. "It is wrong," she admitted. "But doing nothing is all the more wrong. Sometimes there isn't a 'right.' Sometimes you have to do something even though it's wrong."

Something had fallen out of Mia's backpack—a slightly

squashed, but very dignified paper crane. Another one! It gave Agnes an idea. Not all paper was created equal. She had said what she could, but maybe she could do more. She opened a drawer, got another envelope out and started counting banknotes onto the desk.

Fifty. A hundred. A hundred and fifty. Two-hundred.

Mia watched wide-eyed.

"This is just paper too," said Agnes, smiling. "Take it. You can go wherever you want, do whatever you want. But if you go to Andy Collins, he'll help you find somewhere to stay. And a real job."

Agnes leaned back in her chair, suddenly leaden with fatigue. "Do what you want," she said. "Do what you really want."

She closed her eyes. Despite the mess that Sunset Hall was currently in, she felt strangely content. There was no perfect solution here either. Everything was wrong, varying shades of "wrong," but Agnes was determined to do her best, and if doing her best meant murdering the Sugar Man, then that's what she would have to do.

45
STAB IN THE DARK

"It's rather unconventional," Charlie protested. She didn't usually have anything against "unconventional." But no matter how you looked at it, eliminating the Sugar Man was hardly something you could put on YouTube, no matter how much you grinned or how great you looked doing it.

Charlie Tries Murder. It was more than just wacky.

"See it as our wedding present to Bernadette," Agnes persisted. "And the Sugar Man is a heartless killer. We're not just doing Bernadette a favour; we're doing practically the whole world a favour. If you really think about it, it's a good deed."

"But . . ." Charlie played nervously with her pearl necklace.

"No buts!" Now that Agnes had finally got over her own moral misgivings, she was convinced it was the right thing to do. "The good thing about it is that the trap is tailored to the Sugar Man. The chance of somebody else walking into it is as good as zero."

"As good as . . ." Charlie muttered.

Charlie was still blissfully unaware that Christopher might be the killer. Agnes had decided that it would be better to present Charlie with proven facts. Then they could surprise her with two bits of good news: for one, the killer would be no more; for another, Charlie would be well rid of a disloyal lover, who had just been using her to get close to his target. And there were plenty of other men online, after all.

Agnes allowed herself a smug smile and looked quietly around at them all.

"Any other questions?"

Nobody had any questions, not even Edwina. They had discussed it endlessly. The room was ready, the tortoise and the snake had been fed, Brexit was staying at Charlie's grandson's for the night, and the boot of Charlie's car was lined with cling film.

Marshall seemed preoccupied, Winston chipper, Edwina bored and Charlie nervous. Jack looked like a fighting penguin; Bernadette looked a bit tired, probably because they'd done a load of tests on her at the hospital; obviously they hadn't found anything.

"Then, we should take up our posts now," Agnes declared. "It'd be best if we all go to the loo again beforehand, and please think about drinks and snacks; unfortunately, we don't know how long we'll be waiting for."

That was one of their plan's biggest uncertainties. They knew the Sugar Man would turn up at some point—but they didn't know when. In an hour? In five hours? Today? Tomorrow?

Agnes tried a cheering smile. "We're having pizza from the freezer tonight, but we'll have to eat in two shifts. Just hold your nerve. As long as we all keep to the plan, nothing can go wrong."

She immediately regretted the final sentence. If she'd learned anything in the course of her long life, it was that something could always go wrong, especially if you claimed the opposite out loud.

~

THE SUGAR Man had spent an enjoyable day following the goings-on in Sunset Hall from a distance. Even the weather was playing along, dry and mild, but not too warm or too sunny either. All he needed was a bit of patience and a good pair of binoculars—none of this newfangled nonsense that people wasted their time with these days. The old ways were still the best. The nutcases over there were far too fixated on their stupid plan to see him hiding behind the trees. The Sugar Man smiled thinly. The childish trap that the dinosaurs had set for him was almost an insult. But it would also be the last insult of theirs he would ever have to endure.

The idea that he was a dinosaur too didn't even occur to him. He had gone into prison a young man and had walked out a young man. At least in his head. Other people might get old, but him—he was ageing like a fine wine.

It gave him a certain sense of satisfaction to see how the ravages of time had chipped away at them all. Jack. Samantha. Silly old Dotty.

Fat and ugly.

Or scrawny and ugly.

Ugly, in any case.

Nobody was as beautiful as the Sugar Man. After all, beauty came from within and inside him everything was cold and still and clear.

A hazel branch tickled his temple. The Sugar Man snapped the young wood, then squashed the lush green of the budding leaves between his fingers. It was wet and disgusting.

To distract himself, he touched the pistol in his pocket. It was the gun he had taken off silly old Dotty after he had stabbed her between the ribs. He personally didn't think much of the knife-between-the-ribs method. It was too boring. You saw hardly anything and, even worse, the victim hardly felt a thing. Everything was over in a few seconds.

But obviously it had its advantages.

He pulled out the gun and weighed it in his hand. He wasn't sure if he would use it today, but it had led him here, and he wanted to show his gratitude. Scrawny old Dotty could hardly wait to run after Samantha and dangle the supposed evidence under her nose. Luckily the Sugar Man still had friends—well, maybe not friends as such—but people who didn't dare disappoint him, at least. It was basically the same thing.

One of the friends had hacked into Dotty's computer. That was the right word for it, wasn't it? *Hacking*. The Sugar Man liked that word. He didn't like computers, but they had their uses. The friend had been able to see everything that Dotty had been up to online: the videos she'd been watching, the tickets she'd been buying.

By the time the scrawny old bat got on the train, she was no longer any use to him. But she would be a nuisance to Samantha, and the Sugar Man thought that was no bad thing.

On the whole, Dotty had been a real stroke of luck. Goodness knows he'd had enough bad luck in his life. Why shouldn't he have a bit of good luck every now and then?

But even now, after all the years of scorn, the universe still seemed to have it in for him. Whom did he have to run into at the bloody wedding? Stick-up-his-arse Stout! Of all the arseholes he'd come across in prison . . . It had to be Prison Officer Stout, who had always seemed to be on his back, and never believed in his remorseful-sinner routine. One word from him to one of the dinosaurs, and that was it—game over. Luckily, the Sugar Man had been on his A-game. On his instruction, one of the apron-clad youngsters had lured Stout into the maze. It had been ridiculously easy.

Then the Sugar Man had got to work. He'd set the crappy tortoise free and quickly sneaked into the maze during all the commotion. Then he'd done away with Stout, rushed back to the chapel and sat there looking innocent. What should have been a calm moment of pleasant anticipation had been rather hectic, and then that posh cow had thrown a hissy fit. But the main thing was that Stout was out of the picture.

And if the universe really was against him, then sooner or later it would come to regret it. That's the way the cookie crumbled.

He realised he was smiling, shoved the gun back in his pocket and raised the binoculars to his eyes. All quiet, just somebody standing at the window on the first floor. Large. Motionless.

His smile broadened to a grin.

Jack.

No doubt he was waiting for him.

He'd be waiting a long time.

That morning the lovebirds had come home from the hospital with quite a fanfare. The fainting fit had been rather entertaining, but what had they gained from it? A two-day reprieve to put their ridiculous plan into action. So what?

The Sugar Man, who now knew Sunset Hall inside and out—from the videos online and his own personal experience—also knew what they were up to. The trap was the room upstairs, where Jack was. They expected him to wander through the house in search of Samantha. And where would poor, sickly Samantha be? Why, she'd be with her loving husband, Jack, of course, who just so happened to be looking out of the window. The traitor!

The fact of the matter was that they had hidden Samantha somewhere else and would ambush him on the way to Jack. Separating the lovebirds—that was their trick!

The Sugar Man sniggered indulgently. He would keep as far away from their trap as possible. Not that it mattered. There was a flaw in the dinosaurs' logic. They thought he was only after Samantha! Ha! Far from it!

They were all getting on his nerves now. The way they did everything together: eating, drinking, laughing. The way they stuck together and merrily hatched their stupid plans instead of patiently waiting for death as would be right and proper. The way they ignored him and didn't take him seriously. The way that old bat had bossed him about, while he had to pander to her every whim.

That was the end of that.

They all had to go.

The Sugar Man grinned into the twilight.

It was showtime!

THE SUN was already setting. Out in the garden the resident blackbirds were boldly singing their spring song again, but inside Sunset Hall the mood was more sombre. They had eaten their snacks. They had been to the loo umpteen times. The first round of pizzas was bubbling away in the oven; Charlie got some plates out of the cupboard; Winston was playing solitaire in the dining room. Jack appeared dutifully in the upstairs window every now and then, like the cuckoo in a cuckoo clock; Marshall and Bernadette were still at their posts.

There was no sign of the Sugar Man.

None of them had expected murder to be this dull.

"Hettie's bored," Edwina grumbled. "Oberon's bored. And I'm bored. Couldn't we just . . ."

"No," said Agnes decisively. "It's important we make sure it's the right person."

"I don't want to do it anymore," moaned Edwina. "Hettie doesn't want to either, nor does Oberon . . ."

"It's not about what we want," Agnes interrupted her, exasperated.

Edwina stuck out her bottom lip and trotted out of the kitchen. "I'm going to check on Hettie." Edwina was checking on Hettie far too often for Agnes's liking. After all, they were in a crisis situation, not at the annual convention for reptile enthusiasts.

Then, just as Agnes was about to fish the pizza out of the oven, the doorbell rang.

She exchanged surprised looks with Charlie. Nobody had reckoned on the Sugar Man just ringing the doorbell.

Charlie poked her head out into the hallway.

"It's not the Sugar Man," she cried excitedly. "It's Christopher!"

Before Agnes could say anything, her friend was already opening the front door. Agnes bit her cheek in annoyance. This was not what they had discussed! On the other hand: How were they supposed to take out the Sugar Man if he didn't come into the house?

And Christopher was already standing in the hall, an impressive bouquet in his hands and the usual smile on his lips.

"Surprise!" he chirped, beaming.

Then the lights in Sunset Hall went out.

46
PIZZA

A simple power cut? Unlikely. Christopher must have found a way to cut their supply. Why hadn't they thought of that possibility sooner? Agnes glared into the oven, which was now dark, then got out a pizza with the oven gloves. The pizza was pretty hot and currently the best thing she had at hand to defend herself with.

She straightened up and rushed into the hallway, armed with the ready meal. It was gloomy in there, but not completely dark yet. Grey afternoon light seeped through the glass in the front door. Grey light also crept through the doors to the adjoining rooms, across the floor, along the walls.

Agnes raised the pizza. The plan was a distant memory: now it was just about saving Charlie and immobilising the Sugar Man. As Agnes got closer, Christopher carried on blabbering to Charlie.

Agnes thought for a moment. How far would a pizza travel? Probably not particularly far. If she wanted to achieve the desired effect, the hot cheese would have to hit Christopher right in the face. As soon as he was incapacitated, she would drag Charlie into the lounge. Close the door. And then maybe they could go back to the plan . . .

Christopher didn't seem fazed by the sudden gloom or by Agnes, who was slowly but surely heading towards him, pizza raised.

He was holding the bouquet in his hand, chewing Charlie's ear off.

". . . I'm so sorry, sweetie pie. I didn't mean to just desert you. It was very rude of me to suddenly disappear like that. Can you forgive me, honey bun? I was really . . . I've never ever felt as rough as that. And it came on so suddenly—I've spent the last two days in bed . . ."

He finally seemed to realise that there was something amiss. He fell silent and gazed over Charlie's shoulder at Agnes. A look of horror crossed his face.

Next moment Christopher had dropped the bouquet and was beating a hasty retreat. A retreat? Well, it was more like a panicked escape, really. He ran across the veranda and along the drive.

A car door slammed. An engine revved. Gravel sprayed up. Charlie stared open-mouthed at the heap of red roses at her feet.

"I . . . What on earth was that all about?"

"No idea." Agnes lowered her weapon, at a loss. Had she really just scared off the Sugar Man with a pizza?

She realised that Charlie was no longer mourning her roses and was staring at Agnes.

Or at something *behind* her.

She turned around, an uneasy feeling in the pit of her stomach.

Winston, who had been waiting for the pizza in the dining room, had rolled into the hall. His phone was lying in his lap, and the torch function was on, so that you could see his features clearly.

He had a broad grin on his face.

Next moment Agnes knew that there was something not quite right about the grin. It was too low down, not on his face, but right across his throat.

Not a grin. A gaping red gash.

Winston's chin was pointing upwards, his hands lay limply on the arms of the wheelchair.

Agnes's pizza squelched to the floor.

Winston?

Dead?

Just like that?

She took a breath.

In. Out.

For a moment she didn't feel a thing, then something made its way to the surface through the fog in her head.

Strangely enough, it wasn't fear, or even sorrow.

It was a sense of cold, fierce determination.

A few things had become clear to her.

Christopher wasn't the Sugar Man.

But the Sugar Man was here.

And he would soon come to regret being here, at least if she had anything to do with it.

She grabbed Charlie, who was paralysed with fear, moved away from Winston, towards the lounge door, and peered frantically inside.

The lounge looked particularly cosy. Edwina had been busy lighting candles after the power cut. It was like Christmas in there. Better than Christmas, to be fair. Agnes had had no idea that they had so many candles in the lounge. Edwina was sitting on the floor. Oberon was around her shoulders, Hettie on her lap. All three of them looked a bit bad-tempered, but seemed completely unharmed. Agnes's eyes darted around the room. The sofa. The table in the bay window. The chair in front of the fireplace.

He wasn't in here, anyway.

She allowed herself a moment of relief, then pulled Charlie into the room, shut the door and wedged a chair under the handle.

"The heat lamps have gone off," Edwina complained. "Oberon's cold. And Hettie's . . ."

Agnes rushed over to her and shook her by the shoulders.

"For once, it really doesn't matter what's going on with Hettie," she hissed. "He's here. And Winston's . . ." She tried to find the words, but could only manage a silent scream, so she mutely trailed her finger across her throat.

Edwina understood instantly. Wide-eyed, she put Hettie onto the rug and soundlessly leapt to her feet.

"My God . . . Winston!" Charlie made a strange noise, somewhere between a sob and a retch. "And Christopher . . ." She flung open the drinks cabinet.

Agnes knew how she must feel. There was a silent killer on the loose in Sunset Hall, and Charlie's lover hadn't made any attempt to protect her; he hadn't even considered taking her with him.

If Marshall had done that . . .

Agnes's already stressed heart leapt in her chest. Marshall! He, Bernadette and Jack were still upstairs, completely in the dark. Literally and figuratively.

She stood up straight and took the bottle from Charlie, who was trying to pour herself a gin, her fingers trembling.

"Not now. We need to keep a clear head."

"A clear head is just about the last thing I need right now," Charlie spat. She obediently let go of the bottle anyway. "What now? What on earth are we going to do?"

Edwina had already plundered the cutlery drawer and found an oyster knife with a ridiculous handle. Now she gently laid Oberon on the sofa, pushed the chair that Agnes had put under the door handle to one side, and grabbed a candle.

"What do you think?" she said, a glint in her eye.

"Edwina, we . . ."

But Edwina was already out of the door. Agnes could hear her bare feet padding along the hall. Then silence.

"Now we're in for it," Charlie whispered.

Agnes thought for a moment. Edwina was right. How was barricading themselves in the lounge and letting the Sugar Man take the initiative going to help? The others needed to know that they had all misjudged the situation. They had worked on the assumption that the Sugar Man would go through the house looking for Bernadette. Nobody had banked on him merrily murdering the residents of Sunset Hall as he went—not because they'd believed in the killer's sense of basic human kindness, but because it was lavish, risky and time-consuming.

But obviously the Sugar Man operated differently.

"Marshall . . ." she said. "Could we just call him?" After all, Charlie always had her stupid phone on her.

Charlie frantically patted her body down. "I haven't got it! I haven't got it! I must have left it in the kitchen."

Agnes huffed in disbelief. So much for "useful in emergencies." Was there a bigger emergency than this? And obviously, the stupid thing was nowhere to be seen!

"We've got to go upstairs," she said matter-of-factly.

"Out there?" hissed Charlie. "Have you completely lost your . . ."

"If we're going to stand any chance at all, we've got to stick together," said Agnes firmly. "Winston was alone in the dining room. That was the mistake. We've underestimated this guy, Charlie. But I'm not going to underestimate him a second time!"

She dragged Charlie out of the room without thinking about it too much. In some situations, thinking was the opposite of what was needed!

Into the hallway they went. Agnes tried not to look in Winston's direction, but obviously her eyes wandered . . . Only there was nothing there. No Winston and no wheelchair either.

Like the ground had swallowed them up.

She parked herself on the stairlift and frantically pushed the green button. Charlie was already haring up the stairs beside her.

The stairlift started moving extremely slowly. Because the power was out, it was running on the battery. Agnes restlessly wriggled about on the seat, but at least it gave her some time to think. Why had Winston suddenly disappeared? Maybe he wasn't . . . ? Wishful thinking, nothing but wishful thinking! He'd looked incredibly dead, hadn't he? She suddenly remembered Edwina and her ketchup murders. Maybe Winston had . . . There were normally a few sauces in the dining room, weren't there? But it had looked so *real*, nothing like Edwina's attempts. She remembered what Marshall had whispered into her ear during their surprisingly successful dance. *I'm over seventy too. Winston's over seventy.*

Winston? The Sugar Man? Impossible! Or was it?

"Agnes! Agnes, come on!"

Charlie was shaking her arm, and Agnes looked around in a daze. She realised they had arrived on the first floor and quickly slid off the stairlift. It was so dark already! And it was getting darker with every passing second. Agnes regretted not having thought of a candle like Edwina. But they were almost there. They just had to make their way along the landing, to Marshall's room . . .

There!

Marshall's door!

Hopefully everything was all right in there!

Charlie was about to fling open the door, but Agnes grabbed her sleeve at the last moment.

"The knock!" she hissed.

"Knock? What knock? Shit! What was it again?"

"Slow. Fast-fast. Slow," Agnes whispered. Why did nobody ever listen to her?

Charlie knocked and a small eternity later the handle went down.

Marshall flung the door open and pulled Agnes and Charlie inside.

For a moment Agnes stood there, stunned. There was Bernadette busily knitting away in an armchair, and there was Marshall, right in front of her, alive and well. The whole room was bathed in a bluish light because Marshall's computer had a battery and so hadn't been affected by the power cut as yet.

Agnes felt a lump in her throat. She wanted to tell her friends about Winston, but instead, she grabbed Marshall and wrapped her arms around him. Tears streamed down her face.

Marshall patted her back, comfortingly but also probably a bit helplessly, while she heroically battled the stupid tears. Over his shoulder she had a good view of the computer screen, where she could see what their security cameras had picked up. There was a dark shadow on the video of the back door.

"Agnes," said Marshall into her ear. "You won't believe it. I recognised him. It's . . ."

Just then there was another knock at the door.

Slow. Fast-fast. Slow.

47
SITTING DUCKS

Oberon and Hettie had stayed behind in the lounge. At first, they just sat there, stunned, united in their outrage. Just being left in the lurch by the Lettuce-Hands and the Lookout-Shoulders—that had never happened before. After sulking together for a while, they remembered their places in the food chain.

Oberon was a lovestruck predator.

Hettie the object of his affections.

The tortoise got going first and stalked resolutely away from the sofa, towards the hallway.

Oberon flicked his tongue a little indecisively, then he plucked up some snake courage and slithered off the padded furniture after his prey.

Yuck, the ground was cold.

Normally he would have quickly caught up with Hettie, but the tortoise had an unlikely ally: the cold. The sudden cool temperatures bothered her, too, but Oberon was from the tropics and far more sensitive to the cold. He could feel himself getting slower, more lethargic, less himself with every extension and contraction of his powerful muscles. He started to forget things. Trees and branches, wind and water, and—worst of all—the sun.

The sun was the source of all warmth; without it he would gradually become less and less snake-like, ever more lifeless, like a branch maybe, or a stone.

But he wasn't there yet. His love of prey was still there. It kept him warm, like a stone that had lain in the sun, still holding onto the warmth when the sun had long since disappeared from the sky.

Oberon followed Hettie from the lounge into the hallway, from the hallway into the kitchen, from the kitchen into the utility room.

In the utility room, he finally managed to summon the last vestiges of his warmth and snakiness to draw level with the tortoise and flick his tongue towards her.

Hettie froze, then immediately barricaded herself in her shell. Legs in, head in.

Oberon started to slither through his customary hunting sequence, but after a few awkward and half-hearted attempts to swallow Hettie, he had to admit that hunting tortoises wasn't nearly as simple as he'd imagined.

Again and again, his smooth snake body slid off her shell, and even when he found purchase, there wasn't much to grab hold of. The shell just didn't yield, no matter how much he tried.

Maybe he should just swallow her as she was? It seemed rather ambitious, but not completely impossible. If need be, he could open his mouth nice and wide! Oberon widened his jaws and got Hettie's back legs and a bit of her shell into his mouth. But finally, he had to concede defeat—the tortoise was too big for him.

In the end, the two reptiles sat side by side, exhausted, both getting colder and colder.

THE SUGAR Man hadn't had this much fun in years. Decades, actually—since his arrest in the seventies. There was something refreshing about a plan coming together so smoothly, when all of the waiting and hiding and watching bore fruit, and something beautiful, round, and complete emerged.

Christopher really had turned up with a bunch of flowers, just like he'd suggested to him in a message, and in doing so provided him with the perfect distraction.

It had been easy to befriend the snob at the wedding.

Easy to exchange mobile numbers and to be there for him via text as he bemoaned his stomach and relationship problems.

You should surprise her, Christopher. Just pop over with a bunch of flowers!

Back in his day you hadn't been able to send the little pictures. There hadn't been text messages or mobile phones either, but in this case the Sugar Man didn't mind moving with the times.

The little pictures were ideally suited to faking feelings he didn't have in the deep, dark abyss inside of him.

People were so stupid!

While Christopher had been waving his flowers about at the front door, the Sugar Man had elegantly gained entry through the back door. Through the utility room to the kitchen. Through the kitchen to the hall. He had already known where the fuse box was. And then: *click* and the lights had gone out.

It was a shame that the cripple had crossed his path—a

shame for the cripple at least. The Sugar Man hadn't thought twice. And ultimately it didn't really matter. When he was done, there wouldn't be much left of Sunset Hall anyway.

Under the cover of darkness, the Sugar Man had crept back into the utility room and from there down into the cellar, where his research had told him the boiler was.

The boiler was central to his plan.

After his work was done, he struggled back up the cellar steps.

Rather steep, those steps.

More exhausting than he'd expected.

Back in the kitchen, he had to rest for a while, but that didn't matter. It was just in time to witness the two old crows flee upstairs. It was too gloomy to see their faces properly, but the way they moved and the muffled voices spoke volumes.

They were no longer thinking about their stupid plans.

They were scared.

The Sugar Man absorbed the fear like a sponge.

He followed the old crows at a distance. Why stress yourself out when you could get a guided tour? He was a bit surprised to find that the cripple was no longer in the hallway, where he had left him, but never mind—you couldn't control everything. No matter where he was, he couldn't do much harm anymore.

While he stood at the foot of the stairs and was wondering whether he should use the crappy stairlift himself, he heard whispering on the first floor. And then a secret knock.

Slow. Fast-fast. Slow.

A door opened directly above him, then it closed again.

The Sugar Man grinned. Now he knew which door it was, and he knew the secret knock.

After all the years of scorn, luck was finally on his side.

~

AGNES, CHARLIE and Marshall stared mutely at the door.

Marshall took the safety catch off his gun, a rare but probably not very reliable collector's piece.

Bernadette had stopped knitting and was listening.

"It's him," Agnes whispered.

"But the knock . . ."

"He heard the knock before." Agnes was weirdly sure of herself. But maybe it was just wishful thinking. If, after so many setbacks, the Sugar Man were to fall into their trap—that would at least be something.

"What if it's Edwina?" Charlie asked.

Agnes shook her head. "Edwina will have forgotten the secret knock ages ago. She wasn't even listening properly in the first place. *You* weren't even listening properly. The fact that it's the correct knock is proof that it can't be Edwina."

"And what about Jack?"

Now it was Bernadette's turn to shake her head. "Jack's in the other room. He'll stay at his post. It's not Jack."

After lots of back and forth, they had decided on a rather rudimentary trap. The simpler the better, especially when there were so many variables that they couldn't really control. There were two rooms. One right and one wrong—at least that's what the Sugar Man should believe.

In truth, both of the rooms were the wrong room, at least for the Sugar Man.

The killer would come to Sunset Hall looking for Bernadette, they knew that much, and he would be on his guard, particularly against Jack. So, they had to do something that gave him a false sense of security. Position Jack in plain sight, for example.

But Jack wasn't the trap—*they* were the trap.

~

AS HE patiently and almost a bit jubilantly waited at the door, all sorts of things went through the Sugar Man's head.

The time had come.

How often had he imagined this moment? Daily. Hourly. He pulled Dotty's pistol out of his pocket and absent-mindedly stroked the stock.

The door handle moved.

One of the crows opened the door. The head crow. Agnes.

The Sugar Man already had his foot in the door. Rusty? Him? Pah!

Behind her was Samantha, bathed in blue light. She was sitting there knitting.

The Sugar Man was just about to raise his weapon when he realised that there was something amiss.

The crow in front of him should have looked terrified—instead she was grinning like a Cheshire cat.

Next moment he had something red and sticky all over his face. It stank. Paint. He couldn't see a thing. He took aim at Samantha all the same. He didn't need to be able to see to get rid of her; he could do it with his eyes shut.

But just as he pulled the trigger, he felt a dull thud. Then there was something amiss with his head.

He heard a shot. The pistol leapt out of his hand.

Something was running down his face again, but this time it was warm.

What was going on?

The Sugar Man was experienced enough to know that the tide had turned against him. He beat a hasty retreat, staggering towards the landing. After all, there was still the boiler! Ha! It was all about the boiler. The rest was just bells and whistles.

"You didn't get him properly," a voice behind him moaned. "I thought you knew how to play golf!"

"Golf, yes," hissed a second voice. "With balls! Not with heads!"

"He won't get far in that state," said a third voice.

The Sugar Man had reached the stairs. Thanks to constant blinking and a lot of tears he could see a little, albeit double and triple. Everything was spinning. He wasn't completely sure which way was up and which was down.

He heard a scream behind him, then a horrified "Bernadette!" Had he hit Samantha? Of course he had! Even in his battered state, the Sugar Man allowed himself a euphoric grin. But when he heard a voice call for Jack, he decided to sit on the crappy stairlift and push the button. Jack was the last person he wanted to run into right now.

The torch he'd used in the cellar must have fallen out of his pocket, and in the darkness the journey on the stairlift seemed like the descent into hell.

Was he heading towards fire?

The Sugar Man blinked.

Yes. At the foot of the stairs stood a little figure waiting with a flickering flame in her hand.

"Hello, Edwina," said the Sugar Man almost fondly.

"Hello, Richard," Edwina replied.

48

AT THE SHARP END

Richard the Sugar Man reached his hand into his jacket pocket and grasped the handle of a scalpel. Edwina, the batty old bint with the reptile obsession! Just in time! He hadn't forgotten how she'd bossed him around for days on end, humiliating him. And he'd had to play the lovestruck fool. As if he'd ever go with a nutty old bat like her! It was beneath him. But the Sugar Man was a professional; he had done what had to be done. Endlessly dragged the tortoise around. Told boring stories about crappy plants and crappy holidays. Eaten a concrete biscuit. He'd been served a lot of disgusting food in prison, but that biscuit had been rock bottom. Quite literally.

It was a stroke of luck that he'd even managed to get in touch with the dinosaurs. He'd only joined the dating agency to keep an eye on Charlie.

When Agnes had contacted him out of the blue, he had almost fallen off his chair. Of course he'd met up with the old hag—she was his ticket to the wedding.

After all, he wasn't made of sugar.

Edwina raised her candle and looked at him curiously.

"Richard, look at you!" she said in high spirits and offered him her hand to help him off the stairlift.

The Sugar Man relaxed. As expected, the old bat didn't have the slightest clue what was going on. It would be easy to . . .

A sudden pain erased all of his thoughts. He looked around, confused. What was going on now? It took a moment for him to spot the handle sticking out of his chest. Was that . . . an oyster? He didn't understand the world anymore.

What was an oyster-shaped handle doing there? It really hurt!

Edwina was still shining light in his face with the candle and looked at him chidingly.

"You murdered Winston," she said reproachfully. "Now he's got to go in a tin."

He could tell by the look on her face that she wanted him to be in a tin too. A sudden sense of dread came over him.

He leapt off the stairlift with unforeseen vigour despite his injuries. He had to get away! Anywhere but here! He didn't want to end up in one of Edwina's tins!

Where was the utility room? He slipped on something—pizza—then skidded against the wall, but managed to get up straight again. What was a pizza doing on the floor? What sort of house was this?

Boiler, boiler, boiler! He felt his way along the wall through the darkness.

Hall. Kitchen. A gentle glow. There was the cripple, dead in candlelight. Someone had rolled him to the kitchen table and lit a few tea lights for him. Now he was sitting there staring towards Richard like a sinister heathen deity.

Richard shuddered.

Onward!

The utility room!

He tripped again, this time on a long white snake. Dammit.

What was going on? At least the cellar door was in front of him. He didn't manage to get back up onto his feet, but he doggedly crawled on. All he had to do was set the timer he'd placed on the boiler.

Suddenly, something big was flying through the darkness towards him. An enormous . . . tortoise?

It got bigger and bigger.

Then everything went black.

Richard made a gurgling sound and just lay there.

EDWINA GAZED regretfully at the remaining fragments of Hettie III. The baked tortoise hadn't survived the impact with Richard's skull. But the Sugar Man wasn't looking particularly perky anymore either.

She thought for a moment, then gave his lifeless body a little nudge and watched as he bumped down the cellar steps in the candlelight.

She closed the door.

Edwina picked Oberon and Hettie up from the cold floor and carefully carried them into the kitchen, where the oven was still slightly warm from the pizza.

AGNES WAS waiting upstairs for the stairlift, simmering with impatience. The thing was devilishly slow. Like a snail!

In Marshall's room, Bernadette was bleeding all over her blouse and wouldn't stop reassuring everyone that it was just a tiny scratch. Jack and Marshall, who had recently completed a first-aid course, were busy applying pressure and wrapping her arm with a makeshift bandage. Charlie was flapping about like a motivated, but useless peacock butterfly, doling out advice.

Agnes, however, had borrowed a golf club from Charlie

and a torch from Marshall and was following the blobs of paint on the floor.

If the Sugar Man got away from them now, it would all have been for nothing.

All of the coral-red blobs of paint made it easy to tell that the killer had used the stairlift to make his escape. Agnes was annoyed. Why hadn't things gone to plan? First a pot of paint in the face, then a whack with the golf club. That should at least have put him out of action, shouldn't it? Who would have thought that Richard the Lizard had such a solid skull?

Maybe they would have been better off with Marshall's gun after all, but nobody knew how good his shooting skills would be with his hand in plaster. And apart from that, there was something so final about a gunshot. A little whack had seemed a bit more sporting, and could maybe be passed off as a household or DIY accident if anything went awry with the disposal of the body. Fell off a ladder when he was painting and hit his head on the doorframe . . . or something like that. A gunshot wound was a bit more difficult to explain away.

But it seemed like the whack might have been too fair and sporting, and it had given Richard the chance to make a getaway. Fortunately, he had left a coral-red trail. She would soon catch up with him, and then . . . Agnes's doubts had persisted. Even though there were so many reasons to justify it—would she really manage to take a human life?

But now she was all out of doubts.

He had come here. To her house.

Winston was dead.

Bernadette was bleeding all over Marshall's prized Afghan rug.

Enough was enough.

The next blow would land; no matter how little Agnes knew about golf.

The stairlift had finally made its way up and beeped encouragingly at her.

Agnes slid onto the paint-covered seat and pushed the button. Even the button was now coral-red.

Then she was—far too sedately—on her way downstairs, still absolutely livid, with herself amongst others.

Richard, her blasted "date," was the Sugar Man!

In a strange kind of a way it made Agnes complicit in the whole sorry affair.

The signs had been there, but she had been far too bothered about being embarrassed and reassuring Marshall, rather than being on her guard. She should have realised from the start that Richard wasn't really a man; he was more of a caricature of a man. Walking holidays, houseplants and that was it—and she'd believed him?

And in addition to everything else, he'd eaten one of Edwina's biscuits. Love alone wasn't enough for that. That required iron discipline and nerves of steel.

Now that she thought about it, Christopher hadn't been the only one to run out of the chapel searching for the rings. Richard—seemingly duty bound—had gone looking for them and returned rather red in the face.

Agnes had been fixated on Christopher the whole time—because she thought he was slimy. Because Richard seemed like a harmless idiot with a load of sad hobbies.

But when they were in the Garden Room, the alleged houseplant fanatic hadn't shown the slightest bit of interest in the magnificent palms and ferns. Obviously, Agnes had been busy with Marshall at that point, so it was maybe excusable . . . No! The name alone should have made her ears prick up. Sugar Man? Edwina had stirred seven cubes of sugar into Richard's tea, right in front of her. That was extreme—extreme enough to earn him a nickname, even in criminal circles.

The stairlift beeped. Agnes had arrived on the ground floor. She slid off the seat and shone her torch. Coral-red blotches led away from the front door towards the kitchen.

A squashed pizza.

More coral blotches, but also something darker. Was that blood? Richard's blood? Hopefully!

Agnes got to the kitchen and lowered the torch. There were Winston and Edwina, bathed in soft candlelight. A familiar, strangely homely image, and for a second Agnes hoped . . . But no. On closer inspection, Winston was just as dead as she'd feared.

Edwina was standing at the cooker trying to warm Oberon and Hettie up with her breath.

"What they really need is a couple of heat lamps," she groaned when she saw Agnes.

"Have you seen Richard?" asked Agnes nervously.

Edwina nodded. "He was in the utility room. I battered him with Hettie III. Now he's in the cellar."

Agnes held on to the doorframe. That was rather a lot to digest.

"Is he dead?" she asked quietly.

"Yes!" said Edwina confidently. "I don't know," she then added a bit more quietly. "But Hettie III was pretty heavy."

"Richard's tough as nails," Agnes responded. "We need to find out if he's really dead."

"Okay." Edwina covered Hettie with a tea towel, and then put another one over Winston's head. "I'll check."

"Let's check together," Agnes suggested. "You light the way with the candle, I'll hold the golf club. Either he's dead or . . ."

". . . or he will be," said Edwina, nodding.

THE SUGAR Man opened his eyes and could see—absolutely nothing. Pitch blackness.

Was he blind?

Was he dead?

He was lying on his back, resting his head on something hard, he knew that much.

Stone floor beneath him.

It was cold.

So cold.

His head hurt. His chest hurt. There was even a throbbing pain in his hip. The blackness tugged at him as if it was trying to swallow him up.

On the one hand, the Sugar Man would have quite liked to let himself be gobbled up. Anything was better than the cold.

On the other hand, there was this smell: nauseating and familiar.

The smell reminded him of something important.

He tried to focus.

The boiler.

Gas.

Panic gripped him and washed away all of his pain, and even the cold. Suddenly he knew exactly where he was and he didn't like it one bit. He had come down the cellar steps himself, had found the boiler and opened the valve. The cellar had been filling with gas since then and as soon as the detonator was triggered the crappy house complete with its crappy dinosaurs would be resigned to the past.

So far, so good. The only flaw was that, for some reason,

he himself was now in the cellar with all of the gas. How had that happened? He had to . . .

He felt sick.

Up above him he heard a creaking noise, then a soft light swept through the darkness. He saw the steps. He saw a bucket and loads of preserving jars.

And he saw a flickering flame making its way down the cellar steps towards him.

No! Please no! No, Edwina!

But instead of words, all he could muster was a wet gurgle.

Then he heard a hiss.

A blazing bright light filled his head.

49
OUT WITH A BANG

Four figures were sitting on a bench, at their feet a beautiful grey wolfhound with a wistful look on his face. Normally, dogs weren't allowed in the cemetery, but nobody seemed to be bothered about that today.

It was an enchanting, warm spring day. The birds had given up singing and were busy building nests. Bees were getting their fill from the still-very-fresh wreaths and floral tributes. A blue sky puffed out its chest.

The four figures were sweating in their black clothes.

At first, they'd snivelled a little, sniffed and passed tissues around, but now they were just staring mutely at the grave poking out of the grass, which was almost completely covered in wreaths.

Agnes Sharp was written on the wooden cross.

Charlotte Courtenay.

Edwina Singh.

Winston Wood.

And: *Marshall.*

If it had been up to them, they would have squeezed *Hettie* and *Oberon* onto the wooden cross too, but it was a small miracle that the cemetery management had allowed so many people to be buried together. Obviously, the shock at the terrible accident had helped. *It was such a tragedy!*

The four on the bench privately agreed that the deaths of a gang of octogenarians couldn't really be described as a tragedy, no matter how you looked at it. Painful—yes. A tragedy—no. In actual fact, that's exactly what Sunset Hall had been there for: A dignified farewell. Going out with a bang. They could say with absolute certainty that Agnes and her friends had gone out with a bang.

"There really are a lot of flowers," muttered Charlie's grandson melancholically.

He was right. The hippies of Sunset Hall might not have been very popular when they were alive, but after the explosion, which had destroyed the whole house, the residents of Duck End went all out with wreaths and sympathy cards. Somebody had even left an enormous, strangely mournful looking paper crane.

Now, a few days later, peace had finally been restored, and the four of them could start the grieving process.

The grandson's partner got a picnic basket out from underneath the bench and offered them canapés. They were agreed that nothing could happen without canapés. There was a sausage for Brexit too. They passed out champagne glasses and went about opening a bottle of bubbly.

The cork popped.

"It was meant for me," whispered Bernadette, not for the first time. "And if he hadn't shot me and you hadn't driven me straight to hospital, we would have been in there too. He was trying to kill me. But in reality, he saved my life when he shot me."

Jack put his arm around her shoulders. "It's not your fault," he said, also not for the first time.

"I know." Bernadette bravely swallowed her tears and held her champagne glass out towards Charlie's grandson.

Champagne fizzed.

"To Agnes. To Charlie and Winston and Marshall. To Edwina and Hettie and Oberon! And to Sunset Hall!"

They clinked glasses.

"I'm sure they're drinking champagne somewhere too," said Bernadette quietly.

Brexit optimistically wagged his tail.

Something like hope unexpectedly took hold.

It was spring, after all.

EPILOGUE

HEAVEN

Agnes lowered her knitting needles and cast a critical eye over the fruits of her labour. She was pleasantly surprised. The hat, knitted in a lush military green, seemed perfect; it looked good, was soft and would definitely suit Marshall.

She put her knitting things onto the side table, got up out of her armchair and made her way over to the fireplace.

So, this is heaven, she thought sceptically, wiping her finger across the mantelpiece. Dust! Even there. Nothing in this world was perfect, not even the afterlife! But the dust on her fingertip was rosy like candy floss and felt silky and pleasant to the touch. Agnes even thought she could see a subtle sparkle every now and then, like trapped sunlight.

The fact that she could see anything clearly at short distance was a small miracle in itself. She touched her nose; she wasn't wearing glasses. Yet she could see everything, near and far, in technicolour detail: the trees outside the window, the long hallway that someone had pepped up with a sumptuous Berber rug, the front door gleaming coral-red, and of course the dust on her finger, which was in the process of fizzling away, sparkling.

Agnes went to say something critical, but nothing occurred

to her, and even stranger was the fact that she didn't really want anything critical to come to mind. That was new! She would rather explore the house, her house, Sunset Hall. She knew it like the back of her hand, yet everything seemed new and exciting. The wallpaper: an elaborate pattern made up of creeping vines and mischievous doves that seemed like they moved as soon as they caught Agnes's unusually sharp eye. She could have spent hours looking at it, but then she wouldn't have noticed the elegant china. The table was laid, candles flickered and light shimmered through velvety lampshades. An appetising aroma wafted through the room, warm and homely. Apple pie, maybe, or a sponge.

Then she heard something. Gurgling and whispering. The sound was so familiar to her that she almost welled up.

She rushed over to the lounge, and there, in the flower window, framed by the most magnificent African violets Agnes had ever seen . . .

"Lillith!"

Her friend turned from her houseplants, lowered the watering can and beamed at Agnes.

"Agnes! I'm so glad you're here!"

They silently looked each other up and down, and Agnes was a bit embarrassed. The last time she had seen Lillith had been outside in the shed. Lillith had lain outstretched on the floor, flies buzzing around her, grey-faced and dead, with a bullet in her head. Something like that was hard to forget, but Lillith seemed to have recovered quite well. She looked radiant. Red cheeks, silky hair, a dress that really suited her, and clean rubber boots. She seemed healthier and somehow perkier than Agnes had ever seen her when she was alive. Almost unrecognisable, you would have thought, but the very opposite was true: Lillith was unmistakeably herself. If anything, she was actually *more* Lillith than usual, as if her insides had folded out like a hatched butterfly.

It made Agnes wonder what she herself looked like. She cast a furtive glance in the mirror. There floated her spitting image, unusually ethereal. Her hair was done! She had a waist! She even had an elegant green silk dress with matching pearl earrings! As if she'd just got off the *Titanic*—and that's pretty much how she felt too.

She could feel her heart pounding. So, she still had a heart then.

"Lillith! You're not in the tin anymore!" Edwina had breezed in, completely unchanged, her hair short and hedgehog-like as ever, her eyes gleaming, in one of her tatty old sweatshirts again. TIME TO DIE emblazoned in rainbow colours. So it was: even in heaven there was an Edwina, and as usual she didn't mince her words.

"I'm in the tin *too*," said Lillith, smiling enigmatically. "But not just in the tin!"

But Agnes wasn't listening anymore. The folding doors in the lounge had opened, and between them, with his hand on the polished brass doorknob, stood Marshall, looking dashing, elegant, suave, devilish and charmingly bashful. Medals dangled from his uniform jacket. Not too many. Not too few. Just the right amount. Everything about Marshall was just right, just like Agnes had maybe imagined before, but not actually seen yet. The way he stood and strode and smiled, and casually but assertively put his arm around her newly acquired waist.

She felt herself blush and could see in his eyes that it suited her.

"Kids, what fun, huh? Agnes, darling, that dress is fab-u-lous!"

There was Charlie, dramatic as ever, and obviously she looked magnificent as usual, but—for the first time in Agnes's eyes—not *too* magnificent. Suitably magnificent, just like everything else here. Charlie pressed champagne glasses into Agnes's and Marshall's hands. Of course! There was champagne in heaven too!

"That's a wrap," cried Charlie, passing glasses to Lillith and Edwina. "Winston? Are you coming?"

Only now did Agnes notice the soft music coming from the kitchen.

Let's fall in love . . .

Agnes turned her head out of curiosity. She could see a couple through the open hatch, dancing in a close embrace. One of the dancers was wearing an old-fashioned suit and had dark distinguished eyebrows and pomade in his hair. The other dancer was Winston. Agnes almost wouldn't have recognised him, not just because he'd obviously left the wheelchair behind, but also because of the magnificent head of curls crowning his once bald head.

But on second glance, it was quite clearly Winston—more Winston than ever before. He looked happy, happier than Agnes had ever seen him.

Winston spotted her and nonchalantly strolled into the lounge, a wooden spoon in one hand, the hand of the young man with the distinguished eyebrows in the other. Winston swapped the wooden spoon for a champagne glass without once letting go of the hand.

Then they all drank a toast, even Edwina, whom Agnes would normally have advised to avoid alcohol. But what was normal here? Not much it seemed—and that was no bad thing! Hettie and Oberon were bustling about on the rug in front of the fireplace. Hettie stalked mischievously away from Oberon, who play-hunted her, wrapping himself around her shell. You could see that both of the reptiles were enjoying it.

"Once a member of Sunset Hall, always a member of Sunset Hall!" Charlie declared. "Fabulous!"

Agnes was just about to nod when something made her pause.

"Where are Jack and Bernadette?"

"On honeymoon," Charlie explained.

"And where's Brexit?" asked Agnes with concern. The presence of the shaggy wolfhound was important for Sunset Hall, more important than she had thought.

Charlie leaned over towards her and placed a reassuring hand on her shoulder.

"Don't worry, Agnes. Brexit's coming."

A LITTLE while later, as Agnes sat on the sofa, tipsy on champagne and the close proximity of Marshall, her hip pain a distant memory, there was a knock at the door.

"I'll go!" she cried, jumping up and rushing to answer it. She might even have skipped a little.

Outside stood someone in pale clothes, their hair golden and their face as white as a sheet. Agnes instantly noticed the bloodstains on their sleeve and the look of shock in their sky-blue eyes.

"Back there!" the person whispered in shock, pointing eastwards, where fluffy hydrangeas disappeared amongst cotton-wool clouds. "Battered to death! With a . . . with a . . ."

The person made strange, plucking motions.

"With a harp?" Agnes guessed. She felt something blossoming inside her.

So, there were murders in heaven too—and somebody had to solve them!

NOTE FROM THE AUTHOR

Tortoises (and snakes) are animals with specialised requirements, and as with every pet, research should be undertaken before getting one to find out exactly what is needed for the—very long!—happy life of a tortoise. Depending on the species, it can vary greatly.

It goes without saying that only a minority of tortoises enjoy being handled and carried around as much as Hettie, and hibernation in the crisper drawer is (as is well documented) a rather unusual practice.

The keeping of animals in all its forms is a huge responsibility and shouldn't be approached lightly.

ACKNOWLEDGEMENTS

Thanking . . .

. . . my agent Astrid Poppenhusen.

. . . my publisher Soho Press, especially Rachel Kowal and Lily DeTaeye, who always look after me so well.

. . . my fantastic translator Amy Bojang. Working on the text with her is always a fun and enlightening experience.

. . . and all my readers, who have accompanied the Sunset Hall gang on their adventures.

It has been a pleasure!